HIT AND RUN

Also by Diane Hester

Run To Me

HIT AND RUN

DIANE
HESTER

Slender Thread
Publishing

This book is a work of fiction. All names, places, characters and events are products of the author's imagination. Any resemblance to actual people, living or dead, events or locales is purely coincidental.

Cover art by SelfPubBookCovers.com/Shardel

For Michael

CHAPTER 1

The rock ledge trembled beneath her feet, quaking with the force of the tons of water surging over it. On the falls' far side saplings clung to the sheer cliff face, its tree-lined summit looming above her, silhouetted by a three-quarter moon.

In the presence of such a wonderment of nature Raina felt small, insignificant. Salvation Falls. Boundary between chaos and calm. Gateway between the tranquil waters of Jessop's Lake and the churning rapids of Moosehead Run. Drawn by the hypnotic lure of its power, she stepped to the granite's edge and looked down.

Moonlight shimmered off the cascading flume, shattering into a thousand diamonds in the canyon plunge pool far below. Not the largest of Maine's many falls – its mouth a mere twenty-foot cleft in the rock, its drop a paltry two-and-a-half stories – but the boulders heaped about the pool's edge would ensure any misstep would be her last.

She inched closer. Loose pebbles rolled underfoot. A flurry of pine needles, nudged by her toe, fluttered soundlessly over the edge.

She closed her eyes. At once phantom laughter echoed

around her, remnants of the childhood memories forever linked to this special place. The touch of Rick's hand. His shy smile. The way his hair dried to a tangle of curls whenever they emerged from a swim. Shared afternoons of guileless ease that held no hint of what was to come.

She opened her eyes and stared once again at the pool below. Wind off the lake pressed at her back, compounding the urge to lift her arms and lean toward the gulf until oblivion rose to take her.

What held her in place she couldn't say. Cowardice or a vestige of hope? Whatever the reason, it seemed she wasn't yet ready to embrace the release held forth in that final step.

With a last look at the beckoning drop-off she started back the way she'd come, negotiating the moonlit ledge with newfound caution. She followed the series of granite outcrops to the wooded track where she'd left her car, drove the quarter mile back to the road, and turned for home.

Her detour to the falls had been spur of the moment. A mistake, she now realized, giving her a chance to contemplate the state of her life in far too remote and dangerous a setting. She should've gone straight home after the movie.

In the dark she groped along the console in search of a CD to jam in the player. She grabbed the first one her fingers lighted on and promptly dropped it. Leaning aside to feel where it went, she never saw the shadowy figure that darted from the woods.

Until it bounced off the side of her car.

CHAPTER 2

On the dark wooded road she screeched to a halt and sat clutching the wheel in a death grip. That sickening thud. That jolt of something hitting her fender, something big. A deer? Had to be. Oh god, what if she'd killed it? Worse, what if she'd only injured it?

Raina looked in the rearview mirror and felt the air in her lungs turn to ice. Bathed in the bloody glow of her brake lights, the body lying in the road was human.

No! "Oh my god! How could… Where did…"

Her heart battered against her ribs.

Seconds to grope for a rational thought, then she snatched up her bag. With trembling hands she rifled through its contents; fumbled, dropped, recovered her phone—

Light flooded the car's interior. She squinted as the passenger door swung open. A rush of cold air. A figure folded itself through the opening, collapsed on the seat.

And a stranger sat there staring back at her.

She caught but a snapshot of his face – wild dark eyes,

patrician nose, features twisted in a grimace of pain... Then the door swung shut, plunging them into darkness again.

"Drive," he said.

Shock and disbelief held her frozen. Tearing her gaze from the aberration, she checked the mirror. The body lying in the road was gone.

"Are you crazy? You shouldn't be walking around. Wait till the ambulance gets here before—"

"No ambulance." The man looked back. "Just drive, damn it."

"What, to the hospital? I can't leave the scene of an accident. I have to report this, I have to call—"

Ripped from her hand, her phone went sailing out into the night. He turned from the window, the gun he clutched aimed at her face. "I said 'drive'."

A mile down the road her thoughts were in turmoil, her breath coming in short punches, the steering wheel greasy with sweat. A man with a gun. Sitting in her car. A man peering back over his shoulder.

"What's back there?"

"Nothing."

"Then why won't you let me call an ambulance?" In the feeble glow of the dashboard lights she saw him wince, his jaw clench tight.

"This is insane. You're obviously hurt. You need help. You could be bleeding internally, go into shock. At least let me take you—"

"What part of 'just drive' don't you understand?" The gun waved closer.

She swallowed. "Fine. Drive where?"

No answer this time. He turned away. With a stifled groan he leaned toward the door.

Raina stole glances aside as she drove. He looked to be wearing a tweed jacket and pleated pants. Clearly not a hiker or fisherman. His jaw was clean-shaven, his dark hair longish but not unkempt. If they'd met on the street she might think him a teacher, a businessman maybe.

So where had he come from? She'd seen no car. No houses out here as far as she knew – this side of the lake was undeveloped. Not even cabins. Just a few boat shacks engulfed in acres of primal forest.

She peered at the tree trunks strobing past. What could be roaming these woods that would frighten him? Force a grown man of thirty, thirty-five, hale and hearty – until she'd slammed into him – to run out on the road without even looking. The gun, though hardly a hunter's weapon, would still protect him from scavenging bears, the odd coyote, a rutting moose. Unless...

Oh, god, those dilated pupils. Shock or delusion? Crack? Something harder? A drug-crazed madman had hijacked her car? An escaped lunatic? A wanted crim—

She yelped when something flopped in her lap. His hand. The gun still gripped lightly in his fingers. His body slumped against the seat.

She held her breath, fighting not to panic at the feel of the dead weight across her leg. If she startled him now, if he jolted awake, he might squeeze the trigger and accidently shoot her.

She leaned forward to glimpse his face. His eyes were closed. Out cold by the look. But no way to tell how deeply. If she moved would he wake? Then again, if her shriek hadn't roused him...

She straightened, twisting her grip on the steering wheel. This could be it. Her one and only chance to get him to the hospital.

Or pull the car over and get the hell out!

CHAPTER 3

Gravel crunched beneath the tires. Raina eased the car to a stop on the shoulder and cut the engine.

The man beside her still hadn't moved. Was he dead? No, in the silence she could hear him breathing.

Beyond the window darkness beckoned, the safety of the forest just a few feet away. A refuge she would never reach unless she could get his hand off her lap.

With the tips of her fingers she pinched a fold of his jacket sleeve, careful not to catch the flesh beneath, and slowly lifted his hand from her thigh. The gun slid to the floor with a clunk.

She froze, his cuff still gripped in her fingers.

Nothing. No movement, no fluttering eyelids, no change in breathing.

She lowered his arm across his lap.

When he didn't stir, she eased her handbag from the space between them, slid the keys from the ignition, and curled her fingers around the door handle.

The light! She reached up and switched it off.

Door open, she regarded the stranger one last time. Grab the gun? Throw it away and head for the hospital? Even without a weapon, if he woke and became enraged…

The man beside her let out a groan.

She launched to her feet and ran blindly into the forest.

* * *

Pain. A razor slashing his side, prying a tortured groan from his throat.

He reached for the source. Sticky wetness suffused his shirt. He raised the hand before his face but could make out only its basic outline in the mire of shadows filling the car.

As he stared, his fingers and the blood they were smeared with came into focus, awash in a strengthening glow of light. He straightened and turned in the seat.

Headlights were coming up the road behind him.

His heart leapt to a thready gallop, furnishing a burst of mental clarity. Beside him the driver's seat was empty, the woman gone – he leaned to grope along the steering column – and she'd taken the keys.

Another look back. His pursuers were still a half mile off but coming up fast. How far would he get on foot? Maybe if he could staunch the bleeding…

An open box sat on the car's rear seat. He pulled it toward him, felt inside and came up with a handful of woolen hats. Stuffing the handful into his shirt, he clamped it to his side with his elbow and opened the door.

He lifted his legs out, tried to stand. Blackness not of the night engulfed him. He dropped back, clenching his jaw till it passed.

He squinted at the light rapidly turning night into day. He had his answer – he'd never outrun them. The best he could hope for was to keep them from finding the thing they were after.

He pulled it from his pocket and shoved it beneath the

seat.

The moon stippled sallow light through gaps in the forest canopy. Enough that Raina could make out the trunks of trees but not their lower clawing branches. Her face was stinging and raked with scratches before she'd gone a dozen yards. Still, she was safe. Even if the man revived, he'd never find her out here in the darkness.

A flicker of light through the trees caught her eye. Out on the road a car was approaching, coming from the same direction she had. It cleared the bend a short way back and began to lose speed.

Holding her breath, she watched it slow and veer off to pull up behind her own. Someone thinking she'd broken down, stopping to help?

The engine shut off. Car doors slammed. Footsteps on gravel.

She stood twisting the strap of her handbag. Go back? Call out to them? Reveal herself? They'd have a phone. She could get help.

No, she felt safe where she was for the moment. They'd look in her car, see the injured man and call 911. And when the ambulance and police arrived, *then* she'd come out and show herself.

And if the man with the gun woke up before that? Started shooting? Took these people hostage in place of her? And if they had a child in the car...?

"Damn!" She started back for the road.

Ahead through the trees, in the wash of headlights, something moved. A figure walking from her car to the one behind. The injured man or one of the others?

The person got in behind the wheel and slammed the

door.

She quickened her pace.

The engine revved.

She ran for the road, stopped short of stepping out on the shoulder, and stood frowning as the car sped away. How could they just drive off like that? Hadn't they seen the injured man?

She turned to the darkened hulk of her car. No silhouette in the passenger's seat.

She eased closer, damned the crunch of her shoes on the gravel, and leaned down to peer through the driver's door.

Empty.

A bolt of fresh fear. She straightened and scanned the forest around her, straining to see into the impenetrable shadows. Was he there? Watching? Or had he run off? Considering the state he was in, how far could he get?

From across the road – the snap of a twig. Rustling, as something moved through the undergrowth. Something big.

She jumped in her car, locked the door, and sped for home.

CHAPTER 4

Her neighbors' houses, what few there were on her quiet cul-de-sac, huddled back among the trees in darkness. As did her own. No-one waiting up to see she got home all right. No-one to get her a nice tall brandy and sit holding her hand while she drank it, relating the startling events of her evening.

Raina buzzed the garage open, coasted inside and cut the engine. In the deafening silence she sat taking long deep breaths as the garage door slowly closed behind her.

Somehow she'd managed to make it home, despite the tremors that rocked her frame, the painful knot that twisted her gut. Reactions totally understandable. She'd had an accident, been car-jacked on a deserted road, and had a gun aimed in her face. Naturally she was upset, who wouldn't be?

She gripped the wheel tighter and closed her eyes. But of course that wasn't it at all. It wasn't the man or the road or the gun. It was the memories this night had evoked.

A sob fought to crawl up her throat but she swallowed it down. Incredible how all the old feelings, lying still and dormant so long, could be so easily resurrected. And all by a single unanswered question: had she caused another man's death?

She thumped the steering wheel with her fist. "It wasn't my fault. He came out of nowhere. He never even looked!"

The words did nothing to ease her distress. What did it matter that circumstances were different this time? Who would believe she wasn't to blame? *Who would believe it could happen again?*

In her rush to grab her handbag she knocked it off the seat instead. It landed upside down, spilling everything onto the floor. She bent and swept it all back in.

And spotted the dark wet stain on the carpet.

Her breath choked off. *You have to report it. He might still be there, lying unconscious in the woods somewhere. They'll send someone. Maybe they'll find him, take him for the treatment he needs.*

And then?

With a shudder she straightened, clutched her handbag to her chest. She climbed from the car, crossed the garage to the breezeway door, and entered the house. In the kitchen she tossed her bag on the counter, grabbed rubber gloves from under the sink, cleanser and paper towels from the cupboard, then returned to the garage.

Her feet dragged her slowly toward the car. Hand on the door, she steeled herself and yanked it open.

Spatters of blood down the side of the seat trailed to the larger blotch on the floor. For a moment the sight held her transfixed. What part of her car could've cut him so badly? Perhaps it had happened when he'd hit the pavement? Or maybe when…

She shook herself mentally. What did it matter? The blood was here; she had to get rid of it. She swallowed hard and set to work.

With every spot of gore she removed, she felt a bit calmer. Her thoughts at last like a normal person's, like those of someone without a past. Call the police? What would be the point? The guy had run off. She'd offered to help him and he'd refused. End of story. She'd done all she could.

She wadded up the soiled paper towels, dumped them in the bin, and closed the lid. All she'd accomplish by going to the police would be to get herself in trouble. If they didn't find the man – a distinct possibility – how could she prove he'd had a gun? That he'd *forced* her to leave the scene of an accident?

And even if they found him, how could she be sure he'd confirm her version of what had happened? He could tell the police she'd run him down and then driven off. It would simply be her word against his. And with her history, who were they more likely to believe?

She stepped around to the front of her car and slid her hand along the fender. A slight depression marred the finish. The point of impact. She'd expected the dent to be much larger. But then she'd only sideswiped the guy, not hit him full on.

Still, the evidence was plain to see. And if a forensics team went over the interior they'd no doubt find the traces of blood she hadn't quite managed to scour from the carpet. And because she'd tried to remove those stains her actions would look all the more suspicious.

She bowed her head and breathed through a sudden wave of dizziness. Clearly she wasn't thinking straight after all. She needed to talk this through with someone. Someone who'd always been good in a crisis. Someone who'd once said he'd always be there for her.

Moments later, seated in the kitchen, house phone in

hand, she listened as her call stopped ringing and a distant answering machine kicked in. The sound of Brad's voice drove a spike through her chest. She hung up without leaving a message.

Eleven fifteen on a Friday night. Where could he be? Not two months ago—

She pushed to her feet. The hell with Brad. She could handle this herself. It wasn't that big of a crisis anyway. *You can't ever tell.* She'd hit a man but he was all right. *They'll never believe.* He couldn't have run off into the woods if—

She stopped. *And the blood?*

Her gaze returned to the phone on the wall. But no matter how loud her conscience screamed she couldn't bring herself to pick it up. It didn't matter how different the circumstances were this time. In a town the size of Brockton Mills people didn't forget such things. Nor did the police.

She closed her eyes. Especially the police.

CHAPTER 5

In the depths of his pain the woman came to him. "Get up," she whispered. "Keep moving, don't sleep. They might come back."

He reached a hand toward her glowing countenance. The image dissolved. In its place, the moon shone down through the trees.

Gritting his teeth, he pushed himself to a sitting position. The forest shadows were silent around him. His angel of mercy, the woman from the car, had been a delusion of shock and pain. Worse things to wake up to he supposed.

Like not waking up at all.

Delusion or not, her words had been wise. He battled to his feet and worked his way slowly back toward the road.

At the shoulder he peered out from the undergrowth. No cars visible in either direction. He was safe. For the moment. Of all the blind incredible luck. If one could call being hit by a car *lucky*.

In relief, he lowered himself to a log, using the moment to summon his reserves. Yes, she might not have done it intentionally but his guardian angel had saved his life; not once but twice.

Though he'd had the presence of mind to grab the gun before fleeing her car, he'd dropped it soon after and hadn't been able to find it in the dark. Not a dozen steps further he'd collapsed half conscious to the ground and there he'd lain, unable to move. A sitting duck. Watching one of them check her car as the other drove on. Listening with his heart in his throat to the sound of the man's approaching footsteps.

His pursuer had nearly been on top of him when the woman had returned and driven off, drawing the man back to the road. There he'd placed a frantic call and a moment later his accomplice returned and the two had taken off together. Leaving the very person they were hunting lying just paces away in the shadows.

He closed his eyes. Yes, if not for the woman…

His relief took a hit. Though her timely arrival had been fortunate for him, the same could hardly be said for her. If the men had caught up with her, if they'd even just gotten her license plate number…

As he fought to blot out the ensuing thoughts, he recalled the woman's huge frightened eyes, her cowl of flame-shot auburn hair. He hadn't meant to drag her into this but what choice had he had?

He pushed himself up, turned from the road, and started walking, enveloped once more in the forest stillness. Not the direction he wanted to go but he had no choice about that either. He couldn't go back. They might be waiting. They might…

For an instant a pain far worse than his injuries choked off his breath. The thought of simply walking away, leaving behind…

No, he had to keep going. The thing he'd left in the woman's car was his sole objective now. That's all that mattered, getting it back. More importantly, making sure *they* never got it.

But how would he ever find her again? He hadn't even noticed the make of her car let alone her license plate number. All he remembered was a little toy moose dangling from her rearview mirror. What hope would he have…

The box on her back seat appeared in his mind.

A box. So what? What could that tell him?

Not an empty box, a box of items all the same. *Like an order that might get sent to a shop.*

He reached in his shirt, pulled out the mass of half-sodden wool. The hat closest to his skin was soaked through with blood, but the other two had barely a spot. He discarded the first and held a second one up in the moonlight – to reveal a name embroidered on the side.

CHAPTER 6

Raina slid the box from her car's back seat and kicked the door closed with her foot. Light autumn rain misted her face as she crossed the parking lot to her shop's back entrance.

Inside, she switched off the security alarm, set the box on her desk in the office, and went to the kitchen. With the electric kettle started for coffee, she headed for the front to open up.

Shadows slithered and writhed about her as she crossed the shop. Racks of clothing slouched toward the aisle trying to shoulder her off balance. The mannequin on display at the end reached with bony fingers to grab her.

The effects of too little, too troubled sleep.

She paused to fold some sweaters on a shelf, blinking the gritty feel from her eyes. Several times during the night she'd gotten up and gone to the phone, but each time she had stopped herself placing the call. Too much time had elapsed since the accident. The man was surely long gone, she'd reasoned.

And still her sleep had been plagued by dreams.

Oddly, this morning, her attitude toward last night's affair had begun to shift. Her guilt had acquired an edge of anger. Just how much did she owe a man who'd pulled a gun on her, hijacked her car? The jerk had scared her half to death. She hadn't run him down on purpose. What happened had been just as much his fault as hers.

With the front door unlocked, the 'Open' sign turned to the glass, and the lights on, she returned to the kitchen to get a desperately needed coffee.

As she poured hot water into her mug, a thought occurred to her, one she'd not considered before. What if the people who'd stopped to help had actually taken the injured man with them? In the time she'd been standing back from the road they could've easily helped him out of her car and into theirs.

Then again, why would they? Why not simply call 911? Unless they didn't have a cell phone.

She heard the back door open and close, and a moment later, in a swirl of crisp autumn-scented air, Julie Cramer swept into the kitchen. "How was the movie?"

Raina blinked. Last night's movie. The one she wouldn't have gone to at all if not for this woman talking her into it. The one she'd ended up seeing alone when Julie had to cancel at the last minute. After all that had happened since, could she even remember what she'd seen?

"Uh…yeah, not bad. Better than I expected actually."

"Told you you'd like it. I'm just sorry I couldn't have seen it with you." Halfway through sloughing off her jacket, Julie looked over. "I'll make it up to you, I swear."

"No problem; it wasn't your fault. The question is, how's Lorraine?"

Julie's happy expression darkened. "She'd lost her cat. That's what the big *emergency* was. Can you believe it?" She jammed her coat onto a wall peg. "The damn thing was stuck up a neighbor's tree and wouldn't come down."

"Oh dear."

"By the time Jason and I got over there it was safely back in the house eating Puss'n Boots off its silver dish."

Julie whisked the crocheted hat from her head, revealing another new stud in her left ear and short black hair moussed into spikes. She stepped to the counter, grabbed a mug and started making herself a coffee. "We'll do something together next week, I promise. Maybe that nightclub in Bangor I mentioned."

Raina fought to maintain her smile. As much as she loved her, Julie just couldn't seem to accept that she wasn't ready for nights on the town. Still, her intentions were only the best.

"Hey, what's this?" The woman leaned closer to peer at her face. "You lose a fight with a hedge or something?" Raina touched her cheek self-consciously. The trees. Running through the forest last night... "The bush by my back door. The light was out when I got home after the movie and I walked straight into it."

She felt a brief urge to recant her lie and tell the truth. If there was one person in her life besides Brad she could talk to about what had happened... But telling her best friend about the accident wouldn't be the hard part. Explaining why she hadn't reported it would.

"Next time take a flashlight. You'll scare the customers looking like that." Julie added cream to her coffee. "So you do anything after the movie?"

Raina straightened. "Why do you ask?"

"Thought you might've stopped off somewhere afterwards for a bite. Maybe run into somebody interesting?"

Oh, she'd run into someone all right... "I ate before I went to the movie. I came straight home again."

Julie sighed. "You know you're not going to get your life back on track unless you make an effort."

"I know, I will. I just need more time."

The woman studied her, shaking her head. "That bastard has a lot to answer for."

"Don't call him that."

"He's an ass! Three years to build a relationship, a ring on your finger and he dumps you just—"

Raina put a hand up.

Julie took a breath and blew it out again. "Me and my big mouth." Mug in hand she walked from the room.

In the hall she spotted the box on the desk and stepped into the office to have a look. "What's this?"

"That order of hats that went missing. They delivered it to my house by mistake."

"I hate to say this but I think you might have to send it back."

"Why?" Raina joined her at the desk.

"Have you looked at these?" Julie held up a sample to show her. "Something must've spilled in the box. Some of these are stained. It's on the outside here as well." Out in the shop, the front door beeped. "I'll get it," she said and left the room.

Raina felt a chill as she stared in the box. It had been on her door step yesterday afternoon when she'd gotten home from work. Knowing she'd be bringing it to the shop today, she'd put it straight onto the back seat of her car. *After* she'd thoroughly inspected its contents, which she always did when new stock came in.

At the time the merchandise had all been fine. Now several hats had dark brown blotches. As though a bloody hand had pawed through them.

CHAPTER 7

He stifled a groan as the truck hit a turn, pressing him hard against the door. Every bounce and pot hole was torture. Still, he'd made it this far. Farther than he'd ever expected to get.

Last night when he'd stumbled into that roadside motel, having washed his hands in a filthy stream and hidden the blood on his shirt with a newspaper plucked from the bin outside, he wouldn't have placed any large bets on his odds of waking up this morning.

He'd gone to his room and gotten his first clear look at the damage. Thankfully the bullet had passed right through, but it had left a ragged wound in his side, above his right hip. He'd used the motel towels to pack it, replacing the hats he'd taken from the woman's car. But by then he'd lost a fair bit of blood.

After passing out on the bed, he hadn't re-surfaced until nearly noon. With a sense that it was days later he'd clawed his way from a dreamless sleep – a black hole in time with the dubious bonus it had spared him briefly from remembering.

Gazing from the motel window, debating how he could venture forth in the state he was in, he'd caught his first break of the day. In the process of loading their car, the elderly couple in the room next door had left their open trunk unguarded. He'd slipped outside, grabbed a small overnight case, and been gratified to find it full of men's clothing. As well as a razor. He'd freshened up, used a clean T-shirt to pack his wound, and left the case behind in his room.

In the motel's office he'd taken the last of the breakfast muffins and a lukewarm cup of bitter coffee, then stepped out into the parking lot. And there scored his second break of the day – a trucker just climbing into his cab willing to give a stranger a lift.

A lift to a place called Brockton Mills.

Now spotting the name on an approaching road sign, he drew himself up. They rounded a bend and the town's main street stretched before them, a broad promenade of quirky cafes and assorted vintage New England shops.

"Anywhere along here is fine, thanks," he said.

They rolled to a stop beside a park with a white rotunda. Maple trees in full autumn glory spread carpets of russet over the browning grass. Hiding his pain, he climbed from the cab. But the impact when he hit the pavement nearly doubled him over.

"You gonna make it, buddy?" the trucker called down to him. "Looking a little green around the gills there."

He forced a smile. "Gotta lay off the damn Turkey is all."

The trucker laughed. "I hear ya, bro."

As the semi drove off, he started up the sidewalk toward what appeared to be the center of town. He was looking for a gift or clothing shop, the kind that catered to seasonal tourists. The kind that would order a box of wool hats with the town's name embroidered on their hem.

CHAPTER 8

"Bangor hospital. Emergency."

Even though the woman on the line couldn't see her, Raina straightened as she spoke into the phone. "Yes, I wonder if you could help me. I was at a party last night and there was a man who was very drunk – I'm afraid I don't even know his name. I tried to stop him driving home but he got away from me. I'm a little concerned and I wonder if—"

"You want to know if there were any accidents last night and if someone meeting his description was admitted."

Raina breathed a sigh of relief. From the responses she'd gotten so far, her request wasn't that outlandish after all. "It would certainly be a relief to know nothing happened to him. He had dark brown hair. Medium build. About thirty, thirty-five?"

"Well, I've only been on since this morning but I know we did have one gentleman come in last night, about that age."

Raina clutched the phone. Of the three such calls she'd made that afternoon, this was the first hospital to give a positive response to her query. The relief she'd been feeling dissolved in an instant.

"I can't give you the details of course," the nurse explained, "other than to say his injuries were minor and he left the hospital a short time later."

She opened her eyes. "You mean...?"

"If he was your friend, he was very lucky. Next time try taking his keys away from him."

"Yes, I'll do that. Thank you. Thank you so much."

She set the phone down and stood giving silent thanks. Of course there was no way to be sure the man they had treated was the one she'd hit. But neither of the other hospitals she'd called had treated a man of his description. The odds looked good he'd escaped unscathed.

And the blood?

She hurried from the office back into the shop, opened the register and started on the day's takings. The blood didn't necessarily mean the man had been seriously hurt. Any number of minor injuries could bleed a lot. Scalp wounds were notorious for that. In fact, once when she'd cut her forehead ice skating—

She looked up when Julie nudged her arm. "You know her?"

Her friend gave a tiny jerk of her chin toward the figure standing inside the front door. No more than sixteen, with stringy blond hair, the girl was short and couldn't have weighed a hundred pounds soaking wet. Her interest in the rack of clothes she was perusing seemed desultory at best.

"I don't recognize her. Why?"

"She keeps looking over here. I think she's watching for a chance to steal something."

Raina went back to bagging the coins. "You think everyone under thirty's a shoplifter."

"Well, look how she's dressed. Does she look like she can

afford to *buy* anything?"

Raina glanced over. It was hard to tell if the girl's torn jeans and wrinkled shirt were a fashion statement or the mark of poverty. "Maybe she thinks she knows you from somewhere."

"Let's find out." But the instant Julie stepped from behind the counter, the girl turned and disappeared out the door.

"Just my imagination, eh?" she said turning back with a satisfied smile. Only then did she notice what Raina was doing.

"Hey, I thought you were going to knock off early today." She hurried back around the counter making shooing motions with her hands. "Go on, I can take care of this. You head off home."

Raina opened her mouth to protest. But the thought of soaking in a nice hot tub, with maybe a glass or two of red, followed by some mindless TV...

"Thanks. I could do with an early night."

Moments later she closed the shop's back door with an air of finality, firmly placing a symbolic barrier between herself and the worries of her day. Surely after a good night's sleep she'd be able to convince herself the man she'd hit was perfectly fine and put the whole affair behind her. Then her life, as empty as it was, could go back to normal.

She strode from the steps with a sense of purpose, got halfway across the lot, and stopped.

The spot where she'd left her car was empty.

She looked around. Three other shops backed onto the narrow strip of asphalt with parking spaces lining its curb. Julie's car was in its usual space. As were those of the owner of the café next door and one of her regular waitresses. The florist's van stood further along, flanked by various other vehicles, presumably customers. None was a steel-grey Camry station wagon.

Frowning, she walked the length of the lot. Nothing was parked behind the van. *What the...?* Had she left her car somewhere else today and totally forgotten? Could a single night of broken sleep cause memory loss this profound?

She turned in a circle, surveying the lot of the neighboring strip mall, the thin slice of road she could glimpse between shops. With reality finally beginning to dawn, she started back.

"Why are you still here?" Julie called to her, coming down the steps with a bag of rubbish bound for the dumpster.

"You're not going to believe this." Only as she spoke them did her words hit home. "My car's been stolen."

CHAPTER 9

Raina paced the width of the parking lot trying to settle her unraveling nerves. By the time she'd walked around the block, up and down the street in front of the shops and through the parking lot across the road, she had to believe it. Her car was gone. Vanished. Stolen.

For the briefest moment she'd considered not reporting the crime. But her car wasn't insured against theft and she couldn't afford to buy another one – she hadn't yet paid off the loan on this one. Her only hope of getting it back was if the police could find it and return it to her. Which meant she'd had to let Julie call them.

She stopped and put a hand to her head. How could this be happening? Years of taking every precaution – never one mile over the speed limit, never a drink before she drove, not so much as a parking ticket – and suddenly the stars were aligned against her. First last night's accident and now this. It seemed if fate couldn't get her one way, it would do it another.

"How are you doing?"

She turned to find Julie walking toward her from the back

of the shop. "I just can't believe this is happening."

Julie gave a look of commiseration. "You sure you didn't leave the keys in the ignition?"

"I couldn't have gotten in the shop this morning if I had." She blew out a sigh. "Though I might have done something equally stupid. I kept a spare key in one of those magnetic holders under the fender."

"Oh, Rains."

"I know, I know. I put it there ages ago and meant to remove it but I never got around to it."

"Well, at least the thief wouldn't have had to damage your car in order to steal it. Hopefully it'll still be in one piece when you get it back."

"You mean *if* I get it back."

Julie wrapped an arm around her. "Hang in there, kid. Things'll work out."

Soothed by her presence and comforting words, Raina felt herself starting to relax. Until the woman spoke her next sentence.

"The cops'll be here any second; they'll take care of you."

At the sound of crunching tires behind them, Raina turned. Her stomach twisted at the sight of the patrol car stopped on the street. She gripped Julie's arm when a tall uniformed man climbed out.

"If he's hot, I'll give you first dibs," Julie whispered.

"Oh god, please don't…"

The rest of the sentence died in her throat. The officer was walking toward them. A figure looming larger by the second. And as his features grew more defined, his face more distinct, her heart stood still. It couldn't be.

Stopped before them, the man touched a finger to the brim of his hat. "Deputy Farrington. One of you call about a car being stolen?"

With the name, all remaining doubts were destroyed. Here it was then. The encounter she'd avoided and dreaded for years. Craig Farrington. Officer first on the scene of her accident all those years ago. The man forced to deal with the bloody aftermath of her drunken stupidity. Who'd then gone on to present that evidence against her in court.

Having to face only one other person could've been worse.

"So you're the car's owner?" His gaze crawled over her.

For a horrifying moment no words would come. "I… I'm…"

"Yes, she is," Julie supplied, giving her arm a gentle nudge.

He pulled out a notebook and poised to write. "Whenever you're ready."

It didn't take long to relate what had happened, even with all her stammers and stutters. But when her explanation ground to a halt – her throat gone dry – he prodded her with another question. "When did you first notice it missing?"

"Just after five," Julie filled in.

He wrote down the answer, then looked back at Raina. "Does anyone else have a key to the vehicle? Anyone you can think of who might've taken it?"

When again she faltered, Julie said, "She recently split up with her fiancé. A real jerk."

The comment finally goaded a reaction. "Julie!"

"Well, he was. *Is*."

Farrington calmly wrote in his book. "You think your ex might have taken the car?"

"No. No way."

"Would he have borrowed it?"

"Absolutely not. He..." Raina felt a rush of heat to her face. "He doesn't want anything more to do with me."

As Farrington paused to write again, Julie leaned toward her. "You never told me Brad said that. And you don't think that makes him a jerk?"

Farrington completed his notes by recording all Raina's contact details. When she stated her name she watched his face, searched for the flicker she knew would be there. Nothing. He was either a consummate actor or he didn't remember.

"We'll be in touch if something turns up." He slipped the notebook back in his pocket and walked away.

Watching the man return to his car, Raina felt Julie press to her side. "Are you okay?"

The truth was nearly out of her mouth before she managed to choke it back. She forced a smile. "If this day gets any better I'll have to go home and get roaring drunk."

"Sounds good to me. Come on, I'll drive you."

Together they started across the lot.

"Look, I know you're upset but you were acting pretty strange just now." Julie nodded toward the departing patrol car. "Did you know that guy? I mean, the look on your face when he first came over..."

Raina straightened and marched ahead. "Never saw him before in my life."

CHAPTER 10

Raina walked briskly down the hill from her house. It was a good two miles to the nearest group of stores but she needed the outing to help clear her thoughts. She also needed a bottle of milk and a new cell phone and without a car she hadn't any choice but to walk.

She kicked through the dead leaves lining the road, breathing in their sweet earthy scent, a seasonal pleasure she'd enjoyed since childhood. Her neighbors' houses nestled in the trees on either side, lights aglow in the crisp autumn night. Potted chrysanthemums graced every porch. A few early pumpkins, soon to be Jack-o-lanterns. The temperature bracing. Her favorite time of year.

Yet the tensions of her afternoon lingered.

She caught herself absently rubbing her face and forced her hand back down to her side. She could still feel Farrington's gaze on her skin, tingling like an allergic rash. He'd studied her openly, taken in every angle of her face. Yet there'd been no spark of recognition in his eyes.

Was it possible? Granted, she'd changed in the last ten years. They both had. Even so, she couldn't believe he hadn't remembered her. She sure as hell remembered him.

She drew a deep breath and let it out slowly. The important thing was she'd managed to keep their encounter brief, got him on his way before he'd made the vital connection. With luck it would be another ten years before they crossed paths again. Hopefully never.

The wind at her back hastened her step, carrying with it the sound of footsteps, the crunch of dry leaves. She stopped and surveyed the road behind her, her gaze drawn to a section darkened by a missing street light. One of her neighbors out walking their dog?

"Hello?" she called.

Nothing but a whisper of wind in reply.

She continued on, her mind swinging instantly back to Farrington. It wasn't just running into him that unsettled her. It was the timing. To go all these years without an encounter and then see him less than twenty-four hours after her recent accident…

She raised her collar to a sudden chill gust. It was almost as though her resurrected guilt had summoned him. As though, if there was such a thing as karma, she was still paying her dues. Head bowed, she hugged herself. But of course that was nonsense. It was just coincidence.

Another crunch. Closer this time.

She swung back. "Is someone there?"

A breeze stirred the branches of the maples overhanging the road. Shadows scurried across the asphalt, rippled beneath the shrubs on the lawns.

She turned and went on. Walked a bit faster. A few steps further, broke into a jog.

Around the next bend the collection of shops came into view at the bottom of the hill. She never slowed till she reached the bright lights of the intersection. Forced to stop to wait for a light, she finally looked back.

Nothing. No person. Not even a dog. *All in your head.* Still, she might splurge and take a cab home.

CHAPTER 11

From back in the trees the girl stands watching, waiting as the woman crosses the road and disappears inside the store.

Alone with her thoughts, the memories return, never far from mind. A scenario to which she grimly clings, trying to convince herself it's real.

But, no. She is sure. It happened this way. These things she remembers…

Stumbling through the clinic doors. The waiting area, normally thronged with the lost and the hopeless, empty for once. Relinquishing her grip on the door, shuffling forwards, doubling over.

Her cry reaches the reception desk and a face appears. "Erin!"

Nurse Kilburn, a matron of few kind words, rushes out, takes her arm. A rare show of caring. Who is it for?

"Foolish girl! Why didn't you call an ambulance?"

Clutching her belly. "It started at work. I…I thought I'd have time. It went so fast…"

"Well, you're here now. Luckily Doctor Manheim hasn't gone home yet. Wait here while I get you a—"

She grabs for the woman's liver-spotted arm. "I'm two weeks early. Maybe three. The baby—"

"Don't worry. We'll take good care of him."

In the delivery room Manheim appears, a specter in white. "Well now, it seems this little one is in a hurry to meet you." He examines her as gently as always. "Everything looks fine. You're quite dilated so it won't be long. Nurse, would you prepare—"

"All ready, Doctor." Kilburn holds up a large syringe.

Manheim turns back. "Erin, we're giving you something for the pain."

"No, I don't want—" Gritting her teeth cuts off the words.

"There now, just lie back and let us help you."

Kilburn already inserting the needle.

"Will it hurt the baby?"

"No, it's very mild. Just something to take the edge off. You'll still be able to push when the time comes."

She feels it the minute the drug hits her veins. Suddenly her head is packed in cotton, the pain still there but a long way off, somebody else's.

The moment comes. They tell her to push, cheer her efforts. In that one shining moment she is all the things she'd hoped to be. On a rush of exquisite purging pain her child comes.

Tears sting her face. She sobs her relief – the journey complete. She hasn't failed! Emotion beyond all her experience.

She lifts her swirling head from the pillow. And receives a club of fear to her chest. Manheim's face is taut with concern.

"What is it? What's wrong?"

He nods to the nurse. Kilburn quickly adjusts the drip.

"Is he all right? Tell me, please!"

Losing her grip. Clawing for purchase. Sliding into the well of darkness, she hears her baby's first cry of life...

Alone on the street, back in the shadows, waiting for the woman to emerge from the shop, she wipes the rush of tears from her eyes. Yes, she is sure. This much she remembers.

These treasures she will not let them steal.

CHAPTER 12

He hadn't planned on stealing the car, merely searching it. But finding the spare key under the fender had changed his mind. With his own car still back at the lake – or wherever the hell they'd ditched it by now – he needed some wheels. He couldn't keep hitchhiking everywhere. Finding the key meant not having to break a window, draw attention. Better still, it meant not having to hot wire the thing, something he knew little about. In the end it had been all too easy.

After leaving the woman's shop – just the sort of place he'd imagined with its souvenirs and memorabilia from the illustrious state of Maine – he'd seen to other matters first. Things he couldn't put off any longer. Like picking up some heavy-duty pain killers – the strongest they'd sell him over the counter – bandages, antiseptic, another shirt, some bottled water.

With his supplies safely stowed in the car, he'd pulled into the parking lot of this disused diner and driven around back to conduct his search. A search he'd expected to last only minutes. Yet here he was a half hour later, after three exhaustive goings-over – lifting the mat, combing the carpet, poking into every nook and crevice – and coming up empty handed again.

He straightened from pawing beneath the seat. How could the damn thing not be here? Had he stolen the wrong car?

No, it was hers, he was sure of it. For one thing it had a dent in the fender from where she'd hit him. For another it had the same stupid miniature moose dangling from the rearview mirror.

A chill washed over him. Could his pursuers have gotten hold of it? Could the man who'd checked her car on the road have found the object, even as he himself lay in the forest less than twenty feet away?

No. Surely they hadn't had time. The woman had returned and driven away before they'd had a chance.

Which left only one other possibility. *She* must have it.

He swore at the prospect. Another delay. Another chance of his being spotted.

Could he risk approaching the woman at her shop, a public place? Better to do it somewhere private, someplace he could keep her quiet if he had to.

He slid gingerly onto the passenger seat, opened the glove compartment and began sifting through its contents. After a moment he pulled out an envelope and held it to the light. Car registration. With the owner's full name and address on the front.

CHAPTER 13

Raina looked over at the nightstand clock. Eleven-ten. An indulgent hour to be climbing out of bed, even for a Sunday morning. Yet she could barely summon the energy to stir.

Her night had been troubled, her sleep broken almost hourly by a repeating dream. A dream with no images, sounds or meaning, just the stifling sense of being smothered. Born of a past of which she had no conscious memory, an event long gone, the details of which had been filled in by others.

She threw back the covers and swung to sit up on the edge of the bed. She'd not had the dream in many years but was hardly surprised it had resurfaced. The accident and her run-in with Farrington were no doubt the cause. How long would it take for those ancient demons to return to their graves and leave her in peace?

She rose and headed into the bathroom.

Out in the kitchen after her shower, she switched on the radio. Even the news was better than eating breakfast in silence. These days she often caught herself with the radio, TV and stereo going in different rooms all at the same time. Anything to keep her thoughts distracted. Anything to fill the awful stillness of a barren house.

Halfway through her first cup of coffee she felt a bit better. In sleep she was easy prey to her demons, but awake, she could use logic against them. She began by reminding herself of the facts.

Not a single hospital within fifty miles had admitted anyone meeting the description of the man she'd hit, suggesting he hadn't been seriously hurt. And if he *had* been hurt, she'd done everything in her power to help him and couldn't be blamed that he'd refused her assistance.

As for running into Farrington, it had been bound to happen sooner or later. In a town the size of Brockton Mills you couldn't expect to go your whole life without having some contact with the police. The timing had simply been unfortunate. And that was all. There was no deeper meaning to the fact it had happened so soon after the accident.

As she stirred sugar into her second coffee, her gaze shifted to her new cell phone sitting on the counter. She'd tried calling Brad again last night, and again had gotten his answering machine. She'd be lying if she said she wasn't interested to know where he'd been, who he'd been with. Whether he'd managed to forget her so quickly, succeeded in shifting his affections elsewhere as easily as he bought a new pair of shoes.

Of course there was always the chance he'd been away for the week. A conference or something to do with work. Which meant he was probably home by now and could give her his thoughts on—

Swearing, she tossed the spoon in the sink, then smiled at the depths of her self-deception. Who was she kidding? Wanting to talk to him wasn't as much about seeking his counsel as the desire to unburden herself. To plead her case and hear him tell her she wasn't to blame. The same desperate need she'd had for ten years.

She stepped to the fridge, opened the door, and pulled out the bottle of milk. From the radio behind her the reporter's words snagged her attention.

"In breaking news, local police have recovered the body of an unidentified man from the woods southwest of Jessop Lake."

She turned toward the radio.

Jessop Lake.

The temperature in the room dropped sharply.

"The man, in his thirties, is believed to have died either late Friday night or the early hours of Saturday morning. Anyone with information is asked…"

She felt the bottle slip from her hand. From far, far away she heard it smash on the kitchen floor.

CHAPTER 14

She didn't remember calling a taxi, or even leaving the house for that matter. For all she knew she'd left all her doors wide open, the puddle of milk and shattered glass spread across her kitchen floor. All she'd been able to think at the time was where she must go and the person she would have to confront.

Raina stared numbly from the cab's back seat at the passing landscape. Postcard scenes of rolling green hills, white steepled churches, and red gabled barns. Flame and gold maples stretching their limbs toward a cloud-studded sky impossibly blue. With the fear of losing it all so real, she wanted to fix each image in her mind.

The Maine countryside. A place where life was defined by the seasons and tradition was valued more than technology. A place of orchards and cascading streams, pumpkin fields and road-side stands. Of lobster shacks and cider houses, covered bridges and pot luck dinners. The place she'd been born and lived all her life.

A place she should have left ten years ago. One way or the other, maybe *this* time she would.

At the town square the driver turned left, following the

road past the back of the hospital. Spotting the patrol cars parked in the lot, she suddenly straightened. "Stop here, please."

The cabbie pulled to the curb and looked at her. "Thought you wanted the Police Station."

"I did, but this'll do." She fumbled her wallet from her bag. Her hand shook as she passed him the money.

"You okay, lady?"

"No," she whispered and climbed from the car.

She crossed the lot with heavy steps – the condemned's halting march to the gallows. At the door she paused to read the writing on one of the patrol cars. Chief of Police. She was in the right place.

Inside, officers, doctors, reporters, and gawkers crowded the waiting area. All there to learn more about the body that had presumably just been brought to the morgue.

Across the room, standing head and shoulders above the rest, was the man she'd dragged herself here to see. A man who'd be every bit as pleased to see her.

In a blink she was nine years old again, recalling the first time she'd ever laid eyes on him...

The front door opened and a giant stood before her. She nearly turned and ran down the steps.

"Hello, Chief Scanlon. I'm Raina Wilkins, I'm here to see Rick."

The giant stood taking her in for a moment. "Hello, Raina, nice to meet you. Rick told me he met you at the pond the other day."

"That's right. We were catching tadpoles."

"Yes, so he said." His brows descended. "I'm going to have to have a stern word with you two. You know technically it isn't tadpole season."

"It isn't?" Her stomach clenched. *"I didn't know tadpoles had a season. Honest, Chief Scanlon."* She swallowed a lump the size of her fist. *"Are you going to arrest me?"*

The twinkle in his eye turned to a smile. "No, sweetheart, I'm only teasing. Come on in and we'll go find Rick."

Shoving the unwanted memory aside, she pushed through the crowd and came up behind him. "Chief Scanlon?"

The giant turned.

She caught the slightest jerk of his head, his flinch at the sight of her. No trace of that long-ago smile now, no twinkle in his eye. Just a thinning of lips and a tic in his jaw.

"Miss Wilkins." The words as hard as his gaze. All further reaction instantly shut behind the cop mask.

Before she could speak, the nurse at the counter signaled him. "M.E.'s on the line for you, Chief."

"Ask him to hold." He looked back down at her. His hair a bit greyer, his gut a bit softer, but still the stark imposing figure.

She cleared her throat. "I need to speak to you."

"I'm a little busy."

"I'm sorry but… It's about all this."

He spotted one of his men rushing past. "Hendricks, get them out of here." Waving his hand at a group of reporters, he turned back to her. "Well?"

"I… I heard on the news about the body that was found. An unidentified man in his thirties. In the woods near Jessop Lake."

He narrowed his eyes. "You have something to share?"

"I do." She swallowed, forcing her next words past her lips, words she would have imagined speaking only in her blackest nightmare. "I can't tell you who the man is. But I killed him."

CHAPTER 15

Scanlon took her arm and ushered her down the nearest empty corridor. Halfway along it, with no-one in earshot, he stopped to face her. "All right, Wilkins, what the hell is this?"

"I killed him. I didn't mean to but I did. It was dark and he ran right out in front of me; I just couldn't stop. It was…an accident."

She saw his shoulders tense at the word. He turned his face, revealing the muscle at work in his jaw. Then he forced his feelings back under control. "Okay, let's have it."

As calmly as possible she gave him the facts. The collision. The gun. The man passing out. The people that had stopped to help. Finding her car empty again after they'd left.

When she finished, she stood holding her breath.

Scanlon glared, impatience etched in every line of his face.

She frowned at him. "What?"

When he gave no reply, she felt confusion edging toward anger. Was there any need to drag this out? What was he waiting for? If he was going to arrest her, just get on with it.

"I underestimated you, Wilkins. That you can play games

about a thing like this—"

"Games? What are talking about?" As if she would choose to stand before him admitting to an act with the grimmest associations for both of them. "I don't know what more you want me to say. I've told you everything."

"So at what point did you shoot the man?"

"Shoot him!" The words exploded from her lips, echoing along the empty corridor. At the end, out in the waiting room, heads turned toward them.

She lowered her voice. "Shoot him? I didn't shoot anyone! I don't even own a gun!"

"You said *he* had one."

"Yes, but he took it with him when he left. I never saw it – or him – again."

He studied her, clearly searching for tells. The human lie detector. A gift rendered useless by the past they shared.

She threw up her hands. "I don't believe this. I hit him with my car. That's all, I swear it. My god, isn't that enough! I'm here because I thought he died from his injuries. If someone shot him, it wasn't me. You have to believe me!"

"Calm down." An order. No comfort in the words. Again the dark, deliberating stare. A glance up the corridor. Setting his jaw. Then he took her arm and started marching her back toward the waiting room.

She stumbled along with him. Finally getting around to arresting her? Taking a statement? Sending her home? "Where are we going?"

"To view the body."

She stopped, jerking her arm from his grasp, for a moment unable to move or breathe. Yes, of course they'd ask her to view the body. What had she expected? Yet the thought of stepping into that room…

"Please. I can't."

"It's not a request. I need to know if the man on that slab is the one you hit. If it is and *you* didn't shoot him, it means we've still got a killer to find."

"And if it isn't him?"

He baulked at the thought. "Then we're looking at two separate crimes."

Two separate crimes. What were the odds? Still, if true, it meant *her* man could still be alive.

She straightened and lifted her chin. "All right."

Faces blurred as Scanlon pushed her through the crowd. Another corridor lined with people. Large plastic doors swinging aside. No time to think, her panic rising with every step.

Nearing the room, his hand at her back, driving her inexorably forward...

"Wait!" She looked up. "How...how bad..."

"He's dead, Wilkins. What do you think?"

"I mean... You said he'd been shot."

"His face is unmarked. That's all you have to see."

And still the panic was building inside her.

"A bit different, isn't it?"

She blinked at him. "What?"

"Actually seeing the damage you've done."

The sob caught in the back of her throat. So much for compassion.

"You got off lightly last time, Wilkins." He opened the door... "Can't expect the same break every time," ...and pushed her through it.

Chill air enveloped her. The smell slapped her face. Steel, Vicks, a bouquet of chemicals. And something all the rest couldn't mask.

Before her, a table. Staff and officers talking in clusters, falling silent as they noted her presence.

The sea of men parted as Scanlon moved her through their midst. At his nod, someone stepped to the bag, unzipped the side, drew back the flap.

Raina stood frozen. Their gazes like insects swarming over her. In a voice she hardly knew as her own, "It's him."

"You're sure."

"Yes."

She continued to stare as they drew up the shroud, assuring herself the truth of her words. A stranger, yes. Someone she'd never seen till that night, and with whom she had shared but ten minutes of her life.

And yet just for a moment, the starkest instant, she'd seen someone else. Not a man, nor a stranger, but a boy of eighteen she had known very well.

CHAPTER 16

Raina sat on the bench beside Scanlon – a quiet spot further along the hall, yet near enough that he could oversee activities in and around the morgue.

He'd kept her waiting for over an hour before finally joining her. Now, as she finished her second run-through of what had happened, he looked as skeptical as he had the first time.

"Tell me again, what exactly did the guy say to you?"

"Not a lot. Pretty much all he said was 'drive'."

"Drive. That's it."

"Look, I only spent about ten minutes with him before he passed out."

"Did he seem upset? Frantic? Scared?"

"He looked a bit dazed, but seeing as he'd just been hit by a car that wasn't surprising. He did look over his shoulder a few times, but overall he seemed more in pain than afraid."

"So the place where he ran out of the woods – could you find it again?"

She shook her head. "It was dark; there are no lights out there, no houses, nothing. I know roughly where it is – somewhere between the track up to Salvation Falls and the junction with route twenty-three. But I couldn't show you the exact spot. I hit the brakes pretty hard so there might be skid marks."

She held her breath. The stretch of road she'd described was little more than five miles long. Surely they could find what they needed. Enough to prove she was telling the truth.

"What about the people who stopped to help – you get a look at them?"

"I saw shadows, movement, nothing distinct."

"Not even if it was a man or woman?"

"No. Sorry." She stopped herself picking at the cuff of her sleeve.

Scanlon sighed. "Any clue, at least, how many there were?"

"I heard two doors slam so I assumed there were two of them, but I can't be sure."

"No, of course not." He leaned back and regarded her with grim amazement. "And after they left, you simply hopped in your car and drove off."

She shifted. "Yes."

"Just cruised on home. Never bothering to call the police."

"He threw my cell phone out the window. How was I supposed—"

"You didn't think to call them when you got to your house?"

"And report what? The guy was gone. There wasn't anything anyone could do. How was I to know—" Under his scrutiny, she slumped on the seat. "All right. The truth is, I was afraid. I didn't think anyone would believe my story. Which, clearly, you don't."

His lips pressed tighter. "*Had* you been drinking?"

"No. I swear it."

"No way to prove that now though, is there."

She closed her eyes. What would be the point in arguing?

"Anyone go to the movie with you?"

"No." Would the man never let up?

"Anyone *see* you there?"

"Yeah, the guy who sold me the ticket." She shot to her feet. "And I'm sure he'll remember me because I look so different to the fifty other women he served that night."

"Sit down," he hissed.

"Why? You've obviously—"

"I said, sit down."

She lowered herself, waiting in silence for the hammer to fall.

After what seemed an eternity he spoke. "All right, here's what I'm going to need from you. Number one, you are not to leave town."

She blinked at him. "You mean you're not—"

"Two, I want a full statement. My people are all tied up at the moment so make it tomorrow. Come to the station, report to either me or Deputy Farrington. Then I'll decide if there are any charges."

Raina exhaled. Farrington or Scanlon. It seemed only fitting they'd be the ones to tighten the noose.

As if her thoughts had conjured his form, Farrington appeared at the end of the hall, striding from the waiting room toward the morgue. She turned slightly so he wouldn't see her.

"And, three, we'll need to impound your car," Scanlon went on. "Even if you didn't kill the poor sap, you're likely the last person to have seen him alive. Forensics will need..." He trailed off when he saw her expression.

Raina stared back, his request having claimed her full attention. She'd barely got him to look into her story, let alone believe it. How would she convince him...

"What?" he snapped.

She opened her mouth but no sound emerged.

Halfway up the hall, his hand on a door, Farrington spotted them and changed direction.

"Wilkins!" Scanlon had reached his limit.

"You can't have my car. It's...been stolen."

"Stolen." The word fell from his lips like a stone.

"I know how it looks, but I swear to you—"

He put up a hand. "Let me see if I have this straight. You hit a pedestrian, seriously injure him, fail to report the matter to the police, and now you've lost the vehicle involved."

"Not lost, I told you—"

"And when did this theft supposedly occur?"

"Sometime yesterday afternoon."

Farrington had closed the gap between them. Perhaps sensing the tension in the air, he stood, silent, a few steps away.

"Less than twenty-four hours after the accident," Scanlon challenged.

"That's right. I drove it to work in the morning and it was gone when I came out at the end of the day."

Scanlon pinched the bridge of his nose, then threw up his hands. "Right, that's it. I'm through messing around with you, Wilkins." He grabbed her elbow and pulled her to her feet.

"No, wait. Please! I reported it stolen."

"To who? The bag lady in Paradise Park?"

Raina looked up at the man standing next to him. The man who might just hold her fate in his hands.

Farrington returned her gaze, like any good cop, his expression unreadable. The moment drew out. Then he turned to his boss. "To me, Chief. She reported it to me."

CHAPTER 17

Hunched beneath the ambulance portico, Raina peered out at the driving rain. Only in New England could the weather go from fine and sunny to blustery and wet in under three hours – the time she'd been inside talking to Scanlon. She'd called a cab to ferry her home but been told she could have an hour's wait.

Through the sliding glass doors behind her, the reception area was quiet now compared to the chaos when she'd first arrived. Most of the investigative and media people had already left. But Scanlon was still in there somewhere and she wanted to get away while she could, before he changed his mind about letting her go.

Frowning, she recalled their conversation. Why hadn't he charged her? Obviously he hadn't believed her story. Was he deliberately drawing things out, delaying the inevitable to prolong her torment, knowing she'd go home, lie awake nights, waiting for his knock on her door? Clearly he'd derived great satisfaction from forcing her to view the body. But could even Scanlon be that vindictive?

Could she honestly blame him if he was?

She closed her eyes and still the face of the victim was there, seared in her mind. Whoever he was, two days ago he'd been alive. With friends, family, dreams and regrets. Another life cut tragically short. At least it hadn't been her fault this time.

She shot another quick glance through the doors. Whatever Scanlon's reasons for sparing her, her nerves couldn't handle another encounter. She needed time to think, maybe call a lawyer. She needed to regroup.

She needed to get the hell out of here!

Scanning the sky, she saw not the slightest break in the clouds. How desperate was she? She could walk to the diner four blocks away and get the cab to pick her up there. Wait in comfort and relative safety far from cops and morgues and dead bodies.

Movement drew her gaze to the doors; she caught her breath. Deputy Farrington was coming up the corridor, nearly to the exit.

As the doors slid open, she moved aside, hoping to fade back into the shadows. Farrington emerged and took all of three steps before catching sight of her. Their gazes met for an instant, then thankfully, the man walked on.

At the edge of the portico, however, he paused, about to step out into the elements, then turned back. "Need a lift?"

The question stunned her. So harmless a gesture, yet coming from him... A baited snare into which she might stumble?

In the sepia light of the fading afternoon, she studied him closely. He'd changed in the ten years since she'd seen him last. Back then he'd been a rookie fresh to the force, a stranger to the folks of Brockton Mills. The intervening years had clearly been ones from which he had grown. With his athletic build and easy manner he'd never been a bad-looking man. But experience had added strength and character to his features, forging a commanding presence indeed.

She drew her thoughts back. "I've called a cab. Thank you anyway."

"In weather like this it could be a while. Come on." He jerked his head toward the parking lot. "I just got off, I'll take you home."

She stood her ground, fighting for a fraction of the self possession these men seemed to have in such abundance.

He took a step closer. "Look, no questions, okay. I promise. I give you a ride, we're just two people who live in the same town being neighborly."

"Is that what you were being ten years ago?" The words slipped out before she could stop them. The minute they had, she wanted them back.

He drew a deep breath. "No, Ms Wilkins, back then I was only doing my job."

She stared at her feet. So he did remember. "Thank you, I'll walk."

She made it as far as the end of the parking lot before a car drew up along side her.

Keeping pace with her purposeful strides, Farrington rolled down his window a crack. "Thought you called a cab."

"He's picking me up from the diner," she shouted over the drum of the rain on his roof.

"That's a fair hike. You sure you don't want—"

She stopped and faced him. "Walking in the rain is a crime now, is it."

"Look, I'm not hassling you. I just thought you might not enjoy getting drenched."

She stood before him hugging herself, hair plastered

against her scalp, cold water streaming down her face and finding every gap in her collar. She gazed along the rain-lashed street, then up at the sky.

Then she dashed around to the passenger side, opened the door and threw herself in.

CHAPTER 18

Seatbelt fastened, hands in her lap, Raina sat staring straight ahead out the windshield, determined she would not be drawn into conversation.

She shifted uncomfortably, aware of Farrington's gaze on her face. Why the hell weren't they going anywhere?

"You want to give me a hint?" he said.

"About what?"

"Where you're living these days?"

"Oh." Heat flared in her cheeks. "Off twenty three, just past the bridge."

For a heart-stopping instant she thought he was reaching to put his arm around her. Instead his hand vanished behind her seat, came up with a terry cloth hand towel and dropped it in her lap. "Doesn't look it but it's clean, I promise."

She mumbled her thanks as he finally put the car in gear and drove from the parking lot. But as she mopped her face, a band slowly tightened around her chest, her breath growing short. After the chill wind blowing outside, the closeness of the car's interior – not to mention the man himself – had her feeling claustrophobic. This was a mistake.

DIANE HESTER

"You okay?" he said, looking over.

"I'm fine."

He gave her a second then tried again. "That must've been rough back there, thinking you'd killed that man."

Her head snapped toward him. "You mean *another* one, don't you?"

At the sound of her voice, she bowed her head. What was she doing? What happened those years ago hadn't been his fault. He was right – he'd only been doing his job. What would she have had him do, lie to protect her?

Still, it was hard to think of those days without feeling like a kid again. A terrified, vulnerable eighteen year old, sick with a guilt so malignant it turned her soul inside out. A guilt she'd not lived a day without since.

Yes, all these years she'd been kidding herself, she could see that now. Her defiance, her outward displays of indifference – all a charade. Just a skin-thick layer beneath the surface her guilt had been crouching in wait all along, as pitiless as the day it was forged. And after her confrontation with Scanlon, even that thin barrier had been ripped away.

"I'm sorry," she said. "You're right, it was upsetting viewing the body. One of the hardest things I've ever had to… I didn't mean to take it out on you."

"Forget it."

She settled back, her breath coming easier, but not by much. "Thank you, by the way. I appreciate your backing me up with Scanlon about my car."

"You reported it stolen, I filed the report. What else would I tell him?"

She stared at the towel she was twisting in her hands. In truth a part of her had half expected him to deny her claim just to make things difficult for her. But of course that had just been her old guilt talking.

As if reading her mind, he said, "You thought I'd hang you out to dry?" He gave a short laugh. "First of all, I'm not in the habit of lying to my boss. And second…"

Steering with his wrist draped over the wheel, he shook his head. "Could you honestly believe I derived even the slightest pleasure from putting together that case against you… what is it now, ten years ago? Giving evidence, seeing you day after day in court." He lowered his voice. "Knowing what you'd already lost."

With the question hanging unanswered between them, she took in his profile. In all these years, she'd never considered he might have regretted what he'd had to do.

"One young life had already been destroyed," he said. "You think I was eager to ruin another one?"

"That young life was your boss's son."

"So what, you thought I was out to avenge Scanlon?"

She added another twist to the towel. "No. I never thought that."

"I'm glad to hear it." He drummed his thumb on the wheel for a moment. "And just so you know, even if I hadn't had to back you up with Scanlon about the car, I still would have."

She swallowed. "Why?"

He stared at the road for several seconds. "Because you looked pretty much backed into a corner. And, despite how corny it sounds, I think everyone deserves a second chance."

She turned away and closed her eyes. How long had she waited to hear someone say that to her? *Thank you.*

"What I don't get – and you don't have to answer, because I promised I wouldn't ask you about it – was why you didn't report hitting that guy the night it happened. Didn't you realize how that would look?"

"In case you hadn't noticed, I've kept a low profile these last ten years. Or tried to. I pretty much do everything I can to avoid all contact with you guys."

His expression softened. "Cops in general or me in particular?"

Incredibly, she felt herself smile. "You and Scanlon were the top of my list. I decided it was either keep my distance or move away. And I like it here."

He nodded. "Me too."

She gazed out the window finally finding the courage to speak the hope she had nurtured for ten years. "I thought if enough time went by people might forget what happened."

"I think you'll find most of them have."

She stifled a huff, her hopes collapsing in on themselves. *And Scanlon? You think he'll ever forget?*

CHAPTER 19

The rain was beating down even more heavily by the time they pulled into Raina's driveway.

Farrington shut off the engine and grabbed an umbrella from the back seat. "I'll walk you." He was out of the car and slamming the door before Raina could utter a protest.

Shielding them both, he escorted her up the path to the house. She opened the screen door, reached to put her key in the lock and gasped when the door swung back at her touch.

Farrington handed her the umbrella. "Wait here," he said and moved inside.

She surveyed the living room from the threshold as he disappeared deeper into the house. Nothing looked amiss. No furniture overturned, no papers disturbed on the writing desk, no empty spaces on the mantel or shelves.

That's when it hit her.

"It's okay!" she called. "My mistake!"

She stepped inside and closed the door, set the umbrella on the entryway's flagstone floor. She'd shrugged off her jacket and was hanging it on the clotheshorse to dry when Farrington reappeared from the kitchen. "House looks clear. I can't really see where anyone got in."

"They didn't." She shrugged, embarrassed. "No-one broke in. The door was open because I didn't close up."

"You go out and leave your doors unlocked?"

"Not normally, no. I just wasn't thinking straight when I left." She looked at her hands. "I'd just heard the news about the body being found and I guess I was a bit upset."

He digested her words then took a step closer. "And now? You okay?"

"Yeah, I'll be fine." Oddly a smile wasn't too hard to summon. "Thank you for the lift."

"You're welcome." He looked around. "Nothing else I can do or get for you before I go? You don't want to call a friend to come over?"

"No, I'll probably just watch some TV. Go to bed early."

They stood a moment in awkward silence, then he nodded and joined her at the door.

"Well, I'll see you tomorrow then for that statement." He bent and picked up the umbrella.

"Can I ask you something?"

He turned to her. "Shoot."

"Yesterday when you came to the shop, about my car…" She hesitated, choosing her words. "I wondered, did you…"

"Recognize you? Yeah, I did."

She looked up, surprised. "I'd never have picked it. You didn't let on."

"You get good at hiding your feelings in this job."

"I imagine you would." Even today, since leaving the hospital, his expression had given little away, his strong features set to cop default sending a clear don't-mess-with-me message. Except for those intriguing moments he'd smiled. "I guess you picked up that I wasn't eager to prolong our encounter."

"I wondered if you might've been protecting someone."

She frowned. "Who?"

"That ex-fiancé your friend mentioned? The one who wants nothing more to do with you?"

"Oh." She blushed. "No, I wouldn't be protecting him."

"I should hope not." He cocked his head. "He really say that?"

"Essentially, yes."

Shaking his head, he turned to leave. "Your friend's right. He *is* a jerk."

CHAPTER 20

Raina closed the door behind Deputy Farrington and stood considering his parting words. The approving remark, driving her home, making sure there was no-one in her house... Indeed his behavior the entire day had taken her completely by surprise.

After what she'd put him through all those years ago, such kindness was more than she'd expected of him. If only Scanlon could be half as forgiving. If only she could.

Her reflection in the entryway mirror stopped her as she turned from the door. A bedraggled specimen. Drowned-rat hair, haunted gaze. A woman unremarkable in every way. Except for the fact she had blood on her hands.

With reluctant steps she entered the living room and crossed to the bookcase beside the hearth. The high school yearbook she pulled from a shelf fell open to a page marked with a photograph.

She smiled at the pair of ragged youths in torn jeans and grubby sweatshirts, recalling the day the picture was taken – the first time she and Rick had ridden their bikes all the way to the general store, back in third grade

They'd met that year. Not in school but at the pond in the woods between their houses, both of them keen to gather the first salamander eggs of spring. She, the taller and willing to wade out deeper in the frigid water, had scored the lion's share. But as her dejected competitor had turned to trudge home, she'd called him back and tipped half of her squishy haul into his bucket.

That had marked the start of their friendship. As that spring progressed they'd invaded the local golf course together, digging up turtle eggs from the sand traps, bringing them home, raising them along side their frog and salamander tadpoles to be released in autumn. The following summer butterflies had captured their interest.

Raina slid the picture between the pages and turned to their junior year class photograph. As teens their interest in the backyard tree house had given way to hiking and camping. It had been on one such outing, at the plunge pool beneath Salvation Falls, two months after her father's death that things with Rick had changed forever. There on a broad plateau of rock, with his shoulder to hers, summer sun warm on their faces, she'd leaned towards him and kissed his cheek.

Never before that golden moment had she sensed their relationship was changing. One day they were third graders, the next young adults poised to venture forth in the world. In a heartbeat, with that one tender kiss…

Barely able to see for her tears, Raina trailed a finger down his image in the photo. What would've happened if not for the accident that had taken his life? Would he have asked her to marry him? Given up the scholarship to Yale, the one Scanlon had been so proud of him for? Would she have accepted? Had she loved him that much?

To this day she wasn't sure. All she knew was her

childhood friend hadn't deserved to die as he had. That if not for her moment of criminal stupidity they would have both had the chance to find out.

She closed the book and returned it to the shelf.

CHAPTER 21

In the kitchen, Raina sighed with relief. No sign of the bottle of milk she'd dropped earlier. Clearly she *had* cleaned it up after all.

For some strange reason she hadn't been happy at the thought Farrington had seen the mess. Further evidence of her fragile state, a weakness she didn't feel the need to broadcast. That she couldn't remember cleaning it up didn't worry her nearly as much. In the state she'd been in when she'd left the house it was hardly surprising.

She crossed the kitchen, opened the cupboard beneath the sink, and pulled out a large bag. Garbage night. Before it got too dark outside she needed to empty all the baskets and take out the bin.

She went room to room collecting the trash from the study and bathroom. In the bedroom, however, the sight of her dressing table drew her up short. Amid the bottles of perfume, her comb and brush, and assorted cosmetics, the contents of her make-up case lay scattered. Even more strange, several of the lipstick lids were off. Not a terribly remarkable sight. Except for the fact she hadn't worn lipstick in several days. At least not that she could remember.

A chill trickled down over her shoulders. Either she was losing her mind – years of repressed guilt breaking free of the safe she'd locked it in and rampaging unchecked through her psyche – or someone *had* been inside her house.

She turned a slow circle, surveying the room. Nothing else appeared disturbed. In the closet, her clothes and shoes were all in order, just as she'd left them.

Retracing her steps, she did another sweep of the house, carefully checking on her possessions. Nothing was missing that she could see.

Back in the bedroom, hands on hips, she stared once more at the dressing table. Why would someone break into her house, move things around and not steal anything? Except for the fact they hadn't broken in, the doors had been open. So maybe it wasn't a thief at all. Maybe one of her neighbors dropped by and…

And what? Finding no-one home, they'd let themselves in and played with her make-up? No, if someone *had* come in, it had to be a stranger.

She stepped to the window and peered out at the gathering twilight. A stranger who'd just happened along the one and only time she'd gone out leaving her door unlocked? Or someone who'd been there all along, watching and waiting for just such a chance? Someone who was out there now, watching her at this very moment.

Her frown deepened. A man hijacks her car at gunpoint, her car is stolen the very next day, and now her house is invaded. Three incidents like that just had to be connected. And yet she didn't see how they could be. The man who'd hijacked her car was dead.

She dropped the curtain, hurried back to the kitchen,

grabbed her cell phone from her handbag, and punched in a number. Surely this constituted a harmless, no-strings-attached scenario. An innocent plea for a friendly ear to—

Half expecting his answering machine, she was startled at actually hearing his voice. She lowered herself into a chair at the table. "Brad. Hi, it's Raina."

They got through an awkward exchange of greetings, how they both were, a cursory update of what was new. Then she took a deep breath and got to the point.

"Look, I was wondering, is there any chance you could come around?"

"What, tonight?"

"If you're not doing anything. There's something I need to talk about."

"About us?"

She winced. Oh god, is that what he thought? "It's nothing to do with you and me."

"Then what is it?"

"Just something it would help me to talk about. A problem I'm having."

A shuffling sound. She heard him speak briefly to someone else.

She swallowed hard. "Are you at home?"

"Can't you just tell me what it's about?"

"I'd rather not discuss it over the phone." Someone in his house? Someone there with him?

"Well, is it urgent?"

She let out a laugh. There was no mistaking his impatience this time. "No, not really. You know me, getting worked up over nothing as usual."

The voice of the other person again. This time closer, a little annoyed. And distinctly female.

The sound of him hushing her and then he was back. "Raina, look—"

"Forget it, it was a bad idea. Sorry I bothered you."

CHAPTER 22

He sat in the car just up the road watching the house nestled back among the trees. The woman's house. The address on the car registration form. Raina Wilkins. He'd come here hoping she wouldn't be home, planning to break in and ransack the place.

Only one problem. Someone else had beaten him to it.

When he'd arrived two hours ago, he'd been just in time to see a hooded figure slip from the trees behind the house and break in through a basement window. He'd waited, more in confusion than fear, until, an hour later, the same figure had reemerged and disappeared back into the woods.

A random burglar? Not likely. The fleeing figure hadn't been carrying any loot that he could see. What were the odds the thief had been after the same thing he was? He thumped the steering wheel. What were the odds they'd already found it?

He'd tried briefly to console himself with the possibility this wasn't her house, that maybe she'd moved or the address on the form was wrong and Wilkins didn't live here at all.

But not two minutes after the thief had run off, a car had

pulled up into the driveway and a man and a woman had gotten out. And while he'd not seen her face he was sure it was her. There was no mistaking that long red hair.

If it had just been her inside the house he'd have knocked on the door and forced his way in. But not with the man in there as well. He was in no shape for any kind of physical confrontation.

And so, once more, he'd sat and watched. Waited until, a few moments ago, the man had come out, gotten in his car and driven away.

Leaving the woman alone inside.

Now was his chance, the best he would get. And still he sat in indecision. Whether she'd intended to or not Raina Wilkins had saved his life. Was there really no other way he could do this?

No. There wasn't.

He reached for the door and froze when a cab appeared coming toward him up the street. It slowed, pulled into Wilkins' driveway, and beeped its horn. A moment later the woman emerged, climbed in the back, and the cab began reversing out.

He drummed his fingers on the steering wheel. Go inside or follow the cab? If the thief had already searched the house, the thing he sought was either now gone or had never been in there in the first place. His only hope was if Wilkins had it on her.

He started the car and pulled out after her.

CHAPTER 23

Raina slid back onto her bar stool and stared down into her half empty glass. Her third tequila in under two hours. Or was it her fourth?

Elbow on the bar, she rested her cheek against her palm. It felt more like six the way the room was swaying. Still, that was the whole point, wasn't it? The reason she'd come here. She just hadn't expected it to happen this fast.

"Just out of practice," she mumbled to no-one and sipped from her glass.

She gazed about at the cheap décor – the tablecloth curtains, the fake wood paneling, the moth-eaten moose head above the door. God, it was like being stuck in a time warp. First Farrington, then Scanlon and now this place.

She could have called Julie to meet her here. Or Val, or Irene; or even Narelle. But for some reason, visiting her old teenage haunt had seemed like something she should do alone.

She peered at the linebacker serving drinks at the end of the bar. Bald, twenty pounds heavier, a few more tats gracing his biceps but still the man from ten years ago. Owner and barkeep, Rod Dempsy. The man who'd served her the night of the accident. Who'd testified how drunk she'd been when she'd walked out the door and climbed behind the wheel of her mother's car.

A car that had ended up wrapped around a tree less than ten minutes later.

Her thoughts flitted back to her recent moment standing atop Salvation Falls. A place she had visited numerous times after that fateful long-ago night.

She hadn't thought about taking 'the step' in a long time. In the beginning the urge had come to her often – sweet release or justice served, either notion just as compelling.

Then one day she'd simply woken and decided she was tired of it all. Tired of walking with her head down, her gaze averted. Of feeling she didn't deserve what joys life might yet have to offer, that all the enmity people extended were judgments she was bound to accept.

At first her rebellion had been in secret. When no-one was looking she would lift her face to the sun, walk with a survivor's joy in her step. After that it hadn't been long before she was greeting people on the street, forcing them to see her, to meet her eyes, daring to think she might one day have what they had. Forgiveness. Love. A family again.

In her naiveté she'd thought she'd managed to put it behind her. But as her confrontation with Scanlon had shown, it was all an illusion. Gazing across the bar room now she could almost see Rick standing there, pool cue in hand.

She cringed at the memory and hung her head. What was she doing here? Punishing herself? Forcing herself to relive every detail about that night. Why? Because Brad had found someone else? Or because the consequences of that long-ago night had been the very reason he'd dumped her?

Whatever the catalyst, it simply seemed fitting to return to the place where it all began. The turning point. The place where her life diverged into chaos, her dreams derailed. The scene of that single moment's negligence that would haunt her for the rest of her days.

She drained her glass and reached for her bag. Enough self-flagellation for one night. Time to blow this popcorn stand. With any luck she'd pass out after the cab dropped her home and not have to face herself in the mirror.

CHAPTER 24

"You call a cab, lady?"

Outside the door, Raina frowned at the man approaching her across the darkened parking lot. She'd only just ducked into the ladies' room after placing her call for a taxi pick-up. "That was quick."

"I was here anyway dropping someone off. I'm over this way."

He turned and started toward the side of the building walking several paces ahead of her. She followed as best she could. The cold air revived her but she was still a little unsteady on her feet.

Around the side, he walked to his cab, opened the passenger door, and stepped back. Only then did she see there was no light on top.

"Wait a minute, this isn't—"

Something came down over her head. Fabric – a jacket, a pillow case. Arms closed around her, pinning her own, lifting her forward. She wheeled, her head meeting something solid with a force that lit up the night with stars.

*　*　*

Seated upright, her body rocked to a gentle rhythm, ears humming.

With a groan she lifted her head and blinked. Blurred lights slowly swam into focus – tiny twinkles of red and blue. Flashes of white through the glass above hurt her eyes.

She closed them again, pushed herself straighter. The tug of restraint across her chest. Seatbelt? Dashboard lights? Yes, the cab. She was on her way home. Too much to drink. She must've…

"You all right?" A man's voice.

She opened her eyes more cautiously this time. Spotted the object dangling from the rearview mirror. A little toy moose. Wasn't that funny – just like the one… She frowned, a thought taking hold in her addled brain. Not a cab, a car. And not just any car, this was *her* car. Which she'd entered when—

She jerked her gaze to the figure beside her. Her eyes widened when approaching headlights lit the man's face. "Oh, my god."

"Relax. No-one's—"

"No. No. This isn't happening." She pushed back away from him. "You can't be here. You're in the morgue. I saw you – you're dead!"

His broad hands twisted around the steering wheel. "Not me, my brother."

The drum of her heartbeat. "Brother," she echoed, tasting the word. The jolt of adrenaline had cleared her head but not enough for this to make sense. "Brother?"

"We look enough alike that you could mistake us, especially in the dark. It's a relief to know they found his body. When did you see him?"

She covered her face, fighting to smother a rush of nausea.

What difference did it make which one of them it was, she'd still been kidnapped!

"You hearing me, or what? I said when did you—?"

"I don't know, this morning I guess." Was it only this morning? It seemed so much longer ago than that.

"You *guess*?"

A small voice told her she should be afraid but the tequilas were speaking much louder. "You practically knock me unconscious, shove me in a car and expect me to carry on a normal conversation?" She took a breath. "So which one of you did I hit on the road that night?"

"That was me. If you don't believe me, I'll show you the bruises."

"Are you suggesting my hitting you was *my* fault?"

"I was fleeing a murder scene at the time; I wasn't exactly watching the traffic."

Fleeing the scene. As in a witness trying to escape? Or the killer trying to avoid capture? "You had a gun."

"Yeah, my brother's."

"Where is it now?"

"What do you care? I lost it in the woods."

"You don't have another one? You're totally unarmed?"

He frowned. "For the moment."

She sat with her fists clenched on her lap, willing herself not to lash out, not to give in to the insane impulse to start punching this man about the head. "Do you have any idea what you've done to me?"

"What *I've* done to *you*?"

"You put me through hell and you're not even dead? You pull a gun on me, steal my car—"

"You think I asked for this to happen?"

"...kidnap me, not once but twice—"

"You think I asked for my only brother to die in my arms?"

The anguished outburst stopped her dead. Whoever he was, he was clearly hurting. For an instant she felt his loss.

The moment passed. "What do you want with me?" Just saying the words ramped up her heart again.

"With you, nothing. I only want what I left in your car. Where is it?"

"What are you talking about? Where's what?" She peered into the darkness beyond the window, searching for any hope of escape.

"A little black tube. A container about the size of your finger. I had it when I got in here that night and left it behind when I got out. What did you do with it?"

Nothing but trees on either side. Even if she leapt from the moving car... "I didn't do anything with it; I never saw it."

"Look, I searched every inch of this damn car and it isn't here. You must have it."

Light bulb on. "Bastard. *That's* why you stole my car."

"I'm telling you, you don't want to hang on to this thing. Not unless you want to end up like my brother."

Her head snapped around. "You're threatening me?"

"Not me, *them*. Don't you get it? That's why they killed him – to get this thing back. That's why they searched your house today."

"What! Who—?"

His gaze had fixed on the review mirror, his face aglow in reflected headlights. Someone was coming up behind them fast.

Before she could look, he hit the gas and her car rocketed into the night.

CHAPTER 25

Blue lights flashed in her side rear mirror. "Police. They must've spotted my car. I reported it stolen."

When the man didn't slow, Raina looked over. "It's okay. I'll explain to them why you took it. You can tell them—"

Her stomach pressed up the back of her throat as they cleared the next rise. There, before them, spanning the road, another cop car stood blocking their path.

With a screech of tires and a spray of gravel he swerved for the forest.

"What are you doing? You can't go in there!"

The car bounced over a ridge at the shoulder and started down a gentle slope. Fifty yards in – further than she ever thought they would get – the growth got too dense. He slammed the brakes and the car skidded side-on into a tree.

She never looked back. Clutching her bag, she threw wide her door, scrambled out, and ran into the woods. Her second flight through a darkened forest in less than three days – and from the same man.

In a tangle of vines she stumbled, fell, pushed herself up. All the while praying her car being wedged against a tree would delay his exit, buy her enough time to reach the road. If she could find it.

As she pushed from the ground a second time, she heard heavy footsteps off to her left. The man in pursuit, trying to outflank her. She veered from the sound, groped another half dozen yards, then fell back against a massive tree trunk.

Straining to listen, fighting to mask the rasp of her breathing, she spotted the lights of the cop car approaching. At least she knew where the road was now.

The same direction the footsteps had come.

Had the man chosen his course deliberately? Gone that way to cut her off, drive her deeper into the forest? Well, they'd just see about that!

She turned and went back the way she'd come, swinging further away from the road, a move she hoped he wouldn't expect.

Ten yards on she squatted down behind a bush, turned her head in all directions. No footsteps this time. Not the slightest rustle.

Out on the road the lights grew brighter. Through the trees she saw the patrol car pull up near where her car had entered the woods. A figure got out, flashlight in hand. Now was her chance.

She pushed to her feet. Inhaled to call out. And squealed when a hand clamped over her mouth.

Her screams smothered, she kicked at the bush, breaking twigs, stirring leaves, determined to make any sound she could.

Until his lips pressed to her ear. "Don't! They find us, they'll kill us both."

She froze for an instant, the words so startling. Surely the lie of a desperate fugitive.

She doubled her struggles.

The hand clamped tighter, stopping her nose as well as her mouth. She couldn't breath!

She shot out her arm, drove back her elbow as hard as she could. They dropped as one, he on his side, moaning in pain; she to her knees, gasping for air.

She looked up, hoping the cop had heard, but he was moving in the other direction. On the road, the second patrol pulled up. All she had to do was get to them.

Before she could rise, a hand gripped her arm. The startled scream died in her throat at the sight of the face twisted in pain.

"The cops are in on it."

"What?"

"They killed my brother. You've got to believe me."

She stared, unmoving. A glint of moonlight sparked in his eyes. This man – a moment ago such a threat – now lying helpless before her. A stranger whose anguish at the loss of a brother had touched her despite all her fears.

"Please...you're the only one who can help me."

He held her gaze in silent appeal. Then his hand slid away and he slumped unconscious.

CHAPTER 26

Raina watched breathless, heart racing, as her car moved slowly back through the forest the way it had entered. The urge to call out nearly overcame her several times but each time something prevented her doing it.

When her car reached the road, the officer behind the wheel stopped to confer with his fellows. Their discussion, lasting all of a minute, included gestures to the surrounding woods, the areas they'd just finished searching. Then the other two men climbed in their patrols and all three vehicles drove away.

She listened to the sound of their engines fading until nothing but darkness remained. In the resounding stillness she bowed her head. "What have I done?"

It was unlikely any of the three had been Scanlon – as chief, he probably relegated to minions such trifling matters as routine patrols and auto theft. But if she'd known for certain one had been Farrington, it might have altered her decision. Two days ago her choice would've been the same, but after her experience with him that afternoon…

Still, she hadn't gotten close enough to see who they were

so it hardly mattered.

She peered at the figure lying beside her, a silhouette barely discernable in the moonlight. Was she a fool? Or did she just have so few people in her life she felt compelled to befriend total strangers? And potentially dangerous ones at that.

A good quarter hour had passed since the man blacked out. A quarter hour in which she'd sat hunched behind her thicket, silently debating whether to believe his outrageous claims. In the end deciding to follow her instincts and *not* reveal their presence to the police.

But perhaps it was more than instinct alone. His despair over losing his brother had moved her. Also the policemen were armed and she wasn't. If the stranger was telling the truth, they'd have both ended up dead and buried in this forest, her car dumped in a lake somewhere, and no-one would ever know.

If he was lying, in his current state he posed far less of a threat to her. Her frown deepened. Especially if she could knock him out with one blow.

She found his shoulder and shook it gently. He let out a moan, mumbled something that sounded like 'Liam' but nothing more.

She groped through her handbag and found her keys. Using the small light attached to the ring, she trailed its beam down the length of his body. Even in the gloom she recognized the stain on his shirt.

With the flashlight clamped between her teeth, she carefully undid the buttons. The source of the bleeding was a wound in his side – just about where her elbow would have caught him – the bandage covering it soaked through with blood.

"Gunshot."

She jumped at the sound of his voice.

"Bullet went straight through. Happened...the night they killed my brother." He tried to sit up but fell back again.

"You're still bleeding. We have to get you—"

"No hospital."

"But if you don't get this looked at—"

"*No* hospital."

She pursed her lips. Hadn't they had this conversation already? "Look, I've got my cell phone. I can—" She cut herself off. Why was she even arguing with him? This man who'd kidnapped her, stolen her car, held her at gunpoint.

"My *new* cell phone, by the way," she added. "Seeing as I had to replace the one *you* threw out my car window. That was an expensive phone, I'll have you know."

"Bill me," he gasped.

Her brows shot up. "Really. Well, if that's how you feel..." She shoved her keys in her bag and rose. "Enjoy yourself with the bears and coyotes."

She got all of three steps before he called out. "Wait."

She kept walking.

"Wait. *Please.*"

She stopped and came back, stood staring down at him.

"I need your help," he gritted out.

She waited, letting him stew in the fact. Clearly an admission he wasn't thrilled about having to make. "I'll bet that hurt as much as the bullet."

She bent and helped him to his feet.

CHAPTER 27

Raina paused to shift the man's arm draping her shoulders. The weight he'd been putting on her had increased steadily the nearer they had gotten to the road. At this rate she wasn't sure he'd make it.

From the description he'd given of the direction he'd driven after leaving the bar, she had a rough idea where they were. The taxi she'd called should be coming along in another few minutes. She needed to be there to flag it down, yet she couldn't get him to move any faster.

When his step faltered, nearly driving her to her knees, she stifled a groan. Why was she doing this? As compelling as his situation might be, she owed him nothing. After everything he'd done, she should've just gone off and left him where he was, lying in woods. She still could. He'd didn't have the strength to stop her. He couldn't even walk without her help.

Which was precisely why she couldn't leave him.

But in truth her reasons weren't totally unselfish. A second thought had begun to emerge, a reason he might prove useful. Scanlon hadn't believed her story and now she had proof. The man himself. She could bring him to the station and insist he tell the police what happened.

And if he refused? If the cops were involved in the death of his brother as he insisted?

She blew out a breath. It was all too much to think about right now. She'd get him back to town and then decide what to do with him. In the meantime he owed her some answers.

"So what's in the case that's so important?"

"What case?"

"The tube you said you left in my car."

"I don't know." A breathless wheeze. "Never had a chance to look inside it."

"Then how do you know—?"

"They killed my brother to get it back. I'd say that was a good indication."

"Who's 'they'?"

"I don't know."

The road was in sight but she needed a rest, as much to regain her strength as calm her temper.

She propped him against the nearest tree. "Now you listen to me. I'm not taking you another step until you tell me what's going on."

"I don't know what's going on!"

The outburst cost him. He grimaced and swore. "Okay, this is all I can tell you. Earlier that night I got a frantic call from Liam saying he needed to see me. We arranged to meet at a friend's boathouse out on the lake."

He paused for breath. "When I arrived, Liam was already there. He told me someone had given him something, some kind of evidence – he's a reporter…" His jaw hardened. "*Was* a reporter – and after seeing it, he was terrified the people it incriminated were going to try to kill him. He showed me the case but before he could tell me what was in it…"

His words trailed off. For an instant she thought he was losing consciousness. Then he continued, his voice strained. "Someone opened fire on us from the woods. Liam was killed, I was wounded. I grabbed his gun and the case, and ran."

Raina shuddered at the thought of such violence. Violence that had invaded her life. "How do you know they were in my house?"

"I saw them go in. One of them anyway. I came to search the place myself but he got there first."

"When was this?"

"This afternoon. Before you got home."

It was getting steadily harder to breathe. If she'd come home alone while the man was still there...

Blocking the thought, she looked toward the road. The cab would be coming along any minute. The rest of her questions would have to wait. "All right, come on." She shoved her shoulder beneath his arm again.

"So why did you leave this thing in my car? Why the hell didn't you take it with you when you got out?"

"I saw their headlights coming up the road, knew I'd never get away on foot. All I could think to do was hide it."

"Hide it," she mocked. "In a car going nowhere. One which they could easily search."

"So sue me, I panicked." He let out a groan. "I was hoping they'd follow me instead."

"How did you ever find me again?"

His voice was weaker, his words growing slurred. Something about the box in her car...

Gravel crunched beneath her feet. The road. They'd made it!

Almost the moment she stepped on the asphalt, the glow of headlights appeared in the distance, a third light dancing atop the vehicle.

A sudden fear gripped her. What if it wasn't a taxi but one of the cop cars coming back?

"You're the only reason I'm still alive."

His words were a whisper against her cheek. She turned to him, their faces inches apart. In the moonlight his features were knife-edged, cut from granite, defined by shadow.

She swallowed. "And don't you forget it."

She looked away. The approaching lights had grown more distinct. She let out her breath, guided him further onto the road and flagged the cab.

CHAPTER 28

Raina paid the driver twenty dollars extra to help her bring the man inside her shop. The stranger had passed out on the way into town and she'd thought it safest to bring him here. If someone *had* been in her house, she wasn't ready to go back there yet.

After relocking the outer door, she returned to the office where they had left him slumped on the couch. She removed his shirt, then eased him back along the cushions and propped up his feet.

The sight of his half naked form stopped her briefly. Despite his resemblance to his brother she could see some differences now. While both had dark hair and similar features, the one before her had the stronger jaw – shadowed by at least a day's growth of beard – with lips and nose more sharply defined. Character was written in the laugh lines fanning out from his eyes. But the furrows creasing that noble brow also hinted at a deep thinker. Or a man carrying a fair bit of anger.

Her gaze strayed lower over powerful shoulders, well-toned chest and firm waist, finally fixing on the bloody gash.

She winced at the sight. Clearly he needed professional care. He could even have other internal injuries resulting from when she'd hit him with her car. What a risk he was taking in refusing treatment. A risk he was now forcing her to share. All she knew was basic first aid. What if he died? How would she explain *that* to Scanlon?

On the other hand, if she called an ambulance, the minute the hospital staff got a look at his gunshot wound they'd call the police. And if the cops had killed his brother as he'd claimed, there'd be no 'ifs' about how he'd end up.

You're the only reason I'm still alive.

The words he'd whispered back in the forest stirred in her ear. Had she really saved his life? Did it matter that she hadn't done it intentionally? Could it still count toward leveling the score, redeem her for the life she'd once taken?

She peeled off her jacket and tossed it aside. "Right. Let's do this."

With soap, water and paper towels she carefully washed the blood from his skin to get her first clear look at the damage.

She swallowed hard. Her first bullet wound. Hopefully her last.

He must have managed to look after it somehow – aside from the fact it was still seeping blood, the wound showed no signs of infection. It might even have started to heal in places. Before she'd driven her elbow into it.

More hopeful about his chances, she applied antiseptic from the first aid kit and covered the lot with a thick gauze bandage. His shirt was a write-off. She tossed it in the bin and dressed him in another from the shop.

With the job complete, she sat back down. Exhaustion instantly threatened to claim her but something niggled at the back of her mind. Something she'd been vaguely conscious of, a memory trying to push to the surface, ever since they'd left the forest.

What do you want with me?

Nothing. I want what I left in your car.

She frowned at the words. She'd told him she'd never seen the thing. She hadn't lied. So why did she feel…

A little black tube, about the size of your finger.

Her frown deepened. He said he'd shoved it under the seat. Surely she would've seen it when she'd cleaned the bloodstains from the carpet. But earlier, when she'd dropped her handbag, and everything had spilled out on the floor…

She jumped from the chair, grabbed her bag and tipped its contents over the desk.

One by one she shoved the items back in again. Wallet. Keys. Cell phone. Hair brush, tissues, papers, pens, pencils.

As the pile dwindled she felt herself slump. No black case.

Down to the dregs: nail file, paper clips, packet of gum, a button that had come off one of her sweaters, and…

A chill washed over her as she gazed at the object that lay in her hand. To a man, nothing but a small black case. To a woman, a familiar item of make-up – a tube of lipstick.

A tube of lipstick that wasn't hers.

CHAPTER 29

Raina stared at the object in her hand. An item very much like the ones sitting on her dressing table back home. The ones she'd found open and scattered across it only that afternoon. Was this what the intruders had searched her house for? She'd had it in her bag all along?

The thought sent shivers sweeping over her. She took a deep breath and pulled off the lid. No Cranberry Red, no Candy Cane Pink, no Autumn Blush.

A flash drive key fell out on her palm.

She turned it over. No label, no markings. Nothing unusual. The sort you'd buy at any office shop.

She looked toward the man passed out on the couch. By rights he should be the first to see what was on it. But since he was in no condition…

She stood debating. Did she even want to know what was on it? That knowledge had cost this man's brother his life. *If* the story he'd told her was true. Looking at the flash drive might confirm if it was. And if the killers had gone to her house in search of it, they must already think she'd seen it.

She pulled the chair back to the desk, sat at the computer,

and inserted the key.

She'd been prepared to wade through dozens of files, examine all manner of information trying to decipher mysterious clues. But the flash drive had only one item on it. A video clip. With the volume set to a whisper she opened the file.

Amateur footage. By the look of it, taken with a cell phone. The viewer approaching a closed door, a hand outstretched easing it open.

Shadows. Movement. A moment to focus.

A dark room. People standing either side of a steel-topped table. The box between them roughly the size of a carry-on suitcase. Only one face visible – a middle-aged woman – the rest just torsos, one beside her, the others opposite.

One of the figures hands her an envelope across the table. She passes it to the torso beside her without even looking. Torso's large hands – clearly a man's – pull a thick wad of bills from the envelope, shuffle through them, slip them back.

The envelope disappears into his pocket. In return he hands over a larger but thinner one. The woman reaches out toward the box—

A shout from the man who pocketed the money. The others tense. Even as the woman looks toward the camera, whoever is holding it retreats.

Shadows and flickers consume the image. Muffled noises.

The footage ends.

The office chair creaked as Raina leaned back, stretching her neck.

She swiveled to regard the man asleep on the couch behind her. She'd been checking him regularly for the last two hours. His bleeding had stopped, his breathing seemed easier, and he showed no sign of developing a fever. By all indications he was simply sleeping peacefully.

If only she were.

She swung back to face the computer screen, reached for her mug and swallowed the last cold dregs of her coffee. With a yawn she hoped would help clear her head, she clicked on the file to watch it again.

She settled back, shaking her head as the footage played. For this a man had lost his life. A video lasting less than two minutes.

She'd lost track how many times she'd watched it now, and still wasn't sure what she was seeing. Her immediate impression had been a drug deal going down. Yet how many drug deals were orchestrated by middle-aged women?

The big question was, what was in the box? It was clearly the focus of everyone's attention, the subject of discussion, the reason money was changing hands. If she knew what was in it, it could tell her at least if what was happening was something sinister or a legal transaction.

She let out a laugh. Legal transaction? Her mind was mush! Of course it wasn't a legal transaction. These people were meeting in a darkened room and had killed the poor soul who'd seen the footage.

So what else could be in the box besides drugs?

She leaned closer and peered at the screen. The woman was clearly the central figure. Whoever she was, she was running the show – talking, gesturing toward the box, giving instructions to the others.

Yet, even with the volume turned up, it was hard to make out what she was saying. Or any of the rest of them for that matter. Raina huffed. Maybe if her computer had better speakers.

When the image began to blur in her gaze, she rubbed her eyes, then opened them again. No good. She still couldn't see straight. Another coffee was what she needed.

With the footage still running, she grabbed her mug and crossed to the door. And froze at a sound that issued from the speakers.

She turned back slowly, heart in her mouth. It was gone in an instant. Had she really heard it? If so, why hadn't she picked it sooner? The different angle she was to the speakers? Or just her wild imagination?

She sat back down, watched the video through from the start. At the end, where the image dissolved into shadows, she cranked up the volume as high as it would go.

The sound came again, stopping her breath. She hadn't imagined it.

CHAPTER 30

Scanlon slipped quietly into the bedroom. He was grateful Peg was already asleep. He'd never have been able to hide from her the feelings crawling in his gut. Concerns roused by the unexpected and most unwelcome encounter he'd had that day.

He eased down onto his side of the bed, removed his slippers, and reclined against the pillows. At once he was back in the hospital waiting room, feeling that hesitant tap on his shoulder, hearing that voice, turning around…

And there she had been. Raina Wilkins. The girl who had destroyed their lives.

He pressed his fist to the center of his chest. The pressure was building, that familiar unseen weight bearing down on him. Seeing her standing there, looking into her upturned face…

God help him, for a minute all he'd been able to see was Rick beside her. A flashback of the two of them in ragged jeans, a butterfly net over her shoulder, a home-made fishing pole over his. A punch to the gut with a weighted glove that had left him reeling, in the end forcing him to turn away before the shock of it completely unmanned him.

In an act that demanded every ounce of control he possessed, he'd listened to her outrageous story, trying to block the intrusive images that continued to flash behind his eyes...

Rick and Raina up in the tree house.

Rick and Raina in their Halloween costumes. Building a snow man. Dressed for the prom.

Rick and Raina, their small hands stained blue after an afternoon of picking blueberries.

Theirs had been a friendship shared from elementary right through high school. A relationship that had deepened toward the end and might even have ended in marriage. If Raina hadn't started on a downward spiral, dragging his only son along with her.

He massaged the muscles, taut as hawsers, along his throat. They seemed to stretch up into his scalp, steely fingers slowly tightening around his head.

Yes, Raina had once been a welcome guest in their home. A friend so often found playing in the yard or flopped on the couch, she'd seemed to belong there as much as Rick.

It had damn near broken his heart watching the girl go to pieces like she had. He'd known her father of course. All the parent/teacher interview nights, the school plays, graduations, sporting events, had brought their families together on more than a few occasions over the years.

Jeff Wilkins had been a good man, a loving father, and Raina had clearly adored him. Little wonder she'd taken it hard when he died. But that could never excuse what she'd done. Or the fact she'd gotten away with it.

As bad as mourning Rick's loss had been, the judge's decision had made it worse. A ruling Peg had never come to terms with and which had challenged to a profound degree Scanlon's faith in the justice system.

In his world of straightforward ethics, a person paid for their mistakes. You caused someone's death, you made amends. No excuses, no mitigation. Yet for the crime of killing his son, Raina Wilkins had practically walked free. How had justice been served in that? How had she learned from her mistake?

The story she'd told him at the hospital today was so incredible he was still trying to make sense of it. Yet one thing was clear. Her days of flouting the law weren't over. By her own admission she'd left the scene of a serious accident, certainly an indictable offence.

Yet seeing as the man she'd hit was now dead, killed by someone else, it would be hard to make any charges stick. Meaning, once again Raina Wilkins would walk away without paying the price.

That was assuming the victim *had* been killed by someone else.

Scanlon let the thought circle in his mind. From what little evidence they'd gathered so far, other crimes had likely been committed relating to the victim's death. While they still had too few clues to get the whole picture, if he could ultimately prove Raina's involvement in those crimes, if he could connect her in any way to what had gone down…

He settled back, feeling the pressure ease in his chest. After all these years and through a totally unrelated event, justice for what she had done to Rick might yet be exacted after all.

CHAPTER 31

Raina lifted her head from the desk and blinked at the figure standing over her. A figure whose hand still gripped her shoulder, shaking it gently.

The double image fused into one – spiky dark hair, studded earlobes, a concerned frown. She squinted. "Julie?"

"Hey, boss, what's up?"

"What are you doing here?"

The woman laughed. "Well, unless you fired me and forgot to mention it, I'm here to start work."

Work? She straightened. "What time is it?"

"Ten after nine."

"In the *morning*?"

The smile vanished. "Hey are you okay?"

Raina raised a hand to her head. No, she wasn't okay. A throbbing headache. Groggy, weak, a little queasy.

The events of the evening came flooding back – her session at Dempsey's, passing out, waking up in her stolen car with a man she'd thought dead behind the wheel. Bringing him here, nursing his wound, leaving him—

She whipped around to look behind her.

The couch was empty.

"You've got to be kidding me."

She rose and wobbled across the room. The cushions were cold. No stains on the fabric. No sign of his bloody shirt in the bin. As though he'd never been here at all. She held her head. Perhaps he hadn't.

Julie stood eyeing her. "Come on, girl, talk to me. What's going on?"

"How long have you been here?

"Just a few minutes."

"Was anyone else here when you arrived?"

"No, just you."

I don't believe this.

She paced the length of the tiny room. Gone. He was gone. What would she do? How would she ever find him again? She didn't even know his name.

"Raina, you're starting to scare me. What is it?"

She stopped. Then again, why did she need to find him? To tell him what was on the drive key, that's why.

She blinked. The key!

She stepped to the desk, checked the computer's USB port. Her finger trailed over an empty slot. *Damn it!*

"There was a flash drive here. Did you take it?"

Julie blinked at her. "I told you, I just got here. Raina, what the hell is—"

"Nothing." She pawed through the clutter atop her desk. Maybe she'd taken the key out herself before falling asleep.

"You look like you've been here all night," Julie said. "What were you doing? Was someone else here with you?"

Yes, someone had been here with her. The ungrateful bastard who'd stolen her car!

She threw down the handful of papers she held. No sign

of the flash drive. He'd taken it. Taken it and simply walked away. No thank-you, no apologies.

Fingers digging into the back of the chair, she stood fuming. After all she'd done for him. Not turning him in, bringing him here – her personal space – dressing his wound, looking after him. And this was how the bastard repaid her?

Julie placed a hand on her arm. "I'll go open up. Give you a minute."

She nodded absently.

"When I come back maybe you can tell me what's going on."

Raina shoved the chair back under the desk. What was she getting so angry about? The man had obviously lied to her. He'd known enough to take the flash drive, which meant he knew more than he'd been telling her. Just as well he was out of her life. Even better that he'd taken his damn evidence with him. Let him have it. She no longer had anything anyone wanted. Her life could go back...

She resumed her pacing. No, that was crazy. She *had* to find him. She had to tell him what was on the video file, what she had heard.

But he has the file. He'll hear for himself.

If he turns the volume right up. And *if* he watches to the very end, past where the visual footage ends.

The sound of her cell phone cut through her thoughts. On the frantic long-shot it might be him, she snatched up her bag and pulled it out. "Yes?"

Hearing the voice at the other end, her speeding thoughts slammed to a stop as abruptly as if they'd hit a brick wall.

She drew herself up, focused on keeping her voice calm. "Thank you. I'll be there in an hour."

CHAPTER 32

Raina sat on the wooden bench in the police station's outer office. The place hadn't changed much in the ten years since she'd last seen it – the same worn desks, the same framed honors lining the shelves of the same glass cabinet, the same faux-antique clock on the wall.

And behind the closed door off to her right, the same old captain manning the helm.

She could've gotten here forty minutes sooner, come directly from the store, but hadn't been prepared to face John Scanlon without going home to freshen up first. Her one and only hangover in ten years and *he* had to be the one to see it!

She worked at keeping her breathing steady, her body still as she watched the seconds tick by on the clock. God, she wasn't ready for this. So much had happened in the last few days, she was still struggling to make sense of it. Getting barely four hours sleep certainly wasn't aiding the process. Nor were the drinks she'd had last night.

Still, in the time it had taken her to get here, she'd come to have second thoughts about the stranger's sudden disappearance. Maybe he hadn't been lying to her after all.

She'd left the lipstick case on the desk – when he'd woken, he would surely have seen it. It probably wouldn't have taken much for him to work out what had been inside it. In fact, for all she knew he'd been lying there pretending to be asleep on her couch while actually watching the video with her.

So why *had* he run off without speaking to her again? If not to thank her, at least to apologize for the trouble he'd caused her. If his story was true, she knew nearly as much as he did about what had happened. What did he feel he had to hide from her? Had his mission to find his brother's killer been that urgent he couldn't have waited another few hours?

You really don't want to hang on to this thing. Not unless you want to end up like my brother.

She frowned at the thought. Was it possible he'd left to protect her? To put as much distance between them as possible; lure whoever these people were away from her? If that was the case, and he hadn't been lying, it meant the police *could* be involved with his brother's murder.

So what on earth was she going to tell Scanlon?

She settled herself with tremendous effort, folding her hands to keep them still. The officer working at one of the desks, a young black woman, kept glancing over at her. Raina didn't want it to get back to Scanlon that she'd been acting nervously before their meeting.

As for the stranger, she was probably just deluding herself, reading good intentions into the man's actions when in all likelihood—

A buzzer sounded on the officer's desk. The woman looked up. "He's ready to see you."

Raina nodded, rose from the bench and turned for the office. Only to stop at the sight of the object laying on the nearest desk. The morning paper. With her photo, taken at the hospital yesterday, gracing the front page, the headlines reading, "Has She Killed Again?"

Seconds flicked by. She realized her mouth was open and closed it, then noted the stares of the officer and a mother and son now standing at the counter. Before the shock could completely unnerve her, she scooped up the paper and marched with it into Scanlon's office.

CHAPTER 33

"Sit," Scanlon said without looking up from the paperwork he was absorbed in.

Raina slapped the newspaper down in front of him. "You want to tell me how this happened?"

The man did nothing but lift his gaze. It was as though he'd shoved her into the chair.

She waited in silence till he finished his notes and put down his pen. Her heart clenched. Whether by a trick of the light, the angle of his face or the set of his features, for an instant not the man, but his son sat before her. *Rick.*

"I'm looking into it." He glanced at the paper. "It wasn't through any official statement I assure you. When I find out who leaked the information…"

She stared, stunned by his angry tone.

"Don't get the wrong idea," he said. "It's Peg I was hoping to spare."

Peggy, of course. Raina wouldn't have wanted Rick's mother to know about the recent accident either. Still, in the moment she'd thought Scanlon's concern had been for her she'd felt a ridiculous surge of hope.

She nodded, letting the matter drop.

Scanlon played the seconds out staring back at her. He looked to have gotten even less sleep than she, his eyes bloodshot, his doughy features deeply lined. But she knew beneath that jaded exterior lurked a mind as sharp as a scalpel.

She cleared her throat. "You said on the phone my car had been found."

"Patrol spotted it last night being driven along one-fifty-four. Unfortunately when they gave chase, the driver ditched it. I'm afraid he got away."

"Oh. Well..." It felt strange pretending she hadn't been there. Strange and unsettling. She had to be careful what she said. "As long as I get it back, I guess. That's the important thing."

He studied her a moment. "Don't you want to know what condition it's in?"

She mustered surprise. "I assumed it was all right or you would've mentioned it. Why, did something happen to it?"

"It appears he used your spare key to get in so there was no damage there. However he did hit a tree. The driver's door is dented."

She blew out a breath, feigning disgust. "Great. There go my premiums."

"Forensics has already had a look at it. They found traces of blood on the floor beneath the passenger seat. Supports your claim about the man getting into your car that night."

The knot in her stomach loosened a notch. "So you believe me now?"

"Looks like you worked pretty hard on those stains, trying to remove them. Any particular reason for that?"

The knot drew tight again. "I should drive around with

blood on my carpet?"

He settled back, picked up a pen. "We've learned his identity by the way."

"Who?"

"The guy in the morgue; the one you I.D.ed as the man you hit. Name's Liam DeMarco. A reporter for the Augusta Sentinel."

There was more, she could feel it. "This isn't just about you finding my car."

"See the problem is, what you told us doesn't add up. The examiner found no bruising on the body. Which you'd expect, seeing as you ran the guy over."

"I didn't run him over, I hit him. In fact I only sideswiped him, so it really isn't that surprising."

"You came to the hospital believing you'd killed him."

"Yes, but—"

"You said he was sitting hunched in the seat as though in pain."

"He was, but—" She cut herself off. He was trying to incite her, pressure her into blurting something to incriminate herself.

She took a deep breath. "When I heard the news that a body had been found I overreacted. I was upset. I felt bad about not reporting the accident."

"And why was that again?"

"I told you, the man had run off. I didn't see much point in calling an ambulance when there wasn't anyone to treat."

"You didn't see a point in reporting that a man had pulled a gun on you?"

"I… I wasn't thinking clearly."

"But not because you'd been drinking."

"No!" She clenched her fists. Despite her efforts she'd let

him get to her.

Scanlon pulled a folder from a stack on the desk. "We've learned something else. The car the deceased's body was found in wasn't his own. It's registered to an older brother, Alec DeMarco."

He slid two photos in front of her and pointed. "That's Liam, that's Alec. Strong resemblance, wouldn't you say?"

Raina stared. Brothers. Just as the stranger... as *Alec* had told her. Little wonder she had confused the two. "Yes, I suppose."

"Could Alec have been the man you hit on the road that night?"

Her mind raced. In the state she was in she couldn't see where he was going with this, the trap he was setting. "I don't know. It was dark and I was looking mostly at the road."

"We've been trying to locate Alec for questioning. So far no luck. He hasn't tried to contact you, has he?"

"Me!" *Too loud.* She laughed off the outburst. "Why would he want to contact me?"

Scanlon stared.

"No, no-one's tried to contact me."

Her gaze was drawn to the photos again. Did Scanlon know more than he was telling her? Did evidence at the scene suggest... "You think he was there when Liam got killed? Maybe he just loaned him his car."

"Liam's body was found in the driver's seat but his fingerprints weren't on the steering wheel. That plus the absence of blood in the car confirms he was put there *after* he died."

She shook her head, still unable to see what he might be accusing her of. "And?"

"*And* there were traces of cocaine in the trunk."

Her mouth went dry. "You think the killing was drug related?" The video on the flash drive. The box on the table. Had Alec been one of those faceless torsos? Then what was the sound she had heard?

"Still sure he hasn't tried to contact you?"

"I told you, no," she said.

"And you see no connection between your hitting one of these men on the road that night and your car being stolen the very next day?"

"I'm not a cop. It's not my job to make connections."

Scanlon leaned forward, taking his time, savoring the moment. "Then you'd see none between this and what happened ten years ago."

She couldn't draw breath. His words had punched the air from her lungs. There could be no connection between the two events, he had to know that. He was simply goading her, bringing up the past in an attempt to unnerve her.

And he'd damn well succeeded!

Just when she felt her lungs would explode his desk phone rang. Without waiting to be dismissed she surged to her feet.

"See Deputy Farrington about that statement before you leave," he said.

She turned from the desk and stumbled to a halt two steps from the chair.

There on the bookshelf next to the door sat a framed photograph. The face of a young man smiling back at her. The face that would forever haunt her nightmares.

CHAPTER 34

Scanlon set the phone down on his desk. He'd hoped it was Peg returning his call but it was just another update from Hendricks. He picked up the newspaper and again scanned the lead article, his chest growing tight as he imagined the impact it would have on his wife.

Earlier that morning when he'd first come in and seen the headlines, he'd called Peg's sister, Maureen, to warn her, asking that she go by the house and take the newspaper out of their mailbox. And in the event Peg had already seen it, to go inside and comfort her in what surely would be a difficult moment.

He hadn't heard from either of them since and when he tried to call them, neither had answered. He closed his eyes, trying to shut out the possible scenarios.

He and Peg had wanted many children but it was not to be. Rick was born only after many years of trying, after they'd all but given up, and Peg had never fallen pregnant again. Rick had meant everything to her. As he had to Scanlon.

Admittedly in the early years Scanlon had feared for his shy only child, wondering if his lack of desire to mix with others signified some deeper problem. From the time the boy had entered school he'd displayed a consuming passion for nature – birds, animals, insects, trees – but even these he preferred to study in the safety of their home.

All that had changed when Rick met Raina, a confident outgoing nine-year-old with the same fascination for living things. Raina had drawn his son from his shell, taken him from enjoying nature through books and on-line, to discovering it firsthand in the forests and streams of the Maine countryside.

John had never minded the jars of caterpillars, the fish tanks of tadpoles and other creatures that cluttered Rick's bedroom. He'd never minded Raina's almost daily presence in their house. At times, God help him, it had been like having a second child.

To Peg, there had only ever been Rick.

Oh, she'd made Raina feel welcome of course. Fed her lunches, tended the various cuts and scrapes that occurred on her watch, even took Raina to the hospital once when she'd broken her wrist falling from the tree house.

But deep down John had always suspected she'd done it in the hope of keeping Rick close. For the simple fact was, once Raina had come on the scene Rick hadn't needed Peg as much any more. A normal healthy step in a boy's development, he'd always thought.

Peg had never quite seen it that way.

Scanlon put a hand to his head. Well, it was only natural really. The loss of a child would devastate a mother in any case. But when that child was her only one…

He winced when, without warning, Judge Latham's ruling whispered through his mind. The man's decision to be lenient, to give consideration to the circumstances prompting Raina's behavior. Her extreme remorse which he believed to be genuine. The suffering, both mental and physical, she would continue to endure.

Peg had collapsed on hearing those words. Soon after she'd done a spell in Wentworth Sanatorium. After that, further grief counseling and years of therapy on the outside.

Her recovery to a functioning state – bearing little resemblance to the joyous lighthearted woman he'd married – had been arduous and fraught with setbacks. Even now, ten years later, he would occasionally come home and find her sitting in Rick's room, drink in hand, poring over some photo albums or other memorabilia. What would an article, stating that Raina had essentially repeated the same offence, do to Peg's fragile equilibrium?

Slowly he lowered his arm to the desk. He closed his hand, crumpling the newspaper in his fist, then slammed it into the rubbish basket.

CHAPTER 35

Raina fled through the outer office, never stopping to speak to the clerk or inquire if Deputy Farrington was free. By the time she burst out the station's front doors she could barely see for the flood of her tears.

She groped down the steps, swung a hard right and slammed into a passing pedestrian. The impact with the solid figure nearly knocked her off her feet. Only the hand that reached out to steady her kept her from stumbling.

"Raina?"

She lifted her gaze as high as the badge on the uniformed chest. Farrington stood like a wall in her path. She tried to step past him, but he wouldn't move.

"What is it? What's wrong?"

Nothing but hiccoughs and stammers escaped her.

The next thing she knew he'd taken her arm and was guiding her across the maple-lined street.

Inside the café directly opposite he settled her into a booth, then stepped to the counter. "Two coffees, please, Mae."

As he waited for his order, Raina fought to get a grip on

herself. The meeting with Scanlon had been charged with tensions right from the start, but the picture of Rick had been the last straw. She couldn't help wondering – was the photo always on Scanlon's shelf? Or had he put it on display especially because he'd known she was coming?

Farrington slid into the opposite seat and pushed a black coffee under her nose. It smelled divine.

"Thank you," she murmured, clutching the mug in both hands. On a mild autumn afternoon she felt chilled to the marrow.

He gave her a moment, letting her settle, letting the silence entice her to speak.

At last she did. "I just had a conversation with your boss."

"Ah." He nodded and took a reflective sip of his coffee. "If it's any comfort, I'm often reduced to a similar state after talking with John."

The image of this strapping officer weeping uncontrollably was nearly enough to elicit a smile. "He called to tell me my car had been found. But when I came in, we ended up talking about...other things."

"The body in the morgue. Yes, I knew he had some more questions for you."

"I think I could've handled that. Unfortunately that wasn't all."

"You mean..." Disapproval thinned his lips. "I'm sorry. It wasn't right of him to bring that up."

"You can't really blame him."

"Yes, you can. It isn't relevant to the current case. If he can't put personal issues aside..." Farrington seemed to catch himself. As though speaking ill of a fellow officer, let alone a senior one and a friend, wasn't something he felt comfortable about. "There's no place for personal vendettas in police work."

She was both surprised and impressed by his ethics, however naïve.

"But then I suppose..." His look turned uncertain. "Is it possible it wasn't what he said that upset you? I mean what happened the other night had to have stirred up some unpleasant memories."

For an instant she tensed. Then it struck her: there was nothing she needed to hide from this man – he already knew her darkest secrets.

She closed her eyes. "It's been ten years and sometimes it feels like it happened yesterday."

He ran his thumb down the side of his mug. "At the trial, back then, you said you couldn't remember much."

"Of the accident itself, no, nothing. I don't even remember leaving Dempsey's that night. Though by all reports I wouldn't have remembered in any case, I was that drunk."

She cast her thoughts back. "The first I knew of what had happened was when I woke up in the hospital, my mother telling me...that Rick was gone. That I'd been driving. That I was two times over the legal limit.

"I remember the police coming to my hospital room a few days later, formally charging me, my mother sitting beside the bed, sobbing. And, of course I remember the court case, Scanlon's reaction when I got off with a reduced sentence."

She cringed as more memories came flooding back. The nurse, a friend of the Scanlon family, who'd refused to treat her at the hospital. The stares and whispers of the other patients and their visitors. Losing her friends. For months afterwards still being afraid to leave her house for all the comments and emails she'd received.

"It must've been a tough stretch," Farrington said. "Your

mom died not long after the trial, as I recall."

"Seven months later. Couldn't take the strain any more."

He frowned. "Of?"

She let out a huff. "You've got a short memory. My trouble started long before the accident. The string of underage misdemeanors? The pot, the booze, the drunk-and-disorderlies. You even brought me home a few of times. You can't have forgotten."

His expression told her clearly he hadn't. He waved a hand. "All kids go through a—"

"No. Not like that, not like I did. Mine wasn't your typical adolescent rebellion phase. This was different."

She took a sip of the scalding brew, feeling it burn all the way down. "I was sixteen when my dad had the heart attack. Maybe because he died so suddenly...I don't know...I just went completely off the rails.

"For two years I put my mom through hell and to this day I don't know why or who I was mad at. It just seemed the more she tried to rein me in, the worse I got. I was on a steep downward spiral. A spiral ending with Rick's death."

"Surely your mom understood why it happened, what you were going through."

She stared in her mug, a memory pushing up from the depths, a memory she had never told anyone.

"About a month after the accident, not long after I got out of rehab, I came in the house one day and heard my mom talking on the phone. She was shouting at the person on the other end. I never heard her shout on the phone before. She was saying, "Leave us alone! Hasn't she suffered enough!" Then she slammed down the phone and covered her mouth. And I stood there in the doorway thinking to myself, "It should've been me who died that night."

The Deputy's hand descended on hers. "Raina—"

"I know that's what everyone thought. Even the ones who didn't say it." She shook her head, incredulous. "I never dreamed I'd be grateful my parents are gone. But at least they're not here to see it all catching up to me now."

"Look..." Farrington set down his mug. "No matter what Scanlon said to you, you know that what happened the other night has nothing to do with ten years ago."

"I just get the feeling he sees this as a fresh opportunity. A way to finally impose the justice he thinks I escaped last time." She couldn't keep the desperation from her voice. "He's looking to pin whatever he can on me, I can see it. *And* make it stick this time."

"Don't worry. Please. I probably shouldn't be saying this but it's not you he's after, it's the brother. Alec DeMarco is the real person of interest in this case."

"He is?" She shifted. Alec DeMarco. The man she'd only just spent the night with. From one unsettling thought to another.

"That Liam's body was found in his car is itself suspicious. But the fact we can't find Alec suggests he may have gone on the run."

He noticed his hand was still over hers and gently withdrew it. "In any case, the important thing is, it isn't you Scanlon's after. He was just rattling your cage to see what you know."

She took a deep breath and blew it out again. "That does make me feel a bit better." She looked up to find him leaning closer, his blue eyes intent.

"If Scanlon wasn't in so much pain he'd see that you've changed," he said.

The hope he had kindled the day before flared once

again. "Have I?"

"Your own business. Employer and tax payer..." He tipped his head. "Volunteer at the local hospital. "

She smiled shyly. "How'd you know that?"

"I have my sources. Friend of mine works in the children's ward, says she sees you there sometimes. All of which adds up to a responsible caring member of the community in my book."

She looked down. "A far cry from what I was, you mean."

"What matters is you pulled yourself together. You went off the rails but you got back on again. Many who go that far never do."

He was so convincing she almost believed him. "Thank you, Deputy."

"Craig," he corrected.

The request surprised and strangely pleased her. "Craig," she echoed.

"Well..." He drew himself up. "Ready to go back and give me that statement?"

"I am."

"Good. You go ahead, I'll take care of this."

She watched him get up and return to the counter. A man of principles yet surprisingly forgiving. For so long she'd avoided this link with her past. How odd he should now be providing her comfort.

For a moment she basked in the warmth of his words. Maybe she really could believe him. Maybe things had changed. Then her gaze strayed past him, taking in the customers seated at various tables and booths around the room, all staring back at her. Patrons who'd all read the morning paper.

She slid from the booth and pushed to her feet. She might

not be able to stand up to Scanlon but this she could handle. She returned the gaze of each one in turn, then walked out the door.

CHAPTER 36

The Brockton Mills library was a redbrick monolith standing at the end of the town's main street. Alec had been waiting in the adjacent park since sun-up, a frigid four hours marked by occasional bursts of rain from which he'd sheltered beneath the rotunda.

As the library's opening hour drew near he'd taken up position on the steps of the building and could finally now see, through its front glass panels, a staff member approaching to unlock the door.

Despite his eagerness to get inside, he held back to let several elderly patrons in first. When they'd all preceded him through the lobby, he turned and ducked into the men's room.

In a stall he carefully sloughed off his jacket – the one he'd stolen from the woman's shop – and lifted his shirt. He hadn't yet seen the damage she'd done when she'd elbowed him in the woods last night, but he certainly felt it.

Then again maybe it was just the Advil wearing off. Or both. From what he could see, she'd patched him up reasonably well. Better than he'd been managing to do himself in fact, in the awkward position he had to adopt. He lowered the shirt, grabbed the jacket and stepped from the stall.

At the sink he splashed his face with cold water. Seeing his reflection in the mirror he noted that the shirt was in fact not the one he'd been wearing last night. Presumably Wilkins had dressed him in it after tending his injury.

Brave of her, really, to have done all that for him, a virtual stranger. He wouldn't imagine being kidnapped by someone qualified as getting to know them.

But then look at all he'd learned about her just from their two brief encounters. He'd learned she was compassionate – if not entirely sensible about whom she bestowed that compassion on – resourceful, levelheaded, and a bit of a pain in the ass at times. He knew she'd gone to a bar alone but had shown no interested in any of the men who'd approached her. He knew her eyes were the same sunset copper as her hair. And that they sparked with fire when she was angry, but more often seemed dimmed by sadness.

Above all, he would have to call her forgiving, considering she'd helped him despite all he'd done to her – stealing her car, kidnapping her, not to mention the gun in her face. Hell, if *he'd* been on the receiving end of all that, he'd have left the culprit lying in the woods for the bears and coyotes.

Thank god she hadn't.

He grabbed paper towels and blotted his face. When he'd come-to on her office couch and seen her slumped over the desk asleep, he'd nearly woken her to thank her and apologize. But the black tube had instantly caught his eye, returning his thoughts to his primary mission.

From vague recollections of waking briefly during the night, half delusional, and seeing her sitting there staring at the screen, he'd concluded that the flash drive still in the computer must have come from the tube.

He'd retrieved the drive, started from the room, then stopped and – for no other reason than that the impulse struck him, that he wondered what her hair would smell like; or perhaps because, in the midst of this chaos he needed some normal human contact – he gently planted a kiss on her head.

Then he'd gone to the shop, helped himself to one of her jackets and left her without so much as a note.

In disgust he pitched the towels in the bin and set off in search of the library's computer center. He wasn't cut out for this fugitive stuff. Give him a book and a chair by the fire in a nice remote log cabin somewhere. Living on the run, sleuthing after killers, and stealing from good Samaritans were definitely not things he excelled at.

He'd have left her money for the clothes at least. *If* he'd had any. But he'd spent his last dollars on a meal last night and couldn't go to an ATM in case they were watching his withdrawals. No, the way he'd seen it, the best he could do to repay her kindness was to get as far away from her as possible.

Off the main corridor, he came to a room of desks with computers and ducked inside. The simple movement of turning the corner brought a sudden flare of pain to his side. He stopped for a moment to catch his breath.

The pain was definitely stronger this time. Yes, as bad as he felt – about *all* that had happened – he suspected he was going to feel a lot worse before the day was out. The Advil, bandages and clothes he'd bought yesterday had all been left in the woman's car.

He found a computer not in use, eased himself down on the seat, and slipped the flash drive into the port.

CHAPTER 37

By the time Raina returned home – having given her statement, filled out paperwork to reclaim her car, and picked up groceries – it was nearly dark. She would have to bring Julie some brownies tomorrow for holding the fort at work all day.

As she entered the house she took careful note that her front door was locked and showed no signs of having been tampered with. Once inside she went room to room, checking the windows, the kitchen door and the one from the breezeway out to the garage.

Her kidnapper – Alec – had sworn he'd seen someone breaking into her house yesterday. *Breaking* in, not waltzing in through the open front door. Yet she could find no sign of a forced entry. Another lie? Or was he simply mistaken? In any event her house looked secure.

Even then she couldn't relax.

In the kitchen she threw off her coat and started pacing. She'd lied to the police. Not once but twice. If Scanlon found out, he'd think it suspicious at the very least and might find a way to use it against her.

She hadn't wanted to lie to Farrington. Craig, she amended, recalling his request in the café. But after telling Scanlon that Alec DeMarco hadn't contacted her, she couldn't turn around and give a different story in her statement. As much as Craig's words had reassured her, as much as she was beginning to trust the man, she couldn't say the same for the rest of the force. Because if Alec DeMarco was telling the truth, one of them was a killer.

The bottom line was, she had no idea who or what to believe.

From a cupboard she yanked out the mixer and bowl, then went to the pantry to grab the ingredients for Julie's brownies.

The police were currently looking for Alec. Their interest in him suggested they believed he'd murdered his brother, or had at least been involved. Yet from what she'd observed, he'd seemed distraught. Of course he could have been faking it, lying to her. But then so could Scanlon.

Stopped by the thought, she set her ingredients on the counter. Even after all that had happened between them, it was next to impossible to imagine John Scanlon capable of murder. The man she'd known ten years ago wouldn't have been. A man she'd known since the third grade and who'd once been like a second father to her.

But grief could do strange things to people. Let alone vengeance and festering rage.

She removed the wrapper from a stick of butter and dropped it in the bowl. As bad as she felt about lying to Craig, that wasn't all that was worrying her. There was also the video on the flash drive and what she had come to believe might be on it.

When Scanlon told her the police had found drugs in

DeMarco's car she'd suddenly had doubts about her conclusions regarding the video. It seemed more likely that her first impression of the footage was the right one – the scene with the box and the money changing hands *was* a drug deal after all.

Yet somehow her mind kept clinging to the other scenario. Could she have been wrong about what she'd heard? The sound had been short and come only once. She'd had a few drinks and had been so tired she couldn't see straight.

But of course there was no way to know. There was no way she could be sure about anything!

With a muttered curse she turned for the sink and stopped after only a single step. She'd left the door to the breezeway open. In the passage beyond, a shadow was moving along the wall, creeping from the garage toward the kitchen. The shadow of a large hooded figure.

Someone was inside her house.

CHAPTER 38

Raina stood rigid. Run? She'd never reach the front door in time. Scream? Her neighbors' houses were too far away. No-one would hear.

On a charge of cold terror, she lunged to the counter and grabbed the largest knife from the block. Just as the figure stepped into view.

Terror downgraded to highly alarmed. The shadow had been a trick of the light – the figure before her was half the size of that menacing image. A rake-thin girl of no more than sixteen.

For a moment they stood staring at each other. But as Raina took in the worn sweatshirt and grubby jeans she made the connection.

"I've seen you before. You were in my store the other day." She brandished the knife. "Who are you? What are you doing in my house?"

"The stick. Where is it?"

"What stick? What are you—"

"The memory stick. The flash drive. The one in the lipstick case."

Good god, not another one!

"That's all I want." The girl moved closer. "Just give it to me and I'll go away, I'll never come back."

Raina held her at bay with the blade. "I don't have it."

"Don't lie to me! I know you do."

Raina frowned. "What makes you think—?"

"That reporter guy got in your car that night, after you hit him. He must have given it to you then."

Her mouth fell open. "My god, you were there?"

"I haven't been able to find him since. If you helped him escape—"

"I didn't help anyone, at least not intentionally." She shook her head. "I'm sorry, I don't have the thing you're looking for. A guy named Alec DeMarco has it."

"Alec DeMarco." The girl stood blinking. "*Alec* DeMarco. But I gave it to Liam. Liam was going to—"

"Liam's dead."

The news knocked the slight figure back a step. "Dead? No way." A note of panic had entered her voice. "You're wrong. He can't be. I saw him—"

"He's dead. Believe it. The man you saw was his brother, Alec. He has the flash drive."

"Well, where is he?"

"I have no idea. The police don't even know where he is."

The girl threw her head back and turned in a circle. "No, no, no!"

Raina followed each move with the knife, ready to strike if the girl turned violent. But at this point the kid didn't look so much dangerous as distraught.

She swung back to Raina, clenching her fists against her chest. "You don't understand, I have to get it back. My phone was stolen, the stick is the only proof I have."

"Proof of what?"

"I knew the cops would never believe me. That's why I gave it to that reporter. I thought if he could get it in the paper... But they must've found out. They followed him there..." Her face crumpled. "I thought he got away. I was sure he made it!"

She collapsed against the counter, sobbing.

Afraid her actions might be a trick, Raina kept her distance, clutching the knife. "What's on the stick? What's so important—"

"Everything! Everything that means anything to me!" She started to sag, her legs giving way.

Raina dropped the knife and rushed to support her.

CHAPTER 39

With her prowler seated at the kitchen table, Raina poured her a glass of water. She waited as the girl took several sips, then settled onto the seat across from her.

"I'm not sure how much help I can be," she said, "but if I'm going to do anything for you, I need to know what's going on. Take a deep breath and start from the beginning."

The deep breath amounted to a quick gulp of air. "I knew the cops wouldn't believe me so I went to the papers. I went to their office and just picked the name of a reporter off the wall. I put the stick in a lipstick tube and gave it to the secretary with a note to give him."

Raina nodded. Not exactly the beginning she'd hoped for but she could ask her questions later. "Go on."

"I figured if anything happened to the stick, I'd still have the video on my phone, I could make more copies. But then my phone got stolen the next night, which meant the stick was the only copy. I had to get it back. But without my phone—"

When her voice started rising, Raina put a hand up. She couldn't help feeling a rush of sympathy. Whatever this was, the kid had really worked herself into a state. "Breathe slowly and just tell me what happened."

Complying was more of a struggle this time. "I went back to the newspaper office to see if I could talk to the guy. It was after nine, but I thought he might be working late. Just as I got there, I saw him drive out of the parking lot, so I followed him."

With one eye on the temperature gauge, Erin peered out at the thick black forest pressing in on either side of the road. She hadn't been using the car much lately and making only short trips when she did. With a hole in the radiator it overheated like every ten miles and she had to keep stopping to put water in it.

When she'd first spotted the reporter leaving work she'd figured he must have been on his way home – how far could that be? But unless he lived out in the middle of nowhere, that's not where he was going.

In the fifteen minutes she'd been following him he'd just gone further and further out of town. From what she could tell, they had to be out near the lake somewhere. Not a house or street light in sight. Not the best place to be breaking down. Especially without a phone.

"Come on, pull over," she muttered to herself. Her voice sounded scared which only creeped her out even more.

With perfect timing, the red light on her dashboard came on. She let out a curse. Stop now or push a bit further? Another curse. She couldn't risk it. If the engine died she'd be stuck out here. But maybe if she added the water fast enough she could catch up to him again.

She pulled over out of sight behind some bushes just in case they were being followed. As she grabbed the flashlight from the glove compartment she saw up ahead the reporter's car taking a left onto one of the tracks that led down to the lake.

She jumped out, got the jug of water from the back, and hoisted the hood. Then doused her flashlight when another car came along the road. It drove right past but took the same turn-off the reporter had. She watched its headlights wind through the trees and stop at what had to be the shore of the lake.

The lights went out, replaced by a smaller pin-point glow. Another flash light? Was the reporter meeting someone? Voices faint and indistinct drifted toward her on the eerie stillness.

She closed the hood and started toward them. . .

"On foot? In the dark?" Raina had to admire her guts. But perhaps desperation was a better description.

"The light was out by the time I got there but I could see two men standing near the water, next to a boat house. I wanted to go over and talk to them but…"

When the girl bowed her head, Raina sat forward. So far her story matched what Alec DeMarco had said. Had they reached the moment when it all went to hell?

"But what?" she prompted.

The girl looked up, misery etching every line of her face. "I got scared. It was dark and I didn't know who the other man was. I went all that way and in the end I couldn't even…"

"It's okay." Raina reached out and touched her arm. Beneath her fingers, the girl's flesh felt cold and thin. "What happened then?"

This was crazy. It was freezing and she couldn't see a thing. She'd go and see the man at his office tomorrow. One more day couldn't make that much difference. She turned and started back toward the road.

Several minutes later she felt the first stirrings of fear in her gut. It hadn't taken her this long to get there. She must've gotten turned around somehow. She must have—

Something rustled in the branches above her. She stifled a shriek, ran a few steps, collided with a tree, and spun away stunned. Rubbing her shoulder, she peered about at the impenetrable shadows and felt the sharp edge of panic slice through her.

A car! She homed in on the passing headlights and stumbled the last few yards to the road. Here enough moonlight broke through the trees to guide her. She took a guess which way her car was and started walking.

The edge of her bumper had just come in sight when gunshots erupted from back at the boat house.

She dropped to the ground. Cringed in terror for several moments, then lowered her arms.

She held her breath. The shooting had stopped but... Something else now, another sound... Footsteps. Someone running through the woods. Coming straight for her. Nearly on top of her!

The scream had nearly burst from her throat when the figure rushed past her toward the road, lit by the lights of an on-coming car. She watched in horror as the man ran on, the lights growing brighter. Didn't he see...? No. Look out!

Raina closed her eyes against the memory of that awful thud, the screech of her brakes, the impact that had thrown her life off course.

"It was awful," the girl went on. "I thought he was dead. But then he got up and got in the car – your car – and when the light came on inside that's when I saw his face. I was sure it was Liam."

"You must've been standing pretty close."

"You'd stopped practically right in front of me. Then, just

as you drove away, another man ran out of the woods. He stood in the road and aimed his gun at you, but you went around a bend before he could shoot."

Raina slumped back, her heart thudding. In those moments she'd sat arguing with Alec, his would-be killer was stealing up on them. Ten seconds longer and they'd both have been killed.

She looked at the girl. "How did you get away?"

"The man in the road took out a cell phone and talked to someone. A minute later another car came along, picked him up and they drove off after you."

"But how did you know that first car was mine?"

"The name of your store was on the side."

Raina nodded connecting the dots. "Which is why you showed up there the next day."

"I didn't know who to talk to – you or the other girl. I saw your car in the lot out back so I sat there and waited. I figured whoever got in it at the end of the day was the one who'd been driving the night before. But then this guy came along and started snooping around looking underneath it. I couldn't see his face or what he was doing, but the next minute he jumped in and drove away. I only worked out the car was yours when I saw that cop asking you questions."

Utterly drained, the girl sat swiping at her tears with her hand.

Raina got up, snatched the box of tissues off the counter and slid it across to her. She regretted having to press her for more, but there was still too much she needed to know.

She waited a moment then asked softly, "What's your name?"

"Erin," the girl said wiping her face. "Erin Rose."

"Well, Erin Rose, now for the sixty-four thousand dollar

question. What's on the flash drive?"

The girl looked up with red-rimmed eyes. "It shows some people selling my baby."

CHAPTER 40

A shadow fell across Farrington's desk. He'd thought Scanlon had left for the night and was surprised to find the chief standing over him.

"You get Wilkins' statement?" the man asked him.

"I'm typing it now."

"And?"

He shrugged, uncertain what his boss wanted to hear. Raina had insisted Scanlon was desperate to link her to whatever crime he could. Hard to believe of the officer Farrington had respected for years. Still, as one of the family's closest friends he certainly knew what Rick's death had cost him.

"Consistent with what she told you at the hospital," he answered at last.

"With the rest of her lies, you mean." Perusing the pages already typed, Scanlon lowered himself to a chair at a neighboring desk. "She's involved in this somehow, you can bet on it."

"You mean other than hitting DeMarco with her car?"

"I mean with the drugs, the murder, everything."

Farrington kept his tone impartial. "I thought we found skid marks on the road where she said."

"We did. Just out from where the body was found."

"Well, doesn't that support..." He paused to piece together a scenario. "The DeMarco brothers go to the lake to score a deal. Things turn sour and Liam flees. Raina hits him, he forces her to drive him from the scene and the killers grab him when she ditches the car."

Scanlon waited.

After a moment Farrington nodded. "So how does Liam's body end up back at the boathouse in Alec's car?"

Scanlon tossed the pages back at him. "Because it wasn't Liam who ran, it was Alec. Liam was already dead at that point. And she didn't *run into* Alec on the road, she was out there waiting to pick him up."

"If that's the case, then why'd she come forward? Why'd she confess to hitting Liam?"

The big man shrugged. "Could be she's being forced to take the fall for someone else, somebody higher."

"And the blood in her car?"

"Lab's got it now. Twenty to one it's Alec's, not Liam's."

Farrington studied the man before him. Veteran cop doing his job, or grieving father blinded by vengeance? "But she I.D.ed the body in the morgue as Liam."

Scanlon's eyes narrowed. "I'd have thought, of all people, you'd be the last to go soft on the girl."

Farrington grimly held the man's gaze. Hell, it might already be too late. Why hadn't he seen what was happening sooner? "I know the connection you're making here and I just can't see it. You figure because she started down the wrong path ten years ago she must still be on it?"

"She was into drugs then, it's only one small step to

dealing. Probably been doing it all along."

"Then why haven't we picked her up before now? Come on, John, what teenager doesn't smoke a bit of pot? How many of them go on to deal coke?"

"Not every teenager does what she did." The words hissed out between Scanlon's teeth. He rose from the chair. "Put a tail on her. I want somebody watching her house. Better yet, you do it."

Farrington nodded, surprised by his eagerness at the thought. If it had to be done... "I'll get over there as soon as I finish this."

Scanlon rested a hand on his shoulder. "Look, Craig, I don't want you to ever think I didn't appreciate what you tried to do for Rick. And me and Peggy. The fact Wilkins got off ten years ago wasn't because of anything you did or failed to do."

"I tried to do my job as best I could, John."

"Course you did." Scanlon withdrew his hand. "At the same time, I'm making you a promise right now – if Wilkins is involved in this, she's not going to get off again."

So there it was. A declaration of Raina's worst fears sweeping all remaining doubts aside.

Scanlon slapped his shoulder and smiled. "By the way – almost forgot – it's Peg's birthday on Wednesday and we're having a few people around for dinner. We're hoping you can join us."

"Love to, John." Farrington turned back to his typing. "Tell Peg thanks for the invite."

Back in his office, Scanlon picked up the photo from his desk – a shot of Rick on his seventeenth birthday. He normally kept it at home on the mantel but found he liked having it here at work. It reminded him of his quest for justice and firmed his resolve to follow it through.

He especially liked the impact the picture had had on Raina that morning – the very reaction he'd been hoping for. The very reason he'd brought the picture here in the first place. Some things should damn well never be forgotten and Rick was one of them.

He set the photo back on the desk, recalling that not long after it was taken, Raina's father had died and her relationship with Rick had escalated from friendship to love.

He'd wondered at the time if that deepening affection would have developed anyway, or if it stemmed more from Raina's unconscious desire to be enveloped in the folds of a complete family.

He'd not been averse to serving as a surrogate father to her. On the contrary, she'd been one messed up kid at that point and he'd secretly hoped that opening their home and hearts to her would give her the stability she so desperately needed.

Little had he known at the time how she would eventually repay them.

CHAPTER 41

With a tree at his back to cut the wind, Alec stared out across the deserted park. No doubt he was feeling the cold more because he hadn't eaten all day. And without money to buy a beer or even a cup of coffee he couldn't linger in a bar or café.

He'd stretched his welcome at the local cinema, sitting in their lobby for hours pretending he'd been stood up by his date. But when the last movie-goer had left, they'd ushered him from the premises as well.

At a gust of wind he drew his jacket closer around him. If he'd known he was going to be camping out he'd have stolen a hat and gloves from Wilkins's store as well. And some long johns!

Thinking of the woman brought to his mind the image of her sitting at the bar last night. How sad she had looked. Sad yet beautiful. Even if she hadn't been his reason for being there, she'd still have captured his attention. As she had every other man in the room.

When one of them had slid onto the stool beside her, refusing to be put off from buying her a drink, Alec had nearly

140

intervened. Luckily the bartender had sorted it out before he'd completely blown his cover. Still, that had possibly been the first moment his thoughts had strayed from Liam since what happened out at the lake.

A flurry of dry leaves swirled around him and he pulled up his collar. Maybe he should go back to her shop. Maybe she'd be there, working late. With his money gone and no leads to follow…

He recalled the feel of her in his arms as he'd settled her on the seat of her car. The look in her eyes as he'd pleaded his case to her in the forest later. Why had she done it? Why hadn't she called out to the police? What had made her feel she could trust him?

He took a deep breath and blew it out again. Whatever her reasons, she sure as hell wouldn't be glad to see him again. Not after everything he'd done. And as much as he might want to go to her, he couldn't risk dragging her any deeper into this than he had already.

Leaning his head back, he stared at the stars. Not a cloud in the sky. The night would be cold.

Hard to believe how his life had changed in the last few days. In the blink of an eye he'd gone from an ordinary – some would say boring – bachelor existence to sleeping in the open, not a cent to his name, battling a grief that sickened his heart, and with no idea how to proceed from here, how to bring those responsible to justice.

He pushed to his feet. Another circuit around the park might help warm him up.

Thrusting his hands deep in his pockets, he felt the flash drive in one of them. He pulled it out, stared at it as it lay on his palm. The video it contained had told him little. Liam must've had other information to prove whatever crime he'd uncovered. Evidence that had been lost along with him, making the flash drive utterly useless.

As he stepped past the bench he reached out to drop the device in the rubbish. On a whim, little more than a voice in his ear, he stopped and returned it to his pocket.

CHAPTER 42

Fog filled the hollows beneath the trees when Raina stepped out her front door the next morning. She crossed the lawn, damp from the night's soft rain, and headed for the plastic-wrapped newspaper lying halfway down her driveway.

She wasn't expecting Erin back for another two hours so she could have slept in. But memories and fears had plagued her sleep and woken her early.

After hearing Erin's story, she'd vowed to help the kid however she could. Ordinarily – despite her pre-existing aversion – she'd have gone to the police. But without the flash drive they had no proof. And if Alec was right and the cops killed Liam...

No, the safest course, at least for the moment, was what the girl was already doing – trying to get the flash drive back. But the only way to locate it was to track down the man who had it, something even the police hadn't managed.

It had seemed to both of them their prospects were grim. Until, somewhere on the dawn side of midnight, hours deep into their discussion, the answer had come to her. Today was Liam DeMarco's funeral – she'd seen the notice in yesterday's paper. If her guess was correct, Alec would find some way to attend. Even at the risk of being spotted by the killers.

With nothing else to go on, they'd arranged that Erin would return this morning and together they would go to the cemetery for the service at eleven. What they would do if they actually found Alec DeMarco, she hadn't a clue. They'd just have to wing it from there.

She straightened from picking up the newspaper and noticed a car parked up the street, half concealed behind a shrub. Though not visible from her house, its occupants would have a clear view of anyone entering or leaving her property.

The sight instantly put her on guard. Most houses in her neighborhood had long driveways and few people left their cars on the road. And at this early hour it suggested the car had been there all night.

Someone keeping tabs on her movements?

Under the guise of checking her mailbox she walked to the very foot of her driveway for a better view. She didn't recognize the old-model Taurus sedan as belonging to any of her neighbors. If this *was* someone keeping tabs on her, what would they do if she confronted them?

Across the road, the door of the nearest house swung open and Mr Bachman emerged with his poodle setting off on their morning walk. She returned his wave as she started forward, comforted by the knowledge he saw her. Surely if someone was in the car, with a witness around, they'd drive off rather than take a shot at her.

The closer she got, the more out of place the vehicle looked in the carefully-maintained suburban street – a rust-streaked wreck, with a cracked windshield and balding tires.

She slowed her approach. The windshield was foggy. Condensation from someone's breath. Yes, there was definitely someone inside.

Another step.

She couldn't see anyone in the driver's seat. Was the person hiding? Waiting to shoot her at close range the moment she drew level with the window, witness be damned?

Every instinct told her to run.

And yet her feet kept taking her forward.

With a steadying breath, ready to drop if anything stirred within the car, she eased up beside the driver's window. Nothing but bags of rubbish in the front and a pile of old rags in the back.

A pile that began to move as she watched it.

She bit back a shout and turned to flee, then hesitated. Amid the heap of tangled fabric a face had appeared. Peaceful. Sleeping. Not the face of a wanton killer but that of a scrawny teenage girl.

Raina's breath went out in a whoosh. *Erin*. She bent till her nose was touching the glass.

On closer inspection the stuff on the front seat wasn't rubbish but bags of clothing, the mound under which the girl was nestled, not rags but old blankets. Other items filled in the gaps: bottles of water, packets of food, take-away wrappers.

Good god was this—?

She straightened, unable to tear her gaze from the woman-child asleep on the seat. She'd offered Erin a bed for the night but the girl had refused, insisting she had a home to go to. But by the bags and belongings crammed in around her, it appeared this was it.

Raina silently backed away. If the kid would rather sleep in a freezing car than accept her help, she wasn't about to embarrass her. She'd return to the house, wait for Erin to arrive as planned, and say nothing about what she'd seen.

The image of the girl huddled in her nest of grubby bedding tugged at Raina's heart as she walked away. But it was the glimpse of the teddy bear clutched in her arms that brought the sting of tears to her eyes.

CHAPTER 43

Twenty minutes before their arranged departure for the cemetery, Erin knocked on Raina's back door, declined the breakfast she had prepared, and all but pulled her out of the house. More than eager, the girl seemed frantic; so keen to get going, it would clearly be torture to keep her waiting. Raina reluctantly threw on a jacket and joined her outside.

Once tactfully advised that her Taurus might be a bit conspicuous – not to mention unreliable – Erin agreed to go in the Camry.

Buckled in the front, staring through the windshield, Raina paused before starting the engine. "Erin, I'm sorry but I have to ask you—"

"No."

"No what?"

"No, my parents won't help me." The girl turned toward her. "That's what you were going to ask, wasn't it?"

The kid was perceptive if nothing else. "Are you sure they won't? Have you talked to them at least?" When the girl looked away, Raina said gently, "Erin, I know these things can be complicated but—"

"It's not complicated, it's real simple. My dad split before I was born and my mom's a lush."

"That doesn't mean—"

"Yeah. It does." The words were fists punching the air, Erin's eyes bright with defiance.

Raina hesitated. If she pushed too hard, she could lose the girl. "What about extended family? Does your mom have any—"

"You know what? *This* is getting too complicated." Erin threw open her door. "If you don't want to help me—"

"Now hang on, I never said that." Raina withdrew the hand she had placed on her arm. "I'll do whatever I can, I swear. I just thought maybe we'd have some back-up, that's all."

She waited but the girl didn't move. "Close the door, please."

Still no movement. Small as it was, this could be the moment of their first power play. She'd issued what, to this girl's ears, had to have sounded like a command. Would Erin concede or walk away?

The door slammed shut.

Raina hid her smile. Definitely shut.

"How come you're doing this?" the girl challenged.

"I think it's terrible what happened to you and I want to help."

"That the only reason?"

"Well, no, it's not the only reason, but—"

"What are the other ones?"

Their conversation the night before had focused mainly on Erin's experience. Now Raina related her own – her encounters with Alec after the accident Erin had witnessed. How the man had stolen her car to get back the flash drive he'd left behind. The steps he'd taken when he couldn't find it, and how he'd vanished again the minute he had.

"And he never said anything about where he was going?"

Raina shook her head. "He was simply gone when I woke up." Erin's look was so despondent she quickly added, "But you and I know where he'll turn up, don't we?"

The girl's nod was hardly convincing.

Raina started the car and backed out the driveway.

"So..." Erin stared at her lap. "You saw what was on the memory stick? You watched my video?"

"I did. Several times." Raina stopped the car and shifted to first.

"Then you believe me? About what happened to me at the hospital?"

Though parts of her story had seemed a bit odd, Raina had no doubt the gist of it was true. "Yes, I believe you." She touched the gas and started up the road.

Erin slumped back, clearly relieved. After a moment her pale brow furrowed. "So Alec DeMarco stole your car, crashed it in the woods, knocked you out and kidnapped you twice."

"Don't forget pointing a gun in my face."

Eyes wide, the girl shook her head. "No wonder you want to find him again. If some jerk did all that to me he'd be missing some teeth."

Raina let out a bark of laughter. She was starting to really like this kid.

CHAPTER 44

Raina clutched the umbrella's shaft as another gust threatened to rip it from her hands. The squall had come up on their way to the cemetery and only intensified since their arrival. She angled the canopy into the wind in a futile attempt to shield the girl huddled beside her.

The graveside service was nearly over and still they hadn't spotted their man. The rain was making things doubly difficult as every mourner had been issued an umbrella by funeral staff.

Drenched and shivering, Erin continued to scan the crowd, oblivious to the driving rain. "How will we find him? You can't see their faces."

"Follow me; stay close."

Raina led the way down the line of mourners standing three rows back from the grave. As they passed each one, she cast a quick look up at their face, wondering what relation they were to the deceased. How deeply they would feel the loss of his passing, the tragedy of his untimely death. How this single act of senseless violence would impact on so many other lives.

Each face bore the ravages of grief, but none was that of the man they sought.

At the end of the row, they climbed the steps of a small mausoleum and turned to scan the graveside gathering. Even with the height advantage all they could see was a sea of umbrellas.

Erin gripped her arm. "What if we miss him? What'll I do? I'll never find him again!"

With their backs to the wall of the marble structure their voices carried. Several mourners had looked over at Erin. If she created a scene, she'd draw more attention. And if the killers had had the same thought as Raina – that Alec would come to his brother's funeral – *they* were somewhere in this crowd as well.

Pulling the girl with her, she stepped back into the mausoleum's pillared entrance. The rain and wind cut off at once, giving them a sheltered alcove in which to regroup.

"You need to calm down. We've still got time."

"But how—"

"We'll wait here until the service finishes, then move down and stand where we can see everyone go past as they leave. Trust me, we'll find him."

Erin took a shaky breath and nodded.

With one eye on the crowd, Raina tried to keep her distracted. "You never told me how you got into my house last night. Everything was still locked up when I got home."

"Through the cellar. I smashed a window." She shrugged. "Sorry."

Raina shook her head. She'd never given a thought to the cellar – no adult could fit through the narrow windows. Someone the size of a child however...

"I smashed it the first time but you still hadn't fixed it so

—"

She put up a hand. "Hang on, what do you mean the first time?"

"A couple of days ago. You were out and I thought the flash drive was in your house so I went in and looked."

"That was *you* who went through my lipsticks?"

The girl had the decency to look sheepish. "You left a real mess on your kitchen floor – a broken bottle, milk and glass all over the place. I cleaned it for you." She hung her head. "I also took some food from your pantry. I'll pay you back."

Raina didn't plan on holding her breath. "The crazy part is, you didn't have to break in at all. I'd gone out and left my front door open."

"Oh. Sorry."

Raina frowned. "That was Sunday, two days ago. What time did you go in?"

"Afternoon. Four o'clock maybe."

Four o'clock. The same time Alec had said he'd been there, planning to break in himself. A plan he'd had to back off from because someone had already… She nearly laughed. Erin was 'the killer' he'd seen going in!

"It's over. People are starting to leave." Erin pointed down at the gathering. Mourners were beginning to file past the grave, throwing flowers onto the casket.

"Come on."

They hurried down to the head of the line, then turned to view the face of each person as they started back to the row of cars parked along the cemetery's narrow laneway. In a steady procession, the crowd filed past.

All but one.

"I think I see him." Raina nodded toward a large hunched figure walking off in the opposite direction.

Before they could take a step in pursuit, two other men broke clear of the group and started after him.

Whether he sensed he was being followed or just to check, the target looked back. And in the instant before he took off running, Raina glimpsed the face of Alec DeMarco.

CHAPTER 45

"Hurry! Get in!"

Even as Erin slammed her door, Raina threw the car in gear and took off. The sound of her tires screeching in protest drew angry stares from the cluster of mourners.

"Can you see him?"

"There." Erin pointed out her side window at the man weaving a parallel course through rows of headstones. Two other figures not far behind mirrored his every feint and dodge. Whether they were killers or plain-clothed cops, they'd abandoned their charade as grieving relations and were now in flat-out pursuit of their target.

"They're gaining on him!"

Raina drove faster down the narrow lane, straining to keep her man in sight. DeMarco was clearly in trouble, his pace lagging. He ran with one arm clamped to his side. The gunshot wound! He wouldn't out-distance his hunters for long.

"Look out!" Erin cried.

A woman in their path leapt for the grass as Raina jerked the wheel to avoid hitting her. Raised voices from another group of mourners followed them as they sped toward the gates.

The three men were starting to veer away toward a smaller pedestrian exit. At the rate DeMarco was losing ground…

"Roll down your window. Yell to him. Try to get his attention."

Erin leaned out and shouted his name. The fugitive ran on oblivious.

"All right, hang on."

Raina hit the gas for the last thirty feet, then slowed as they passed through the open gates. To a medley of blaring horns and driver curses she swung right into flowing traffic.

Twenty yards on, above the stone wall that bordered the cemetery, she caught her first glimpse of a running man. Too soon, two others appeared behind him. DeMarco's pursuers were nearly on him.

She drove toward the spot where their paths would converge. With DeMarco still twenty feet from the wall, she skidded to a halt in front of the exit. "Open the back."

Erin reached around, unlocked the back door and pushed it out – just as DeMarco stumbled into view.

At the sound of the two of them shouting his name, he fell back, alarmed. A precious second to make sense of the sound, recognize Raina, then the man dived into the back of her car.

By the time the others burst out the gate, Raina was already turning the corner. She checked the mirror, praying they'd not caught her license plate number, then slumped back against the seat in relief.

"The flash drive. Where is it?"

She turned to her passenger. "Erin, for goodness' sakes, give him a chance to catch his breath."

The girl ignored her. "The memory stick. Tell me you have it."

Hunched and gasping, clutching his side, DeMarco looked in the rearview mirror, met Raina's gaze, and nodded the thanks he couldn't yet voice.

"Hey, jerk-off! You hear me? I'm talking to you."

His focus shifted to girl in his face. "Who are you?"

"Never mind. Just give me the stick."

"Why?"

"Because it's mine. I made it. And it's the only copy."

"Yours?"

Raina looked up at the change in his tone. Something shifted behind his eyes, a shadow passing over his soul.

"*You* gave that thing to my brother?" He seemed to be growing, filling more of the view in her mirror. "*You're* the one who got Liam killed?"

"Easy, DeMarco," Raina cautioned. But as he'd just come from his brother's funeral, she imagined his feelings were pretty raw.

Erin faltered. "I didn't think they'd go after him, I swear."

"Go after him? They didn't *go after* him? They *murdered* him!"

His shouts struck like blows. The girl shrank away and broke into tears.

Taking her hand, Raina looked back. "You do still have it, don't you?"

DeMarco sat fighting to govern his rage.

"Alec! The flash drive."

"Yeah, I've got it."

She let out her breath. "And? Did you watch it?"

"Only about a dozen times. Doesn't show a damn thing." Wincing, he drew his hand from his side and checked it for blood. "As evidence it's totally useless. Except for the woman, you can't see a single one of their faces. Meaning my brother died for nothing! Just a bunch of nameless drug dealers with no way to—"

"Drug dealers?" Erin twisted around in her seat. "What are you talking about? It's not about drugs."

"Then we're talking about two different clips. The one I've got shows people in a room, a box on a table, money changing hands—"

"Yeah, that's it. That's my video. But it's not about drugs."

Frantic and distraught the girl launched into a disjointed account of her experience. Even Raina, who'd heard the story only last night, had trouble making sense of her words.

Alec pressed a fist to his brow. "Someone had better explain this to me in a way that makes sense because I've had just about all I can take."

Raina caught the look that passed between them – the desperation in Erin's eyes; the pain, grief and fury in Alec's. Though she'd so far managed to hold herself together, she was struggling with feelings of her own. She had to defuse the situation or they'd all be at each other's throats.

"Okay, people, here's what's happening." She gave them a moment to shift their focus. "I don't think it's safe to go back to my place but I know somewhere else. We're going to go there, have ourselves a nice little chat and sort this out. Calmly and like reasonable people."

Beside her, Erin turned to face forward.

In the back, jaw clenched, Alec gave a huff and looked out the window. "Good luck with *that*."

CHAPTER 46

Despite the slight risk of being spotted, Raina opted for a public place – Chappy's Diner – in the hope it would help them keep a lid on their emotions.

Set back from the highway, surrounded by forest, the diner was frequented mostly by truckers and tourists on route to Sugar Loaf Mountain. Inside, she chose a booth at the back, away from the lunchtime crowd at the counter. Alec took one side of the table and she slid onto the other seat with Erin.

They waited in silence as the waitress poured them each some water then handed out menus.

The instant she left, Alec set his aside. "Well?"

Raina gently touched Erin's arm. "Just tell him what you told me last night and try to stay calm."

With little of the brashness she'd shown in the car, the girl took a breath. "A year ago I was living on the streets, doing whatever I could to get by. When I got pregnant I found out I could get money from the government and a place to live. So I decided to have the baby and keep it."

Alec gave a huff of disbelief. "How old are you?"

She straightened. "Eighteen."

He shook his head and the girl continued.

"I started going to this clinic. They gave me all my checkups for free. Everything was fine until…" She balled her hands into fists on the table. "Ten days ago I went to the clinic and had my baby. When I woke up afterwards, they told me he'd died."

Raina slid her arm around the girl's slim shoulders. Hearing the story a second time was proving no easier than the first.

"I told them they were wrong, he couldn't be dead – I heard him cry right before they knocked me out. They said I only imagined hearing him, that he was stillborn and never made a sound."

"Look, I don't need to hear all this," Alec said. "Just tell me what's on—"

"She's getting to that; just give her a minute." Raina prompted the girl to continue.

"When I asked to see my baby, they told me it wouldn't be a good idea. Like there was something wrong with him or something. When I said I wanted to see him anyway, that's when they knocked me out again."

"You mean they sedated you when you got hysterical," Alec translated.

"Well, of course I got upset. They wouldn't let me see my baby!"

Raina urged her to lower her voice.

"When I woke up the second time it was two days later. They told me there'd been some kind of complication, an infection or something, that I'd been unconscious most of the time with a really high fever."

"Which of course you didn't believe."

"If I'd been as sick as they said, I would've known it. They just kept me knocked out with drugs so I wouldn't cause trouble."

Raina shot Alec a warning look and Erin went on.

"When I asked again to see my baby they looked at me like I was nuts. The doctor said, "But you've already seen him; don't you remember?"

"You didn't remember seeing your baby?"

"I didn't remember because they were lying. They never showed him to me. I don't care what Dr Manheim said!"

Raina gently settled her again. "What *did* Dr Manheim say?"

"He said that sometimes..." Erin swallowed. "Because of the trauma of losing a baby and...because of the extent of his..." She covered her mouth.

Deformity. Raina read the word in Alec's face. And the unspoken conclusion that followed: Was it any surprise? A girl on the streets – drugs, sex, god knew what else...

"They thought you'd blocked out the memory of seeing him," Alec supplied.

"But I didn't! I didn't block it out! They never showed me!"

He threw up his hands. "Okay, they didn't. What happened next?"

"I told them I didn't care what they said, I wanted to see my baby again. That's when they told me I couldn't see him because he was gone."

"Gone where?"

Erin put a hand to her head. "That's the part that just doesn't make sense. I never would have signed that paper. Not ever."

Alec's face cleared in understanding. "They showed you a form giving them permission to dispose of the body. Which *you* had signed."

"But I didn't sign it. It looked like my writing but it couldn't have been. I would never let them take him."

Raina tried to get her to lower her voice.

"No!" Erin slapped off her hand. "You think I would let them throw him away like a piece of garbage?"

At the sight of the waitress coming toward them, Erin fell silent. She bowed her head in a fight for control as Alec looked up. "If you could just give us another few minutes."

The waitress nodded and walked away.

Wiping her eyes, Erin leaned toward him. "My baby's alive. He's *gone* because those people stole him. They took him and sold him to somebody else, and *that's* what's on the memory stick."

He shook his head. "Not the one I watched."

"*Yes*, the one you watched."

"I'm telling you there is nothing on—"

"That's because you didn't watch far enough." Raina held the man's startled gaze. Considering he'd just lost his only brother she was prepared to cut him a bit of slack. But this girl had her problems too – ones she was far less equipped to deal with – and she wasn't about to let him badger her.

He quickly recovered. "I watched it till there was nothing left to see."

"Then you didn't listen. Right at the end, about five seconds after the image blacks out, there's a sound. It's short and you have to have the volume turned up to hear it."

He blew out a breath. "A sound, eh? The sound of what?"

Raina swallowed. "A baby's cry."

CHAPTER 47

Scanlon walked back behind his desk, slammed a drawer shut and sank into his chair. "You want to tell me how you managed to lose them?"

Farrington gave him a moment to settle. As if it would help.

"You had me keeping tabs on Wilkins. At nine-fifty this morning she had a visitor – a scrawny-looking kid in a beat-up Taurus. Female, Caucasian, late teens, blond. We ran the plates but the car isn't registered."

"Stolen?"

"No. Just not in the system. The two of them left the house a short while later in Wilkins' car. I tailed them to the cemetery where I was surprised to meet up with Hendricks."

Scanlon waved a hand. "Yeah, I sent him. Thought there was a chance Alec might show for his brother's funeral."

Scanlon looked away, briefly distracted; by what, Farrington hadn't a clue. From his haggard appearance and haunted gaze, this case had clearly ripped open old wounds.

"And of course you were right," he said. "Alec did come. But we didn't spot him till the very end – too hard to see for all the umbrellas."

Scanlon continued to stare into space.

"When we finally did see him, Hendricks and I took off after him. I was aware of a car on the cemetery drive paralleling us toward the south exit. But it wasn't until we got out on the street and DeMarco got into it that I saw who was driving."

Scanlon's gaze sharpened with a predator's focus. "Raina Wilkins."

"Yes."

He frowned. "And the kid was still with her at that point?"

"Unknown. She was there at the gravesite but we don't know if she got back in the car."

The chief thought a moment, then leaned back. "So... The second time Wilkins helps DeMarco escape and you still don't think she's involved in this?"

"Hendricks and I weren't in uniform. She only saw us from a distance so she could've thought we were someone else, the men who shot Liam maybe."

"Then why'd she lie to me yesterday? To both of us? Why'd she say, in a sworn statement, she hadn't been in contact with Alec?"

Though each question had grown more demanding, Farrington kept his voice steady as he answered. "Maybe at that point she hadn't seen him. Maybe she only met up with him at the funeral."

"How did she know he'd even be there?"

"Maybe a hunch, same as you. Maybe she'd been looking for him before that, just like—"

Scanlon thumped the desk as he rose. "The question is *why*. Why is she looking for him if not because she's hooked up in this?"

Farrington fought down a sense of futility. Clearly nothing he could say would change the man's mind.

Of course he understood how Scanlon must feel. He'd seen what losing Rick had done to them over the years, him and Peggy. In a way he felt almost disloyal to them for his own changing sentiments toward Raina. Hell, Rick had been like his own kid brother.

But at the same time he'd meant every word of what he'd said to her – that everyone deserved a second chance. That if a person could find the strength and courage to change their life, their past should be laid to rest. And Raina had changed. If he could only make this man see it.

Scanlon turned and stepped to the window, his broad shoulders tense, head bowed. "That girl took everything from me." The words barely audible. Had he even realized he'd said them aloud?

Farrington eased closer, stood within reach of the man's bent back. This mentor, this hero, he'd admired so long was falling apart before his eyes.

He reached out. "John…"

Scanlon shrugged off the hand on his arm and turned to face him. "Put out an APB on her car."

CHAPTER 48

Alec stared in the men's room mirror, inspecting the circles under his eyes. Three days growth of untidy beard couldn't hide his unhealthy pallor.

He'd cleaned his wound and packed it with a handful of napkins, hoping to hold them in place with his shirt. The pain was taking a toll on his strength. A pain of the heart as much as the body. He washed his hands, then left and headed out the diner's back door.

After Erin's repeated outbursts they'd decided it best to eat outside. With the weather chilly they had the entire back porch to themselves and could talk more freely. There was also less chance of being spotted.

He started for the pair seated at the furthest picnic table. Their claims about what was on the flash drive had brought him up short. He'd not heard the sound to which Wilkins had referred. He'd been so focused on what he was seeing, he might well have missed some belated cry. *If* it was there.

He slid onto the bench across from them and fixed his gaze on the shivering girl, her burger sitting untouched before her. He'd let her ramble on inside but now he intended to get some details.

As though reading his thoughts she drew herself up, bracing for the next barrage of questions.

"Where and how did you make the video that's on the key?"

She carefully folded her hands on the table. "After the second time I woke up, I pretended to believe what they were telling me – that Cody was dead." She looked up at their startled expressions. "That's what I named him. Not then, just since I left the hospital."

Raina nodded. "It's a lovely name."

The girl's slight smile died in an instant. "I figured if I kept getting upset they'd just knock me out again so I—"

"Hang on," Alec put up a hand. "*They*. Can you be more specific? Who were these people? What were their names?"

"Doctor Manheim and Nurse Grace Kilburn. They did all my pre-birth exams and they were the ones who delivered the baby."

"Just those two. You never saw any other staff at the clinic."

"No, just them. That's why I couldn't figure... I mean... They'd been so nice to me up till then."

"Right." He huffed. "That's the only thing puzzling me at this point."

The sarcastic remark drew a look from Wilkins.

He stared back, stopped by a thought. Raina Wilkins. His guardian angel. What was her stake in all of this? Why had she helped him at the cemetery? What was she even doing there? And when had she teamed up with this girl who clearly had unresolved mental issues?

"I had to find Cody," Erin was saying. "I was sure he was still somewhere in the hospital. I thought if I could find him I'd steal him back and run away with him before they caught me."

"Why did you think he was still there when they'd told you he was gone?"

"Because I didn't believe them. Because..." She shrugged. "I don't know, I just *felt* it, that's all."

Another warning look from Raina. Clearly she saw what he thought of that statement, and was telling him, with her pointed stare, to watch his step. To go easy. Why would she care?

The girl went on. "That night after they turned out the lights, I got dressed in my street clothes, grabbed all the stuff I'd come in with, and snuck out of my room. Naturally the first place I checked was the nursery, but the cribs were all empty. I guess mine was the only birth that week."

Her voice grew faint. "It was sad seeing all those tiny beds empty." She bowed her head. "That was the first time..."

"The first time you thought they might've been telling you the truth," he finished. "That your baby was dead."

She raised her chin. "I decided I had to know for sure. I followed the signs and went down to the morgue. I had my cell phone. I thought, if I find him, I'll at least take his picture to bring away with me.

"When I got down there it was really dark. And cold." She shuddered. "I hated to think of him alone in that awful place. Then I saw a light under a door. I walked up real quiet and pushed it open." Her gaze grew fierce. "And that's when I saw. That's when I knew I'd been right all along."

Before he could speak, Raina leaned toward her. "How, Erin? The video doesn't show us that. How did you know? What did you hear?"

"They were talking about papers."

"Papers. You mean like a birth certificate?"

"I guess so, yeah."

Raina cast her gaze his way, "The envelope they handed over," then back at Erin. "Did you recognize any of them?"

"Only Nurse Kilburn."

"What else did you hear?"

The girl looked down. "My baby. I heard him crying."

"You heard a baby," Alec corrected. "There's no way you could know it was yours."

"Even if it wasn't," Raina snapped, "it's a pretty strange place to find one, wouldn't you say? In a box, on an autopsy table in a morgue?"

Conceding her point, he turned back to Erin. "What then?"

"I used my phone to film what was happening. But one of them saw me and I had to run."

This he couldn't let go unchallenged. The man on the video who'd run toward the camera had been fit and able-bodied. In pursuit of a feeble teenage girl – one supposedly recovering not just from a difficult birth but a post natal infection…

"How'd you get away?" he said.

"There was some kind of trolley outside the door. I pulled it across behind me when I ran and he fell over it in the dark."

"Didn't he get up? Didn't he come after you?"

"The door to the parking lot was just up the hall. I made it to my car and drove away before he could catch me."

She turned to direct her next words to Raina. "I couldn't go back to my apartment; I knew they'd come there looking for me. So I slept in my car. I guess…" She looked down. "I guess I've been living in it ever since."

Raina patted her hand. "It's okay."

The pair looked up, awaiting his judgment.

Alec fought to keep his voice calm. "And after acquiring this damning evidence you felt the best plan was to give it to my brother."

"I didn't know what to do with it," Erin said. "My phone was out of credit so I couldn't send it to anyone. I went to the library and made a copy so I'd have one, just in case. It was only later that I thought to give it—"

"If you were on a computer, why didn't you just upload it to YouTube?" Despite his efforts his voice was rising.

"I didn't think anyone would pay attention. I needed someone important to help me so people would listen, so they'd believe me."

The girl rushed on, relating the story she'd told Raina the night before: how she'd given the flash drive to Liam, and later followed him to the boathouse. How she'd heard the shots, seen someone run out onto the road, get hit by a car and—

"You're telling me you actually saw the killer?" Alec sat up. "Why the hell didn't you say so? Who was it? Did you know him? Could you identify—"

"No, it was dark. I couldn't see his face."

"You said he was standing right in front of you! How could you not—?"

"The same reason *you* didn't," Raina cut in. If those copper eyes of hers flashed any hotter they'd set him on fire. "Because she'd be dead now if she had."

CHAPTER 49

Raina watched the man walk away and stand overlooking the pond behind the diner. She gave him the moment he obviously needed, then slid Erin's plate back in front of her. "Stay here. Try to eat a bit more."

The girl took her arm as she started to rise. "He doesn't believe me, does he?"

"Give him time. He's just lost someone he cared about."

"So have I."

Reluctant to make any false promises, she squeezed the girl's hand and pushed to her feet.

Slowly she walked toward the lone figure standing unmoved by the scene before him – the shimmering birch trees reflected in the water, their gold-coin leaves studding its surface. Balsam and rain scenting the air, with mist-shrouded mountains in the distance.

Bracing herself, she came up beside him. "A bit hard on her, weren't you?"

Alec cast a look at the girl on the porch. "Where did you find her?"

"She found me. She broke into my house looking for the

flash drive. In fact she's the one *you* saw breaking in."

"What?"

"Basement window? Sunday, around four o'clock? That was her."

His frown deepened as he watched the girl.

"Doesn't look much like a killer, does she?" Raina said. "Anyway, she came back last night and I told her you had the flash drive."

"Thanks a lot." He directed his gaze back over the water.

Raina rejected the urge to ease closer. "Look, I'm sorry about your brother. But can't you understand why a kid like that might need someone? Why she'd be afraid to act on her own?"

"What I don't understand is how you can buy into her story so completely. Did you ever stop to think…"

He turned to give her his full attention. "How do you know everything they told her at that hospital wasn't true? A young kid, all on her own, her baby's born dead – worse, it's deformed… They're not going to want to show him to her, are they? Even if they did lie to her, even if they drugged her, they might simply have done it to spare her."

"*Spare* her? You think it's right—"

"I'm not saying I agree with them, just that their reasons might not be as sinister as she imagines."

Raina gave that a moment's thought. "Well, if this has nothing to do with her baby, then what's on the video?"

"Just what I said."

"A middle-aged woman dealing drugs?"

"A nurse would certainly have plenty of access."

"And what about the cry?"

He tipped his head. "Ah yes, the cry. This mysterious sound that only you heard."

She held his gaze in lieu of an answer.

He blew out a breath, reached in his pocket and pulled out the flash drive, studied it as it lay in his palm. "We need to go somewhere and watch this again."

CHAPTER 50

Raina closed her phone and leaned against the side of her car. The drizzle had stopped but thick clouds still hung low in the sky, giving a premature sense of dusk to the mid-afternoon.

She straightened when Alec appeared from around the back of the diner heading toward her, hands thrust deep in the pockets of his fleece-lined jacket, shoulders hunched – a man with feelings held tightly in check. She could see now how those frown lines had formed.

Somehow his quiet intense demeanor suggested a man of a different era, a scholar more at ease with a book in his hand than his fingers flying over a keyboard or tablet. A bit of cleaning up, dressed in a tux, he'd look downright aristocratic. Educated and refined, with a deep moral conscience.

Or was she just seeing what she wanted to see?

His actions and attitudes, especially toward Erin, hadn't yet lived up to that noble impression. Of course, if his story was to be believed, he was a man in considerable pain at the moment, both emotionally and physically.

But that would only get him so far.

He stopped beside her. "You call your friend? She going

to help?"

"Julie agreed to look after the shop until she hears from me. If anyone asks, I've got the flu." She eyed him uncertainly. Something about the jacket he was wearing…

"What about the money?"

"There's just over two hundred dollars in the safe. I'm meeting her at Dempsey's after she closes and she'll give it to me there." That jacket. She frowned. Rust-colored suede, classic Marlboro man design…

Alec huffed. "Two hundred dollars. That won't go far."

"Enough for food and a place to stay for the three of us for a couple of nights. I know some rental cabins not far from here. Cheap and remote. Best of all, each one has its own computer."

"Sounds wonderful."

She cocked her head. Was that a complaint? "I don't see you pitching in anything."

"Hey, I wasn't being sarcastic. As for paying my way, I told you, I ran out of money two days ago. I haven't wanted to use my card in case they were tracking it."

A valid point. And one which now applied to her as well. The very reason she'd gone to Julie instead of the nearest ATM. Still—

Alec jerked his thumb at the diner. "That meal in there was the first I've eaten in forty-eight hours."

"A meal *I* paid for."

One of those expressive brows arced upwards. "How ungallant of me. And on our first date too."

"Well, you might show a bit of gratitude. I don't *have* to be doing this, you know. And while we're on the subject," she turned to face him, "in case it escaped your attention, I saved your ass back at that cemetery."

The full force of his gaze engulfed her, a glint in his eye. Amusement? Annoyance? "So you did."

"Well, the quaint backwoods custom in these parts is to say thank you when someone saves your life."

"Thank you." His dark eyes narrowed. "Why'd you do it?"

"Erin wanted her flash drive back and you had it."

"But how did you know I'd be at the funeral?"

"I figured you'd want to say goodbye to your brother. You took a big chance doing it, you know. Those guys nearly had you. Any idea who they were?"

"My bet would be the men who killed Liam." He winced at a sudden twinge in his side. "If I'd been in better shape I'd have stuck around and had a little talk with them."

"And been found tomorrow floating face down in a lake somewhere." Spotting Erin rounding the diner, Raina dropped her cell phone back in her bag. "And just so you know, I didn't like lying to my friend just now."

His gaze fixed on the girl coming toward them. "There's not much I like about this whole situation."

"So what's the plan?" Erin said, joining them.

Raina explained about the cabin. "It'll be safe. We can hole up there while we figure out what to do next."

"Okay, but I gotta go get my car first."

"You don't need your car," Alec dismissed.

Erin squared off, preparing for round three. "Everything I own is in that car; I'm not leaving it."

"You can get it later. I need to look at this video again."

"Why? I already told you what was on it?"

Raina put a hand up to cut short the argument. Another time the girl might've been more accommodating, but in her current state… "Okay, we'll drop you off to get your car first, then pick up some supplies and meet you at the cabin."

She nearly laughed at the smug look of victory the girl flashed Alec as she got in the car.

Alec on the other hand looked anything but happy. "So I get no say in this."

"You just had it." Raina opened the driver's seat door. "But the person with the money and car calls the shots. Now get in."

CHAPTER 51

"Don't go to your house. Let me off around the block."

Having just signaled to make the turn, Raina frowned at the girl leaning forward between the car's front seats. "Why?"

"In case those guys at the cemetery saw your license plate and know where you live."

Raina looked aside at Alec. "Smart kid."

He responded by clenching his jaw even tighter.

Around the circular cul-de-sac, she pulled to a stop before the property that backed onto hers.

Erin got out. "See you at the cabin."

"You remember how to get there?" Raina called after her.

With a wave, the girl ran up the driveway, and veered into the trees behind the house.

Raina watched till she disappeared, then swung a U-turn. At the corner where the cul-de-sac met the next road, she pulled to the side and peered up the street toward her house.

"Why are we stopping?" Alec said. He could feel the flash drive burning in his pocket. All he wanted was to watch it again and instead had to face these further delays.

"I want to make sure she's all right," Raina answered.

"Why wouldn't she be? *Her* car wasn't at the cemetery."

"Just making sure."

He sighed. "Is this really—"

"You're welcome to get out and walk if you want."

He stared out the windscreen. Maybe he *should* just walk away. He could go back and watch the video in the library as he'd done before. But after that? As this woman so rightfully pointed out, a man with no money had limited options. And – call it a weakness – he was rather fond of eating occasionally.

Leaning forward to see around him, Raina briefly looked down at his clothes. The connection she'd been searching for earlier at the diner suddenly hit her. "By the way, nice jacket."

He followed her gaze and let out a huff. "Okay, yes, I stole it from your shop. We get out of this alive, I'll pay you for it."

"I notice you didn't take one of the cheap ones. Pigskin suede, fleece-lined. For a fugitive you've got excellent taste."

"I'm sorry, okay; I needed something warm. And I didn't exactly have a choice about stealing it."

"There's always a choice."

He stared, incredulous. "You saying I shouldn't have taken it? The nights have been freezing and I spent the last one on a park bench."

"Then you know what it's been like for Erin, don't you."

As he chewed on her words she looked past him again, shaking her head. "Something's wrong. This is taking way too long."

You're telling me. "Well, seeing as we're sitting here, how about answering a question for me. The other night after we left Dempsey's, you told me you didn't have the case I'd left in your car. So how come it was lying on your office desk when I woke up there the following morning?"

"Turns out I did have it, I just didn't know it." She explained about scooping it into her bag along with the rest of its spilled contents.

"You expect me to believe that?"

Her gaze snapped back to him. "I don't care if you believe me or not. Look, let's get something straight, DeMarco – you dragged me into this. I don't have to explain myself to you."

He took a deep breath. No, of course she didn't. He was acting like a total jerk. Yes, he was in strung-out shape, desperate for answers, but this wasn't how he'd wanted this or any conversation between them to go. "Look, Raina—"

"Something must've happened. This isn't right." She'd resumed her surveillance, peering up the road. "We should see her by now."

Alec looked around to follow her gaze. "Maybe she went out the other way."

"There is no other way. It circles around and comes out here. If she's not—"

"Wait." He put up a hand. "You hear that?"

She stopped and listened, her eyes growing wide. "Sirens."

"Right, that's it, let's get out of here."

"What about Erin?"

"She'll be fine. The cops aren't after her."

Raina's jaw dropped. "If they killed your brother to get *her* video—"

"She can leave in her own car."

"*If* she can get to it." Raina strained to catch more of the sound. Definitely sirens. Definitely louder and coming their way.

"Get out of here. Now!" Alec insisted.

"I'm not leaving her." Despite the words, her panic was

growing. Even if Erin did get away, what would Scanlon make of the fact were *she* apprehended in this man's company?

He opened his door. "If you're just going to sit here—"

"Wait." She reached out and grabbed his arm. Her breath burst out in a rush of relief. "It's not the police."

They looked around to see a fire truck coming up behind them and swinging wide to turn up the street. *Her* street. Just when her fears had begun to recede... "You see any smoke? Can you see where it's stopping?"

"No, but it looks like the girl got her car."

She leaned toward his window, the man a solid cushion beneath her. The car that had veered to let the fire truck pass was now coming toward them. The same rusted wreck Erin had slept in the night before.

CHAPTER 52

Quaking aspen lined the road, their branches tangling overhead in a vaulted avenue of sulfur and gold. They were well out of town, no houses in sight and very few cars. When Erin pulled off the road behind her, Raina braked and did the same.

"Now what?" Alec said.

"I'll find out." She shut off the engine and opened her door, then reached back and pulled the keys from the ignition. "Just in case – been having trouble with car thieves lately."

Funny. Alec rolled down his window, rested his arm out and watched the pair in the side mirror.

The girl, also now out of her car, retrieved something from the back seat – a large plastic bottle – and carried it around to the front. When she lifted the hood he heaved a sigh, got out and started back to them.

The girl had the cap off the radiator and was pouring in water from the bottle. She seemed to have things under control – clearly it wasn't the first time she'd done it.

He let his gaze wander over the vehicle. "*This* is the car we had to come back for?"

"I told you, everything I own is in here." Her head poked out from under the hood. "At least I didn't *steal* it."

Another comedian. Alec caught the smile on Raina's face – a break in the clouds all too brief before concern darkened it again.

"Erin, did you see where the fire was on my street?" she said.

"There wasn't one. False alarm."

The woman frowned. "How do you know it was a false alarm?"

"Because I called it in."

Raina's jaw dropped. "You called the fire department to my street when there wasn't a fire?"

"It looked like some cops had staked out your house. I needed to distract them to get to my car."

Raina looked toward him and lifted her brows. *Told you she was smart.*

Erin slammed the hood and started for the back.

Alec didn't move from her path when she reached him. "I had a pretty good view of the street. Damned if I could see a patrol car."

"I never said it was a patrol car."

"So how did you know they were cops?"

"You try living on the streets for a year. You'd know too." She walked around him, threw the empty bottle in the back, and climbed behind the wheel.

"Look, there's something else I have to do." She started the engine. "Don't bother following, I'll meet you at the cabin."

Before Raina could utter a protest, the girl drove off. They stood on the road, shoulder to shoulder watching her bomb disappear up the road.

"How does a girl that young get a license?" Alec said.

"She said she's eighteen."

"If she's eighteen I'll eat this jacket."

"Well, how does a girl that age end up pregnant and on the streets?"

He looked down at her. "Want me to draw you a diagram?"

Lips pursed, she started to turn when he took her arm. "Why would the cops stake out your house?"

Raina waved a hand. "Despite what she claimed, she couldn't know for sure they were cops."

"But you didn't seem real surprised when she said it."

She pulled her arm free. "I thought you were in a hurry to get to the cabin."

CHAPTER 53

Alone in the office with the shop doors locked, Julie counted out the day's takings. She set aside the bare minimum for tomorrow's register, then slipped the remaining two hundred and twenty dollars into an envelope. With the register money locked in the safe and the envelope stuffed in her bag, she grabbed her jacket and headed for the back door.

She was feeling more than a little unsettled. Raina had called her at home that morning to say she'd be attending a funeral and wouldn't get to work until after lunch. When she still hadn't arrived by four o'clock, Julie had grown concerned. But her friend's second call to explain her absence had only compounded things, despite all her protests and denials.

"Can you look after things for me for a while. I have to go away. I'm not sure how long – hopefully just a couple of days."

"And you're not going to tell me what this is about?"

Raina's request that Julie meet her at Dempsey's and hand over all the money from the safe had only stirred up deeper concerns. That she'd lost her wallet might explain the request, but when taken with other aspects of her recent behavior...

"Okay what's going on?"

"Nothing. I told you—"

"You're going away, but you can't say why."

"Julie, please..."

"Look, I'm worried about you. You've been acting really weird lately. Falling asleep in your office the other night. The way you acted when that cop was here about your car. Taking off with no explanation... This isn't like you."

"Trust me, okay. I'll explain it all to you when I get back."

Yet somehow Julie felt not the least reassured.

At the end of the hall, she activated the security alarm and stepped out onto the shop's back porch. She turned from closing the door to start down the steps and gasped at the large figure blocking her path.

"Sorry, didn't mean to startle you," he said. "Deputy Farrington. I was here the other day about your friend's car."

She slumped in relief. "Yes, of course. I didn't recognize you out of uniform."

"Is she here? Raina? I've been trying to call her on that number she gave me but her cell phone doesn't appear to be working."

"No, I'm sorry, she..." She cut herself off. Did Raina's instructions to tell no-one her whereabouts include the police? Why did they need to see her anyway? A follow-up regarding her stolen car? They'd already returned it to her, hadn't they?

"Raina didn't come into work today," she answered. "Touch of the flu. Said she was spending the day in bed."

"Really? That's funny, I went to her house but she wasn't there."

Julie stared back. And why would a policeman go to her home? Was Raina in some kind of trouble?

"You wouldn't know where she might have gone," he said. "It's important."

"If she wasn't at home, I'm afraid I wouldn't know. Is something wrong?"

"To be honest, yes, there could be. I really need to speak to her."

She studied him in the gathering dusk. His tone hadn't sounded entirely impartial. "As a policeman or as a friend?"

He paused, seeming to weigh his words. "It is a police matter but... I'm not here in an official capacity."

Which didn't really tell her a lot. Except for the fact this handsome cop appeared as concerned about Raina as she was.

"What about you?" he said.

"Excuse me?"

"I assume you don't just work for Raina, you're also her friend. If you care about her, you need to tell me where she is."

The man still hadn't moved from her path. Rather then let her come down the steps to speak with him on equal ground, he'd chosen to keep her on the porch, essentially trapped. Intimidation or a reflection of the depths of his concern?

"I'm sorry, I don't know. If she wasn't at home maybe she went to see a doctor."

He blew out a sigh. "All right, thank you." Seeming to note he'd been blocking her way, he stepped aside to let her pass.

Julie started for her car.

"Look, if you hear from her..." He pulled a scrap of paper from his pocket, wrote on it, and handed it to her. "My number. Tell her to call me, please. Tell her, if she wants to come in, *don't* go to Scanlon. She was right, he—"

He caught himself, then shook his head. "Just tell her to call me."

CHAPTER 54

From the lane behind the row of shops, Farrington watched Julie Cramer get into her car and back from her parking spot. The woman was lying; every instinct he had was telling him. The question was, who was Raina hiding from? Had she told Julie not to reveal her whereabouts to anyone or to the police specifically? With her fears regarding Scanlon's obsession, he could understand if it was the latter.

When Cramer drove from the parking lot, he pulled out behind her and followed at a measured distance – close enough to see if she lifted her cell phone to her ear. The fact she hadn't yet used her phone suggested she might be planning to talk with Raina in person. With luck she might actually be heading to meet Raina now. All he had to do—

When his own phone rang he checked caller ID and muttered a curse. He could ignore it, let it go through to voice message, continue on his current mission. But that might just create more problems in the long run.

He answered the call. "Farrington."

"Craig? John. I need a favor. I've been a bit distracted lately – I forgot to pick up the wine for tonight. Stop off on your way over, would you, and grab me a couple of bottles. You know the one Peg likes so much."

He frowned. Tonight? Peg's favorite wine? "The Chablis?"

"That's it. I'll be in deep shit if she thinks I forgot. She's really gone overboard with this dinner."

Damn! Peg's birthday dinner. He checked the time. The one he should've been at ten minutes ago.

"How about it?" Scanlon said in his ear. "Figured you must be on your way. I'll fix you up as soon as you get here."

He could see Cramer's car just up ahead, but pulling further out in front of him. He could make some excuse, lie to his boss, stick to his plan. But in the state Scanlon was in these days, better all around to keep the man happy.

"No problem, John, leave it to me. Be there shortly."

He flicked on his blinker and took the next right, watching Cramer's car continue on in the other direction.

CHAPTER 55

Julie had been waiting ten minutes when Raina walked through the door of Dempsey's. She'd spent the time staring into the drink she ordered but hadn't yet touched. As she watched her boss approach her table and take the seat opposite, she wondered if she knew this woman at all.

"Do you have it? The money?"

Spoken like a genuine fugitive. Julie slid the envelope across to her.

"Jules, you're a life saver. Thank you so much." Raina slipped the packet into her bag and glanced toward the door. "Look, I'm really sorry but I can't stay; someone's waiting for me." She started to rise. "I swear I'll explain everything to you when all this is sorted out."

"Just tell me one thing. Does it have anything to do with this?" Julie set yesterday's paper before her.

Raina took one look at the headline and slowly sank back onto her seat.

"It was on the table when I came in," Julie said. "I hadn't seen it yet – you know how I am with papers. I have to say it was a bit of a surprise."

When Raina just stared down at the headline Julie leaned forward. "You hit a man on the road that night – the night we were supposed to go to the movie – and you didn't even tell me about it? I don't understand, I thought we were friends."

"We are."

"And this other business…" She tapped the article. "It says you had an accident when you were eighteen. DUI, your boyfriend killed, you were charged over it…" She shook her head in disbelief. "I've known you two years and you never once mentioned any of that."

Raina rested her face in her hands, rubbing her eyes. "I was trying to forget. Can't anyone understand that?"

Julie reached out and touched her arm. "I do understand. If that's the real reason. I just… I'd hate to think you didn't tell me because you were afraid it would make some kind of difference. It wouldn't. I don't think anything could."

Raina exhaled and squeezed her hand. "Thank you."

"But look, there's something you need to know. That cop who took the report about your car came back to the shop today."

Raina's face paled. "Farrington? When was he there? What did he want?"

"He showed up just as I was leaving to meet you. He wants you to call him, says it's urgent."

Julie handed over the paper and watched her friend struggle with her conflicting emotions. "You did know him, didn't you? That's why you reacted that way when you saw him."

Shaking her head, Raina tucked the paper into her pocket. "Believe me, it's not that I don't want to tell you…"

Julie waited but she didn't go on. "He said something else. Or started to. He said, "Tell Raina if she wants to come in, *don't* go to Scanlon." I didn't get it at the time, but after reading this..." She touched the newspaper. "He means if you want to turn yourself in, doesn't he? Turn yourself in for what?"

"I'm sorry but I really have to go."

"You're in some kind of trouble, aren't you?" When Raina got up, Julie rose with her. "What can I do? Tell me; how can I help?"

"Just...keep the shop open, carry on as normal and don't tell anyone you've talked to me."

"Even the police?"

"Especially the police." Raina met her startled gaze. "It's a lot to ask and you could get in trouble. Which is one of the reasons I don't want to get you involved."

"Okay. Don't worry, I won't say a word."

Julie reached up and gave her a hug. "Stay safe. And call me if you need anything else. Anything at all."

CHAPTER 56

Raina unlocked the cabin door, shouldered it open and flicked on the light.

A couch, an arm chair, a TV on the chest of drawers opposite, a basic kitchen, and – most importantly – a computer on the desk by the window. She stepped inside and held the door.

Laden with the bags of provisions they'd bought, Alec headed straight for the kitchen. He set them on the tiny table, took a look around, then started unpacking.

"What happened to your little friend?"

Raina fought to conceal her fears. She'd not been happy letting Erin go off on her own. Since leaving the girl, she and Alec had purchased provisions, rendezvoused with Julie at Dempsey's, and checked into the cabin. More than enough time, she would've thought, for Erin to perform her single errand and meet them here.

"You think it was a mistake to let her go?" she said.

"That's the least of your mistakes with that kid."

Poised to condemn his lack of concern, she froze at the sound of a car pulling up outside the cabin. The air whooshed out of her. "Here she is now."

A moment later Erin walked in bearing her own tattered bag of belongings.

Raina stared down at the two license plates she dropped on the coffee table. "What are those?"

"For your car. Like I said, those guys at the graveyard might've seen yours."

"Where did you get them?"

The girl started for the back of the cabin.

"Erin?"

"Okay if I have a shower?"

Raina slumped. Clearly she wasn't getting an answer. In truth she wasn't sure she wanted one. "Hang on a minute."

As the girl turned back, Raina lined up three phones on the table. "I got one for each of us. They're just cheap burners but I thought we should be able to contact each other in case we separate. I've already entered into each one the numbers of the other two."

Erin nodded, picked up a phone and continued on in search of the bathroom.

Alec grabbed one as he went by in the other direction. "I'll move your car around back and put these on it." He held up the plates and went out the door.

And all at once she was standing alone. "You're welcome," she said to the empty room.

She busied herself stowing the perishables in the fridge. The news Julie had relayed at their meeting, that Craig had come to the shop looking for her, his warning that Scanlon was gunning for her, was deeply disturbing.

She'd known about Scanlon already of course, but the fact Craig could now see it too meant the Chief must be making no attempt to conceal his objective. At least not with his most trusted officer and friend.

Having met with Julie alone, she hadn't yet shared this news with the others. She couldn't deny a strong inclination to comply with Craig's request to call him. But that wouldn't go over well with Alec who believed the police were involved with his brother's death.

She looked around. The place was too quiet. No sound of water running in the shower. She went to the bathroom and found it empty.

Poking her head into the bedroom she smiled at the sight of Erin lying curled up on one of the beds. She took a blanket from the closet shelf and draped it over her, then returned to the kitchen. Just as Alec was coming back in.

"Where's the kid?" he said.

"Her name is Erin. She's asleep. Poor thing must be exhausted. Living in that car, she probably hasn't had a decent night's sleep in—"

"So are we going to check out this flash drive, or what?" He stepped to the desk and pulled off his jacket.

"There, you hear it?" Raina asked a few moments later when they'd finished watching Erin's video.

Alec stared back at her incredulous. "That's what you've been going on about? *That's* what you think is a baby's cry? For god's sake that could be anything – a bit of machinery, a squeaky door, someone's shoe even."

"What are you talking about? Listen again."

She started it again and turned up the volume. When the screen went dead a second time, she sat back vindicated. "That is clearly an infant's cry.

Alec shook his head in amazement. "You've got better hearing than I do."

She waited as he stalked to the window and stood in

silence peering out. Then abruptly he turned, grabbed his jacket from the back of the chair, and started pulling it on again.

"What are you doing?"

"What's it look like?" He yanked the flash drive from the computer. "There is nothing on here that could lead us to the people who killed my brother." He hurled it aside.

"There has to be!"

As he stalked to the kitchen she retrieved the drive from the trash where he'd thrown it. "Why else would Liam have been so frightened the night he called you? Clearly *he* thought there was something on here. Evidence someone would kill to get back."

Alec stood grabbing selected items from the stash on the counter – the Advil, bandages, antiseptic cream. "Liam was an investigative journalist. And he was good at it. He must've uncovered something else, something he never got a chance to tell me, and *that* was the evidence he was talking about. Not the video."

He took a couple of shirts from a chair and started shoving his goods in a bag. "Look, you can stay on this ride if you want, but this is where I get off."

"You're making a mistake."

"Not from where I stand."

"And what about Erin?"

He stopped for a moment and blew out a breath. "My brother was the champion of hopeless causes, not me."

"So you're just walking out."

The last of his items went into the bag. He pulled it from the table. "Frankly I suggest you do the same. Because that kid in there has some serious problems."

He marched for the door.

CHAPTER 57

Out on the porch, Raina called to the figure striding away from her across the lawn. "Where will you go?"

Alec kept walking.

"It's not just the killers who are after you, you know."

The man never slowed.

She charged down the steps and stopped at the bottom. "The police found Liam's body in your car."

That did it. He stopped, turned and waited.

"They found him sitting in the driver's seat."

"What are you talking about?" He took a step toward her. "Liam was shot in the open. I left him lying on the ground near the boat house."

"Someone put him in your car and drove *his* car away from the scene. Not only that." She moved toward him. "There were traces of cocaine found in your trunk."

"What! That's insane! I've never had any kind of... They must've... They..." He wound down like a spinning top. The arm he'd raised dropped to his side. "They did it to make it look like we were dealing and that I killed Liam."

"Which is exactly what the police now believe – the ones

not involved with what your brother was trying to uncover."

As though all the strength had been sapped from his body, he slumped onto the bench at edge of the driveway. Bending forward, he threaded his fingers through his hair.

Raina walked over and stood before him.

He looked up, frowning. The cabin cast its long shadow over them, deepening his look of utter despair. "How do you know what the police found at the scene?"

"Chief of Police Scanlon told me." She lowered herself to the space beside him. "When your brother's body was found I went to the hospital and confessed to killing him."

He straightened. "You *what*?"

"I thought it was him I hit on the road that night and that he died from his injuries. When I found out he'd been shot I retracted my confession but by then I had trouble convincing Scanlon I wasn't involved."

He shook his head as though trying to clear it. "But…if the cops have pictures of Liam and me, surely they can see how you might confuse us."

She blew out a sigh. "I've dug myself in a bit deeper since then. Yesterday morning the police called me to say my car had been recovered. When I went to the station to pick it up, Scanlon asked me if I'd seen you. I told him I hadn't."

She felt his dark gaze taking her in. "Why would you do that?"

"You said the police killed your brother. Seemed like a pretty good reason to me."

"And you think they found out you lied to them?"

"Somehow they must have."

"Which explains why they were watching your house." He leaned back and sighed. "So the cops are after you now as well. And here I thought you were just being nice."

They sat in silence, the question pressing at the back of her lips. "You never explained how you know the police are involved in this?"

"Liam told me. At the boathouse, before they killed him."

"Well, how did *he* know?"

He opened his mouth then closed it again, staring back. Why would he hesitate? Didn't he trust her?

"Look, don't you get it," she said. "We're in this together. Erin wants her baby back and you want to find out who killed your brother."

In the shadows his eyes were wells of suspicion. "And what do you get out of it?"

"You mean apart from getting the police off my back?"

"That doesn't explain why you're helping the girl; you don't even know her." He shook his head. "The cops have nothing to pin on you. No matter how this all pans out, when it's over you can just walk away."

She nearly laughed. *Just walk away.* If only. "So you're not going to tell me."

His answer was silence.

Frustration drove her to her feet. "You know I wouldn't be mixed up in this at all if it wasn't for you. If you hadn't run out in front of me that night—"

He rose to confront her. "The next time I'm fleeing from my brother's killers I'll be more careful."

She watched him heft the bag to his shoulder. "I don't believe this. You're still leaving? Even after what I just—"

"As far as I can see, nothing's changed."

CHAPTER 58

Raina watched Alec walk away into the twilight. She knew once her buried emotions surfaced they would hit her hard, but for now mental and emotional overload seemed to have blunted the moment's impact. She turned and started back to the cabin.

Halfway up the steps she spotted the face peering from the window and felt her heart drop. She'd hoped Erin might've slept through her encounter with Alec but clearly the girl had witnessed their exchange. Indeed, her gaze still followed the man as he strode down the track heading for the road.

Steeling herself, Raina entered the cabin.

The girl turned from the window to face her. "What's happening? Where's he's going?" When she got no reply, she lowered her voice. "Right. He's not coming back, is he?"

"Erin, you have to understand, he's upset. His only brother—"

"Yeah, yeah, I get it." She waved a hand. "He thinks he's better off without us. Like I haven't heard *that* before."

"Look, the important thing is we got your video back. We don't need him. We can do this ourselves, just you and me."

Erin jerked away from her touch. "You don't have to make excuses for him. It doesn't mean squat to me if he leaves." She stormed to the door and yanked it open.

"Where are you going?"

"Getting something out of my car."

"You need any help? I—" The door slammed shut.

Raina hurried to the window and watched Erin walk to her battered Taurus. Was she upset? Despite her insistance she didn't care, deep down she could view Alec's leaving as just another form of abandonment. How many had there been in her short troubled life? Damn DeMarco!

Erin opened the car's back door and began rummaging through her belongings. Not getting in. Not driving off. When she straightened with a box in her arms and kicked the door closed, Raina let out the breath she'd been holding. She was just turning away from the window when she heard the girl give a loud shriek.

In a heartbeat she was out the door and down the steps. "What is it? What wrong?"

Erin stood clutching her hands to her throat. "In the box." She shuddered.

Raina looked for the source of her terror. Though some of the contents had spilled on the ground nothing looked out of the ordinary – shampoo, soap, a tube of toothpaste...

Movement caught her eye. Incredulous, she bent and pointed to the finger-long creature with black and red stripes inching along the rim of the box. "Is this what's worrying you?"

Erin shrank back. "Get rid of it. Get it out of here!"

Raina flicked the caterpillar onto her palm where it curled in ball. She carried it away from the car and settled on the edge of the cabin steps.

Erin gathered her scattered belongings, casting anxious looks her way. Hefting the box, she moved toward the cabin but stopped at the sight of the insect now inching across Raina's hand. "How can you even touch that thing?"

"It's a Wooly Bear. Hard to be afraid of something with a name like that, don't you think?"

"I'm not afraid. I just don't like them, that's all. They're gross."

Eager to relieve the girl's anxiety, perhaps distract her from all that was happening, and connect on any level she could, Raina considered the insect and smiled. "I know it sounds crazy but every time I see one of these, I think of my Dad."

"Your Dad's fuzzy with black and red stripes?" Erin huffed. "You're right, that's nuts."

"You know they say you can tell how bad the winter's going to be by a Wooly Bear's stripes."

"I thought *all* winters in Maine were crap." Erin edged closer, eyeing the bug with a bit less revulsion. "Why do they remind you of your father?"

"My Dad was the kindest, most soft-hearted person I ever knew." She held up the caterpillar. "In autumn when these guys were crossing the roads he'd steer around them whenever he could."

Erin rolled her eyes. "Sounds like 'crazy' runs in your family."

"One time we were out somewhere and there were a bunch of these on the road. Somehow he managed to miss every one. The only problem, a policeman saw him and pulled him over for drunk driving."

A hesitant smile turned the girl's lips. "Did you tell him what your Dad was doing?"

"Yeah, we all did. He didn't believe us."

The girl set a foot on the bottom step. "Cops aren't big on believing, are they."

"He couldn't understand how anyone would care that much about a bug." Raina shrugged. "But that was my Dad."

Erin watched the insect a moment longer then continued up the stairs. "I wouldn't know what my Dad was like – never met him."

CHAPTER 59

Alec barely made it out to the road before the second-guessing began. He'd always been good at split-second decisions; once they were made, for better or worse, he could normally live with them.

This one was proving a bit more difficult to put from his mind.

Had he done the right thing in walking away? As he'd known from the first time he'd watched it, there was absolutely nothing on the girl's video that could help him find Liam's killer. Her story about her baby being stolen was sheer fantasy. Still, if she'd been there the night Liam died out at the lake, she might know something she wasn't telling him. A clue she might not even realize she knew.

And Raina. It seemed he'd put her through more than he'd realized. Not only had he placed her at possible risk from Liam's killers, he'd caused her a nasty confrontation with police. What would it have been like for her to believe she'd killed a man with her car? Even though it had been an accident, she couldn't have helped blaming herself. And then to have the cops on her case even after she'd told them the truth…

On the edge of the winding wooded road he stopped and ran a hand through his hair. The sun had long since dipped below the trees and a damp chill was creeping out from their shadows.

He looked back along the distance he'd walked, perhaps a mile or so from the cabin, and wondered yet again…

As crazy as the girl obviously was, as prickly as Raina could be at times, was it wise to just leave them? Never mind that they were all on their own. *Or* that Raina had saved his life. Wouldn't combining their meager resources serve them all better in the long run?

Or would turning around be admitting that he'd begun to feel…

He forced himself to resume his march. Fog drifted across the road. Arms of mist reached from the forest to caress his face with cold clammy fingers. Up ahead, the lights of a small camping and bait shop flashed in the murk. With no other destination to draw him, he headed toward it.

Yes, of course he was making the right decision. The last thing he needed was to get tangled up with a contentious female and a delusional teenage runaway.

He blew out a breath. All right maybe contentious wasn't the word. Naturally Raina had her moments – protective of the girl now in her charge, mothering instincts fully engaged. But it was all complications he didn't need and simply couldn't handle right now.

He quickened his stride across the bait shop's tiny parking lot. Keep going, keep moving, don't look back. He had his Advil, he had his bandages, he had some clothes—

And that was all.

He stopped in his tracks. No money for food and no place

to stay. Oh, yeah, he'd really thought this through.

With a muttered curse, he reached for the door of the shop and noted the object adorning his wrist. His Laurent Ferrier. With its midnight blue dial and white gold hands, its calf leather strap and cushion design. A gift from Liam. Worth far more in memories and sentiment than he could ever get for it in cash.

Bowing his head, he let out a sigh. Then pulled back the door and stepped inside.

CHAPTER 60

The Scanlons' dining room had been festooned with balloons and streamers in honor of Peg's sixtieth birthday. Friends and family had gathered to celebrate, donning hats and forced smiles. But even with their concerted efforts the festive atmosphere had deteriorated through the course of the evening.

Peg had clearly had a few drinks before Farrington even arrived. And the bottles of wine he'd picked up at John's request were emptied soon after – mainly into their hostess's glass. Now, as her sister Maureen cleared the plates, Peg leaned toward him across the table.

"Craig, dear, I wonder if you can help me with something. I keep asking this question but no-one seems able to give me an answer."

At the head of the table, adjacent to them both, Scanlon flashed her a warning look, which she purposely ignored.

Though he had his suspicions what it might be about – and no desire to discuss the subject – Farrington had no choice but to answer. "Of course, if I can."

"It's about that accident, the man who was killed. The one

involving that wretched girl." She gave a huff. "Well, I suppose she's not a girl any more, is she. That woman then. That Raina Wilkins." Hand to her throat, she lowered her voice to a slurred whisper. "I won't tell you what *I* think she is."

Farrington gripped the stem of his wine glass. Oh, yes, he'd stepped into something all right.

"Hadn't you better get the coffee started?" Scanlon said. "Lois and Dave want a cup before they—"

"Maureen's getting it," Peg dismissed, and turned back to Craig. "See, what I can't understand, what I just can't seem to get my head around, is how someone like that can kill two people with their driving and go unpunished on both counts."

"Peg," Scanlon cautioned. "Craig doesn't want to—"

"No, no, I want to hear his thoughts on this. After all, who knows better than he what the woman's capable of. Isn't that right, dear?"

Craig watched his fingers turning the wine glass.

Peg leaned forward and took his free hand. "I mean you were there, weren't you? The first on the scene all those years ago. You *saw* what she did." Her features tightened. "You saw what that miserable drunken tramp did to my beautiful—"

"Raina didn't kill the second man." The words burst out before he could stop them. He felt Scanlon's glare like the sun on his cheek.

Peg seemed more bewildered than angered. "She confessed to it, didn't she? The newspaper said she walked into the hospital of her own free will and openly admitted to running him over."

"At the time she *believed* she'd killed the man, yes, but—"

"Because she hit him. With her car. Another act of criminal negligence. Not only that, she just drove off again;

never stopped to help the poor soul. No-one knows what state she was in because she didn't even report what happened."

"Yes, that's true, but the man didn't die from—"

"I just don't see why no-one is doing anything about this. What does it take before a person like that is brought to justice?"

Scanlon reached over and gripped her arm. "Peg—"

"No!" She threw off his hand. "I want to understand this, John. I want someone to explain to me how this is possible." She got unsteadily to her feet. "How many times does this have to happen before something is done? How many people does she have to kill!"

When she lapsed into tears, Scanlon rose to escort her from the room.

She shoved him back with surprising strength. "If you'd been any sort of father, you'd have made sure justice was done ten years ago."

Scanlon stood speechless as she ran from the room. Just as Maureen emerged from the kitchen with a birthday cake, candles alight.

CHAPTER 61

Raina straightened at the computer keyboard, suddenly aware of a presence standing over her. She blinked to clear the sleep from her eyes.

"You." Was she dreaming? She must've nodded off and the sound of him entering the cabin had woken her. "How did you—?"

Alec held out the cabin door key. "Forgot to give it to you when I left before."

When you ditched us, you mean. When you begged for my help and then walked away the minute you had it.

"So you just came back to return it, did you? Fine. Thank you." She plucked it from his fingers. "Now get the hell out of here."

He settled into the seat beside her. "Actually I thought I'd stick around."

"And what if we don't want you here?"

"Well, if it makes any difference, I'm not empty-handed this time." He set a bottle of beer on the desk and pushed it toward her.

"What's that supposed to be?"

"Peace offering." He looked around. "Where's the kid?"

"Erin," she corrected. "Her name's Erin. She's gone to bed so keep your voice down."

She glanced beyond him toward the kitchen. His jacket was slung on a nearby chair, his pack on the table. He really was staying.

"You're a piece of work, you know that, DeMarco. You think you can just walk away and then waltz back whenever it suits you?" She leaned to within an inch of his face. "We don't need you."

"But I need you."

She held his gaze, trawling the depths of those dark hooded eyes for a glimpse of the man he was asking her to trust. She knew the words he'd just spoken meant nothing to him. Yet her pulse had done an annoying skip at hearing him say them.

As though sensing their effect, he said them again. "That's right, I need you. Both of you. I realized it once I stopped to think about it. There might not be a lot to go on, but without you I've got no leads at all."

"Not to mention, no money. Right?" She jerked her chin at the bottle of beer. "So how'd you buy that?"

"I hocked something."

She stared at the glistening frosty bottle and licked her lips. Sam Adams Oktoberfest. She could almost taste it.

She tore her gaze away and glared at him. "Erin saw you leave before, you know."

"So?"

"You can't play games with a kid like that, she's been hurt too much. You either accept that or you leave right now."

He settled back, beer in hand. "Playing games is the furthest thing from my mind."

She studied him a moment, convincing herself he meant what he said. She was right to be annoyed at him for leaving, but perhaps a bit of the anger she felt was aimed at herself. What had she been thinking, talking about how wonderful her Dad had been to a girl who'd clearly had a rough home life?

Signaling she'd accepted his return, she grabbed the bottle and took a deep swig. Alcohol was probably the last thing she needed, but nothing had tasted as good in a long time.

"So what are you doing?" He gestured to the blank computer screen. "Don't tell me you're still going over that video."

She clicked on the file. "I spotted something that might be of help, something I didn't notice before." She let the video roll for a moment, then paused it and zoomed in on the man's waist.

"See this guy's belt? It looks like it might have a fancy buckle." She leaned closer and squinted at the image. "I think I can make out a moose on this side."

"That would certainly be unique in the state of Maine."

She exhaled loudly and threw up her hands. "Well, then you were right – the flash drive is useless. If you don't accept that the sound at the end is a baby's cry—"

His warm hand closed around her wrist. "Okay hang on. Just listen a minute." He pointed to the screen. "What if we look at this from a different angle? We know these people are up to something. We might not know what, but we *do* know the identity of one of them."

Raina sat up. "The nurse; Grace Kilburn." Her mind was suddenly leaping ahead. She turned to the keyboard and began typing.

"What are you doing?"

"What I should've done right at the start. Searching the

names Manheim and Kilburn."

"Manheim? But we don't know the doctor's involved in this."

"According to Erin he damn well is."

He sighed. "I thought we were sticking to what's on the video."

Despite his protests, Alec leaned forward to study the data that came up on the screen. The warmth of his body pressing against her spread down her side. She fought to ignore it.

"Look here," she pointed. "Manheim and Kilburn both work at the same two medical facilities – the welfare hospital where Erin had her baby, and the Baxter Memorial Fertility Clinic."

"So?"

Raina pressed her folded hands to her chin, waiting as a half-formed idea took shape. "All right, I know you don't believe her, but let's assume just for a moment that Erin is telling the truth – they stole her baby and sold it to someone. What if…"

Her eyes widened as she turned to face him. "What if it wasn't a one-off thing? What if it's an on-going racket – couples come to the fertility clinic and Manheim fixes them up with a baby from a mother at the welfare hospital?"

"A bit far-fetched. Why wouldn't the couple just adopt a kid legally?"

"Sometimes they can't. Maybe one of them's too old or has a criminal record or some other black mark against them. Adoption agencies can be very picky."

He thought for a moment. It was the first hint of a lead they'd had. "Even if you're right, how would we prove it?"

"If it is a racket, Manheim would have to keep some kind of records – details of both the birth mother and the adoptive parents. All we have to do is get our hands on it and turn it over to the FBI."

"That's all, is it? So what do you propose – we break in and tear the place apart? Torture Manheim till he hands it over?"

Raina exhaled. She was tired and stressed and had had just about enough of his nay-saying. "Well, if you've got any better ideas, I'm listening."

Alec frowned as he studied the screen. She could almost see his mind ticking over – her theory was nuts, but since there were no other leads at the moment…

"How about this?" he said. "You and I go to the fertility clinic posing as a couple unable to have children. We let it slip that we'd adopt a baby if we could, but we're ineligible for whatever reason. We rig up some way to record the meeting and if the good doctor suggests an alternative to legal adoption, we've got our proof."

She blinked. Not bad. Not bad at all. But she damn well didn't have to tell him as much.

"Better than sitting around on our hands," she said grudgingly. "I'll call tomorrow and get us the first appointment I can."

CHAPTER 62

The minute they'd finalized their plan of action, Raina felt a crushing fatigue settle over her. She would finish her beer and head off to bed.

Beside her at the desk, looking no less exhausted, Alec leaned back in his chair. With his attention now switched from the computer to her, he sipped his beer thoughtfully. "I take it you're not married."

She gave a short laugh. How had he come to that conclusion? "What, am I wearing a sign or something?"

"The only person you called was your friend. I figured if you were involved with someone you'd need to report in." He waited. "So are you?"

"Married? No. Involved? No. Anything else you'd like to know?"

He arched a brow. "Didn't mean to hit a nerve."

Wincing, he rose, grabbed the pillow from the arm chair, and tossed it to the end of the couch. He eased himself down onto one of its cushions and began taking off his shoes. "What about family?"

"My parents are dead."

"Brothers or sis—?"

"Look, there's no-one, okay. How many ways do you want me to say it?"

"Hey, I was just wondering if someone's likely to show up looking for you."

"Well, now you know."

She took a deep breath and blew it out slowly. Yes, the tensions were taking their toll, making her touchy and short tempered. But she had no desire to discuss with this stranger – a man with no qualms about walking away if the urge possessed him – how empty her life was at the moment.

Shoe in hand he continued to study her. "You were married once though."

She hung her head. Clearly he wasn't going to let it go and she hadn't the energy left to argue. "Not married. Engaged." She downed a generous gulp of beer, pushed to her feet, and stepped to the window. "He broke it off about two months ago."

Silence descended. Maybe he did know when to stop after all.

"*He* broke it off. So what went wrong?"

She turned to tell him to mind his own business and found herself staring at his outstretched form. An impressive sight, even with smudged jeans and a wrinkled shirt. The image of him lying half-naked on her office couch flashed in her mind and she felt herself flush.

She glanced away. "He's not going to show up looking for me, if that's what you're worried about."

"I'm not. I'm interested. So what happened? Cold feet? Another woman?"

She heaved a sigh. "He thought I lied to him."

"Did you?"

"No." When he gave no reply, she looked around and noticed the smile he was battling. "Did I say something funny?"

"Just hearing things I guess."

"Such as?"

"The two little words you left off that sentence: *not really*. You didn't say them, but they were there. So what did you *not really* lie to him about?"

She stared at him a moment, then thumped her empty bottle on the desk and walked to the kitchen. If they were going to do this she needed more fortification.

From the fridge she pulled out another beer and wandered back. "I told Brad from the very beginning I never wanted children. Only natural he didn't pay attention at first – we were just dating, who knew at that point where things would go."

Pacing slowly before the couch she sipped from the bottle. "When things turned serious, he started bringing it up more and more. Often in a joking way, as though I just hadn't heard my biological clock ticking yet, or it was an opinion I might outgrow." She stopped and pointed a finger at him. "My response was the same on every occasion. I never gave him the slightest reason to think or hope I'd change my mind."

"And yet somehow…"

"When he asked me to marry him I figured he'd come to terms with the fact. But one night the subject came up and it became clear he hadn't accepted it and that he was still expecting I would change my mind. We had a fight and I finally made it clear – so clear even Brad could understand – that it was never going to happen."

"So how is that lying?"

"That's what I've been saying, I didn't lie. He just believed what he wanted to believe."

Alec yawned, watching her now through half-closed eyes. Clearly her story had moved him deeply.

"But other than that you two were good?" he said.

"Good? Oh, you have no idea. A match made in heaven. We never argued, he did all the housework and I had to have my toes surgically straightened after we had sex."

The instant the words were out of her mouth she cringed in horror. How had a man she barely knew managed to goad her to such a point? Or perhaps, the better question was, how had she let him? The beer no doubt had something to do with it.

She set her bottle down on the coffee table. "Guess you can tell I'm not a big drinker."

"You looked pretty accomplished knocking back those Tequila's at Dempsey's the other night."

Her jaw dropped. "Are you trying to start a fight or are you always this charming?"

"If you've got no real thing for kids, how come you're so keen to help Erin find hers?"

All at once his gaze was sharp, his focus intent. Had his line of enquiry had some other purpose? In her muddled state – half exhausted, half drunk – what else had she said that she might regret? And his last question. Phrased differently but pretty much the one he'd asked her outside. *What do you get out of it?* Could he make his distrust of her any more obvious?

She shrugged. "Just a stand-up gal, I guess. Same reason I'm helping you. Though in your case I'm having second thoughts."

She flopped down into the chair beside him. If he could get personal so could she. "All right, my turn."

CHAPTER 63

"What did you mean when you said Liam was the champion of hopeless causes?"

Alec looked away from the woman's face and gazed instead at the cabin ceiling. A familiar voice spoke up in his mind, cautioning him not to reply to her question. It was a subject he wouldn't have discussed with anyone let alone a total stranger.

Yet with their lack of preconceptions, strangers were sometimes the easiest to talk to. And oddly, he found he wanted to talk. Prevented from mixing with family at the funeral, denied the rituals of communal grief – the shared anecdotes, the fond reminiscing about the departed – it seemed there were things he desperately wanted to say about his only brother. No need to tell her everything of course.

"From the time Liam and I were little he was always looking out for others. If he saw some kid getting bullied at school he'd always weigh in, no matter who or how many he might be up against." A sad smile twisted at his lips. "I can't tell you how many fights the little creep dragged me into."

"So you weighed in too."

Her tone implied she was surprised by the fact. Clearly he hadn't impressed her with his behavior so far. Yet how much could he have done differently?

He shrugged. "My kid brother. Couldn't let him go it alone."

"Doesn't that make you a champion as well?"

Her tone this time had held something different. Mockery? Challenge? Something he couldn't quite identify. Caught in the ambient light from the kitchen, her eyes gleamed as she took him in. Interest for a person she wanted to know, or assessing him for potential threat?

"The difference was in our motives, I guess. I was just looking out for Liam. If *Liam* decided something was wrong, he'd speak out for anyone. Probably the whole reason he got into journalism – to expose wrongs and defend the weak."

Surprisingly, speaking the words seemed to help. Telling the world, even in this small way, how noble Liam had been in life, somehow felt like honoring him. Even if he never told the whole story. Even if no-one would ever—

"What else?"

Raina's words brought him back with a jolt. "That's pretty much it."

"No, there's more; I can see it in your face."

The voice in his head had started again. Perhaps he'd better listen this time. "Your imagination."

"You hear things, I see them. And I can see you've got more to say about Liam." She studied him. "Something happened between you, didn't it? Or *to* you."

He returned her challenge with a warning glare. "Let it go."

"Like you let my failed engagement go?"

His jaw was aching, the voice still whispering. And yet

some part of him wanted to answer. To finally release this ultimate confession. Something only one other person besides himself had ever known.

He took a deep breath. "Our dad used to knock us around – me, Liam, and our mom. She tried for years to leave him but he always found us. It was only because of Liam that we finally got away from him.

"Case went to court, Mom and I were too scared to talk, but not Liam. I can still see him sitting there in that huge chair, answering the judge's questions without batting an eye. He just told it straight out, our old man sitting there glaring at him the whole time."

He cleared his throat, the rough sound drawing him back from the past. "So, like I said, Liam was your champion, not me. Even if I did have to step up once in a while to watch his back." He swallowed. "Always knew his damn convictions would get him into trouble one day."

His words died away. The silence stretched.

"Well, I guess that explains it," she said at last.

He frowned at the woman who'd risen before him. "Explains what?"

"Your reaction to his death. Clearly it was your fault, seeing as you didn't protect him this time."

The sucker punch caught him square in the gut. As he fought for breath, struggled to muster the sense to answer, she turned for the bedroom.

"My guess is, if Liam was here, he'd tell you to get over yourself."

CHAPTER 64

In the dream she is always watching what happens. A distant if not impartial observer, never performing the actions herself.

She'd always assumed this stemmed from the fact she had no true recollections of that long-ago night – either she'd passed out behind the wheel before impact, or lost control and blocked what happened from conscious thought. The result was the same – she remembered nothing of the accident in which Rick Scanlon had died.

Her ignorance hadn't spared her however. In the endless days she'd lain immobile in the hospital afterwards, her mind had vengefully filled in the gaps, providing her vivid imagined reflections of squealing tires, the car rolling over down the embankment, the final impact that had thrown him from the car.

Those horrid impressions, precise or not, had become her experience of the event. Ones she'd relived nearly every night for months after leaving the hospital. A dream that had yielded ground only grudgingly, until one day she'd dared believe it was gone for good. A hope she'd been granted all the years since. Until tonight.

With her breathing still slowing, Raina dragged her thoughts from the receding nightmare and focused on the hand gently touching her shoulder. She followed the line of the bare muscled arm, to a corded neck, to concerned dark eyes in a now-familiar face.

She pushed herself up from where she'd been slumped over the edge of the desk – the third time in as many days she'd fallen asleep in front of a computer.

Alec was squatting beside her chair staring up at her, his dark eyes intent. "You were crying in your sleep," he said.

She swallowed, unsure how her words would emerge. A tension born as much from her dream as the man's proximity. "Sorry. I didn't mean to wake you."

He released her arm and pushed up into the chair beside her. With the room in darkness, his clean-cut features were bathed in the bluish cast of the screen saver. "I thought you'd gone to bed," he said.

"I did. Couldn't sleep. I came out to check the news on-line." She watched him as she revealed what she'd learned. "The police have extended their search. For both of us."

He nodded, less troubled than she had expected. "How about we deal with that in the morning."

She squinted at the monitor. Four-fifteen. "It's nearly that now."

The intensity of his gaze unsettled her. Was he still angry with her for her earlier remark? It was a tactic she'd often used with friends – say aloud the fears you knew they were thinking and it made them see how ridiculous they were. It usually worked. But given the fiery look he'd flashed her, she feared in his case the strategy had backfired.

Then again...now that she thought about it, why would she even waste such a gesture on a man she hardly cared about. Normally she reserved such acts only for the people she—

"So what was it about?"

She blinked at him. "What?"

"Your nightmare."

"Who said I had a nightmare?"

"I'm pretty sure I know what one sounds like."

She closed her eyes. The dream had been slightly different this time. A hybrid of the distant past and an event only three days old. *One* of which she was prepared to talk about. Or did he already know about the other? Had he seen the newspaper?

"You," she whispered. "The accident."

"You mean hitting me on the road the other night? Hardly worth having nightmares over."

No mention of the other incident. He must not have seen the article in the paper. "I thought I'd killed you."

"But you didn't. See, I'm right here." With his arm on the desk he leaned closer. "Besides it was only a glancing blow. I'd been shot; in the state I was in I hardly felt it."

It was the first time she'd seen anything approaching a smile on his face. The first time he'd shown the slightest regard for anyone besides his brother. Was he trying to be kind, absolve her of blame? Return the gesture she'd extended him earlier? Maybe he did understand after all.

"I keep hearing that awful thud," she said.

His hand settled on her shoulder, found the knot at the base of her neck and began kneading it. "As you rightfully pointed out, the accident was my fault."

"Yes, but maybe..." Head to one side, she relaxed toward his hand. She could smell the faint hint of beer on his breath. "Maybe I wasn't concentrating as much as I should've been."

"I doubt it would've made any difference." His fingers worked their way up her neck, into her hair, sending shivers over her scalp. She felt the effect down to her toes. *So tired.* She stifled a groan.

"I ran out less than ten feet in front of you." His voice was a murmur. "There was no way you could've stopped in time."

No way to stop. No way to...

Her eyes flew open. He'd pulled away, withdrawn his touch. The spot he'd been kneading felt instantly cold.

She turned to find his face inches from hers. His gaze, just moments ago so concerned, now hard and remote.

"I...I'm still responsible," she blurted. "The driver is always—"

"No. They're not."

With this firm pronouncement he rose and hobbled back to the couch. "Go to bed. And if you have to dream, do it quietly."

CHAPTER 65

Alec lay back against the pillow and shoved both hands behind his head. With Raina now returned to the bedroom he was free to contemplate his jumbled thoughts and confusing behavior.

He'd implied that Raina's nightmare had woken him, but in fact she hadn't disturbed him at all. He'd been lying awake, too sick with grief and anguish to sleep.

When he'd heard her slip back into the room, in his sleep-deprived state he'd experienced a spark of excitement at the thought she might be returning to *him*. An image half-dream had burst on his mind of her sliding naked beneath his blanket, her lush hair tumbling across his chest. True desire? Or an attempt to mitigate his grief by whatever pleasures were currently available?

He didn't know what angered him more – that he hadn't stopped such thoughts there and then, or that he could have them at all at a time like this.

When he'd heard her crying out in her sleep a short while later, he'd rushed to her side, eager to comfort her in her nightmare. He certainly hadn't planned to then drive her from

225

the room. But when he'd caught himself wanting to do more than comfort her, he had to put some distance between them. He couldn't allow himself to become distracted from his mission to find Liam's killer. And Raina Wilkins was a definite distraction.

Though they had angered him at the time, it hadn't taken him long to realize the true intent of her words to him earlier. He appreciated her attempt to shock him to his senses despite the fact it hadn't worked. The truth was, she wasn't that far off the mark. Rational or not, deserved or not, he did feel a measure of responsibility for Liam's death.

Which was why he couldn't let anything or anyone stand in the way of his finding who killed him.

CHAPTER 66

Raina stepped out onto the porch, cast a look back at the man lying asleep on the couch, and drew the door softly closed behind her. Clouds obscured the mid-morning sun. In the darkened cabin it had felt much earlier. Between that and the depths of the man's exhaustion he would hopefully sleep until she returned.

She descended the steps and headed for the woods.

Despite his insistence she get some rest, she'd barely slept after going back to bed the second time. It hadn't been dreams that had kept her awake but concerns over the extended police search to find them. Clearly suspicions had escalated regarding their involvement in Liam's death. Suspicions fueled by actual evidence or manufactured by Chief John Scanlon?

There was only one person she could go to for help and she wasn't about to ask permission from Alec, a man she wasn't yet sure she could trust.

She could excuse everything he had done – pointing a gun at her, stealing her car, kidnapping her – as efforts to find his brother's killers. Even his brusqueness, his inexplicable behavior last night, his lack of compassion where Erin was concerned (things that secretly bothered her more) she could attribute to the pain of a grief-stricken man. *If* she was sure that's what he was.

Was she missing something? In her stressed state it was certainly possible. If it wasn't for Erin saying she'd given the flash drive to his brother would there be any real reason to believe him? And even if he was telling the truth, she wasn't sure she could count on the man. By his own admission he wasn't the hero type.

She walked through the woods that flanked the cabin till she reached the road at the back of the campgrounds. A short distance further she came to the small camping and bait shop they'd passed getting there the day before. Several cars were parked out front, including a pick-up with four fishing rods fixed to the roof.

Inside the store she spotted what had to be the pick-up's passengers – four men in fishing vests with fly lures stuck in their canvas hats. Three were perusing the snack foods on offer as the fourth struggled to talk on his cell phone while getting a coffee at the self-serve counter.

Raina worked her way up the aisle. When she reached the fourth man she stopped beside him, pretending to study a packet of granola while watching him from the corner of her eye. The man said goodbye to his caller, set down his phone, and turned to add cream and sugar to his coffee.

She whisked the cell phone from the counter and headed for the door.

CHAPTER 67

Alec jerked awake on the couch when something feeling remarkably like a baseball bat jabbed his ribs. He grunted – thankfully it wasn't his injured side or he'd have done a lot more – squinted up at the girl standing over him, then down at the object in her hands. Not far off. She was holding a broomstick.

"What the hell are you doing here?" Erin demanded.

"I thought I was sleeping. My mistake."

"Last I saw, you were tripping off down the road. Couldn't get away fast enough. What'd you come back for? Forget something?" She leaned closer. "You weren't worried about us, were you? 'Cause I can set you straight about that: we don't need you."

"So I've been told." Braced for an onslaught of now-familiar pain, Alec slowly sat up on the couch. Possibly just his imagination but the fire in his side felt better this morning, a mere smoldering ember compared to the blowtorch heat of yesterday. Thank god for Advil.

Erin was still glaring down at him.

"Look, my decision to leave wasn't anything against you

or Raina." Aside from the fact this girl had gotten his brother killed and he couldn't look at her without his guts twisting in knots. "I just didn't see the point of—"

"So what changed your mind? You suddenly remember Raina's your meal ticket?"

He let out a sigh. "Are you sure you two aren't related?"

"Just 'cause we both know a dirt bag when we see one doesn't make us sisters."

"I was thinking more along the lines of mother and daughter." It was a throwaway comment. He was still half asleep and had meant nothing by it. Yet he saw from her face the remark hit a nerve.

"So where is she?" All trace of civility had left the girl's voice.

"Where's who?"

"Raina. Who else are we talking about?"

"How should I know? I've been asleep." He scratched his head. "She must be here somewhere."

"You think I'd be asking you if she was? I've looked everywhere, she's not here."

He lowered his arm. "What are you talking about?"

"You did something, didn't you? What did you say to her? What did you do to piss her off?"

"Nothing. I haven't even seen her since..." He sat up straighter. Shit. Maybe he had pissed her off.

He threw back the cover and rose from the couch, padded to the bathroom, checked the bedroom, then returned to the kitchen.

Erin greeted him with an incredulous scowl. "You really don't believe a word I say. I'm telling you, she isn't here."

He scanned the room – the table, the chairs, the couch, the desk. Raina's handbag was nowhere in sight. Wherever she'd gone, she'd apparently done it of her own free will.

But his next concerns were no less disquieting. *Where* had she gone? And why had she needed to sneak out without telling anyone? As he'd pointed out to her several times, she was under no obligation to help either him or the girl. Had she finally come to her senses and bailed on them?

As though the girl had read his thoughts, her voice quavered. "She left, didn't she? Just like you did."

Frowning, he gazed toward the locked cabin door. Just last night he'd walked out that door himself. Why would it be such a tragedy if Raina had?

"Damn it, answer me." The girl waved a hand in front of his face. "Hello. Come in. Earth to Dirt bag!"

He pushed past her and rushed out the door. The porch was empty. But surprisingly Raina's car was still in the driveway. He stepped back inside.

Erin confronted him. "What did you say to make her leave? What did you do?"

"Relax, her car's still here. She hasn't gone far."

"How do you know? You don't even know where she went?"

The crack in her voice made him look over. She wasn't going to start crying was she?

"Okay look…" He put up his hands. "You're right, I barely know either of you. But one thing I'd be willing to bet my life on is that Raina would never just walk away." He gave her a moment to swallow her tears. "Come on, it's okay. She'll be back, I promise."

The girl shook her head. "It isn't that."

He lowered his hands. "Well, then what? What's wrong?"

She dragged a sleeve across her face. "I remembered something I need to tell her."

"Something to do with my brother's death?"

She nodded.

Alec grabbed his shirt from the back of the couch and shrugged it on, then pulled out two chairs at the kitchen table. "Fine. Tell me."

CHAPTER 68

Outside the bait shop, Raina used the fisherman's phone to call the number Julie had given her the day before.

A familiar voice answered after three rings. "Farrington."

"Craig. It's Raina."

"Raina, my god! Where are you? Are you all right?"

Despite the urgency of his tone, after speaking her name his voice grew hushed. Clearly she'd caught him in the presence of others. Was Scanlon one of them?

"I'm okay," she said. "But I can't tell you where I am, not yet."

"I've been looking everywhere for you. Everyone has. You know Scanlon ordered the search for you and Alec DeMarco—"

"I know, I saw it on the news."

His sigh whispered over the line. "I just don't understand. Why did you do it? Why did you help DeMarco escape?

She frowned. The only way he could know that…"That was *you* at the cemetery?"

"Scanlon thought DeMarco might show up there so he sent Hendricks and me to watch for him."

"I had no idea. I thought—"

"That's what I figured. It's what I told Scanlon but he didn't believe me. But, Raina, why on earth did you intervene? Did DeMarco force you to? Does he have something over you?"

"No. No, it's nothing like that." *Not exactly.* "Look, I can't tell you yet what's going on because I'm not sure myself. The reason I'm calling... I just need you to know..." She took a deep breath. "You have to believe me that I had nothing to with Liam DeMarco's death."

A heartbeat of silence. "I've been pretty sure of that all along."

She closed her eyes, touched by his faith in her – even with what he knew of her past. "And I don't think his brother, Alec, did either," she added.

"Is that what he told you? Raina, for god's sake, you're not still with him."

"What happened has nothing to do with drugs, I can tell you that much. Whoever killed Liam planted the traces of cocaine you found to implicate Alec."

"Raina, listen to me. You don't know this man. He could be lying to you so you'll help him. He could be dangerous."

"Craig, I need you to do something for me. It's a lot to ask and I wouldn't if there was any other way. I'm looking into something that could tell us what really happened that night, the night Liam DeMarco was killed. I need you to keep Scanlon off my back for a while. Just a few days."

The silence stretched so long she thought they'd been cut off. "Craig?"

"Scanlon's convinced you're involved in this. He can't see any other possibility. Frankly, your abetting this guy hasn't helped matters. In the state Scanlon's in... I've never seen him like this. I think he would actually go so far as to manufacture evidence to prove your guilt."

"Oh god." Just what she'd feared.

"I'm doing what I can, but I guarantee you it won't be enough. Your best bet is still to turn yourself in. Come to me, Raina. I'll help you, I swear. I'll arrange it so Scanlon isn't there."

She clutched the cell phone. *Come to me*. Was there more to those words than pertained to the crime? "I can't. Not yet. This isn't just about me. Or Alec. There's someone else involved. A girl. I'm trying to help her."

"A girl. What girl?"

"If what she says is true—"

"Raina, you're the one I'm worried about. Please, just meet me. We'll work out a plan. If you turn yourself in—"

"Thank you, Craig. Not just for what you've done, but for believing in me."

"Raina, wait, listen to me—"

"I'll call you as soon as I know something." She closed the phone on his plea to dissuade her.

Back in the store, she returned the phone to the coffee counter, then stepped to the check-out to purchase some freshly made cinnamon doughnuts.

The four fishermen, engaged in a search for the missing phone, were at the same time abusing its owner for leaving it lying somewhere as usual.

On her way out the door she heard one of them say, "Here it is, Frank. Right where you left it."

CHAPTER 69

Erin sat across the table from Alec. "You think I'm crazy, don't you?"

"I never said that."

"You didn't have to, it's obvious. You think I'm making it up – having Cody, someone stealing him, all that stuff that's on the flash drive."

Alec stared down at his hands on the table. He'd listened to the girl's latest revelation with the same reservations he had about the rest of her story. Since there were no other leads to follow he was prepared to look into her claims at least. But he couldn't lie and deny he had doubts. As well as a host of other feelings. Better simply not to reply. Anything he said would only antagonize her.

She leaned toward him. "Well, you know what? I don't care if you don't believe me. It's all true, every word of it. And not only do I have a baby, I even know who the father is."

She caught the reaction he thought he'd disguised and let out a laugh. "Oh yeah, there's that look again. How could a slut like me know who the father of a my baby is? Right?"

He bowed his head, shamed by her brutally honest

reading of his thoughts.

"Well, you're wrong. I do know him." She deflated slightly and lowered her voice. "*Did* know him."

Alec wasn't sure he wanted to hear more. No good could come of getting too involved. Nothing she could say about the father of her child would bring him any closer to finding Liam's killer. He had to stay focused. Naturally, even after all she had done, he'd help the girl if he could, but his primary aim...

Cursing himself he blew out a breath. "So who was he then?"

"A kid from my school."

She was silent a moment, the lines of her face slowly softening. "I'd had a crush on him for years but never had the nerve to tell him. After I left home I figured I'd never see him again so I tried to forget him."

Her gaze fixed on a distant point. "One day, months after I hit the streets, I saw him in a coffee shop. He was all alone so I thought to myself, why not? I'm cool now, a woman of the world and all that. I can at least talk to him, right? Tell him how I used to feel about him."

Alec stared at the transformation. Without the familiar belligerent mask she looked years younger.

"So I go up to him and say the usual, "Hi. Remember me? Erin from English class?" She shook her head. "Those were the coolest words out of my mouth. Everything after that was dribble. I made a complete idiot of myself."

Her smile died. "I just suddenly thought, why would someone like him want to talk to someone like me? I started to leave but he held me back, asked me to stay. I said, "You don't know what I'm like anymore. I've changed since I left." But he just answered that it didn't matter, that he was glad he'd found me again. He said he'd always wanted to be with me, he just never got up the nerve to tell me. "

"So you got together."

Her smile returned. "He used to meet me after school. He'd bring me books and tell me what they were doing in class." She laughed at the thought. "All those times I wanted out of there and there I was wishing I could go back."

Alec scratched at a chip in the table top. "Where is he now?"

She shrugged. "Who knows? Quillen found out he was coming to see me and scared him off." She winced. "Or worse."

"Quillen?"

"The guy who used to think he owned me. Never found out what he actually did, I just know Ryan never came back."

She didn't explain further so he let it go. "Did Ryan know you were pregnant with his child?"

Another shrug. Another failed attempt to portray indifference. She couldn't believe she was fooling either of them. "I went by the school a couple of times to see if I could find him but I was too embarrassed to stick around."

Alec enlarged the chip with his finger nail. "Maybe when things settle down and this is all over..."

She laughed. "What? You figure I can go look him up? Knock on his door, ask his mom if I can come in. Sit down and tell him, "Hey, guess what..."

She shoved back her chair and folded her arms. "Good one, DeMarco. Now who's crazy?"

CHAPTER 70

Farrington returned his phone to his pocket and looked about the police station office. Everyone was going about their business; no-one seemed to have noticed his call or his reaction to hearing Raina's voice.

Her plea for his help still whispered in his ear. Unethical or justified under the circumstances, it made little difference. He'd come too far. His feelings for the woman had changed too much.

As Hendricks walked past, he put out a hand and drew the puzzled man aside. "We still got that APB out on Wilkins' car?"

"Yeah. Nothing yet."

He leaned a bit closer. "Do something for me. If there's a sighting, give it to me the second it comes in." He met the man's gaze. "Before you tell Scanlon."

Hendricks frowned. "You saying you don't want me to tell him?"

Farrington cast a look through the door at the man sitting hunched and still at his desk. "I'm worried about him." Not entirely a lie. "You saw what happened at dinner last night.

On top of how *he* must feel about all this, he's under enormous pressure from Peg. This whole thing is tearing open wounds that never really healed. For both of them."

Hendricks nodded. "Last night was grim, I'll give you that." He glanced toward their boss. "And I've noticed he's definitely feeling the strain. Nearly bit my head off before over some minor slip with the roster."

"It's more than that. In the state he's in, I'm worried..." He shook his head. "I just wonder how impartial he can be under the circumstances."

Hendricks' frown deepened. "You're not suggesting—"

"No, no, of course not. All I'm saying..." Hand on his shoulder he leaned to his ear. "Look, why take the risk? I just don't want to chance it, that's all. If he did do something, it wouldn't just ruin the case, it would finish him. He'd regret it for the rest of his life."

Hendricks stared through the door at his boss. "You really think...?"

"Well, how would you feel if you were in his shoes? What would you do to settle the score if the situation presented itself?"

"Shit." Hendricks scrubbed a hand across his neck.

"Look, I'm not asking you to keep anything from him. Just give me a heads-up first, that's all. A little bit of time. And that goes for anything else that comes in on this. I'll soften the blows as best I can for him and make sure everything gets done by the book."

"You'll back me if the shit hits the fan?"

He slapped the man's shoulder. "You know it."

Hendricks exhaled. "Okay fine. I'll let you know."

CHAPTER 71

"Where the hell were you?" Alec demanded the minute Raina stepped through the door. He hadn't expected such a rush of relief at hearing her footsteps on the cabin porch. Relief now venting itself as anger.

"And good morning to you too," she tossed back. With barely a glance at him she crossed to where Erin sat at the table.

"Where did you go?" the girl asked, managing to convey with her fearful tone all the concern Alec had been fighting to hide.

Raina brushed a curl from her face. "Were you worried? I'm sorry. I thought I'd be back before you woke up." She set a paper bag in front of her. "I got you some breakfast."

Arms folded across his chest, Alec stood leaning against the counter. The woman still hadn't answered his question. "We're supposed to be keeping a low profile. That means staying out of sight as much as possible."

"I wanted to make that appointment we talked about last night," she said, looking over. "I couldn't get any reception on my phone so I walked up the road."

At last a plausible explanation. Did he believe it? "You shouldn't be using your phone anyway. I thought we agreed we'd only use them to talk to each other. Burners or not, it's still possible they could track the call."

"Yeah, well, in the end I used someone else's."

"Someone else's phone? Who the hell—"

She straightened to face him. "Look, I handled it, okay. The important thing is I got us an appointment at the clinic. They had a cancellation for twelve-thirty today so I booked us in."

He studied her closely. Her gaze didn't flinch. Whatever she'd done, she wasn't stupid. If she said they couldn't track her call, he believed her.

He looked at the clock. "We better get moving then."

"What's the rush? It's only eleven."

"It looks like we're stopping off somewhere else first."

She followed his gaze to the girl beside her.

"I remembered something in the middle of the night," Erin said. "I nearly woke you but I thought it could wait."

Sensing her tension, Raina took the chair beside her.

"A year ago when I was on the streets I met this girl, Naomi, who'd just had a baby at the Manheim clinic. She was all messed up because it had died. I never thought anything about it at the time, but last night it suddenly hit me...what if it wasn't just me they did it to? What if they stole other babies as well?"

Raina shot him a meaningful look. The info definitely supported her theory.

"Alec told me what you found out last night," Erin went on. "About Doctor Manheim working at that other clinic and that you two were going there to see him. I decided while you're doing that I'll go back and look for Naomi."

"Go back?" Raina paled.

"Yeah, you know, to the area I used to live. Maybe there's something Naomi could tell us. Maybe there are other girls too."

In her eagerness, Erin had risen to her feet. "Alec said I should go with you in your car 'cause mine isn't all that reliable." She looked over at him. "I'm ready now if you want to get going. I'll just grab my coat."

Raina sat stunned, watching Erin walk from the room. The conversation had happened so fast she hadn't had a chance to voice her concerns.

She turned to Alec. "What is wrong with you?"

He blinked at her. "What?"

"You're just going to let her walk into that awful neighborhood all by herself?" She rose and stepped toward him. "Do you know the area she's talking about?"

"Hey, it was her idea; I'm not forcing her."

"Well, you sure as hell aren't trying to stop her."

He pushed from the counter to meet her approach. "She wants to go. And anyway what's it got to do with me? She's not my kid."

"Oh, that's right, I forgot. You're not a champion of lost causes. Or anyone else but yourself, it seems."

Clenching his jaw, he pointed toward the bedroom. "In case you forgot, *that* lost cause got my brother killed."

"She's trying to get her baby back."

"I'm not convinced she ever had one."

Erin stepped back into the room and stood looking from one to the other. "You two aren't having a domestic, are you?"

Raina fought to speak her fears calmly. "We're not sure it's such a good idea for you to go back there. At least not alone."

"We?" Alec muttered.

"Why not?" Erin challenged.

"It could be dangerous."

The girl laughed. "Bit late for that. Don't worry, I can take care of myself."

"Erin, I don't think you—"

"Forget it. I know my way around down there, I'll be fine." She took their silence for further dissent. "Look, I'm doing this, okay. Don't try to stop me." She squared her slim shoulders. "So are you driving me or am I driving myself?"

"We'll take you," Alec said.

"Erin, please—"

The girl wrenched her arm from Raina's grasp. "I lived in that shit-hole for over a year. Who do you think looked after me then?"

Raina watched the girl leave the cabin, then swung her glare back to Alec.

He shrugged. "You heard her; she can take care of herself."

CHAPTER 72

Alec climbed into the passenger seat of Raina's Camry and slammed the door. With Erin sitting glum and silent in the back, he was left with little to think about but his latest confrontation with Raina.

Few, if any, women he'd known had her knack for getting under his skin. Admittedly their current situation was fraught with inherent tensions. Yet somehow he doubted it would be any different had they met under less difficult circumstances.

That's right, I forgot. You're not a champion of lost causes – or anyone but yourself, it seems.

He focused on a pair of hawks circling in the cloudless sky, trying to regain a bit of composure. His life had been simple up until now. Structured. Low-key. Just how he liked it. The greatest stress he had to contend with was getting his papers graded on time, his end-of-year reports submitted.

He'd dated of course, known his share of women. But never one that had moved him to the point he'd considered changing his solitary lifestyle. Never one whose view of his character, whose complaints that his guarded exterior hid none of the warmth they had hoped to uncover, had given him even the briefest pause.

No, never a one like Raina Wilkins.

In their single evening together he'd opened up to her more than anyone he'd ever known. Exhaustion? Grief? Mortal danger? Even their combined effects couldn't entirely explain such a lapse.

What was it about her? Aside from her looks, looks that would turn any man's head. Did her protectiveness for a girl she hardly knew remind him of Liam in some way? Was it that courage, that devotion to defending the weak – traits he'd long found wanting in himself – that intrigued him about her?

From the backseat, Erin's voice cut through his thoughts. "Where's Raina? Isn't she coming?"

"She'll be out in a minute, she's getting changed."

In the side-view mirror he saw the girl slump back against her seat and stare out the window, biting her cuticles. Nervous about her impending mission or troubled about her blow-up with Raina?

It was hard to believe the two of them had only known each other a few days. Though the girl was trying hard not to show it, she was clearly becoming attached to Raina. And perhaps that's where her anger resided, in the fear of letting herself need someone. Still, little wonder. She looked barely more than a kid, let alone the eighteen-year-old she claimed to be.

A frightened, vulnerable, defenseless kid, despite all her bluster and bravado.

Alec took a deep breath and blew it out softly. Hell, what was wrong with him? Yes, Erin had given Liam evidence of something that had gotten him killed. But that didn't mean Liam wouldn't have gone after that evidence all on his own if he'd known about it.

Even if her claims about her baby being stolen were pure delusion, did that make her pain any less real? As bad as he felt losing a brother, wouldn't losing a child be worse?

"Don't know what bug crawled up her ass all of a sudden," the girl muttered. "Treating me like I'm some kind of baby. I've been looking after myself for two years. I don't need her or anyone else. What's she getting so worked up about anyway?"

"I'd say it's because she cares about you."

"Yeah, right. Unlike *you*."

He looked away from her glare in the mirror.

"Yeah, I heard what you said in there. You're just like the rest of them; think I'm worthless. Nothing but another addict, a whore, no good. Well, I'm not a whore. Not any more. And I never was an addict, not ever. I'm not going down the path my mom did."

She pushed herself forward. "You know what else you don't know about me? I'm not dumb. Before I left home I was making good grades. Good enough to maybe get in college one day." She thumped her fist on the back of his seat. "You think people choose to live on streets? You think that was the life I dreamed of? I was going to get an education. *I was going to be a writer some day!*"

Her voice finally cracked. She slammed back against her seat and returned to staring out the window.

Again he studied her through the mirror. A writer. Like Liam. Perhaps she'd have been a champion too. Exposing wrongs. Protecting the weak.

And maybe it was just another delusion.

When she dragged her sleeve across her face, he reached in his pocket, pulled out his handkerchief, and handed it back to her.

She snatched it from his hand and blew her nose noisily. "I'll bet you never spent one night on the streets. Nowhere to stay, nothing to eat. My friend had a name for guys like you. Orchids. A flower raised in a hot house, too delicate for the real world. You wouldn't last one week where I've been."

He thought of his single night in the park, his one and only day without food, medicine, or the support of someone who cared. As bad as things had been with their old man when they were kids, he and Liam had still had their mom. What would it have been like with no-one?

"All I can say is, I'm sorry. *Again*. I never meant for your brother to get hurt." She glared in the mirror at him. "And if you don't believe me, go screw yourself!"

He stared silently through the windscreen, her words ringing in his ears. Then he opened the glove compartment, pulled out a small plastic spray bottle – an item he recalled from having searched Raina's car when he'd stolen it – and handed it back over the seat.

"What's this?" Hesitantly she reached out to take it. "Bug repellent. You're worried I'll get a mosquito bite?"

"Sprayed in the eyes it'll blind a person for a minute or two. Keep it in reach where you're going today. Might come in handy."

Another laugh. "Oh, this'll be a great against Quillen's stiletto."

"What was that?"

"Forget it." She shoved it into her pocket.

He blew out a breath. "Look, maybe Raina was right about this. Maybe you shouldn't—"

"Aw, you're worried about me now too? Gee, what am I going to do with all this parental supervision?"

He arched a brow. She certainly had a better vocabulary

than your average street kid. Leaning aside, he pulled out his wallet and handed her all the bills it contained.

"What the hell is this? I told you I'm not—"

"Shut up and take it." He shoved it into her hand. "The girl you're after might need some incentive to talk."

Puzzled, she held his gaze in the mirror. Her eyes narrowed. "You told Raina you didn't have any money."

"I didn't at the time. I sold my watch yesterday."

She noted the empty wallet in his hand and held up the bills. "This is all you got."

"Take it." He closed it and returned it to his pocket. "Bring me back what you don't use."

She laughed. "Sure thing." And pocketed the cash.

CHAPTER 73

Steering her car through the mid-day traffic, Raina looked out at the lively sights of Portland's central mercantile district – the stately maples lining the road, the high-end merchandise in store-front displays, colorful awnings and flower boxes gracing every café and restaurant window. Even the rubbish bins were immaculate.

A far cry indeed from the pot-holed streets, derelict buildings, and forgotten residents of the area in which they'd just dropped Erin.

Her knuckles whitened around the steering wheel. She was angry with herself for failing to dissuade the girl from her mission. Angrier with Alec for not even trying. Her only comfort was that Erin had agreed to call them if she needed help and to let them pick her up in exactly two hours whether she'd located Naomi or not.

The urge to check her phone for messages became too great and she flipped it open – the fourth time since they'd dropped Erin off less than twenty minutes ago.

"Will you quit worrying," Alec said from the seat beside her. "She'll be fine."

"She's just a kid."

"With more street smarts than you and I put together."

"No doubt she has. Far more than anyone her age should have to have. That doesn't mean she'll be all right. And even if she makes it through this untouched, her situation is far from fine."

She threw the cell phone back in her bag. "You know what I can't understand? How you can be so devastated about losing your brother and not care a whit about someone like Erin. You're right, you really are different from him."

She regretted the words the instant she said them. In her rising frustration a part of her had wanted to wound him. From what little he'd told her he'd clearly had deep respect for his brother, their differences a sensitive issue for him. Was it fair to use such knowledge against him? Information he'd divulged in a vulnerable state, in implied confidence?

She glanced aside and nearly laughed. She needn't have worried. He was staring out the window, completely unmoved.

On the far side of town they found the address. The Baxter Memorial Fertility Clinic. A two-story building of barn-red brick, black-shuttered windows, and a faux widow's walk adorning the roof. They pulled up in front of the entrance walkway and sat staring up at the impressive façade.

"I'll let you do all the talking," he said. "Less chance of us mixing up our lies that way."

"Thanks a lot."

"But just so we have our stories straight... We've been married six years, our names are Annie and Peter Marks, we're not insured and we're paying cash."

She nodded as she climbed from the car. "I just hope we have enough money."

CHAPTER 74

It was the stuff of nightmares. A setting in shades of gun metal grey, not a tree or blade of grass in sight. These crumbling streets smelling of rubbish, piss and decay. Streets that had been her home for a year.

Erin walked toward a familiar corner, the donut she had forced down for breakfast threatening to rise in a bilious mass from the pit of her stomach. Across the street a cluster of women ranging in age from jailbait to post use-by date strutted their stuff for passing motorists. A circle of which she had once been a part.

She'd vowed she would never return to this life. But that had been for her baby's sake. With Cody gone, her home and financial support along with him, would she just end up right back here again?

She clenched her fists and squeezed shut her eyes. No, she would not. Because Cody wasn't gone. Wherever he was she would find him again. She wouldn't let herself consider any other possibility. She had already stumbled on some useful information she hadn't expected. If she could just find Naomi she might finally have something to go on.

She took a deep breath and started across the street

toward the women.

A stick-figure blond noted her approach and turned to confront her, the only color in her bloodless face, a smear of claret across her mouth. "Hey sweetmeat, this spot's taken."

"I'm not here to cut in." Erin stood tall as the others gathered in close around her. *Remember Cody. Remember why you're here.* "I'm looking for someone. Naomi Giles. Any of you know her?"

A redhead with freckles and big yellow teeth, a Marlboro stuck to her bottom lip, looked her up and down. "Who's asking?"

"A friend. I used to live here. Naomi and I used to hang out."

Yellow Tooth squinted, taking her in. "Yeah, I remember you. You're one of Quillen's, aren't you?"

"*Was,*" she corrected.

One of the relics, thin-lipped and gaunt, stuck out her jaw. "And how'd that happen? Quillen don't let his girls walk away."

"I didn't ask him."

This drew a round of snickers and jeers.

Yellow Tooth hawked up a bit of tar. "So where you been, honey? Taking a vacation?"

Laughter from the others.

"I moved uptown. So you know her or not? Naomi Giles."

"Yeah, I know her." Yellow Tooth sucked on her coffin nail and blew the smoke skyward. "You want to see her, it'll cost you."

Erin pulled two twenties from her pocket and handed them over. "Two more when we get to Naomi."

The bills vanished into Yellow Tooth's cleavage. "Follow me."

CHAPTER 75

Manheim wasn't what Raina had expected. A fatherly figure with kind grey eyes, a gentle manner, and comforting voice. Across his large mahogany desk he shook both her and Alec's hands, then motioned them into the seats before it.

"We've been trying for five years to start a family without any luck," Raina told him in the line she'd rehearsed. "We heard your clinic has a high success rate with couples like us so we wanted to come and discuss treatment options."

"Have you consulted any other physicians as yet about your problem?" he asked.

"No, you're the first."

"Well, we'll certainly do everything we can to help you. But we'll run some preliminary tests to see where we stand before we start talking options. First, I'll get some details about your history and general health."

His questions were pretty much what she'd expected. Had she ever miscarried? Had an abortion, STDs, infections, etc.?

She answered negatively to each, all the while feeling a mounting anxiety – a swimmer treading water as a dark shadow slowly circled beneath her. Back at the cabin, a world away, she'd been sure she could do this. Yet now…

She balled her hands into fists on her thighs. *Stay focused on why you're here.*

When Manheim paused to record her replies, she sat forward. "You must really love your work, Doctor."

He looked up and smiled. "It's deeply satisfying to help couples achieve their dream to have a family."

"Does it ever not work? The procedures you do?"

"Naturally there are situations where no amount of intervention can produce a satisfactory result. But as you stated, our clinic has a very high success rate. I think you'll find that reputation is well deserved."

As he went back to writing, she looked aside. Alec gave her a slight nod. *Keep going; I'm ready.* She glanced at his hand, resting casually on his thigh, and saw him hit record on his phone.

She took a deep breath and turned back to the man behind the desk. "It must be difficult those times you fail though. For everyone."

Manheim's look was sympathetic. He'd seen this fear in his patients before. "Let's not get ahead of ourselves. The solution to your particular problem could be quite straightforward."

"Yes, but it does happen, doesn't it? Despite all the things you can do these days, there are still some people you just can't help."

The doctor set his pen on the desk. A man prepared to address his patient's darkest fears, however irrational. "If that situation arises and we're certain we've exhausted all other options, there's always the alternative of adoption."

The moment of truth. She saw Alec slide the phone toward his knee.

"Always, Doctor? Not everyone is acceptable, are they? I mean…what does a couple do if they can't have children and, for whatever reason, can't adopt?"

By his frown she feared she had gone too far, been too obvious, aroused his suspicions.

At last the fatherly smile returned. "Try not to worry. We'll do our very best for you, I promise." He pushed back from his desk and gestured to a door on his left. "Now, if you'll come this way we'll do your internal."

"Internal." Alec sat up in his chair. "As in exam?"

Manheim turned to him. "You're welcome to come in and provide your wife support if you—"

"No!" the two of them said in unison.

The doctor looked from one to the other.

"I…I'd prefer to do it alone," Raina said.

"Whatever you're most comfortable with. Well, then…" Manheim stepped to a cabinet, pulled out a specimen container, and handed it to Alec. "Since you won't be joining us, I'll get you to take care of your side of things in the meantime."

Alec blinked at him. "My…?"

Manheim pointed to the door behind him. "Right through there you'll find everything you need. Just be sure to lock the door."

Despite her unease, her mounting dread, Raina fought a smile at Alec's expression as she walked from the room.

CHAPTER 76

Erin followed Yellow Tooth down barren streets of broken facades and forgotten souls.

After several blocks, in an area she had rarely been, they came to an abandoned canning factory and pushed through a hole in the fence surrounding it. Judging from the path worn through the weed-choked yard and the board they slid past to gain access to the building, it was an entrance not unknown to squatters.

Inside, cold damp air enveloped them heavy with the scent of urine and mold. Wordlessly Yellow Tooth moved through the labyrinth, leading her now past occasional signs of habitation – a cluster of old lawn chairs, up-ended crates serving as tables, a legless couch, the odd mattress.

Deep in the bowels of the derelict world, they stopped before the doorway of a shadowed room. On hearing their movements, a woman pacing the floor within whirled and rushed forward, her face captured in the light of the hall. Haggard, filthy, bathed in sweat. A face Erin knew but hardly recognized. *Naomi.*

Even the feeble light made her squint. "Stix, is that you?"

"No, hon, it's Pam," Yellow Tooth answered. "Brought you a visitor."

Ignoring her completely, Naomi slumped. "I thought it was Stix. You seen him, haven't ya? He hasn't forgotten me."

Something shifted in the older woman's face, a softening of the lines about her eyes. "I'm sure he's on his way."

As Naomi withdrew into her darkened lair, Yellow Tooth's mask slipped back into place. She pulled out a cigarette and lit it with fingers the color of her teeth. "I'll take the rest of that money now."

Erin handed her the other two bills.

Pocketing the cash, the woman jerked her head toward the open door. "How long since you've seen her?"

"About six months."

"A life sentence in this place." Smoke formed a shroud over Yellow Tooth's face as she called through the door. "You hang in there, hon, you hear."

CHAPTER 77

Alec stalked back into Manheim's office and set the container down on the desk. With the room to himself he gave vent to his frustrations and began pacing in front of the bookcase.

Of all the ridiculous, humiliating, pointless... How had he gone from tracking down his brother's killer to giving a sperm sample in a fertility clinic?

He shot a look toward the exam room opposite, the door through which Raina had vanished with Manheim. His plan certainly hadn't played out as he'd expected. Still, Raina had agreed to it. Could *she* have suspected what was in store for them in coming here? Would she actually have made the appointment knowing...?

The door opened, Raina stepped through and calmly returned to her seat by the desk.

He stared at her stoic profile a moment then sat down beside her. "Where's Manheim?"

"He just stepped out to take a phone call. He'll be right with us."

He shifted. "But he... You had..."

"Yes."

Far from stoic, up this close she looked shaken and pale. He shook his head. "You didn't have to go through that. I mean I know you want to help the girl but no-one expects—"

The door opened and Manheim walked in, taking the seat behind his desk. He shifted some papers, then looked up at Raina. His smile was gone, replaced by an air of puzzled concern. He seemed to be waiting.

When Raina just kept staring down at her lap, Alec felt a chill wash over him. "What is it? What's wrong?"

Manheim took a steadying breath. "I believe I've found the source of your problem." He looked back to Raina, his frown deepening. "You knew what I'd find before I examined you. You've known all along. You must have."

Alec's gaze shot to the woman beside him.

"I thought there might be something you could do," she whispered. "Some new treatment."

"Treatment." The doctor all but laughed. "The damage is irreversible. There is no treatment."

Alec sat forward. This wasn't in the script they'd rehearsed. "What damage?" he blurted.

Manheim's look turned to sheer disbelief. "Your husband doesn't know?"

Raina sat a moment, clutching her bag, then pushed to her feet. "Thank you for your time, Doctor."

As she stepped out the door, Alec looked back. "What don't I know?"

Manheim closed the file before him. "I'm sorry but it's up to your wife to tell you."

CHAPTER 78

Erin stared in horror at the figure pacing before her. The girl she'd known had been bright, pretty, and a smart dresser, however limited her income had been. The one before her was a lost soul. Gaunt, hollow-eyed, and clothed in rags. She shuddered at the thought this could've been her.

The shudders deepened. It could be still.

She checked the time on her cell phone. She was due to meet Raina and Alec four blocks away in less than ten minutes.

She took a step deeper into the room. "Naomi, it's me, Erin."

The woman stumbled to a halt and stood blinking. "Who?"

"Erin Rose. Don't you remember?"

A spark in the vacant gaze at last. "Erin, yeah. Sure, I remember." She raised her arms.

Erin returned the feeble embrace, then stepped back. "I have to talk to you. I need your help."

"Erin." Naomi frowned, still getting her mind around the fact her old friend was standing before her. "What are you doing here? If Quillen sees you—"

"I won't be here long. I came to ask you about something that happened a few years ago." *If you'll even tell me.* "I need to know what happened to you at that clinic, the one where you had your baby."

The girl's watery smile dissolved. She took a step back.

"Please, Naomi, I need to know…"

"I don't want to talk about that."

Erin took her arm. "You have to. I need—"

"The hell I do!" Naomi pulled free, then lowered her voice. "Go away. Why did you even come back here?"

"You remember why I left, don't you? I was pregnant and I wanted to give my baby a decent life. I went to that clinic, the same one you did."

The girl turned away, shaking her head. "I don't want to hear this."

"You will, damn it!" Erin spun her back around. "They took him, Naomi. I had my baby and they said he died but I don't believe them. They took him and gave him to someone else."

For a moment it seemed she had broken through, that Naomi was processing her words. Then, incredibly, she gave a short laugh. "What do you want me to do about it?"

"I want you to help me. Answer my questions."

The girl closed her eyes. "Why are you doing this?"

"Because it's important!" Erin stepped closer and took her arm. "Please. Just tell me and then I'll go. How did you first find out about the clinic? Who told you about it?"

The girl bowed her head in defeat. "A lady at some church."

"What church? Where?"

"I don't know, Saint Martin's or something, a few blocks

from here." She looked up, incredulous. "That was two years ago, how do you expect—"

"All right, all right, just tell me what happened."

"When I found out I was pregnant I went there to pray." Naomi smirked. "Yeah, I know. Not what you figured, right, someone like me. I was sitting their, crying, and this woman came up and asked me what was wrong. When I told her, she said she could help me. She said if I agreed to give the baby up for adoption she knew a place I could get everything for free."

Erin hesitated. If Naomi had arranged to give up her child willingly perhaps her experience wasn't related after all. "So that's what you decided?"

"Yeah, at first. But then, as I got closer to the time, I decided I didn't want to give up my baby, I wanted to keep it. The woman got really mad when I told her. She kept trying to talk me out of it, said all the arrangements had been made, that the baby would get a really good home."

"But you didn't change your mind."

"No. I thought..." She looked down and shrugged. "It would be nice to have someone of my own, you know. Someone to..." She waved off the thought. "In the end it didn't matter anyway. My baby died."

Erin took her shoulders. "Naomi, listen to me, this is important. Are you sure it died?"

Her eyes filled with horror. "Are you crazy, of course I'm sure. The doctor told me."

"Yes, but did you ever actually see him?"

Her body went limp, all fight drained away. "Her," she corrected softly. "My little girl. No, I never saw her. They told me it wouldn't be a good idea."

Erin's heart skipped. The very same thing they had said to

her. "Who told you that?"

The woman had drifted away again, her focus on something beyond the door. Though their experiences differed – Naomi had been 'recruited' to the clinic, while Erin had stumbled on it by accident – the same personnel may have been involved.

"Naomi, who was your doctor? Who delivered your baby?"

Rubbing her arms, the girl continued to stare at the door. "Where the hell is he? What could be keeping him?"

Spying something on the floor, Naomi dropped to her knees, fumbling with a small bottle. With frantic fingers she popped the top, but nothing tipped out into her hand. She swore and hurled it against the wall.

Erin saw other bottles now. Months' worth of empties strewn about the floor. One for each month of the life they'd destroyed.

She picked one up, read the label, then helped her friend back to her feet. "Naomi, my god, what happened to you? How did you get onto this stuff?"

The girl's gaze hardened. "Weren't you listening? I just told you what happened." Just as quickly, her look grew confused. "She gave them to me at the clinic. All the extra bottles the nice lady gave me to take home."

"Nice lady? What are you talking about? You mean the nurse?"

"The nurse, the lady." She waved a hand. "The one from the church."

Erin gripped her arm. "You're telling me the woman you talked to at the church, the one who told you about the clinic, was also one of the nurses there?"

"I figured that's how she knew about the place."

Erin reached up and took both her shoulders. "Naomi, please, try to remember. What was her name?"

"That was two years ago. How do you expect—?"

"Would you know it if you heard? Was it Kilburn?"

All the color drained from her face. She covered her mouth. "Oh, god. It was. I know because...at the time, in the hospital, I remember thinking..." Her hand fell away. "It rhymes with stillborn."

CHAPTER 79

Alec burst out the clinic doors. Across the parking lot he spotted Raina sitting in her car with the engine going. He couldn't see her face through the glare on the windscreen but judging from her haste in leaving the building, something was wrong. He walked over and got in beside her.

Before he'd lifted his foot from the asphalt she was driving off. "What's the rush?"

"We're late to meet Erin. We're supposed to be there in ten minutes."

"Don't worry, she'll wait." When she swerved past a car backing out of its spot he studied her profile. Was it Erin she was hurrying *to* or her encounter with Manheim she was rushing *from*?

Giving her a moment, he checked the recording he'd made on his phone. "I don't think there's anything on here that'll help us."

No comment from the woman beside him. He'd essentially declared their mission a failure, their efforts wasted. For all purposes they were back to square one with nothing to go on. Yet she seemed totally absorbed in her thoughts. What could take precedence in her mind over her earlier obsessive need to help Erin?

"Looks like Manheim wasn't our man," he said. "Just like I've been saying all along." Still testing the waters.

Still no response.

He waited, trying to hold himself back. He'd been stunned to learn there was something wrong with her. Even more surprised to find he wanted to know what it was. He barely knew her. It was none of his business. And yet…

"Are you going to tell me what that was all about back there?" He gestured toward the building they were leaving behind.

"Nothing you need to concern yourself with."

Finally a reaction. "I'm just wondering why we bothered with this. If you knew before we came there was something wrong with you…" The circuit connected. He looked aside at her. "That's why you let Manheim examine you. You knew what he'd find."

"It seemed the best way to convince him our situation was genuine."

He gave a huff. "You might've told me that was the plan."

"I didn't know how good an actor you'd be. I thought it better to make it a surprise."

"Well, it was certainly that."

He continued to study her. The red-rimmed eyes, the shaky voice, the tremor in the hand now wiping her brow. "So you really can't have kids."

He waited but she ignored the statement. It seemed they were back in lock-out mode. If he wanted answers he'd have to push harder. "You told Manheim you'd never had an abortion."

"I haven't."

"Well, if it wasn't a botched abortion or any of those other things he asked you about—"

"Just drop it, okay."

"Sure."

He waited for all of five seconds. "It's just I'm a little confused, that's all. If you knew you can't have kids, and you've known it for a while...then what you told your fiancé, that you didn't *want* them—"

"Has absolutely nothing to do with you."

He put up his hands in a show of surrender. Perhaps this wasn't the best time anyway. At the speed she was going, he'd rather she kept her eyes on the road.

CHAPTER 80

The fragile figure in Erin's arms finally stopped shaking. She eased back, holding her friend by the shoulders, taking in the tear-streaked face, the pain she had caused. "I'm so sorry. But I had to know. Thank you for helping me."

Arms hanging limp at her sides, Naomi stared blankly toward the door.

Erin checked the time on her phone. She was already late. But how could she leave?

"Naomi, I have to go. I have to meet the people I came with."

Nothing. Had she even heard?

Erin touched her arm. "You could come with me. This guy and woman are helping me. I trust them. Well, the woman anyway. Things are a bit of a mess at the moment but when they're all sorted out, you and I could—"

"Go away." The tone as dead as the look in her eyes.

"But, don't you see what this means? If what we think is true, your baby might still be alive as well. We could—"

"Get out of here!"

Erin fell back at the force of the words. Before she could move, Naomi's eyes flew open wide. She shoved Erin aside and rushed to the door where a tall thin boy with long stringy hair had just stepped through.

"Stix!" She snatched the paper bag from his hands and tore it open.

Another bottle. Just like the ones that littered the floor.

"Naomi, wait." Erin tried to reach her but the boy stepped between them, glaring down at her.

She backed away. She had to leave, but not like this. "Naomi, please."

The boy pressed forward, forcing her steadily toward the door.

"I'll come back, I promise," she called around him.

Her friend never answered. Her last glimpse of the woman she'd known was Naomi downing some of the pills.

"Take care of yourself," Erin whispered and turned up the hall.

She started back the way she'd come, checking her phone. Ten minutes past the rendezvous time!

She ran a few steps, then slowed to a walk, deliberately reducing her strides. So what; she was late. Raina would be worried – big deal. The woman had no control over her. Let her wait.

And if she doesn't wait? If Raina decides you're too much trouble, too much of a pain in the ass?

All at once she was walking faster.

Halfway down the hall a phantom dog snapped at her heels. Her gentle trot became a jog.

With every step her following grew – not one, but a whole pack of rabid curs, snarling, slavering at her feet.

Wait! Don't go. Don't leave me here!

She charged to the end and around the next corner.

Straight into Quillen and two of his thugs.

CHAPTER 81

Raina pulled the car to a stop at the corner where they'd arranged to meet Erin. Her breakneck driving had gotten them there only ten minutes late. The fact Erin was nowhere in sight caused an instant spike in her blood pressure.

"Can you see her anywhere?"

"Don't worry, she's coming," Alec said from beside her.

She pulled out her phone, checked it for messages, then sat scanning the street in dismay. "You think she was here and left again?"

"Got tired of waiting you mean? I don't think so."

"This *is* the right corner?"

"Relax. She got hung up, that's all. Just like we did."

Easy to say when you don't care. She forced herself to sit back in the seat.

"Manheim was actually pretty convincing as the kindly physician." Alec reflected after a moment. "Hard to believe he'd be mixed up in an adoption racket."

The man's words managed to snag her attention. Her encounter with Manheim had been upsetting, yes. But those feelings had quickly taken a back seat to her concerns about meeting Erin on time.

She'd hoped the girl would be here waiting, annoyed with them for being late. Hell, she could've handled that. Forced instead to sit here confronting the sights and horrors of Erin's former world – a world which the girl could yet return to – her concern had escalated to all-out fear. Was Alec trying to distract her from it or so self-absorbed he didn't notice?

Still, she'd thought much the same thing of Manheim herself. "He seemed to genuinely want to help people. Not the type who'd be in it for the money."

"Well, I wouldn't go that far. You don't spend all those years studying to end up treating people for nothing."

She gave a wry laugh. "That's what I like about you, DeMarco. You're such a believer in human nature. Giving free treatment is exactly what he does at the welfare clinic."

"What he *appears* to do. Those selfless acts could be serving him some other way. Providing him a resource he can tap to earn big bucks elsewhere." He nodded toward the women on the nearest corner. "A resource like their babies perhaps."

Raina frowned. Here she was arguing against her own theory while he argued for it. "You just said you couldn't see Manheim being involved."

"I said it was difficult, not impossible. It could mean he's just a really good actor."

"He seemed pretty sincere to me."

"Which is exactly how he'd get away with it. They'd trust him. Girls like Erin, kids who've never had a break in their lives, they'd flock to him just for a glimpse of that fatherly smile. And once he's got them where he wants them…bye bye baby."

She turned to stare at him. "I thought you didn't believe

Erin's story."

He shifted. "I'm not saying I do. It's just… If Manheim *is* in the business of stealing babies, his bedside manner would be a definite asset."

She studied the man a moment longer. Just when she thought she had him figured… Then her fears dragged her back to the present situation.

She checked the time on her phone again. Erin was now more than twenty minutes late. Her palms felt itchy against the steering wheel. Should they go looking? Drive up and down the streets hoping to spot the girl?

And if she came here, there'd be no-one waiting.

Raina gripped the wheel. *Erin, where are you?*

CHAPTER 82

"Well, well, look who it is. My little rose."

Quillen made a show of trailing his gaze the length of Erin's body. "Sissy came and said she saw you around. There I was thinking she must be high and damned if she wasn't telling it straight. Here you are, just like she said."

Erin recoiled as much as she could with the wall at her back. The face of the man who'd once claimed her as his – the scraggly beard, crooked teeth, mug-shot stare – repelled her almost as much as his breath.

Yet revulsion was taking a back seat to fear. Memories of the things she'd seen this man do – his unprovoked displays of cruelty, his violence toward the girls who dared to defy him, or worse, tried to leave him – threatened to undermine her courage. She'd known the risks when she'd chosen to come but had convinced herself she could ask her questions and get out again before he spotted her. She hadn't counted on one of his other girls turning her in.

With one arm keeping her pinned to the wall, he pressed in closer. "Didn't think you'd have the guts to come back after shafting me the way you did."

She swallowed hard. "I'm not *back*."

"Hear that, boys? Rosie's not back." His smile died. "Sure looks that way to me."

Again his gaze roved over her body. "Lookin' good, too. Except for the threads. You know I think you filled out a bit. Especially these."

She slapped his hand away from her breasts. A reflex she was sure to regret.

He only smiled. "Yeah, I heard you got knocked up. You know I'd of taken care of that for you. Guy I know does it real cheap. You'd of been on your back again in no time."

He laughed at his joke. She had the feeling it wasn't the first time he'd used it, making it all the more sickening.

She tried again to pull from his grip, managed to get a foot from the wall before he slammed her back up against it.

He leaned to her ear. "Looks like we're going to have to get you in the swing of things again, remind you who calls the shots around here."

He looked to his goons. "Give us a minute, would ya boys." When they hesitated, he flashed them a grin. "Don't worry, you'll get your turn."

Quillen watched them retreat up the hall and vanish around the corner.

In the moment his attention was diverted, Erin pulled the bug spray from her pocket. But when the man turned back, his leering face so close to hers, his foul breath wafting across her cheek, her courage faltered. She'd never resisted, never stood up to Quillen before.

But perhaps that would work to her advantage now.

As his hand began moving over her body, she closed her eyes, fixing on the thought of holding her baby and all that this man was trying to steal from her.

Taking the gesture for defeat, Quillen relaxed his hold on her throat. With a cry of rage that astonished them both, Erin raised the bottle and sprayed it point blank into his eyes.

CHAPTER 83

"There she is!" Raina shot upright in the driver's seat when Erin dashed out from behind a building across the street. An instant later two men careered around the corner after her. "Oh my god!" She reached for her door.

Alec gripped her arm. "Stay in the car. Start the engine." He climbed out leaving his door open wide.

She did as he'd said. But his gunshot wound! In the state he was in he'd be little good against a single opponent, let alone two. She gasped when another man rounded the corner. Make that three!

Head down, hands in his pocket, Alec started stumbling up the sidewalk, weaving an erratic course toward the four approaching targets. What was he doing? Erin made a bee-line for the open car door, running straight past him.

When the first man reached him, Alec blundered into his path. With no time to veer, the man went sprawling.

Babbling apologies, Alec bent as though to help the man up but instead swung to greet the second pursuer with a fist to the gut.

Erin jumped into the front seat beside her, then turned to

277

look back. "Oh my god, what do we do?"

The first man, already on his feet, spun Alec around to face him. By the time he'd ploughed a fist in his jaw the second thug was up as well. The man pinned Alec's arms behind him as his partner moved in.

"Do something! You can't just leave him!"

Warring voices screamed in Raina's head. *Protect Erin, she's your main concern. But Alec can't hold up against both of them.* On seeing the third man coming up behind him, switch blade in hand, the voices united in a single command.

She stamped on the gas. Accelerating, she jumped the curb and aimed for the knifeman. At the sight of the car hurtling toward him he dove from her path.

The roar of the engine startled the others. She screeched to a halt on the sidewalk beside them; Alec pulled free and threw himself into the back of the car. One thug recovered enough to charge, but lost his grip on the door handle when Raina swung back onto the road.

Two blocks away she recovered her voice. "Everyone okay?"

On the seat behind her, Alec appeared in the rearview mirror, a shiner already blooming on his cheek, and gave a thumbs-up.

She nearly yelped when Erin flung herself out of her seat and threw her arms around her neck. "You didn't leave me."

On a rush of tearful giddy relief, Raina clutched the girl to her shoulder.

The moment shattered when a police car came around the next corner heading straight for them.

Raina pushed the girl away. "Erin, sit back. Fasten your seatbelt." She quickly slowed to the speed limit and drove as inconspicuously as possible.

The patrol went past.

After a moment holding her breath, watching the car grow smaller in her mirror, Raina felt herself relax once again.

Until the cruiser swung a three-sixty, put on its lights, and hit the siren.

CHAPTER 84

Farrington saw Hendricks leave the dispatch room and knew instantly something was up. He rose from the desk where he'd been typing a report, caught the man's eye, and gestured him toward the empty hallway at the rear of the squad room.

Alone beside the water cooler, just two colleagues shooting the breeze, Hendricks filled him in on the latest. "A call came in a few minutes ago. Wilkins' car may have been spotted on Conlon Street, Dawson Flats."

"What's the status? Who called it in?"

"Billings and Laskin. But she got away from them. Must've been flying low by the sounds of it." Hendricks smirked. "Guess that maniac driving of hers comes in handy."

Farrington managed to mask his contempt. For the time being he needed this man. "Dawson Flats?" His stomach clenched. "What the hell was she doing there?"

"Couldn't tell you. Not the safest neck of the woods, that's for sure."

"Wait a minute." Farrington frowned. "What did you mean, *may* have been spotted?"

"The car was the same make and color as hers, but the

plates were different."

"Well, hell, there'd be dozens of silver Camrys around. What makes them think—?"

"The report you filed when her car was stolen said something about a toy hanging from the rearview mirror. Apparently that's what tipped Billings off."

Farrington slumped. *Raina, Raina…you go to all the trouble of changing your plates just to get sprung by some damn trinket?* "A little toy moose. Yeah, I remember her mentioning it. So it was there? Billings saw it?"

"*Thinks* he saw it. They weren't close enough to get a good look. The fact she took off instead of pulling over certainly suggests it was Wilkins. But, hey, you draw your own conclusions."

Hendricks started to move away, then turned back. "Oh and sorry, but Scanlon already knows."

"About the sighting? I thought we agreed—"

"Nothing I could do, man. He was there when the call came in."

Farrington nodded and blew out a breath. "All right, thanks for letting me know."

He stood watching Hendricks walk away, then cast a look through the open door of Scanlon's office, at the figure sitting hunched and thoughtful behind his desk. What would Scanlon make of the information? What *could* he make of it?

The answer came back: nothing good.

CHAPTER 85

Raina carried the cup of hot chocolate to the kitchen table and set it down before her patient. She pulled up a chair beside the girl and returned to cleaning the cut on her hand.

So far she'd managed to stop herself speaking her thoughts – *You shouldn't have gone, I told you it was dangerous*. No-one needed to hear her nagging, especially a girl who was used to looking after herself. But she wasn't about to let Erin's injuries go untreated. With some paper towels and disinfectant she gently bathed the blood from the area. Thankfully it wouldn't need stitches.

At the counter, an ice pack pressed to his cheek, Alec looked on. "Don't anyone worry about me, I'm fine."

"Oh, here." She tossed the box of band-aids at him. If he'd helped her talk Erin out of her mission none of this would have happened.

He caught the box and set it aside. "Thanks."

She watched her patient's face as she worked. Erin had been particularly quiet since returning to the cabin and that worried her even more than her injuries. Clearly something had happened in her search for Naomi. Yet despite being asked, she refused to say who the three men had been and why they'd been chasing her.

"How did you do this?" Raina said softly, dabbing her arm.

"Does it matter?" Seeming to catch herself, Erin took a breath. "Climbing a fence."

Raina suppressed her need to know more. Instead she said, "You really should have a tetanus shot."

The girl's incredulous look said it all.

"Did you find your friend?" Alec asked.

The question seemed to focus her thoughts. She drew herself up. "Yeah, I found her. She told me some things that might be helpful. Plus I heard about another girl, too."

Raina listened in mounting horror to Naomi's experience and to that of the second girl who, after losing her baby at the same clinic, had committed suicide.

"I wrote down their names." Erin pulled out a slip of paper and handed it to Alec. "Maybe the police can do something now."

He took the paper, read it, and huffed. "The testimony of a homeless addict. That'll go far in court."

Erin stared at him a moment, then got up and ran for the bedroom.

Raina watched her go, then swung back to Alec. "You're as sensitive as a dump truck, you know that?" She rose and followed after the girl.

In the bedroom she found her lying on the single bed facing the wall. As she perched on the edge beside her, she saw in Erin's arms the same stuffed bear the girl had been clutching in her car the other morning.

"I got it for Cody," Erin confessed. "Holding it makes me feel like it's him. Except... I don't really know what that feels like – I never even got to touch him."

Raina reached out and stroked her hair.

The girl rolled over, gazing up at her. "Maybe it's better if I never find him."

"Oh, sweetheart, don't say that."

"Well, who knows what kind of mother I'd be. The places I've been… The things I've done…"

Raina placed a hand to her cheek. "None of that matters. You landed in that situation through no fault of your own. And when you found out you were pregnant you conquered tremendous odds to change things. For your baby. Look at all you're going through now just to get him back again."

"That doesn't mean I'd be a good mother. I don't know anything about babies. I might be awful."

"Every new mother has those doubts."

"Really?" She wiped her eyes. "What do they do?"

"They get help. They read books, they talk to people. They get together with other mothers and share their experiences. They tell each other things they've learned and ways to cope." Raina smoothed a strand of hair from her face. "The point is, you don't have to do this alone."

The girl let out a shuddery sigh and hugged the bear closer. "Do you have kids?"

She swallowed. "No."

"You should have some. You'd be a good mom."

"Maybe one day."

Raina blinked the sting from her eyes. She'd always wondered what sort of mother she might have been. In stores, restaurants, other public places, she would often watch mothers engage with their children and be surprised at the strength of her views on their actions – whether they were being too lax or too firm, too inattentive, too overprotective.

But just because she had strong opinions didn't mean she'd do any better herself. Like any relationship, there were things going on between those mothers and children wholly invisible to outsiders. Words spoken with a certain inflection, phrases laden with secret meaning, significant to them only because of their past shared experience. An intimacy she would never know.

Raina reached out and stroked Erin's head, amazed at herself for speaking her prior words of reassurance with such conviction. Who was she to spout views on the subject of motherhood? Despite all she believed to be true, she had no firsthand experience from which to speak. Nor would she ever.

Yet the very fact of her deprivation had given her a kinship with this girl. A woman who could never have a child and a mother whose child had been taken from her. Not exactly the same, but close enough she could feel Erin's pain as keenly as her own.

Soothed by her touch, Erin rolled back onto her side facing the wall. "Was your Mom good?"

Raina smiled. "She was one of the best." *Despite everything I put her through.*

"Guess that's where you get it from." Her voice dropped a notch. "Mine wasn't."

Raina winced. The simple statement made hers seem somehow insensitive. *Alec isn't the only dump truck.* She waited but Erin didn't elaborate. Maybe one day the girl would trust her enough to share her story.

One day. How many more did they have together?

"Erin, whatever your mother did or didn't do, doesn't mean you'll do the same. You're different people."

"Doesn't matter." Blessedly her voice sounded tired.

"Never going to find him anyway."

Raina gave her hair one last caress. "Get some sleep. You'll feel better when you wake up."

The girl heaved a sigh. "Maybe it's best."

CHAPTER 86

Alec sat slumped in a chair on the porch. Raina had been right, he should never have let Erin go into that neighborhood all by herself. Never mind that she wasn't his kid, never mind that she used to live there. He'd been so obsessed with finding Liam's killer he'd compromised the welfare of the very person his brother had been trying to help.

He closed his eyes. Liam would never have let her go. If she'd insisted it had to be done, he would have gone with her, made sure she was safe. That's who he was. That's who Liam would always be. Despite being the younger, he'd been the morally stronger. The one person Alec could always count on.

And this brother he'd so admired and trusted had made it his goal to help this girl, despite the dangers. Erin. Another pint-size warrior. Battling her demons with every bit as much courage as Liam. If Raina could accept her story so completely, why couldn't he?

Yet perhaps Raina's motives ran deeper than simple compassion. He'd asked her several times, in several different ways, what her stake was in all of this, why she had chosen to risk her life for a girl she hardly knew. Perhaps today he'd gotten his answer.

Though she'd tried to hide it, he'd seen how upset she'd been after their appointment with Manheim. The fact she herself could never have a child might explain her need to help Erin find hers. What's more it could account for her readiness to accept the girl's story on so little proof.

Unfortunately, he'd needed a bit more convincing.

The cabin door opened and Raina stepped out onto the porch. She moved to the head of the steps and stared out over the darkening yard.

"Is Erin okay?" he said.

"Asleep finally. The only relief she's got at this stage." She shook her head. "I don't know how much more she can take of this."

"What about you?" He didn't want to say any more. The way she was standing – moonlight on her hair, her lithe body taut with dread – it wouldn't take much for any expression of caring on his part to escalate into something more.

Deaf to his query, she started pacing back and forth in front of the railing. "This is getting out of hand. We're in way over our heads with this. What did we even accomplish today besides nearly letting Erin get killed? We have to accept it, there's no other choice." She stopped before him. "We need to go to the police."

"Weren't you listening when I told you the police were in on this?"

She threw up her hands. "They can't *all* be involved. Surely there must be one among them—"

"*No* police." As he'd hoped, his tone cut short the debate.

"Well, what do you suggest we do next then?" she said. "We got nowhere with Manheim today. As far as I can see we're back to square one."

"Not quite." He pushed to his feet. The longer he stayed out here alone with this woman, the harder it would be to maintain his distance. "Tomorrow you and Erin will go to that church her friend mentioned, find out what you can about the nurse."

She raised her brows. "And while we're doing that?"

"I've got a few things I want to check out."

"Which you're not going to share."

He gazed down into her face, debating. If he told her, she'd most likely want to come with him. They both would. But it was time he started drawing some lines, being the person he wanted to be. A man like Liam. Sending them to a church was one thing. He wasn't going to endanger them again.

"If I find out anything useful I'll tell you." He turned to go back inside the cabin.

"You just can't bring yourself to take the leap, can you?"

Her words stopped him two steps from the door. "What are you talking about?"

"Trust, is what I'm talking about. I thought you'd accepted we were in this together."

She'd moved closer, straining taller to stare defiantly into his eyes. He considered and discarded several responses – the ones that would push him over the line. "Have I ever had a choice?" He might have once, but not any more.

"About some things, no." She took a step back. "If you ever decide about the rest let me know."

Raina watched the door close behind him, then turned to stare up at the stars, trying to get a grip on herself. Her heart was thudding, her body quaking. A delayed reaction to the day's events. Fear expressing itself as anger.

Whether because Erin was ashamed of her past or hadn't

wanted to hear a litany of I-told-you-so's, the girl had refused to answer any questions on the drive back to the cabin. That had left Raina to fill in the blanks – something she was unfortunately all too good at.

She had no trouble picturing Erin poking through condemned rat-infested buildings and fending off all sorts of dangerous characters. Or wondering what would have happened to the girl if they hadn't gotten there when they did, if they'd shown up just a few minutes later.

She shuddered at the thought, then closed her eyes, willing the awful images away. Erin was safe. No point imagining what might have happened – they had enough real fears to contend with.

She succeeded in pushing back all but one image. The one that remained leapt to her fore-mind with sudden clarity – that of a lone man, crippled by a painful gunshot wound, risking his life to save them both.

She opened her eyes. Risking his life?

Whichever way she turned the idea, there was really no other way to see it. Alec had left the safety of the car, insisting she remain behind, and confronted Erin's pursuers head-on so the girl could escape. Had he not, the outcome of the day's events would most certainly have been quite different.

Raina looked toward the cabin door. No matter what he said to her face, his actions spoke louder. Like his brother before him, Alec DeMarco had stepped up when he was needed the most.

CHAPTER 87

In the cabin's small kitchen Alec uncapped the bottle of Advil and dry-swallowed two of the tablets. He doubted the drug would completely eliminate all the fresh aches and pains he'd acquired, but it might at least dull them enough to let him get some sleep.

He set the bottle back on the counter. A night in a real bed might aid in the sleep department as well. Why was it he was stuck on the couch when Raina had a whole double bed to herself? Couldn't they at least—

He shook off the thought. No they could not.

With his bruises muttering complaints, he slowly made his way to the bathroom. His muscles were already starting to seize, his joints to stiffen. While he still had some flexibility left he needed to change the dressing on his wound.

As he reached for the bathroom door, it opened suddenly and a slight figure nearly walked out into him. He drew away, murmuring apologies, as Erin did the same.

Awkward silence gathered around them. He sidestepped further to let her pass, but the moment she had, something compelled him to stop her again. "Hey."

She turned.

"I'm sorry about before, what I said about your friend."

"It's okay. You were right – no-one would ever believe Naomi. Just like no-one would ever believe me." She stared at her feet. A figure so lost, so fragile, so defeated, he felt something tear lose inside him.

"I believe you," he said.

She squinted up at him. "Yeah, since when?"

"Sooner than either of us realized, I guess. Sometimes it takes me a while to see things clearly." He shrugged. "It's a guy thing."

Another moment of awkward silence – a connection desperately trying to be made.

"That stuff you gave me in the car this morning came in handy today," she said.

"What, the bug spray?" He felt a knot draw tight in his chest. Any scenario requiring that level of defense on her part couldn't have been good. How could he have let her—

"And the money," she added. "I wouldn't have found Naomi without that. I've got some of it left, by the way. I'll give it back to you tomorrow."

"No rush."

A further step toward bridging the rift.

She contemplated her feet a bit more, then looked up. "You did good today. Those guys who were chasing me were playing for keeps."

He touched the painful bruise on his jaw. "I got that impression."

"But..." She frowned. "What was all that staggering around you were doing? I didn't even recognize you at first, I thought you were just some drunken bum."

"That's what I wanted *them* to think. I'm not a hundred

percent at the moment so I needed an advantage. I figured if they thought I was harmless, I'd at least have the element of surprise."

"Good move, rooky." She smiled. "You sure you've never lived on the streets, Orchid Boy?"

He smiled back. "Just glad I didn't have to call the fire department."

All too quickly the darkness returned and she was again staring down at her feet, her small body hunched around its burden of pain. Thoughts of her child, the baby she'd lost without ever seeing, could never stray far from her heart and mind.

He reached out and rested a hand on her shoulder. "We'll find him, okay. Try not to worry."

She swallowed, nodded, bit both her lips. Then her toothpick arms were suddenly around him, her face pressed to the wall of his chest.

He held himself still, willing to provide the support she needed but wary of giving anything more for fear the gesture might be misinterpreted. With his arms wrapped lightly around her shoulder, he waited as she cried herself out.

When the tide of her grief seemed to have ebbed, he eased her back. "You okay?"

Wiping her eyes, she nodded. "Yeah."

"Just remember, you're not alone in this."

"That's exactly what Raina said."

He rolled his eyes. "Don't tell me we actually agree on something. She'll be asking for an engagement ring next."

"I think you've got a ways to go before *that* happens."

He smiled, pleased at the thought he'd cheered her enough that her humor had returned. "Hey, tomorrow – seeing as we may have to use it – how about you and I take a look at your car, see if we can patch up that radiator."

"Sure. Thanks." She nodded, taking a reluctant step back. "See you in the morning."

CHAPTER 88

From the shadows of the kitchen Raina watched Erin return to the bedroom. She'd come inside, intending to talk things out with Alec, and been surprised to overhear their conversation.

Surprised and chastened. That this girl with so much pain in her heart, with so much reason to fear and distrust, could see past the man's insensitive manner and recognize the sentiments buried beneath. Sentiments he'd only then openly expressed with his words of comfort – perhaps the biggest surprise of all.

Raina walked to the rear of the cabin. In the bathroom she found him, shirtless, trying to apply a bandage to the wound above his hip, something he'd managed on previous occasions but appeared now to be struggling with.

She stepped to the door. "Need some help?

He looked up, uncertain, clearly wondering if their battle would continue or if her gesture signaled a truce.

"Thanks." He handed her the dressing and presented his side.

She positioned the gauze over the wound and gently smoothed on the tape to secure it. Her hand went a bit further than necessary, straying onto undamaged flesh.

Firm, warm, unblemished skin.

She drew away quickly. "All done."

She studied his face when he turned around but he gave no indication he'd noticed her slip.

He retrieved his shirt from the edge of the tub and gingerly slid his arm in a sleeve. The light caught the side of his face; she spotted the bruise on his jaw and winced.

For an insane moment she found herself fighting the impulse to stretch up and kiss the spot. Something in his bearing cut short the thought – the way he kept turning further away from her, keeping his distance, avoiding her gaze.

Idiot! She murmured good night and headed for the bedroom.

CHAPTER 89

Naomi sat stiffly in the passenger seat growing more and more anxious. It had looked like a cherry gig at the start – decent car, the driver handing her a hundred dollar bill before she even got inside, with the promise of a second to follow.

But the guy still hadn't said what he wanted. In fact, in the ten blocks they'd driven, going deeper into the city's hard-luck district, he'd said not a word. Worse, in the dark, with his hood pulled up, she couldn't see his face. What did he want for his two hundred dollars?

When he turned down another deserted street, this one heading back to the creek they'd just crossed, she summoned her nerve. "Where are we going?"

"I like it private."

The voice sent an icy chill down her spine. Did she know this guy? "You gonna tell me what you want?"

"Sure, I'll tell you." He pulled back his hood and turned to face her. "Has anyone been to see you lately asking about our little secret?"

Her stomach dropped. Yes, she knew him. The man who'd once paid a large sum of money for her silence. A silence that had festered inside her, dark and malignant, ever since.

"How did you find me?"

"Oh, I never lost you, Sweetheart. I keep a close track on my investments. Now answer the question."

She struggled to think. He'd know if she lied. "Yes, someone came, but I didn't tell them anything."

"Who was it?"

"Just a girl. Someone I used to work with."

"This girl have a name?"

Her throat tightened. "Samantha Bishop."

"Naomi." Though his tone was gently admonishing, his smile was chilling. "Try again."

"Erin," she blurted. "Erin Rose."

"That's better. And what did this Erin Rose want to know?"

"About...my baby. But I didn't tell her a thing, I swear."

"Well, of course you didn't." He patted her thigh. "That was our agreement, wasn't it?"

She nodded furiously. "Sure. Right. Absolutely."

At the end of the street, he turned into the vacant lot beneath the railway bridge that spanned the creek. "Where is she, Naomi?"

"How the hell should I know? I hadn't seen her in almost a year. She showed up out of nowhere, talked to me for less than two minutes, and then pissed off again."

Stopping the car beneath the bridge, he shut off the engine. He turned and locked his gaze on her face.

Her heart raced. Not a soul in sight. Sheets of a newspaper sailed ghostlike across the pavement, catching on weeds growing up through the cracks.

"Look, I swear, I don't know where she is. She said some guy and a woman were helping her but she didn't say who or where they were." When his stare didn't waver she quickly added. "I heard that Quillen grabbed her after she left me. Maybe he knows where she is."

The smile was no less chilling this time. He trailed a gloved hand down her cheek. "Relax, I believe you. I know you'd never lie to me."

He reached in his pocket and pulled out a syringe. "And as a reward, I've got something for you."

CHAPTER 90

Wind sighing through the trees carried the spicy scent of balsam. Moonlight glittered on the waters of the lake, silhouetting the figure beside the boathouse. He started towards it.

Shots exploded out of the darkness, seeming to come from every direction. The figure went down, thrown to one side, arms whirling, a spinning top.

He dove for the ground, crawled the last stretch over rocks and twigs, bullets flying. The boathouse shielded him the final yards to the fallen figure.

Awash in moonlight, spattered in gore, the victim stared sightlessly up at the sky...

Alec bolted upright on the couch, damp with sweat, tangled in the twisted bedding. In his dream he'd let out a shout of horror, but he caught no dying echo of it in the room. The cabin was silent but for the labored rasp of his breathing. Hopefully he hadn't woken the others.

Gently he swung his legs to the floor and sat trying to slow his heart rate. He covered his face but the image remained, burned in his thoughts. By some twisted trick of his mind, the victim this time... Not Liam, but Raina.

Still fighting to orient himself in the present, he detected movement at the cabin door. The scrape of the latch, the creak of hinges.

He struggled to his feet and crossed the floor, his bruises more awake than he was. With the door still inching aside, he grabbed the intruder, pulled them through, and pinned them hard against the wall.

Moonlight skewing through the open door gilded a head of long red hair.

At the sight of the woman standing before him alive and unharmed he nearly dragged her into his arms. Instead he demanded, "Where the hell have you been?"

Raina slapped at the hand on her arm. "Damn it, DeMarco, you scared me to death."

And you don't think you did the same to me? "Answer me."

"I couldn't sleep so I went for a walk."

Even in his muddled state he knew it was a lie. "Bullshit. You were with someone."

"Go back to bed." She tried to move past him but he blocked her path. "All right," she relented. "If you must know, I went to meet Julie."

"Who?"

"Julie Cramer, my friend from the shop. The one who gave me the money from the safe."

A glint of moonlight sparked in her eyes, stealing his focus. It was hours ago that she'd helped him apply the dressing to his wound, yet he could still feel her silken touch on his skin.

Only with the greatest effort had he managed to conceal his reaction at the time. Now, as those feelings once again stirred, they brought with them images of a dream he'd had earlier in the night – before the ghastly scene at the boathouse – the two of them making love beneath the stars on the shore of the lake.

He wet his lips. "What did you need to see Julie about?"

"To get more money of course. We spent most of what we had left on that appointment with Manheim and there's no telling how long we're going to be stuck here."

Noting he still had her pinned to the wall, he took a step back. "I thought she gave you everything there was."

"In the safe, yes. This was her own money. A thousand dollars." Raina shoved her handbag at him. "If you don't believe me, check my wallet."

"I believe you."

She cocked her head. "Well, there's a first."

"A thousand bucks." Frowning, he set her bag on the desk. "Where does she come up with that kind of cash in the middle of the night?"

"You never heard of an ATM? I met her at the one on Gibson Street."

A faint disquiet stirred in his chest but just at that moment he didn't know why.

She touched his arm. "Are you all right?"

"Why couldn't you tell me any of this *before* you went out so we could discuss it?"

"Discuss it?" She laughed, dropping her hand. "You mean like how we discuss what *you're* going to do?"

He knew exactly to what she referred.

I thought you'd accepted we were in this together.

Have I ever had a choice?

Not the words he'd wanted to say. He'd told himself it was all to protect her but had there been another reason? "I'm going to see Manheim again tomorrow."

"Manheim? What for?"

"I'm going to try a different approach. See if I can get anything out of him."

She studied him, her expression unreadable. "So what's the big secret? Why couldn't you just tell me that?"

"I thought you and Erin would want to come with me."

"What if we did?"

He turned away, guarding his thoughts, which surely must be written all over his face. "After what happened today with Erin... I just...I can't..."

She stepped in front of him. "You can't what?"

His hand started to rise to her face but he forced it back down. "I can't let anything happen to you. Either of you."

The words seemed to alter the air around them, making it warmer and charged with tension. She eased closer. "So why couldn't you tell me *that*?"

"Raina, I..." His shirt was only buttoned halfway. He could feel the heat of her through her clothes, the swell of her breasts grazing his chest. "I'm not sure this is the best time for...either of us to get distracted from our purpose."

"Sometimes it helps to take your mind off things for a little while."

She hadn't stepped back. Her scent enveloped him. He closed his eyes, trying to think. "How much did you tell Julie?"

"Nothing. She doesn't even know you exist. Or Erin for that matter." The words were all business but her voice was hushed.

"She just hands over a thousand dollars without asking any questions?"

"Oh, she asked heaps of questions, I just didn't answer

them." Her hand returned to his arm. "Are you sure you're all right?"

He swallowed. *Focus.* "And Julie was okay with that? You not answering any of her questions?"

She gave a half-smile. "It's called trust, DeMarco. You should try it sometime."

He half-smiled back, admitting defeat. "I'm working on it. Can't you tell?"

"You know…" She reached up and cupped his cheek. "Sometimes you just have to take the plunge. Leap of faith and all that."

He bent his head. "You think this might be one of those times?"

She stretched up to meet his descending lips. "Yes."

CHAPTER 91

Sunlight capered on the bedroom wall, bearing the promise of a golden day. One in which mysteries could be unraveled, dangers resolved, and loved ones reunited. Raina rolled over and stared at the empty bed beside hers. Erin must be up already.

She lay listening. No sound came from the other room but she could hear faint voices outside the cabin. She climbed out of bed and stepped to the window.

Two figures leaned head-down beneath the open hood of Erin's car. Alec had mentioned something about helping the girl patch up her radiator but for some reason Raina hadn't expected it to actually happen.

For a moment she couldn't tear her eyes from the pair. The sight of them working side by side, talking, sharing an occasional joke, warmed her heart. She couldn't explain her profound delight that, after all the troubles they'd had initially, they were finally getting along. It seemed this man was full of surprises.

She let the curtain drop back in place and stood smiling at the sound of their laughter. A sound so normal, a scene so peaceful, she could almost let herself climb back in bed and— But no. Their situation was far from normal. And those mysteries wouldn't get solved on their own.

She grabbed some clothes and headed for the bathroom.

As she climbed in the shower a twinge of disquiet intruded upon her fragile peace. Despite her relief at Alec's change in attitude, she couldn't help having reservations about him. Or, more specifically, about *them*.

Last night's kiss was hardly unexpected. The tension between them had been building for days – from the moment she'd seen him lying half naked on her office couch in fact. Maybe even before that.

Yet what genuine feelings could she have for a man she'd known less than a week? Crisis and danger were said to bring people together much faster, but what did she actually know about him, other than what he'd told her himself?

You don't know this man. He could be lying. He could be dangerous.

Craig Farrington's words stirred in her ear but she quickly dispelled them. Alec had risked his life to save Erin. That put him squarely in the 'safe' category in Raina's book. He'd shown compassion for the girl's situation and vowed to be more open with both of them. Even if he had been slow to come around initially, his fundamental character had now been revealed. He could be trusted.

Yes, it seemed she did know a few things about him after all. Things more important than where he came from or what he did for a living or what his favorite take-away was.

What was more likely the source of her concern was that not five days ago she'd wondered if she might be developing feelings for Craig. Looking back now she could see his unexpected show of kindness, coming at a time when she desperately needed it, had simply led her to wonder where a friendship between them might lead. An attractive man like

Craig Farrington – what red-blooded girl wouldn't wonder?

But that question had since been answered – for the time being at least – by her growing feelings for Alec DeMarco. Whether those feelings would develop further they would now just have to wait and see.

Assuming they were given a chance to develop.

Showered and dressed, she entered the kitchen a short while later to grab some breakfast. Her handbag lay open on the kitchen table. Its contents appeared to have been moved around – the small address book she normally kept in a zippered pocket sat atop items in the main compartment. Someone had been going through her things? Looking for what?

The cabin door opened and Erin came in.

"How are the repairs going?" Raina asked.

"It's a patch-up job but Alec says it should hold for a while."

"Oh, that's good." Raina peered over Erin's shoulder at the door. "Where is he? Isn't he coming inside?"

"No, he left. Said he had a few things to do. He'll catch us here later after we get back from the church."

Raina looked up at the kitchen clock. Eight-fifteen. A bit early to be meeting Manheim. She looked back at Erin. "Did you go into my handbag for something?"

"No, Alec did."

"Did he say what he was after?"

"I didn't ask. Figured he just needed some money."

Money. Of course. A simple explanation.

As the girl walked off to have her shower, Raina pulled her wallet from her bag. She'd been asleep, Alec hadn't wanted to wake her to ask—

All the money was still inside.

CHAPTER 92

Julie jabbed the last stud through her earlobe and leaned toward the mirror to apply her make-up. It was going to be a rushed job. After getting Raina's phone call and dashing out to meet her in the middle of the night – four in the morning to be precise – she'd been so hyped up with questions and fears she hadn't fallen back asleep until nearly dawn. And had then slept blissfully through the alarm.

She glanced at the clock on her bedside table. Eight twenty-five. If she wasn't out of the apartment in the next two minutes she'd be late opening up the shop.

Not that Raina would mind of course. She'd remarked again what a tremendous favor Julie was doing her by keeping it open. Still, with the trust her friend was placing in her, Julie didn't want to let her down. More importantly – if she were honest – she wanted to be there in case Raina took her up on her offer to come in and chat. And tell her what the hell was going on!

When her mascara clattered into the sink, Julie forced herself to pick it up calmly and take a deep breath.

Her clumsiness wasn't just from lack of sleep. A call from

her friend in the middle of the night asking for money. No explanation why she needed it, or why she couldn't withdraw the funds from her own account. Her refusal to answer any questions, claiming she didn't want to get Julie involved. And, to top it all off, the report Julie had seen on the news that Raina, together with some man she'd never heard of, was wanted for questioning by police in connection with the death of some reporter. A murder no less!

Just thinking about it got her all worked up again. She tried to focus, but her mind wouldn't let the matter rest. Was the dead man the one Raina had hit with her car that night? The news report said the victim had been shot, so how could she be linked to his murder? But if it was an accident, why had Raina gone on the run? And who was the man she was on the run with?

"God, girl, what have you gotten yourself into?" Julie returned the mascara to her make-up case and pulled out her lip gloss.

Words from the newspaper ran through her head…

Ms Wilkins…well-known to local authorities…aged 18… convicted of vehicular manslaughter after killing her passenger, Richard Scanlon, in a single car collision. Wilkins had been driving while intoxicated but escaped with a reduced sentence.

Escaped. Interesting choice of words. In a town the size of Brockton Mills, Julie doubted any teenager could ever fully *escape* the stigma of such a trauma. Whether she'd gone to prison or not, one way or the other, Raina would've paid for her mistake ever day since.

The thought stopped her hand. She stared at her reflection in the mirror. When she'd met Raina at Dempsey's the other night, she'd wanted to broach the topic then but hadn't had time. At their meeting last night she'd wanted to ask again but her courage had failed: did the fact Raina had a criminal record account for why she'd hired Julie to work in the shop?

Not that it mattered either way. She would always be eternally grateful to Raina who had given her a job when no-one else would. And been her closest friend ever since.

Which meant, no matter how much trouble Raina was in now, she would do everything she could to help. Even if the woman never answered a single damn one of her questions!

She shoved her lip gloss back in the case, switched off the light, and hurried from the bathroom. At the kitchen table she threw her keys and phone in her bag, grabbed her jacket, and ran for the door.

Stepping out into the building's corridor, she collided with a figure blocking her path. A figure that grabbed her, covered her mouth and pushed her quickly back inside.

CHAPTER 93

Alec cleared a spot on Erin's windscreen for a better view across the clinic parking lot. He felt conspicuous sitting in the rust-spotted wreck with all the high-end models around him. But he'd wanted Raina and Erin to have Raina's more reliable Camry. Just in case.

Staring up at the clinic façade, he recalled yesterday's appointment with Manheim, how upset Raina had been afterwards, her reluctance to discuss what was wrong with her.

Whatever the issue was with her health, he couldn't see why it would cause her such pain. If she really wanted kids, why not look into adopting one? Being single wasn't the barrier it used to be. Then again, maybe she'd had plans to do it with Brad and their break-up put an end to her dreams.

Not for the first time he found himself wondering what the man had been like? Not very bright if he could let a woman like Raina slip through his fingers. For an instant Alec felt last night's kiss on his lips, a kiss Raina had largely initiated. So soon on the heels of her failed engagement, were her actions nothing but love on the rebound?

He let out a huff. Hell, who said anything about love? It was just a kiss.

Right. And hurricane Katrina had just been a sun shower.

Raina had told him Brad had falsely accused her of lying. Yet from the sounds of it, she *had* lied to him, saying she didn't want children when the fact was she couldn't have them. Had she told Brad that? Was that why he'd broken off the engagement? Some men were so obsessed with continuing their bloodlines they wouldn't even consider adopting. Perhaps that's what had gone wrong between them.

Alec sipped the coffee he'd bought on the way, then looked for a place to set it down. The car was a mess. Erin's belongings covered the console and every inch of the seat beside him.

He began tossing things in the back. From beneath bags of clothing and takeaway wrappers a notebook appeared – tattered, stained, and nearly filled with handwritten scrawl. Without thinking he opened it and read a few lines. Some kind of journal. Erin's diary? He quickly closed it and put it aside, set his coffee in the dashboard holder, and returned to scanning the parking lot.

After a moment his gaze drifted back to the notebook. The lines he'd read had been quite moving. Perhaps it wasn't Erin's own work but things she had copied from other authors. She'd said she wanted to be a writer. Maybe this was how she hoped to learn the craft.

He reached out and opened the book at random. A poem this time, as heartfelt as the first lines he'd read. Surely she'd copied these pieces from somewhere. And yet there were enough misspellings and imperfections to convince him they were a beginner's efforts. The work of one talented fledgling author. A girl who might well have achieved her dream of becoming a writer had circumstances in her life been different.

He closed the journal and placed it on the car's back seat. In the leg space below, he spotted more books. Fiction, poetry; volumes on child birth and infancy. Evidence of the girl's desperate efforts to educate herself despite having no support or stable home life.

At the bottom of the pile, a title stopped him. My Baby's First Year. A scrapbook for recording the milestones of an infant's growth from birth to their first birthday. He stared at the cover a moment longer, then gently replaced the books on top of it.

He turned in his seat in time to see a car pull into one of the clinic's reserved parking spaces. When the driver emerged, he jumped out and ran to intercept him before he went inside the building. "Doctor Manheim!"

The man turned, surprised to see who was hurrying toward him.

"I'm sorry to approach you like this, Doctor, but I have to speak to you."

"You should make an appointment. Though I'm not sure what more—"

"That's what I wanted to speak with you about. I need to ask...about yesterday. Is there *anything* you can do for my wife?"

Manheim turned to face him. "Sir, I thought I made it clear to you both that your wife's condition is untreatable."

"You did, yes. I understand." Alec held the man's gaze like a vise. "I was thinking more along the lines of alternatives."

"Alternatives." Manheim frowned. "I'm afraid I'm at a loss as to what you're asking me. As I said you could always consider adopting."

"What if for some reason we couldn't adopt? Or foster a child. Are there any options open to us then?"

The man's hesitation was longer this time, a glimmer of suspicion edging his gaze. "None within the scope of my services."

"What about beyond your official services?"

Silence. His expression now wholly unreadable. "I think you'd better leave."

Alec stepped in front of him as he turned to walk off. "Please, Doctor, help me. I'll do anything. Pay anything. I love my wife and she so desperately wants a child."

The words came out unplanned and untempered. Yet Alec had the sense he was speaking the truth. On every count.

Manheim studied him for a long moment – so long Alec began to hope this might actually be the turning point.

In the end, the doctor just shook his head. "I'm sorry, there's nothing more I can do for you."

CHAPTER 94

Raina stood in the wide sunny corridor of Saint Martin's church. Her plan was to stare at the poster on the bulletin board – a message about the church's program for homeless women – until someone noticed and came to speak to her.

Fearing Erin might lack the control needed for such a delicate encounter, she'd asked the girl to wait up the hall. She hoped she wouldn't have to stand here too long as she doubted the girl's nerves could take it. When she saw a white-collared man walking towards her she sighed in relief.

Tall and thin with a shock of grey hair, Father Perry greeted her with a kindly smile. She introduced herself as Miss Fletcher.

"You're interested in our outreach program?" He gestured to the poster she'd been studying.

"Uh...yes. I'm curious to know how you go about reaching out to women with problems and what you do for them when you find them."

"Our program was set up mainly for younger women who've fallen on difficult times, or strayed from a healthy righteous lifestyle. Most are homeless, many are addicts.

Through the program we provide them spiritual, financial, and medical assistance to help them get their lives back on track."

She pointed to the poster. "And this is the person the women would contact? Grace Kilburn?"

"That's correct. Grace founded and runs the program, directing the women to the types of services and help they need. She is also a registered nurse on the staff of the local welfare clinic which provides some of the treatment they receive."

Raina forced a smile. "Sounds like a real saint."

"Oh yes, Grace is totally committed to helping these poor unfortunates."

"I wonder what prompts a person to undertake such a difficult mission."

Perry grew thoughtful. "Grace did confide that to me once. As you can imagine, in her profession as a nurse she's been exposed to a great deal of human suffering, especially in lower economic areas. At one point she simply found she'd seen too much. Confronted daily with the horrific results of what these women do, both to themselves and their unwanted children, she decided she had to do something about it."

"That's so noble. Most people would just shake their heads and walk away."

His smile faltered. "Our Grace is a woman of very strong convictions."

The slightest hint of misgiving to the words. How strong was he talking? She kept her tone neutral. "Oh? Strong in what way?"

"Well, as you might expect, Grace is an avid pro-lifer. Understandable of course considering all she's seen. However…"

"Yes?"

"There is one point on which Grace and our church don't entirely agree. She believes any woman who's had an abortion or been a prostitute should never be allowed to have children."

"Or keep a child she's had out of wedlock?"

The man shifted. "Possibly that might be another of her views. I wouldn't know."

"And just how would you go about enforcing such a thing?"

"Well, we wouldn't, of course. As I say, these are Grace's personal beliefs. Naturally the church strives to forgive people their past wrong-doings. *If* they seek such forgiveness of course."

"And if they don't?"

His gaze met hers as though he were seeing her for the first time. "Miss Fletcher, what is it exactly you're after?" He glanced toward Erin standing up the hall. "Were you seeking help for someone in particular?"

"No, I was just curious. Thank you, you've been most helpful."

CHAPTER 95

As Raina started up the church corridor, Erin rushed over and fell in beside her. "You find out anything? What did he say?"

"It's possible we might be on the right track," Raina whispered. "I might've uncovered their motive at least. I'll tell you in the car." They headed for the exit at the end of the hall, to the parking lot at the rear of the church.

"I don't know why you wouldn't let me talk to him with you," Erin said, glancing back at the grey-haired cleric. "I'd have gotten some answers out of him."

"Which is precisely why I asked you to let me handle it."

Passing the ladies' room door, Erin veered toward it. "Meet you outside."

Raina kept walking, contemplating what she had learned. If Doctor Manheim shared Kilburn's view, they could have the same goal in all this – remove babies from unsuitable mother's and give them to...

Give them to whom? How would they locate couples willing to break the law to a give a child a *better* life?

Having reached the exit she stopped and waited for Erin. A door stood open on a large rec room with ping-pong and pool tables, an upright piano, and a low stage with guitars and a drum kit. The venue for the church youth group no doubt.

A television mounted on the wall was playing the news. She stared at it absently, deep in thought. Until a familiar building appeared, smoke pouring from its upstairs windows. She stumbled blindly into the room, rushed to the TV, and turned up the volume.

"...started in an apartment on the second floor at around 9:45 this morning. The occupant, Julie Cramer, is currently missing and police hold grave concerns for her safety."

Raina gasped when the face of John Scanlon appeared on the screen. "Accelerants have been detected on site, confirming that the fire was deliberately lit. At the moment our primary suspects in the arson attack are Alec DeMarco and Raina Wilkins. Anyone with information as to their whereabouts is asked to call the number on the screen."

Rage and panic flooded her veins. She grabbed a pen from the nearest card table and wrote the number on her hand.

When the broadcast moved on to the next news item, she dashed from the room, back up the hall and into an office she'd passed earlier. A startled secretary looked up from her work as Raina snatched her cell phone off the desk. "Emergency. I'll give it right back."

In the hall she punched in the number from the news bulletin. At the sound of Scanlon's voice in her ear, her panic burst forth. "Where's Julie? What's happened to her? What do you know?"

No need to even identified herself – he knew instantly who it was. "I'd have thought you'd be the one to tell me."

"I had nothing to do with this! I saw Julie last night and she was fine."

"Turn yourself in and I'll listen to anything you have to say."

She clutched the phone. Not a question about where or when she'd met Julie. He didn't care about finding her friend; all he could think of was getting to *her*.

"You're damn right I have something to say but you'll listen now. Everything that's happened – Liam DeMarco's death, the fire, Julie's disappearance – it all has to do with the illegal activities at the Manheim welfare clinic. Newborn babies of homeless women are being taken and sold in an adoption racket. The latest victim is a girl named Erin Rose who fled the hospital only last week. You want to find out who killed Liam and who took Julie, check out that clinic."

"And what about Alec?"

His voice, so calm, stopped her a moment. "Alec had nothing to do with his brother's death. The drugs you found in his car were planted there by the real killer to implicate him."

Nothing but the sound of Scanlon's breathing. Then, in a tone she had not heard in years, "Raina, I'm going to give you a chance to do the right thing here. Because of what you once meant to Rick."

The words were a sledgehammer to her chest. Whether because he'd used her first name or mentioned Rick or still had it in him to do something for her.

"What...I don't...?"

"Despite all that's gone down between us, I don't believe you were directly involved in what happened here today. But if you know where Alec DeMarco is, you *must* tell me. Do you hear me, Raina? You have to hand him over to us now."

"Why? Are you suggesting Alec had something to do with the fire and Julie's disappearance? That's insane. He doesn't even know her."

A heartbeat of silence. "We've just watched the footage from the security camera at your friend's apartment block. It clearly shows Alec DeMarco entering the building at 8:48 this morning. An hour before the fire started."

CHAPTER 96

In the lot behind Julie Cramer's apartment building, with the fire crew still cleaning up and Hendricks getting statements from residents, Scanlon closed his phone and sat staring out the squad car windscreen.

Wilkins was clearly protecting DeMarco. The fact she'd hung up without refuting that Alec had been at Julie's apartment this morning had to mean she'd known about it. Either before, in the planning stage, or after, once he'd finished the job.

The question was, why kill the woman? Did Cramer have something on the pair? Had Wilkins told her something she'd later regretted or which Alec decided she shouldn't know? The woman had worked at Wilkins' shop. Been there a little over two years. Surprising she got a job at all with an embezzlement conviction on her slate. But then even as a kid Wilkins had always had a thing for hard-luck cases. Which made the events of the last twelve hours even more confusing.

Resting his head back against the seat, Scanlon rubbed his eyes. Though he still couldn't quite see how or why, one way or the other, Wilkins was in this up to her neck – with the murder of Liam and now the disappearance and presumed death of Julie Cramer.

He lifted his head, slipped a pack of Rolaids from his pocket and popped two tablets. Despite his pressing need to finally bring Wilkins to justice, now that he was convinced of her guilt, he found he took little pleasure in it. In fact, to his surprise, he felt almost a kind of sick horror.

As irresponsible as she'd been ten years ago, he'd truly believed she'd loved his son. Rick's death at her hands had been an accident. Reckless, criminal, unforgiveable, but still an accident. For Wilkins to be involved in what was happening now meant she'd gone from a troubled teen to a cold-blooded killer. A leap even he found hard to accept.

Which in all probability simply indicated he hadn't known her back then as well as he'd thought he did. None of them had.

And yet...

Something in her story, as outrageous as it seemed, had been vaguely familiar, tugging at a distant memory. Babies of homeless women being stolen. Where had he heard...not that exact story perhaps but... He just couldn't make the connection.

His cell phone beeped – a message coming in. As he reached to open it, dispatch crackled over the radio. The body of a young woman had been found.

Matching the description of Julie Cramer.

CHAPTER 97

Raina sat on the marble bench outside the back of Saint Martin's church. She couldn't seem to catch her breath. Alec at Julie's apartment. Impossible!

"You want to tell me what the man was doing there less than an hour before the fire?" Scanlon had pressed her. "Did he take Julie with him, Raina? Is she there with the two of you now? Or did he drive her out to the woods somewhere, put a bullet in her head and—"

That had been the point when she'd slammed the phone shut, her heart thudding wildly. She'd placed a hand to the corridor wall, trying to stop her head from spinning, her stomach from heaving. *Dear God, no.*

She couldn't believe what Scanlon had told her. Not then and not now. It hadn't been mentioned on the news report so he had to be lying, trying to get her to turn against Alec and hand him over. From the very beginning Alec had insisted the cops were involved in his brother's death. Clearly Scanlon was one of those cops!

When she'd first called Scanlon, she'd intended to send him Erin's video in the hope it would give him enough incentive to look into her claims about the clinic. But with her fresh realization she'd had second thoughts. If Scanlon killed Liam, it meant getting his hands on the video had been his objective all along.

In the end, however, after moments of intense debate, she'd done something that surprised even her. She'd sent the video anyway, downloading it from her burner phone to the secretary's and on from there.

She'd reasoned that Scanlon couldn't know what was on it. If he saw there was nothing that could incriminate him, he might back off from trying to kill Erin and Alec.

Yet going over her decision now she wondered if her logic had been sound. Could there be a third possibility? Scanlon had had nothing to do with Liam's death *and* he was lying about Alec being on the security video?

And maybe all her rationalizing was simply an attempt to deny the truth she feared the most. Alec *had* been at Julie's apartment.

She hung her head, wiped her face. Who to believe? A man she'd known all her life who hated her? Or a virtual stranger she had fallen in love with?

CHAPTER 98

Scanlon parked at the end of the street between two abandoned factory buildings. Beneath the railway bridge at the rear, a vacant lot had been cordoned off. He ducked past the ribbon of tape and headed for the dumpster near the banks of the creek.

"What do we have?"

With the body of a young woman sprawled at his feet, Hendricks looked up from the notebook in his hand. "Naomi Giles. Nineteen, homeless, two priors, both for possession. Looks like she O.D.ed."

Scanlon knelt down beside the body. Not Julie Cramer but every bit as appalling a sight. It wouldn't matter how long you'd been in this job, no-one who had ever had kids could look upon a young life wasted and not feel this sickening kick in the chest. "Who found her?"

"Two kids cutting through the lot." Hendricks nodded toward the pair of teens being questioned by Laskin a stone's throw away.

"They touch anything?"

"Said they didn't but who knows."

Scanlon bent closer over the body, taking in the items lying nearby – syringe, spoon, cotton filter. "Her priors." He frowned. "For possession of what?"

Hendricks consulted the data sheet. "Oxy and Vike."

"So nothing injected."

"That she was ever caught with, no."

"And yet she died from a heroine overdose?"

Hendricks shrugged. "Guess she moved up."

Scanlon scrutinized both the girl's arms, uncertainty starting to nag at his memory. Naomi Giles. Did he know that name?

"There are no other tracks here," he pointed out her blemish-free skin. "This would've been her first time with the needle."

"So?" Hendricks frowned.

So maybe Naomi had a little help.

Scanlon rose and started toward Laskin. The minute he ducked back under the tape a gaggle of reporters appeared from behind one of the bridge's concrete pylons. As he pushed through their midst they shouted their questions, none of which he intended answer.

Until one stopped him dead. "Chief, how does it feel to be pursuing the woman who killed your son?"

Slowly he turned to the man who had spoken, the rest of the group falling silent, yet pressing closer to hear his reply.

"Are you hoping to settle an old score?" the reporter said. "You think they'll convict Raina Wilkins this time?"

Scanlon stared, bile rising up the back of his throat. Then he turned and resumed his march toward Laskin.

CHAPTER 99

From the edge of the police station parking lot, peering out the Toyota's window, Erin watched Raina slink along rows of employee vehicles and place her note beneath the wiper on someone's windshield.

Had Raina totally lost it, she wondered. When she'd exited Saint Martin's church an hour ago, she'd found the woman crying softly on a bench outside but unwilling to say what was wrong. What could've happened between the time Erin had ducked in the ladies' room and rejoined her a few moments later?

She'd comforted her new friend as best she could. A strange feeling, to be comforting someone else for a change. Yet she felt oddly pleased she'd been able to return even a small measure of the kindness Raina had so far shown her.

But just when she'd seemed to pull herself together, Raina had suddenly jumped up from the bench, insisting she had to go somewhere, muttering something about 'taking a friend up on an offer'.

Twenty minutes later, when they'd pulled up here behind the police station, Erin had known a moment of panic. Hadn't

Alec said his brother insisted the police were involved in what was happening? While she had no proof of the fact herself, it certainly made sense. Who better than a cop to cover up an illegal adoption conspiracy?

So what the hell were they doing here?

Like a soldier evading a sniper's bullet, Raina slunk back the way she'd come, opened the driver's door, and climbed in.

"Okay, what's going on?" Erin burst out. "What was in that note you wrote? Who did you leave it for?"

"A friend." Raina turned in the seat to face her. "Erin, you have to trust me on this. I know Alec said the cops were involved but there is one I know I can trust. He offered to help us and I decided it was time to let him."

"You've been talking to a cop behind Alec's back?"

"I haven't told him anything up until now. He's been helping keep another cop off our backs."

"So what was in the note you gave him?"

"I've simply passed on our suspicions and asked him to check out Manheim's clinic." Raina reached over and gripped her hand. "You know I would never do anything to endanger you, right."

"Yeah, I guess."

Her grip grew tighter, demanding a more decisive response.

"Yes, I know you'd never endanger me."

"And I'm doing everything I can to help you find Cody."

She looked down and nodded. "I know."

"Then you're just going to have to trust me. Please. And say nothing to Alec for now, okay."

Totally bewildered, Erin sighed. "If that's what you want."

Raina lifted her hand to the girl's cheek. "We're going to

get through this, I promise you. Everything's going to work out, you'll see." Then she lowered her hand, pressed back in her seat, and gripped the steering wheel.

"Just one other thing I need you to do for me." Her knuckles whitened. "Show me where I can get a gun."

CHAPTER 100

Farrington pushed out the station's back door and started down the steps. He needed a break and a hit of double-shot espresso to clear his head after six straight hours at the computer.

His first 'day off' in over a week. A day he might have put to good use if not for Scanlon calling him in. Still, he'd managed to cross a few vital things off his list. And with all that was going down at the moment you had to expect it was all hands on deck.

Shoulders hunched, he started across the parking lot. Dark clouds hung over neighboring buildings, deepening the shadows beneath the trees and creating a premature sense of dusk. A chill breeze carried the ozone scent of an approaching storm. As the first fat rain drops began to fall, he put up his collar and ran for his car.

Even from halfway across the lot he could see the slip of paper under his windshield wiper. Not another damn pamphlet ad. He rounded his bumper, snatched the page from under the blade, and prepared to ball it up in his fist. Then noted it was a hand-written note. And the signature at the bottom.

He turned a quick circle, scanning the lot, then rushed to the curb to look up and down the street. No sign of Raina or her car. He'd been tied up inside since eleven this morning. No telling when she had dropped this off.

He started back, reading her message even as rain drops spattered the page.

Swearing, he stuffed the note in his pocket and pulled out his phone.

CHAPTER 101

Erin eased closer to Raina's side staring up at the forest canopy. The wind was doing strange things to the trees, rattling their limbs like old dry bones, making the leaves hiss and sigh as though the branches were filled with snakes.

The dry husk of a sycamore leaf landed on her shoulder, its curled tips wrapping around it like claws. She stifled a yelp, brushed it off, and shrank closer to the woman beside her. "Tell me again – why are we here?"

Raina lowered the gun she'd been aiming and nodded down at it. "We just bought this from the back of some guy's car, behind a dumpster in a disused parking lot."

Erin shrugged. "You asked me if I knew someone."

"Yeah well I'd like to at least make sure the thing works before I go staking our lives on it." Raina gently pushed the girl back, then resumed her stance, aiming for a tree across the clearing. "Besides I've never even held a gun, let alone fired one."

She pulled off the shot and winced at the recoil that stung her wrist. Together they walked through the ferns and leaves to check her accuracy. At the base of a towering sycamore tree she bent to inspect the hole in the bark.

"Shooting dead stuff is easy, you know," Erin said. "Trees don't shoot back. They don't bleed either."

Raina stared at the weapon in her hands.

"So who are you planning to use it on?"

"I'm not *planning* to use it on anyone. It's just...after what happened to you on the street yesterday I thought we should have some form of protection."

The girl reached out and poked a finger into the bullet hole she'd made in the tree. "Well, at least you know you can hit what you're aiming at."

"Yeah. Except I was aiming at that one." Raina pointed to the tree next to it.

"In that case I'd say you need a bit more practice."

She heaved a sigh. "No, that'll do." *Especially seeing as, if I need to use it, I'll likely be firing it at close range.* With a chill in her heart, she slipped the weapon back in her handbag and lifted her face.

Sunlight streamed in across the clearing, freshened by a whisper of pine-scented breeze. Leaves of birch and silver maple, bright as butterflies, fluttered to the forest floor around them.

"You feel that?"

"What?" Erin froze.

"Sunlight filtered through leaves has a different feel to it. In summer it's cool, fresh. Quenching. Now, when the leaves are changing, it's more golden, warm, gentle on your skin."

Raina paused to savor the feeling. She was in no great hurry to return to the cabin. As always any contact with nature was a welcome respite from her troubles and fears. Anything to distract her thoughts from the decision she might soon have to make.

Erin stood frowning. Whether the wind had suddenly died or the sun got brighter, somehow the forest seemed less threatening. "Who taught you about the woods?" she said.

"My dad. He was a real nature lover. We used to go hiking together when I was young. He'd tell me all the names of the trees and plants, even the flowers."

"When you were young. Does that mean he's not around any more?"

Raina smiled sadly. "He died of a heart attack when I was sixteen. It was very sudden."

"You still miss him, don't you."

"Every day." Her smile faded. She gazed to the distance. "You know the most amazing thing about my dad? He never had to *try* to be good. The rest us struggle to do the right thing, the thing we know we ought to do, to be the kind of person we want to be. He never even had to think about it. He just always knew the right thing to do."

She closed her eyes. *What would you do if you were here now, Dad? Help me, please. Do I trust DeMarco or protect this child at any cost, even if it means... Please tell me, what do I do?*

"Always?" Erin said.

The question brought her back to the moment. "Well, naturally he wasn't perfect. Still..." She shrugged. "If there's one person in this world I would want to be like, it's him."

Erin looked up, suddenly hesitant. "I want to be like you," she whispered.

The words caught Raina's heart in a vise. She reached for the girl and hugged her close, pressed her face to her silken hair. With the fragile figure wrapped in her arms, the rest of the world could be held at bay.

CHAPTER 102

Manheim slumped in the chair at his desk, watching the stout figure pace before him. Never an attractive woman, Grace Kilburn's pinched, deep-set features grew downright fearsome when she was angry.

"He's getting completely out of hand," she raved. "Doesn't even consult us any more when he decides something should be done. What he did to that girl is sure to draw attention. What was he thinking?"

"He knows what he's doing. I'm sure he was careful." As Manheim expected, she heard not a word.

"I'm not saying he shouldn't have done it. Who would even mourn such a loss? He just should've taken steps to minimize the risk." Even though the clinic was closed, the building deserted, she lowered her voice. "For one thing, the body should never have been found."

"I agree with you there but—"

The woman turned suddenly and planted both her hands on his desk. "Have you forgotten the reason we started this, Oran? It wasn't so he could come in and take over. It was *our* vision, yours and mine. You remember that?"

"Of course I remember. Look, the man's been fine up until now – an asset really, you have to admit. And ultimately he shares our view."

"What good is that if he destroys everything we've worked for? Do you fully appreciate what's at stake here? He wouldn't just put an end to our future work, he'd undo everything we've accomplished so far. Years of planning, establishing the network, contacts, sources."

"Grace, what do you suggest I do? We've never had a choice in this."

"Talk to him. Explain to him all that he's putting in jeopardy. He came in after all the hard work was done. He doesn't understand what it took. Get him to see—"

"Yes, yes, all right, I'll try. Of course I will." Manheim clasped his hands at the thought. "Just please, don't antagonize him, will you. Remember last time."

It was rare indeed when the woman backed off. Even rarer the times he'd seen fear in her eyes and felt moved to comfort her. "Don't worry. I'm sure this meeting will resolve all the issues you've raised."

The office door swung open before them and a figure stepped through. "What issues are those?"

CHAPTER 103

Raina piloted her car into the camp grounds and followed the track toward their cabin obscured by trees at the rear. The object in her handbag felt like a time bomb waiting to go off. At one time she'd vowed she would never own a gun, let alone use one. But these were extraordinary circumstances. And it wasn't just herself she needed to protect.

In her heart she still believed Alec was innocent, that he hadn't been anywhere near Julie's apartment, and Scanlon had only been trying to trick her. If the man she'd known these last five days was the true Alec, then her feelings for him were just as true. But if his actions had been a ruse, his words a deception…

When the cabin came in view she rolled to a stop. Erin's car was parked out front, which meant Alec was back, waiting inside.

"What's wrong?" the girl said from beside her.

Raina looked over. While she was prepared to confront Alec herself, she would not put Erin at risk along with her. No matter how many guns she had.

"I need you to do something for me." She pulled her

wallet out of her bag. "When we get up to the cabin I want you to get straight in your car and go and buy yourself some dinner."

Erin stared at the money held out to her. "I'm not hungry."

"Erin, please—"

"I want to stay with you." The voice so needful, so filled with fear, tore at Raina's heart.

Alternatives suddenly flooded her mind. They could take off together, just the two of them. Leave Alec to his fate. Follow the leads they'd uncovered so far and with Farrington's help...

But, no, she couldn't. At some point, without even realizing it, she'd committed herself. To both of them. If Alec was what he appeared to be, he needed her help to find Liam's killer. And to avoid being killed himself.

And if he was lying, if she had given her heart to a killer, she *had* to know.

"You're going to tell Alec about that cop, aren't you," Erin said. "You know he won't be happy."

"You let me worry about that. He'll be fine once I explain it to him." Raina pushed the money into Erin's hand and continued driving.

Pulling up at the side of the cabin, she shut off the engine and turned to face her. "Now this is important so listen carefully. If I haven't called you in an hour, *don't* come back here; you understand? Go back to the police station and ask for Deputy Craig Farrington. Tell him everything we've learned so far and he'll look after you."

"Deputy Farrington. Is that the guy you left the note for?"

"Yes. Now go, get out of here." Raina reached across her and opened the door.

Erin clutched her arm. "Why don't you want me to come

inside with you? You don't suspect Alec of anything do you?"

"I just need to talk to him alone, that's all. It shouldn't take long."

The girl's grip loosened, her face slowly cleared. "Yeah, I know. You just want to jump him, don't you."

"What?"

"I've seen the looks you two give each other. I'm not dumb, you know."

Raina laughed despite herself. "I've never thought that for an instant."

"I could just sit in the living room, turn the TV up really loud while you guys go at it. There isn't much I haven't heard."

Her smile faded. Sadly it was no doubt true. Raina opted to continue the charade. "A bit of privacy would be nice. Now go on, get."

Erin heaved a sigh, climbed from the car, then leaned back through the open door. "Next time get a cabin with two bedrooms."

CHAPTER 104

Alec stood transfixed by the television. Horrified would better describe it. The scene before him defied belief. He didn't want to think what would've happened if he hadn't acted when he had. If he hadn't chosen to obey his instincts and—

The cabin door opened. He quickly shut the television off and set the remote on the coffee table. When he looked over, Raina was standing inside the door staring back at him.

"Something you don't want me to see?" she said, indicating the blank TV.

He waved a hand. "Just rubbish. Nothing worth watching."

He rounded the table, intent on greeting her, but she stepped past him. Hadn't she seen his outstretched arm?

"How did it go with Manheim today? Did you get to see him?"

"I did." He shoved his hands in his back pockets. "I asked him if he could do anything for us, apart from his services at the clinic."

"And?"

"I told him we couldn't adopt or foster a child and asked if he knew of any alternatives." He moved closer, lowered his voice, intent once again on knowing her secret. "That's the truth, isn't it, Raina? That's why you got so upset yesterday. You can't have children and for some reason—"

"This isn't about me." She stepped away, presenting her back, her casual demeanor unconvincing. "Just tell me what Manheim said."

"He said there was nothing he could do for us."

"You think he was on to you?"

"Possibly. I don't know."

She was silent a moment. "What else did you do?"

"What do you mean?"

"Talking to Manheim didn't take all day." She turned to face him.

Only then, with the lamp light full on her face, did he see she'd been crying. His disquiet doubled as a second thought struck him. "What's happened? Where's Erin?"

"She went to get dinner. Answer my question."

A definite edge had entered her tone. Something was wrong. "I went to see someone."

"Who?"

"A friend. I borrowed some money like you did. I didn't think it was right that you should foot the bill for all this." He pulled out his wallet, held it open, showing her the bills it contained.

Raina barely glanced at the wallet. She couldn't tear her gaze from the man before her. *Please tell me something I can believe.* "That was after you spoke to Manheim."

"That's right."

Like dry crumbs, her next words caught in her throat: *What did you do* before *you talked to him?* She opted for others a bit less confronting. "Erin said she saw you going through my handbag this morning. What were you looking for?"

Alec exhaled. Is that what this was all about? "I was going to take some money but… That's when I decided to go to my friend."

Raina shifted the strap on her shoulder, feeling the weight of the gun in her bag. How fast could she reach it if she had to? She opened her mouth, determined to get the question out.

Alec's burner cell phone rang. He pulled it from his pocket and checked the caller.

When he stared in surprise, Raina frowned. "Answer it. It has to be Erin. We're the only two who have your number."

Holding her gaze, he opened the phone and raised it to his ear. "It isn't Erin."

CHAPTER 105

Contemplating Rick's photo on his desk always took Scanlon somewhere different. Some fresh memory revived by the sight of his son's crooked smile. Today's was the fishing trip they'd gone on in honor of Rick's eleventh birthday.

A stream of impressions flashed through his mind. Rick's face as he tore the wrapping from his new rod and reel. The two of them loading the car together the morning of the trip. Their flashlight prowl the evening before that had yielded not a single night crawler but which had given them a chance to discuss the Red Sox's line-up and joke about what they would use for bait instead of worms. Peanut butter! Hostess Twinkies! A bologna sandwich!

Smiling, Scanlon set the frame down again.

How does it feel to be pursuing the woman who killed your son?

A chill washed over him. His smile died. The reporter's words breathed in his ear. *Think you'll finally get to settle an old score? Isn't that really what this is about?*

Scanlon put his face in his hands. The man had been right. He'd lost all perspective on this case, compromised the ethics he'd always prided himself on. All the things he'd tried to teach Rick. He'd been on a one-man vigilante crusade. Had he been so blinded by anger and vengeance he hadn't seen it? Or had he simply chosen to ignore it?

Either way it had to end. He had to get his perspective back – had to get *himself* back – or he'd have nothing left. If Wilkins was guilty, he would bring her to justice. But it would be justice for *this* crime, not for what happened ten years ago. He would not let her turn him into someone he despised.

Drawing himself back to his purpose, the reason he'd returned to the office, he typed 'Naomi Giles' into his computer. Her priors came up and he read them through, but nothing they contained jogged his memory.

Still with a strong sense he knew the name, he extended his search and found something else – an investigation the girl had initiated two years earlier. He clicked on the entry and opened the file.

A knot slowly tightened inside his chest as he read the report. He knew he'd heard the name before.

He sat back, working to see some connection between what he'd just read, the girl's recent death, and the claims Wilkins had made on the phone. There could definitely be something here but he needed more facts to piece things together. Following a hunch was one thing but speculating about something this big...

Only when his cell phone fell silent did he register it had been ringing. Absently he picked it up. A missed call from Peg, a message from Craig... He froze and blinked at the number displayed – and a message from the phone Raina had used to call him earlier, sent moments after their conversation.

Ignoring the others, he clicked on Raina's.

CHAPTER 106

Alec placed the phone to his ear. He greeted the caller, his puzzled expression turning surprised. "Doctor Manheim."

He listened, nodding. "Yes, certainly…Yes, of course, I understand…We'll see you there then. Thank you, Doctor."

He hung up, looking no less surprised. "Manheim's agreed to help us after all. He says he'll meet us to discuss our situation but not at the clinic. We're to meet him at his cabin on Jessop's Lake at eight o'clock." He checked the time. "We better get moving."

Raina stood digesting his words. Jessop Lake. A remote location. The perfect spot for a clandestine meeting.

Or murdering someone and dumping the body.

She watched Alec pulling on his jacket. Had it really been Manheim on the phone? "Why would he suddenly change his mind?"

"Who knows? Maybe he thought someone was watching us today when I approached him at the clinic. Maybe he's just learned of another baby that needs a home."

When she didn't reply, he took a step toward her. "Raina, this is what we've been hoping for. We finally have a chance to nab the bastard and expose his racket, find Liam's killer and get Erin's baby back."

Staring into his earnest gaze, she felt the factions at war within her. Her desire to put her arms around him; her need to protect both herself and Erin. If it hadn't been Manheim on the phone, if Alec had simply sensed her ambivalence and turned a wrong number to his advantage—

"It'll look more convincing if you're there with me." Alec slid his hands to her neck. Hesitation filled her eyes. This woman, whose touch had only last night kindled the promise of a future together, had since erected a wall between them. What had changed? What did she know that she wasn't telling him?

"Okay," she relented. "On two conditions. Number one, Erin stays out of it."

"Absolutely. We won't even tell her." He threaded his fingers up through her hair. "Just leave her a note, say we'll be back in a little while."

"Right. And two—"

He pulled her against him, stopping her words with his mouth against hers. Unable to break through the barriers one way, he would try another.

He lifted his head, searched her eyes, and let himself smile. Perhaps not broken but the barriers had definitely weakened. "The second condition?"

She swallowed hard. "You drive. I'm feeling a little shaky at the moment."

CHAPTER 107

Sitting in the passenger seat of her car, her gaze glued to the cabin's front door, Raina pulled her phone from her bag. She had maybe three minutes in which to call Erin before Alec finished changing and came out to join her.

She opened her phone and tapped in a number. "It's me. Where are you?"

"You told me to go get something to eat."

She couldn't help smiling at the girl's peevish tone. Spoken like a typical teenager. "I didn't think you'd listen to me."

"You didn't give me a lot of choice. So what's the story? Are you and Alec finished *talking*?"

Raina's smile faded at the girl's innuendo. She could still taste Alec's kiss on her lips. Still feel his arms as he'd held her close just moments ago, promising her everything would be all right. God help her, despite all her fears, she'd kissed him back.

The one thing she *had* had the foresight to do was to ask him to drive to their meeting with Manheim. With her hands free, she could get to the gun in her bag if she had to.

"We're going to need more time," she said. "I told you

one hour but let's make it three."

"Boy, you guys are a couple of rabbits."

Another reluctant smile. It seemed this girl could lighten her heart even under the most trying conditions. "If you haven't heard from me by ten o'clock, you know what to do."

"Go and see that deputy guy. And what am I supposed to do until then?"

"It's okay to come back to the cabin. Alec and I won't be here. We're checking something out."

A heartbeat of silence. "I don't suppose you'll let me come with you."

"Not this time."

"Should I be worried?"

"No. Everything's going to be fine." Even to her own ears the promise sounded thin.

"Great. I'll just sit around doing my nails until I you get back." The girl's sulky tone turned suddenly earnest. "Whatever you're doing, be careful, okay."

Erin closed her phone, slipped it back into her pocket and started her engine. She didn't buy Raina's story for a minute. Something was up. Something resulting not just in the woman's tears but in her sudden desire to buy a gun. A weapon purchased from a black market source requiring no permit or proof of ID.

A gun she was planning to use against whom?

Erin sat patiently, the engine chugging. A moment later, Raina's car pulled from the rear of the camp grounds and turned up the road ahead of her.

When it had gone a safe enough distance, Erin pulled from the side of the road and took off after it. She hoped the makeshift repairs to her radiator lasted till they reached their destination.

CHAPTER 108

"You wanted me, Chief?" Farrington stood in the office doorway. The man behind the desk looked beat, the pain of years sitting heavily on his shoulders pressing him deeper into the chair.

"Come in," Scanlon said. "Something I need your opinion on."

Hiding his impatience, Farrington stepped inside but declined the seat Scanlon had offered. He didn't have time for this. He'd finished for the day – a day he wasn't to have worked in the first place. What was so important it couldn't wait till tomorrow morning? "What's on your mind, John?"

Scanlon laid a manila folder on the desk and slid it towards him. "Two years ago. Seventeen-year-old homeless girl gives birth at the Manheim clinic. Ten days later she walks in here claiming staff at the hospital stole her baby. Ring any bells? It should. You were in charge of the case."

"Naomi Giles." Farrington decided to take the seat after all. "Sure, I remember. Retracted her story a week later and disappeared. Probably made the whole thing up."

"Disappeared until today. Her body was found this

morning under the bridge near Hampton Creek. Apparent overdose."

He managed a shrug. "No surprise there. Drug addict, living on the streets. Amazing she lasted this long."

For no apparent reason, Scanlon's focus drifted away, a tendency he'd been exhibiting more and more in recent days. He turned to the picture frame on his desk, reached out and touched it, smiling faintly.

Farrington waited. Had the man forgotten their conversation? Did Scanlon even know he was here? "Sir?"

"Remember that time you, me, and Rick went on that camping trip?"

He stifled a sigh. The poor bastard was losing his grip, his demons finally getting the better of him. A process downright painful to watch, especially with someone he'd once so admired. "I was eating trout for over a month."

"That boy idolized you," Scanlon said.

"Not as much as he did his old man." It was the same line he always said at this point. Following the same recollections from Scanlon. How many times had they had this exchange? How many ways could he drag up the past? Still, if it was what he needed to hear...

"Rick was like a brother to me. He was a good kid."

At last Scanlon set the photo down and looked across at him, his eyes red-rimmed, his expression raw. "Craig, I've never said this before but I want you to know something – no-one could ever take Rick's place in our lives but you came damn near as close as possible."

The admission stunned him, possibly something he'd wished deep down but never dared let himself hope was true. "John, I...I don't know what to say. I'm touched. Truly. You and Peg have been like family to me all these years. I feel—"

Scanlon hit a key on his laptop and turned it toward him. Shadowy images danced on the screen, at last coalescing into recognizable shapes.

Farrington sat immobile, staring. "Where did you get this?"

Scanlon let the footage play out, then rewound to a spot, froze the frame and pointed to something on the belt of the unidentifiable man.

"My guess is if I got the tech boys to sharpen this a little, that buckle would show up nice and clear. You can almost make it out now. See here – the moose's antlers, the line of the bear's back. A gift custom-made. One of a kind." The man's grim gaze returned to Farrington. "The one I gave you for your tenth anniversary with the force."

The clock's dull ticking filled the office.

Scanlon leaned forward onto his elbows. "Here's what I think happened two years ago. In the course of investigating Naomi's claim about her baby, you discovered she was telling the truth. An illegal adoption racket is operating out of Manheim's clinic. You saw a way to make money out of it, so you paid the girl off, blackmailed the staff, and cut yourself in for a share of the profits. You've been working with them every since."

Farrington let a long moment go by. The clock ticked. "Serve and protect. Isn't that what they teach us, John?"

"So Naomi's overdose..."

"She reneged on our agreement; or was about to. I had to stop her before she did."

"And the journalist? Liam DeMarco?"

"He'd gotten wind of things through another girl who'd recently given birth at the clinic. The same one who made that tape I assume. Though this is the first time I'm seeing it. I wasn't sure it even existed until this moment."

Scanlon studied the man before him. His admissions seemed to be coming too easily, his confessions too willing. Could he honestly think their long-standing friendship would safeguard him from the consequences of his actions? "Have you any idea how much I wanted to be wrong about this?"

Farrington deftly tapped a few keys and deleted the file. "It's not what you think." He closed the laptop and ripped out the cord. "And you're not going to do a thing about it."

"Craig, for god's sake, you know I have no choice about this."

Farrington stared across at his boss. He hadn't wanted to play this card. Not now, not ever. If he had his way, the truth would never come to light, for Scanlon's sake as well as his own. But the man had left him no other option. And perhaps it was time he knew anyway.

"You're wrong, John, you do have a choice. And I'm sure it's going to be the right one."

CHAPTER 109

Alec steered the Toyota along the winding wooded road toward Jessop Lake. They'd been driving for more than twenty minutes and were nearly there. With every mile they got from the cabin the landscape grew increasingly wild and remote.

Beside him, Raina sat silent and tense, staring out the windshield. Fearful of their impending encounter, he wondered, or something else? Several times he thought he'd detected her gaze on his face but when he'd turned to her, she'd quickly glanced away again.

"You didn't tell me what you learned at the church today," he said.

She thought for a moment before she answered. Deciding what she could and couldn't tell him?

"Grace Kilburn is not only a member of their congregation but founder of the church's outreach program. She helps young homeless women find shelter, food and medical assistance."

"According to Erin and her friend, that's not all she does."

"It seems a safe bet she's the linchpin in all this, in charge of seeking out homeless pregnant women and directing them to Manheim's clinic. Where – one way or the other – Manheim makes sure their babies stay behind when they leave."

Alec drummed a thumb on the steering wheel. "What I'd like to know is how she lines up the couples who adopt them. They'd have to know it wasn't legal. Are there people prepared take such a risk?"

"Desperate ones, certainly. People who can't get a child any other way."

Knowing her personal stake in the matter, he hesitated. "Perhaps some who should never have one?"

She shook her head. "Something tells me Manheim and Kilburn take great care in finding suitable adoptive couples. According to the pastor, Grace lives the life of a nun, donates everything she earns above a bare subsistence back to the church. If she's getting any money out of this, she sure isn't spending any."

"That we know of." He shrugged. "Maybe the church recruits the parents then."

"That's what I'm thinking. The network could extend all over the country. An underground group of hardcore fanatics taking it upon themselves to remove babies from 'unsuitable' parents and place them with ones they deem acceptable."

He shook his head. "*Unsuitable* parents like Erin."

Beside him, Raina sat clutching her bag. Without the spur of further questions she'd lapsed into wary silence again.

"What's wrong?"

Her gaze jerked toward him. "Nothing. Why?"

"You seem tense."

"Just worried about confronting Manheim. We still have to convince him of our story before we can nail him."

"No, it's not that. You were distant back at the cabin, even before Manheim called. What is it? Tell me."

She turned away, unable to meet his eye.

That's when he knew. He pulled to the side of the road and stopped.

Her attention swung back to him. "What are you doing? We'll be late to meet Manheim."

He twisted the wheel in his hands, staring ahead. Once he said it, there'd be no turning back.

He looked aside. "You know about Julie, don't you?"

Her eyes widened. "Oh my god, it's true. You were at her apartment this morning?" She sat frozen for an instant then lunged for the door. She'd yanked the handle and was swinging it open when he grabbed her arm.

CHAPTER 110

Scanlon sat at his office desk, fighting to breathe. He felt gutted. Bruised. Battered by the words his deputy had spoken. A revelation so astounding, wave upon wave of ramifications were still slamming into him.

No doubt that was what Craig had intended. To leave him powerless, immobilized by shock and despair. Beyond reluctant, wholly unwilling to pursue things further, giving the man the time he needed to go off and complete his unholy plan.

Craig had known precisely what card to play. A wild card that trumped all others, one Scanlon hadn't even known was in the deck. Still, what could have convinced him that would be enough, that Scanlon would simply stand by now and do nothing to stop him?

He closed his eyes. Probably any of their meetings in the last six days. In any of the conversations they'd had since Raina Wilkins walked into the hospital confessing to a crime she hadn't committed. One he had nevertheless determined he would pin on her whatever the cost.

If a nameless reporter could see the truth, a man he'd

worked with for eleven years would've known it from the start. Yes, if nothing else, his behavior since this whole thing began would've shown Craig Farrington how far his ethics and judgment had eroded.

But perhaps not lost beyond all redemption.

He opened his eyes. The picture on his desk swam into focus.

As though waking from a dream, he looked toward the clock. Seven-twenty. He hadn't been sitting here stunned and useless as long as he'd thought. There might still be time.

He reached out and touched the image in the frame. Then he pushed to his feet and ran from the room.

CHAPTER 111

Raina yanked her arm from Alec's grasp and threw herself out the door to the ground. By the time she'd scrambled to her feet, he'd dashed around the car to confront her.

"Wait, please. Let me explain."

She stood her ground. Even after hearing his admission – that he'd indeed been at Julie's apartment – she couldn't bring herself to believe he'd started the fire. Why would Alec want to hurt Julie? Yet what other reason could he have had for going there?

He held up his palms. "Something you said last night bothered me. But I was so tired, so out of it at the time, it didn't hit me until this morning."

She frowned. "Last night?"

"When you came back from meeting Julie. You said she withdrew a thousand dollars from an ATM and gave it to you."

"That's right. So?"

"Given that the cops are looking for you and she's your best friend, did you ever consider they might put a trace on Julie's bank account in case you went to her for help?"

Her mouth dropped open. "You're telling me you went to

her apartment to warn her?"

"I told her to leave town and not let anyone know where she was going."

His words threatened to ignite her anger. Did he think she would swallow anything he told her? "And Julie believed you? A total stranger knocks on her door, tells her to leave town, and she just packs up and goes?"

"You'd already given her plenty of reason to think you were in trouble. Plus she'd seen my photo in the paper and knew we were on the run together."

She slipped her hand inside her bag. "I never told her that."

"No, but it was in the news." He took a step toward her. "Look, it wasn't easy – I had to convince her – but in the end she believed me."

Raina stared back. God help her, it did sound credible. Probable even.

Except for one thing.

"How did you know where Julie lived?"

"That's what I was really looking for in your bag this morning. Her address was in that notebook of yours."

She narrowed her eyes, her hopes receding. Her fingers found the grip of the gun. "I was right there in the cabin with you. Why didn't you just ask me? Why didn't you tell me what you were doing."

"I didn't want to worry you. And anyway you were asleep."

And that was about as lame a reason—

"Look, I know about the fire at Julie's apartment," he said. "I saw it on the news. I assume you did too and I know what a shock that must've been for you. I'm sorry I couldn't have—"

The gun was trembling in her hand, aimed at his heart,

before she realized she'd pulled it from her bag.

He showed her his palms. "Raina, don't do this."

"They said it was arson."

"Which proves I was right to tell her to leave. She's safe, Raina. She was gone before the fire ever started."

She wavered. Did he know how much she wanted to believe him? "And if I called her?"

He lowered his hands. "She won't answer. I told her not to take her phone in case they could get her location from it."

"So there's no way I can be sure she's all right."

"You can be sure because I'm telling you." He eased closer, holding her gaze. "You already are or you wouldn't have come with me to meet Manheim."

She didn't pull back. He was right. She'd made her decision before she'd even returned to the cabin.

Slowly she lowered the gun to her side. "All right, let's go. We don't want to keep the doctor waiting."

CHAPTER 112

Scanlon pulled up at the welfare clinic, one of the two medical facilities where both Manheim and Kilburn reportedly worked.

As he shut off the squad car engine he saw a stout matronly woman rise from behind the desk inside and walk to the door. He paused briefly but she didn't come out, just stood there watching him through the glass. Was he expected?

As he climbed from the car, Hendricks' patrol pulled up beside him. Together they walked for the clinic door, reaching it just as the woman turned the lock.

Scanlon read her name tag through the glass then held up his badge. "Miss Kilburn, we'd like a word with you. Please open the door."

Kilburn stared him in the eye for a moment, then started backing slowly away.

"This is a police matter, Miss Kilburn. Unlock the door."

She turned, walked back around the desk, and disappeared down the corridor beyond.

Scanlon drew his service revolver and raised it, preparing to break the glass. A nurse strode into view from their left, spotted him, and shrank back in alarm. When he held up his badge, repeating his demand for entry, she rushed forward and unlocked the door.

He and Hendricks ran up the hall in pursuit of Kilburn. They opened each door, checking every room along the corridor, but none were sheltering the woman they sought.

Finally at the end of the passage they found her in a treatment room. Steel and glass gleamed all around them – bottles, flasks, scalpels, syringes – potential weapons on very counter top.

Holding his revolver trained on the woman, he ordered Hendricks, "Check the other rooms. Find Manheim."

When the man had run out, he turned to Kilburn. "You know why we're here. Things might go easier for you if you tell me where he is."

The woman stared serenely back at him.

He stepped toward her. "There's a meeting tonight. Or should I say an ambush. Manheim set it up but he never had any intention of going. Where is it?"

Nothing but more defiant silence.

Scanlon felt each second tick by. "We've got you both on a number of charges. If you don't talk now, we'll be adding murder to the list. Now where's Manheim?"

Her blunt features twisted in a grimace of pain. She lifted her chin. "He won't tell you anything. And neither will I."

With a trembling hand, she laid an empty syringe on the table and collapsed to the floor.

CHAPTER 113

Blades of moonlight sliced through the trees, melting and shifting along the dirt track that led down to the lake. Reluctant to drive out on the open shore, Alec parked the car well back from the water in the shadows of the forest. He climbed out and stood rooted to the spot.

"What's wrong?" Raina said, closing her door on the other side.

"This isn't far from where it happened." He pointed to the silhouette of a small building not two hundred yards along the shore. "That's my friend's boathouse right over there. That's where they shot Liam."

She rounded the car to stand with him overlooking the water. "Try not to think about that now. We need to find Manheim."

Despite her words, she made no move to step from his side. She had her own memories of this place; the most recent, the night she'd stood atop Salvation Falls, the lake at her back, the plunge pool darkly beckoning below. The night this whole affair had begun.

Incredible how much had changed since then. Before that

night she hadn't thought about taking 'the step' in a long time. But her break-up with Brad had left her once more with the prospect of a bleak future.

She'd long ago been forced to accept that the family she longed for would likely never consist of more than two. But she *had* accepted it – she had no choice. Brad, on the other hand, did have a choice. And if *he* couldn't accept a childless marriage, what other man would?

What she'd been through these last few days had changed that perspective, she suddenly saw. It had filled her heart with the profound sense that saving a life forged a connection between two people as strong as any familial bond. Even if she never saw Erin again, if she could reunite the girl with her child she would carry that memory the rest of her life. In a sense she would never be alone again.

She found Alec's hand in the darkness and clutched it. "Come on. Let's do this."

Tearing his gaze from the distant scene, he nodded down at her. Together they stepped to the edge of the tree line and scanned the moonlit slope to the water.

"I don't see a cabin, do you?" he said.

"Are you sure this is the right lot number?"

He checked the back of his hand with the flashlight. "It's the one Manheim gave me on the phone. You think he meant that?" He aimed his light at the building at the water's edge. Another boathouse.

"Let's check it out."

They started down the path to the dock. With each step, Alec's feet grew heavier, his heart beating faster. Just like last time, his meeting with Liam. Had his dream of the same fate befalling Raina been not nightmare but premonition? Braced for an eruption of gun fire, he scanned the woods, the protection of which they were leaving behind.

The boathouse loomed dark and silent before them. As they stepped up onto its surrounding deck he spotted the paper taped to its door. He removed it and read it by the beam of his flashlight, then looked up to peer out over the water. "Damn."

"What's it say?"

He pointed to the row boat tied to the dock, then to the dark shape sprawled down the center of the lake. "He wants us to row over there."

"To the island?" Raina said, incredulous. She squinted but could see no lights or buildings. "I didn't know anyone lived over there."

"Maybe no-one does."

"What are you saying?"

He blew out a breath. "I'm saying the good doctor could be setting us up."

"A trap? How could it be? Manheim doesn't know we suspect him of anything. Look, his bringing us here makes perfect sense – he wants to make sure no-one followed us, that no-one else is around when we talk."

"There are other ways to assure seclusion." Alec shook his head. "No, this is all wrong. I don't like it."

"So does that mean you're ready to call the police?"

"No." He shoved the note in his pocket and the flashlight into the waist of his jeans, then turned to face her. "It means I'm going over there alone."

"Don't be ridiculous, I *have* to go. You said yourself it'll look more convincing if—"

"That was for a meeting. This is an ambush."

"We don't know that for sure. And even if it is, I still have to go." She pushed past him, heading for the boat.

He took her arm and turned her back. "I won't let you risk your life for me."

"You still don't get it, do you, DeMarco? I'm not doing this just for you."

He didn't let go.

"All right, look." She turned him and pointed out over the water. "Whatever's over there, we don't have to walk straight into it. On this side of the island there's a jetty like this one. It's the only one, the only place to tie up a boat. If this *is* a trap, that's where Manheim will likely be waiting."

"So?"

"So we won't go there. *We'll* row around to the other side, cut across the island, and come in behind him."

He gazed down into her upturned face. "I still don't like it."

"Neither do I. But he won't be expecting us to come that way. We surprise him, we'll have the upper hand." She reached in her bag and held up the gun. "Plus we won't be entirely defenseless."

She turned to clamber down into the boat. He stopped her with a hand on her arm. "Why, Raina? You've never given me an explanation. Why would you risk your life for either of us, Erin or me?"

She stared up at him. "We get through this and I promise I'll explain it all."

"You believe me though, right? What I told you before about why I went to Julie's apartment."

"Yes, I believe you."

The words sounded a touch too mechanical. Was she simply saying what he wanted to hear? "You still haven't told me where Erin is."

"Don't worry, she's safe."

He smiled at her evasive reply and let go of her arm. "You don't believe me at all, do you."

She sighed. "Want proof?" She picked up his hand and slapped the Remington into his palm. "Now come on, before I change my mind."

CHAPTER 114

From her vantage point among the trees, Erin watched the two figures climb in a boat and start rowing out across the lake. What the hell were they doing – going for a romantic moonlight dip?

The only thing out there was an island and their boat appeared to be heading straight for it. Was something on it? Or someone? She couldn't see any lights or houses. Still, if Raina and Alec were going there it had to have something to do with Cody.

Her breathing slowed. Then stopped altogether. A thought so horrible rose in her mind, for an instant she thought she'd be sick. What if the people who'd taken Cody had decided they didn't want him after all? They couldn't very well bring him back. What if something else had gone wrong? What if – she covered her mouth – they needed a safe place to bury the body? Someplace where he would never be found?

She recoiled a step, trying to distance herself from the thought. It couldn't be. Raina and Alec's presence here might be something far more simple. They'd found a clue. They were meeting someone. Someone who knew where Cody was. Or who'd asked them here so they could return him.

Then why hadn't Raina wanted her along?

She looked around. With no bridge to drive across to the island, she was left with the choice of sitting in her car until they returned or hopping in another boat to follow them.

Having come this far, and with what she now feared, the prospect of waiting was unbearable. She had to know what was happening! It was *her* baby they were trying to recover. She had a right to be there when they did.

As the boat glided further away from shore, she stepped out of the forest's shadows and sprinted down the slope to the dock. There were no other boats tied to its pylons.

She waited, staring out over the lake until she was sure where Raina and Alec were going, until their boat's shadow was swallowed whole by the black sprawling silhouette of the island.

Then she stripped off her jacket, took off her shoes and slipped silently into the water.

CHAPTER 115

Alec dragged the rowboat from the water and helped Raina out onto the sand.

A wall of dense forest rose before them, standing sentry to the island's interior. He started to wind his way inland, aiming the flashlight's beam at the ground, clutching the gun in his other hand.

About fifty yards in, they came to a clearing. Stumps of felled trees lined the perimeter in silent testament to pillaged firewood. A circle of smooth white stones glowed in the moonlight, marking the remains of a cooking fire.

"Looks like an old fishermen's camp," Raina whispered. "The tie-up dock is just through there."

The mournful hoot of an owl met her words. Before they could move in the direction she'd indicated, something rustled in the undergrowth off to their right. Alec swung the gun toward the sound. Then froze at the feel of a cold steel barrel pressed to his temple.

"Nice and easy," a male voice instructed.

As Alec stood immobile, a figure slipped from the shadows beside him and removed the Remington from his hand. Alec lifted the light to his face.

"Craig!" Raina burst out. "Oh, Craig, thank god!"

When the man relieved him of the flashlight as well, Alec stepped back. "You know this guy? What's he doing here? Where's Manheim?"

A sphere of golden light engulfed them as the stranger lit a lantern on a nearby rock.

"It's all right." Raina took his arm. "I'm sorry, I know I should've told you this sooner. Craig's an old friend. He...he's also one of our local deputies."

Alec wrenched his arm from her grasp. "You went to the cops?"

"Craig and I were talking days before you and I hooked up."

"And you didn't think to mention it to me?"

"Just the two of you?" Farrington cut in, keeping his gun fixed on Alec. "Where's the girl? I figured she'd come with you. I was sure she'd want to tag along."

"She did want to," Raina said. "We made her stay behind; we didn't know—"

"Behind, where? Where is she, Raina?"

Alec grabbed her arm before she could answer. "Don't tell him anything."

"Alec, please, it's okay. I told you, he's—"

"Can't you see what's happening here? He got Manheim to set up this meeting so he could ambush us. He's the cop Liam warned me about. *He* killed Liam."

CHAPTER 116

Erin hauled herself onto the bank. The water had been colder than she'd expected, the distance to the island far greater than it had looked from shore.

The minute the night air touched her skin she began to shiver, her teeth chattered. She crawled forward on hands and knees then collapsed in the rushes, catching her breath.

In the silence, she strained to listen. A murmur of voices drifted on the breeze, coming from somewhere deeper in the island's woods. Hugging herself, she pushed to her feet and started cautiously into the trees.

Twigs and pebbles stabbed her bare soles. Branches reached from the darkness to gouge her flesh. The voices, unidentified as yet, drew her like a moth to flame. She caught the warm glow of a lantern up ahead.

Crouched low, she tip-toed toward it. She wouldn't need to show herself. If it was just Raina and Alec talking, she could simply slip back into the water – a prospect she didn't particularly relish – swim ashore, get in her car, and return to the cabin well ahead of them. She'd be showered, dressed, and sitting on the couch watching TV by the time they got back. They'd never even know she was here.

Provided that was all that was going on.

As she neared the source, the voices got louder. One voice anyway – Alec's it sounded like. And not just because she was getting closer, because the man was talking louder. Upset about something. Shouting, in fact.

She slunk to the edge of a lantern-lit clearing and spotted three figures. Raina. Alec. And a man who's face she would never forget. The man who had taken Cody from her and, in the cold depths of that hospital basement, sold him to strangers. The man whose face she had failed to capture on her cell phone recording.

A man who's eyes she would claw from the sockets! If he weren't holding a gun.

CHAPTER 117

Fists clenched, Alec stepped toward the man with the gun.

Raina rushed forward to hold him back. "Alec, please, listen to me. You don't understand, I left Craig a note earlier today and told him about Manheim."

"You *what*?"

"Obviously he went to the clinic, found the evidence we needed, and arrested him. That's why *he's* here instead of…"

She stood a moment then turned around slowly. If Farrington knew why Liam had been killed, why was he holding a gun on Alec? "Craig?"

"I know you've been helping the girl," he said. "You need to tell me where she is so we can put an end to this."

"Put an end to it how?"

The man didn't answer.

"Craig, for god's sake, what are you…" For a moment she feared her legs would give way. "Alec's right? It was you? *You* killed his brother?"

"It was necessary, Raina. There was no other way."

"Necessary? You son of a—" Alec broke off when the gun swung toward him.

"I don't believe it," Raina stammered. "You were so... All that talk about..." Unable to process the magnitude of the man's deception, she choked on the words. "And now you want to kill Erin as well?"

"I wouldn't if there was any other way, believe me."

Comprehension struck like a blow. "That's why you've been offering to help me all this time?" As the truth burrowed deeper she found her confusion turning to anger.

Ignoring the gun, she took a step toward him. "*That's* why you were so willing to forget my past. All that crap about second chances... You didn't care, you just wanted to find Erin and Alec, and you thought I knew where they were."

The man shook his head. "You're wrong. I cared deeply. I still do. So much so I'd be willing to walk away from everything to make you happy, to give you what you've always wanted."

"*What?* What are you talking about?" Her hands balled into fists at her side. "You have no idea what I want."

"Oh, but I do, Raina. I do." The man eased closer. "You forget I was there all those years ago. Not just at the scene of your accident but afterwards, those first few days you were there in the hospital."

The words knocked her back. Yes, of course he knew. He'd always known.

"I was there with Scanlon when they told him. That the accident didn't just kill his son, it took the life of your unborn child – yours and Rick's. A child you didn't even know you were carrying till you woke in the hospital and they told you it was gone. Along with any chance of your having another one."

She squeezed shut her eyes. *Don't. Please.*

Another step closer. "You were too young to understand

the impact it would have on the rest of your life, what it would mean. But you've learned since, haven't you, Raina? All these years you've been alone, unable to have a child, a felony record destroying any hope of adopting. Those things don't mean so much when you're young, but as you get older it starts to matter. It certainly mattered to Brad, didn't it?"

Her eyes flew open. "You bastard."

He was at her side now, all but whispering his words in her ear. "Is that why you've been helping the girl? I understand perfectly if it was. Her baby was already stolen, the crime concealed. Help her find it and you could keep it yourself. Was that your plan?"

Raina gaped at the man in horror. A man she had once thought stable and kind. How could she have been so wrong about him?

"It's okay, really, I understand. A girl like that isn't fit to raise a child. None of them are. That was the whole reason Manheim and Kilburn set up the program."

She didn't know how much more she could listen to. "What do you want from me?"

"You still don't understand what I'm saying. It's not what I want, it's what I can give you." He touched her arm. "A baby, Raina. A child of your own."

Her mouth dropped open. More than cruel, more than self-serving, the man was insane.

"That's what you want more than anything, isn't it? Your own family? I can get you one. I've even made sure Scanlon never bothers you again."

She recoiled. "My god, Craig, what have you done?"

"Raina listen. We could get married, raise the baby together, you and me. In a couple of years there might even be another one."

Alec stood stunned by what he was hearing. He understood now what Manheim had found in examining Raina, her reasons for wanting to help Erin. This man's offer must be absolute torture. Was it too much? "Raina, don't listen."

Craig lifted his hand to her face. "I alone know how much you've changed. Scanlon was blind but I could see. What I said that day in the café... I meant every word. You'd make a wonderful mother. You deserve a child of your own. All you have to do is tell me where the girl is and it can all be yours. Where is she, Raina? Where's Erin?"

Fury rose like venom in her throat. "Go to hell."

The man deflated. His hand cupped her cheek a moment longer, then dropped to his side. "I'm so sorry you feel that way."

His expression hardened. He took a step back. "Last chance, Raina." He lifted the gun to aim at her chest.

"No!"

The three turned in unison to gape at the figure that stepped from the shadows.

"You want me, asshole? Here I am."

CHAPTER 118

Raina swung toward the sound of the voice. "Erin, no! What are you doing here?"

The girl ignored her, her gaze on Farrington. "I know you. You were there that night at the hospital, the night they sold Cody. You were one of them." She took a step closer, oblivious to the gun in his hand. "Where is he? Where's my baby?"

Farrington laughed and turned to Raina. "See, I told you she'd come." His look for the girl held utter contempt. "What are you so angry about? You should be thanking me. He's got a good home. Better than any you could've given him."

"Where is he?" Erin repeated. "What have you done with him?"

With Farrington between them, Raina couldn't reach her to stop her words. But Alec was there. As the girl stepped past him, he reached out and hauled her back, holding her tightly as Raina turned to confront their captor.

"Craig, how could you do this? How could you separate a mother from her child?"

"Mother?" He laughed. "Any ally cat can produce

offspring. Manheim and Kilburn make certain *their* mothers are fit to raise a child."

"So they do all the work and you get the money," Alec threw at him. "Is that how it works?" He was fighting to hold himself back as well, fearful of endangering Raina and Erin, yet wanting nothing more than to get his hands on this man who'd killed Liam.

"You know nothing," Farrington told him. "It's not about money. Not for any of us. It never has been. The parents we select are screened more rigorously than they would be by any adoption agency. We look at everything about them, from income to morals."

Raina stared at the man before her, his voice so impassioned, his body taut with indignation. No, clearly this wasn't about money. Not for Craig Farrington.

"Morals like yours?" Alec challenged him. *Oh please, just give me a chance to get at you.* "Who are you to decide who's fit and who isn't?"

Farrington shrugged. "Who do I need to be? It's simple, really." He pointed to the girl Alec clutched in his arms. "Sluts like her don't deserve to be mothers."

"Screw you!" Erin screamed, making Alec grunt with her struggles.

"Women so doped up they don't even feed their kids half the time," the man raved on. "Don't even know when their child is sick and in need of urgent medical care."

"I'm not an addict!" Erin cried.

In a flash of insight his meaning hit home. Raina stepped toward him, making the connection. "But your mother was. Wasn't she, Craig?"

The circle fell silent. In the lantern light she saw his jaw tighten. Her hunch had been right. "Is that why you're doing this? Your mother was an addict. She left you alone when you were sick?"

She watched his fingers working the gun grip. Had they pushed him too far?

"Not me, my sister." A different emotion now strained his voice. "I came home from school and found her cold and blue in her crib while our *mother* lay doped to the gills in the next room.

"They put me with a foster family after that. A good one." He glared back at Alec. "So don't tell me I don't know the difference. Don't tell me I haven't the right to judge who's suitable and who isn't. I know firsthand the difference a decent home can make. A difference I'm now making in the lives of these kids. Kids in need. Kids like *hers*."

"You're wrong! You don't know anything! I love my baby!" Erin fought against Alec's grip.

Holding his gun on the struggling pair, Farrington moved to gaze down at Raina. "There was a time I thought you were like her," he whispered. "Ten years ago maybe you were, or at least heading in that direction. But you've changed. Anyone could see it if they looked."

His hand rose again to cup her cheek. "You have so much love in you to give. Don't let it go to waste, Raina. Let me make it happen for you. Let me get you the child you've always wanted." He pointed to Erin. "You can even have hers if you want."

With a scream of rage, the girl broke free of Alec's grip and charged her tormenter. In the same instant Raina shoved at his hand, knocking the gun. His shot went wild. The force with which Erin barreled into him, kicking and clawing, drove all three of them to the ground.

He tossed the girl aside like a doll. As Alec pulled her to

her feet, the deputy stayed on hands and knees, clawing the mulch.

He'd dropped the gun!

"Run!" Alec pushed Erin toward the woods and threw himself at the man on the ground.

Rage overrode the pain in his side as they wrestled and fought, but couldn't compensate for his weakness. He was no match for a man in his prime. Not without some kind of—

Pinned beneath Farrington's heaving bulk, he felt a branch jab at his back. He rolled free, struggled to his feet, grabbed up the club, and raised it for a lethal blow.

Just as Farrington pulled a second gun from his pocket.

Grim with defeat, raging inside, Alec dropped the branch and put up his hands. The clearing was empty but for the two of them. At least Raina and Erin had escaped.

Farrington held up the gun and shrugged. "Forgot I had yours." He raised it to fire.

Alec kicked at the lantern beside him. It smashed against a rock and darkness enveloped them.

CHAPTER 119

Raina broke through the last bit of undergrowth and emerged onto the island's rocky shore. It had torn her heart to leave Alec behind, but Erin's safety had taken priority. Yet despite her efforts, she'd been unable to find the girl in the dark as they'd fled the clearing in different directions. And she hadn't dared call out to either of them for fear Farrington would hear.

To make matters worse the man had taken her phone so she had no way to call for help. Their only chance was to make it ashore and get to the car. Hopefully Erin would have enough sense to get off the island any way she could. As Raina now had to do herself.

But which way was it? In her flight, she'd lost all sense of direction. The land she could see across the water might be the *other* side of the lake. In which case, if she crossed here, her car would be miles through dense forest from where she landed.

She scanned the island in both directions. The boat she and Alec had rowed across in was nowhere in sight. If she went in search of it, either combing the shore or back through the woods, Farrington would be sure to spot her. In the water she'd be less of a target. She could swim out till she got her bearings, spotted some landmark, then... Quickly she threw off her jacket and shoes, and ran into the lake.

The minute she was a stone's throw out she turned to scan the island for movement. Nothing stirred. Erin must've come out somewhere else. If Alec had gotten away from Farrington the two of them might even be together. Hopefully *they* would find the boat. And if they didn't, they could swim for it.

Assuming they made it as far as the water.

She pushed back her fear. Of course they'd make it. She hadn't heard any gunshots. The fact she and Erin had run in different directions would surely have given them an advantage. Farrington could only—

A belated perception sprang to her mind. Erin had been soaking wet in the clearing, suggesting she had swum to the island. Would she have the strength to swim back again? And Alec with his gunshot wound?

Raina turned to gauge the distance. As deceptively close as objects tended to appear over water, the stretch before her seemed enormous. Even someone fit and rested would struggle to—

Shots rang out from the woods to her left. *No!*

She swam toward the sound, paralleling the island's shore. Near the spit that marked its furthest reach – from which the sounds seemed to have come – she stopped, treading water, gasping for breath.

She watched for any hint of movement – a figure darting out of the trees, the wink of a flashlight, the flare of more gunfire.

Not a sound floated on the rising wind. Not a shadow stirred at the forest's edge.

CHAPTER 120

Alec groped through the tightly-packed trees, clutching Erin's hand to keep them together.

He'd literally stumbled into the girl after fleeing the clearing. Distressed at finding her so close by, all on her own – he'd hoped she and Raina would be well on their way to shore by then – he was bent on getting her as far from Farrington as fast as the poor visibility allowed.

The shots the cop had fired at them, while surely blind, had come way too close for comfort. Indeed this entire insane scenario was far too similar to his frenzied flight the night Liam had been killed at the boathouse.

Erin tripped, nearly bringing him down as well. He pulled her back up and hurried on, dodging tree trunks, ducking under branches, shouldering underbrush aside. With no idea which way they were going, his aim was to simply run a straight line. If they went far enough in any direction they had to reach the water.

They plunged through a final thicket of undergrowth. Starry sky opened above them. But unlike the sandy bank he and Raina had landed on earlier, a rocky spit stretched before them.

Two steps further, he nearly went down when a stone rolled beneath his foot. With Erin clinging to his side, he reassessed their situation.

In all but the direction from which they'd come, yards of jumbled rock lay in wait to twist an ankle, break a leg. At best their progress would be slow. Worse, they'd be fully exposed till they reached the water. Yet the only other way was back through the forest.

A forest in which a killer waited.

CHAPTER 121

Raina spit out a mouthful of water. Wind was plowing the lake into furrows and hurling foamy crests in her face. Half blown, half by her struggling efforts, she cleared the island's rocky point and started around the other side.

On its shore, two silhouettes emerged from the trees, one slightly ahead of the other. When the larger figure grabbed the smaller she stifled a cry. *No! Bastard! Leave her alone!*

Almost at once they were moving again, starting across the rocks together, the larger clearly *helping* the smaller. Her heart leapt. Alec and Erin!

Raina kicked herself up in the water as high as possible and started waving. She thought she saw Alec's arm reach out, pointing her way, but she couldn't be sure.

For agonizing moments she watched them pick their way over the rocks, arms outstretched like tightrope walkers in their fight for balance. A balancing act taking far too long!

Watching for movement at the edge of the woods, she willed them faster. *Move it, DeMarco. Keep her going. Put her on your back if you have to.*

At last they made it to the water's edge, stumbled out

through the reeds and shallows, and started swimming in her direction. If she stayed where she was they'd soon catch up.

She watched the island shore behind them. No sign of Farrington. They might just make it out of this alive. The deputy would surely have a boat of his own, but without knowing which way they'd gone, he could row around for ages before—

She strained to hear above the lapping of water, the rising wind. From behind the island had come a faint sound.

For a moment nothing. Then she heard it again. The breeze caught it and carried it toward her.

An outboard motor sputtering to life.

Her heart sank. A power boat! With that much speed, Farrington could circle the lake till he found them, then either shoot them where they floated or run them down.

She started waving the others aside. In the water they were sitting ducks. They had to get ashore and fast. Whether they saw her or heard the engine, Alec and Erin appeared to be veering in that direction. She mirrored their course.

With frantic strokes, she fought through the water, then stopped to gauge her new position. She didn't appear to be making much headway. Nor did the others. If anything, they seemed to be moving further from land and drifting out toward the center of the lake.

Something was coming up on her right, a few yards off. A tiny island, no more than a rock with a sapling on top. A point of reference. One she was approaching much faster than she would've expected. And definitely moving in the wrong—

A ragged cry broke from her throat. Not a rock with a tree. The warning marker!

By the time she realized what it was, she was too far past to grab a hold. It hardly mattered. The beacon was for boats anyway, ones with power to fight the current. Any swimmers who'd strayed this far were in its grip and had little hope of turning back.

But Erin and Alec still had a chance.

"Cut over!" she screamed. "Swim! Get ashore. Aim for the marker."

Even to her own ears, her voice sounded weak, a feeble cry lost on the wind and buffeted by an approaching rumble. A strengthening din, a deepening thunder.

The growing roar of Salvation Falls.

CHAPTER 122

Erin floundered, straining her neck, trying to keep Raina in sight. "What is she saying? I can't hear her."

"I don't know. Just keep going."

With a hand at her back, Alec pushed her through the water, the pain in his side flaring with every stroke he took. He didn't want to say, didn't want to *think*, what it looked like to him – that Raina was in trouble. Was she snagged on something? Had she gotten a cramp? The way she was screaming and flailing her arms—

"I thought she was waving us toward the shore," Erin spluttered. "So why's she going over that way?"

Caught by the question, he looked around. "Why are *we*?"

He double-checked and saw it was true. With all their swimming they should've been closer to land than this. Instead they were moving further away.

And as if that wasn't bad enough…

He cocked his head in Raina's direction. "What's that sound?"

Erin's eyes flew open wide. "Oh my god, the current." She grabbed his shoulder. "We have to get to Raina. We have to help her!"

When she tried to swim off, he held her back. "Erin! What—?"

"The falls!" She coughed on a mouthful water. "There's a marker, a sign. Once you pass it the current's too strong, you can't get back. She's nearly there!"

Still clutching her arm, Alec looked past her. He could see the marker now. A pillar of rock in the middle of the lake, looming up fast. They were definitely being pulled by the current.

"We're too close. I don't want you getting caught as well. Head for shore; I'll help Raina."

"No, I'm coming—"

"Don't argue. Go!" His shove propelled her all of two feet. At once she was beside him again. As though an unseen hand had shoved her back.

CHAPTER 123

The roar of the falls drowned out her cries. Raina could no longer see the others. She was barely keeping her head above the surface. The current had spun her around in the water, turned her to meet her fate face-on.

The jagged rim of the lake spread before her. Silhouetted against the night sky, boulders framed the surging spillway, a black hole into which she and everything around her was being pulled, to be spewed forth into open space.

And a two-story drop to the rocks below.

Tossed and dipped, she was carried toward it, a leaf in a storm gutter, fighting to pull from the current's grip. Her efforts useless. The lake rapidly receded behind her as more and more of the sky filled her view. Sky, boulders and—

Yes, something there! A giant hand rising out of the water, fingers of wood. A fallen tree still anchored to land, reaching out from one edge of the spillway. A bare ten feet of wrist-thick branches to which she might cling.

If they were strong enough. If she could reach them.

CHAPTER 124

"Come on, swim!" Alec continued to push Erin forward. His pain was gone, his side numb. A lead weight threatening to drag him under.

The girl tried a few more fruitless strokes, then gave up, clearly needing all her strength just to keep her face above water.

They clung together, the landscape sweeping by much faster. They wouldn't make it to shore, that was certain, but they were heading straight for the warning marker. A tiny man-sized lump of granite with a sign on top. Provided the current didn't drag them off course—

Swimming his hardest, he shoved her toward it. "Grab on!"

She clawed at the rock, fingernails scraping, nearly swept past before finding a crevice. Another handhold. She pulled herself up, wrapped her arms around the sign.

He latched on beside her, gasping for breath.

Panic receded. They'd made it. They'd done it! The current was strong but not overpowering. They could hang on. Even if they had to cling here all night, someone would eventually come and find them.

And Raina?

He lifted his head. At the edge of the world, just a stone's throw further, granite arms beckoned him toward oblivion. But in the waters rushing to fill that void... No figure bobbed. No arms waved. No voice cried out.

Raina was gone.

Before the pain could even register, a sound from behind them. He snapped his gaze back toward the island. To find a motorboat bearing down on them.

CHAPTER 125

Ten feet from the lip of the falls, Raina clung to the fallen tree, its limbs trembling in her grasp. Alec and Erin had not gone past her. Either they'd managed to make it ashore or had reached the relative safety of the marker.

Hand over hand, hauling herself against the current, she pulled herself along the tree. Its smaller twigs had been worn away by the swirling water. A slimy trunk with a few slender offshoots polished smooth were all that remained. The tree lay wedged against one of the boulders that framed the spillway – rock too steep and slick with moss to provide a grip. She worked her way further along, searching for a way to climb up.

At last a toe-hold. She wedged her foot on the nubble of rock sticking out below the surface. Pushed herself up. Slid her hand higher. Groping. Searching—

Gunshots rang out from the lake behind her.

She whipped around. Held her breath. Strained to see anything amid the splinters of moonlight shimmering across the face of the lake.

Two figures swept into view, bobbing helplessly in the

swell, heading for the falls. A larger silhouette close behind –
a man in a speed boat – moving independently of the current.

Scrambling back the way she'd come, Raina rushed to
intercept. The falls were a good twenty feet across and the
branch extended only a few feet out from one side. But if Alec
and Erin saw her in time, they might be able to direct their
course far enough over that she could grab them. *If* she could
get their attention away from the man in the powerboat
shooting at them!

As the pair swept closer, the boat veered aside. Farrington,
no doubt confident the falls would finish them, was opting not
to risk the stronger current near the edge. Having reached the
furthest end of the tree, Raina shouted to Alec and Erin.
Whether they'd heard her, or just blind luck, they were
moving toward her.

The boat had started to circle back. While Farrington was
still turned away, Raina strained forward and stretched out her
hand. Clinging to Erin, Alec fought to close the gap. Not fast
enough! But a last-second whim of the current delivered them
both into her arms.

Together they worked back along the tree to the foothold
Raina had found earlier. Alec climbed up onto the boulder
and reached down for Erin as Raina gave her a push from
below. With the girl safe on the rock beside him, he hoisted
Raina up as well.

Raina peered over the other side. Moonlight shimmered in
the plunge pool below. But nearer... The ledge! A drop of
maybe ten feet at most. And from there a climb down a few
granite tiers to the woods and safety. They could do it if they
worked together. She glanced behind her – Farrington's boat
was nearly around. Not so easy if the man started shooting
again.

"Erin first," she shouted above the roar of the falls.

Alec looked where she was pointing, saw the way, and helped the girl slide down onto the ledge. He jumped down beside her, turned and reached up his arms for Raina.

Poised to take that final leap, Raina screamed and dropped where she stood.

CHAPTER 126

Cold hard dampness pressed to her cheek. A pillow of stone, her head leaning over the side. The sound of a freight train rushing toward her. Fire lapping at her skull.

Raina blinked the scene into focus – two frantic faces staring up at her, mouths open, screams drowned by the roar of the...

Not a train. The falls.

Alec and Erin. Their hands straining toward her from a lower ledge, just out of reach. Beyond them in the canyon below, a plunge pool glittering in the moonlight, edged by the black of surrounding boulders.

Like those swirling waters, her thoughts circled and eddied back, adrift from the present. *Salvation Falls. This was the place. The very spot I stood five days ago, debating...*

With a gasp at the pain, she pushed herself to sit up on the rock. Blood streamed down over her shoulder. She felt for the source. A graze on her temple. From a bullet that hadn't quite found the mark!

She spun around. Farrington's boat was bearing down on her, the man at the wheel taking aim with his rifle.

Before she could dodge, the shot rang out.

Raina felt nothing. Dumbstruck, frozen, she watched instead as the man fell forward across the controls. The boat's engine spluttered and died.

Farrington shot? But who— How—?

Her gaze skimmed the water, the rocks, the shore, then rose to the ledge overlooking the falls.

The silhouette of a lone figure stood staring down at her. A hunter who'd seen what was happening and intervened? Who else but Manheim could know they were here?

Farrington's boat, now caught in the current, was still coming toward her, picking up speed. With the engine stalled and no-one to steer, it was drifting steadily toward the falls. If the man inside was still alive he'd be swept to his death in a matter of seconds.

She scrambled out to the end of the boulder. Flopped on her belly, she reached in the water and snagged the prow as it came within reach.

Anchored by her grip, the craft swung around, the pull nearly dragging her off the rock. The stern swept past. The hull scraped bottom, catching on the granite below as it breached the falls. Not enough to counter the relentless surge.

The boat nosed out over the drop-off. Two feet. Four.

Arms trembling against the strain, Raina held on. From the corner of her eye she caught sight of the ledge below – Alec and Erin huddled together, watching her battle.

Movement drew her gaze back to the boat. The silhouette of the man sitting up. Craig. Alive.

"Get out!" Her scream a whisper in the deafening roar. "I can't hold it!"

He seemed to have heard. The shape rose higher, inching toward her, his movements clumsy in the teetering craft.

She felt herself sliding further off the rock. "Give me your hand!"

His arm reached out. Moonlight glinted off something in his grasp. A hand raised not in want of rescue but aiming his gun. At the pair below.

"Craig, no!"

Fighting for balance to get a clean shot, he fixed Alec and Erin in his sights.

Raina let go, threw herself back.

And watched the boat vanish over the side.

CHAPTER 127

On the far side of the falls Raina clambered down tiers of granite, leading the others toward the safety of the forest. Her head throbbed, her muscles quaked from cold and fatigue. Just a little further and they could rest.

Where rock turned to pine needles beneath her bare feet she entered the shadows in search of the dirt track out to the road. Darkness threw its thick cloak over them where branches entwined to block out the moon.

Up ahead a light appeared moving through the trees. Someone with a flashlight. The man who'd shot Craig? Manheim? Kilburn? Another accomplice? Whoever it was, it was too late to run.

Clutching Erin, with Alec's arms around them both, she winced when the light beam caught their faces. Almost at once it swung away. The large figure aiming it hurried toward them. "Is anyone hurt?"

At hearing the voice, she gripped Erin tighter. Certainly not someone she had expected and hardly a friend. Yet the question he'd asked…

She wiped a drop of blood from her eye. "Just cuts and

bruises I think. Nothing serious."

"All right, sit down then, all of you. Help's on its way."

Help? Was she hearing him right?

The others stood rigid.

"It's okay," she told them. "Do as he says."

Alec whispered close to her ear. "You know him? Who is he?"

Raina nodded. Yes, she knew him all right. But how...? She put a hand to her head.

Erin slumped down onto a log. The man with the flashlight took off his jacket and draped it around her trembling shoulders. She looked up at him. "Who are you?"

"Police Chief Scanlon."

Raina felt Alec tense beside her. "What are you doing here?"

"Following a tip-off."

Her head was spinning. Concussion, blood-loss, delayed shock? A tip-off from whom? Someone had told him about the ambush? That Manheim had called them, directing them here? Said he would meet them but sent in his place...

She caught her breath.

"*You* shot the cop in the boat?" Alec said, putting voice to her thoughts.

Scanlon looked toward the top of the falls. Long seconds passed but he gave no reply.

Behind him, flickers of light pierced the night. Patrol cars pulled up along the dirt tract. "Stay here," he said. "I'll get someone to drive you to the hospital."

CHAPTER 128

She had been here before. Too many times. Sitting on this very station house bench, watching the seconds tick by on the clock. Waiting to speak to Chief John Scanlon. The only difference was, this time Alec DeMarco sat with her.

Raina looked up at Scanlon's closed office door. Questions and fears churned inside her like worms in an apple. Questions only he could answer.

He hadn't accompanied them to the hospital last night but remained at the falls to oversee the scene and the recovery of Craig Farrington's body. She and Alec had given their statements to Deputy Hendricks, but been informed this morning that Scanlon wished to see them following their release from the hospital. Fine. She needed to see him as well. *So where the hell are you?*

"You okay?" Alec squeezed her hand. "How's your head?"

She touched the bandage above her eye. "I'll live." Though the cut had required only three stitches it still throbbed. She hardly noticed. The important thing was Erin had come through their ordeal unscathed. Physically at least.

Raina cast an anxious glance toward the hallway down which the girl had been escorted. When they'd first arrived an hour ago, driven from the hospital by Deputy Hendricks, Erin had refused to be separated from them. Only after repeated assurances that Raina and Alec would remain close by – in the next room speaking with Scanlon in fact – had she agreed to accompany the female officer and social worker to give her statement.

Sensing Raina's fears from the direction of her gaze, Alec slid his arm about her shoulders. "She'll be okay. They'll look after her."

Despite his assertions, Alec was every bit as concerned as Raina. It seemed in his quest to find Liam's killers he'd committed himself to another far greater – to help this girl reclaim her life. To see this courageous persevering soul united with her stolen child.

Raina gave him a half-hearted nod. Yes, Erin was physically safe. Yes, she was being treated kindly, her claims and story finally listened to. But none of them could have any idea at this point just how 'okay' this would all turn out.

She settled herself as best she could, clutching Alec's hand in both of hers. One thing she had come to have total faith in was this man's commitment to Erin. He'd stayed by her side through her admission last night and initial questioning, refusing treatment until the girl was sedated and asleep in bed. Even if nothing more came of their time together, Raina was heartened the two had formed such a bond.

From the corner of her eye she took in the profile of the man beside her. What she wasn't nearly as certain about was where things stood between the two of *them*. A spark ignited under dangerous circumstances might fizzle in the routine of day-to-day life. A matter they would have to shelve for the moment until others more pressing had been addressed.

She gazed toward the door. *Damn it, Scanlon—*

When the chief appeared, trudging grimly through the squad room, she surged to her feet, Alec at her side, and together they stepped to the door of his office. Whether sensing her urgency or planning to do so in any case, Scanlon opened it and ushered them in.

Even as he was rounding his desk, before they'd even taken their seats, Raina burst out with a question that had plagued her all night. "How did you know about Farrington's ambush? How did you know to go to the lake?"

Scanlon motioned them both into the chairs, then took the one behind his desk. "Between what you told me on the phone, what I found on the girl's video, and other evidence we had on file, we had enough to arrest Manheim and Kilburn. We went to the clinic and found Kilburn but unfortunately got nothing out of her. She killed herself before we could question her."

Raina's hand flew to her mouth. "Oh my god." As the ramifications of his words sank in, she rose in her chair. "But Manheim? You found him? He was still alive?"

"Luckily Manheim didn't share *all* the woman's fanatical views. He folded the instant he heard she was dead. I told him things would go easier on him if he cooperated and he confessed to setting up the ambush. Told me where it was and who was meeting you."

Raina sank back into the chair, needing a moment to find her voice. "Then you knew it was Craig when you shot him in the boat."

Scanlon stared down at his hand on the desk. That he would kill a man he'd known and worked with all these years, a man he might well have come to regard as a second son, attested to the depth of his principles. Principles she had once feared he'd lost.

In lieu of an answer he replied, "Deputy Farrington put a track on your friend Julie Cramer's bank account, presumably hoping she'd lead him to you. She rang us this morning by the way."

Raina blinked at him. "You heard from Julie? She's all right?" Another of the matters that had been worrying her.

"She's been staying with a friend in New Hampshire. She saw on the news that the situation here had been resolved and wanted you to know she was all right." Scanlon shifted his gaze to Alec. "According to Cramer, you were the one who told her to leave the area for a while."

"I had a hunch that, as Raina's best friend, she might be in danger." Alec frowned. "So this Deputy Farrington lit the fire in her apartment?"

"We're not certain of his motive at this stage," Scanlon said. "It's possible he was trying to scare Cramer into telling him where you were. Or he may have thought she was inside, and that she knew something and he wanted to silence her. We may never have the whole story on that." He looked back at Raina. "She asked if you had a spare room she could stay in until she finds a new place."

Raina smiled but didn't have long to enjoy her relief. A knock on the door ushered Erin into the room.

CHAPTER 129

Erin stood taking in the man before her. "They said you wanted to see me too."

Scanlon motioned her into the room. "Yes, come in, have a seat."

She settled into the chair beside Raina. Shoulders stiff, jaw clenched, she returned Scanlon's gaze unflinchingly.

The man leaned back. "First of all I want to assure you we're doing everything we can to find your baby."

"Cody," she said.

Something in the tone of that single word turned Raina's head. In their time together Erin had on several occasions alluded to encounters she'd had with the police. By the attitude she was now exhibiting, it would seem those encounters had not been pleasant.

"Cody," Scanlon echoed. "Doctor Manheim has handed over all his records relating to the adoption operation and we're currently following every lead. In the meantime we have another matter to address, primarily where you will reside. Assuming we do find Cody, there's a shelter in Portland for homeless teens that—"

"No, no way," Erin cut in. "I'm not going to any shelter."

Raina reached over and touched her arm. "Perhaps just listen to what he—"

"No! I'm not bringing Cody to a place like that." Her voice was rising. "I won't do it. They can't make me."

"In fact they can." The room fell silent at Scanlon's pronouncement.

Alec leaned forward. "Couldn't she just rent an apartment? If it's a question of money..."

"It isn't that."

"Well, clearly the shelter isn't an option," Raina argued. The thought of further complications after all they'd been through was too much to bear. "How can you force her, she's done nothing wrong. Erin's the victim in all of this."

"No-one's debating that." Scanlon lowered the hand he had raised in a call for silence. "Sadly, she's also only sixteen."

"Sixteen?" Raina turned to the girl beside her. "But you told us..."

Erin hung her head. "Nurse Kilburn helped me lie on the forms so they'd give me money for my own place. If they'd found out I was only sixteen they would've put me in one of those shelters."

"And Manheim and Kilburn wouldn't have gotten their hands on her baby," Alec concluded in disgust.

Erin's look was growing increasingly desperate. "I'm *not* going into another shelter. I swear I'll run away if they make me."

"Your only alternative," Scanlon said calmly, "would be to enter into foster care. But as we currently have a shortage of homes, it's unlikely we'd find a family prepared to take both you and your baby."

"You mean we'd be separated?"

"This is insane." Raina thumped the arm of her chair. "You can't let this happen."

"There's not a lot I can do I'm afraid."

The room fell silent.

"What if..." Erin turned to Raina. "What if Cody and I lived with you? Just until I'm eighteen that is, then we'd move out." The girl gripped her arm. "We wouldn't be any trouble, I swear. I'll take care of him, help out with housework, anything you want."

Seeing the look of hope in her eyes, hearing the desperate plea in her voice, Raina's heart shattered. How would she explain...

Scanlon rose behind his desk. "I'm expecting a delivery. I'll just be a moment."

He went out the door, leaving deathly silence in his wake. Raina stared at his empty chair. Checking a delivery at this precise moment? Or unwilling to hear what he knew was coming?

Erin sat waiting for her reply.

Raina took a deep breath and blew it out again. "There's something I need to tell you. Both of you." She reached for Alec's hand as well. Only with the support of both of them could she speak the words. "Ten years ago I made the biggest mistake of my life. I drove home drunk from a party, had an accident, and killed my passenger."

Erin's eyes widened. She was already bracing herself for the worst. A habit she'd no doubt learned all too well in her short troubled life.

"I wasn't much older than you at the time," Raina went on. "We were celebrating my eighteenth birthday."

"Did you go to jail?" the girl breathed.

"Because I was young and had recently lost my father..." Raina shifted her gaze to Alec, "...and because I suffered permanent life-altering injuries in the crash..." She saw comprehension dawn in his eyes and finished her sentence, "The judge let me off with a reduced sentence. However..." She looked back at Erin. "Vehicular manslaughter, the crime for which I was convicted, is a Class B Felony."

Erin swallowed. "What does that mean?"

"Among other things..." she squeezed the girl's hand, "...it means I can never foster or adopt a child."

As her words sank in, Erin's face crumpled. "You can't take us? Even if you wanted to."

"Oh sweetheart, I do want to, more than anything. You have to believe that."

Erin stared down. "So that's it. They're going to send me and Cody to that place. Well, they can't do it." She surged to her feet. "I'm not going!"

She rushed to the door just as Scanlon was coming back in. Ducking past him, she raced out across the squad room. Behind her, Raina and Alec came to a stop when Scanlon put up a hand to block them. "I just need one more minute with Raina."

Alec nodded after the girl. "I'll take care of her." He rushed out and followed Erin across the squad room.

Raina watched till they vanished from sight. Reluctantly she stepped back inside and returned to her chair. As Scanlon walked around his desk, he dropped an envelope into her lap.

"What's this?" she croaked.

The man took his seat. "Given the circumstances – the impact of what Erin's been through and the extent to which you and she have bonded – Social Services have agreed to allow her to reside with you temporarily."

Raina looked up. "For how long?"

"Two weeks."

She nearly laughed. Two weeks. Just long enough for the girl to feel settled, to feel she belonged, for the first tentative roots to form. Before they yanked her away again, tearing those fragile bonds to shreds.

Raina studied the man before her, his expression giving nothing away, a face divulging not the barest hint of how he felt about the agency's decision.

Did she even need to ask?

Indeed, he'd not said a single word regarding her involvement in the whole affair. Less than forty-eight hours ago he'd been hell-bent on convicting her of the murder of Liam DeMarco. Yet now, with her innocence proved beyond doubt...

Professionally of course he was under no obligation to apologize; he'd just been doing his job. But personally? With the history they shared?

Clearly, in his eyes nothing had changed. He might be prepared to kill his deputy in the line of duty, but when it came to forgiving her the death of his son...

"And Erin's baby?" she managed at last.

"If he's found within that two-week period the child can reside with you as well. There are conditions, of course. It's all in there." Scanlon pointed to the pages in her hand.

"And when the two weeks are up?"

"Provision will be made for them at the shelter."

The pressure continued to build inside her. She leaned forward. "I'd take them both in a heartbeat, you know that."

The man stared back.

Clutching the envelope, Raina rose and rushed from the room.

CHAPTER 130

Raina sat on the hospital couch holding Erin's hand tightly in hers. They were alone in the lounge, not even Alec permitted to join them, much to his dismay. Just two social workers and one police officer standing up the hall. An officer by the name of Chief John Scanlon.

Raina stole glances at the man as she waited. They hadn't spoken since the meeting in his office three days ago. True to his word he'd overseen the search for Erin's baby with all due diligence and had notified them only that morning of a possible lead.

For all the good it would do any of them.

For what had to be the tenth time in the hour they'd been waiting, Erin jumped up and resumed pacing. Raina let her do a few restless circuits of the room, then reached out and pulled her back down beside her.

"I can't sit still," she admitted tearfully. "You really think it's him? You really think they could've found Cody already?"

Raina slipped an arm around her shoulders. As much as she wanted to comfort the girl, she didn't want to build up her hopes. Only four days after Farrington's death, Manheim's arrest, and the exposure of their long-running racket, it did seem soon for any of the stolen babies to be recovered. Still, as the last one adopted out, Erin's might've been the easiest to track.

"Even if it isn't Cody this time," she said, "They're sure to find him eventually."

"Yeah, but...they wouldn't have called us down here if they didn't think... I mean...the test should confirm it, right?"

Raina squeezed her hand. "We'll know soon."

Erin hung her head, emotion suddenly getting the better of her. "What does it matter? Even if it's him I won't get to keep him."

"What are you talking about? Of course you will. Who told you—"

"What I mean is, maybe I *shouldn't* keep him." She looked up to judge the impact of her words. "I want him to be raised in a real home, not one of those places. So I've been thinking..." She swallowed. "Maybe I should just give him up."

"Sweetheart, look...if you really can't bear the thought of Cody in a shelter, you wouldn't have to give him up for adoption. You could put him into foster care. Just until you're old enough to take him yourself."

"And what then? Even if he did want to come and live with me, it'll be like tearing him away from the people he's used to. People who love him." Her head bowed further. "The people he loves."

Raina swallowed, unable to speak.

"I just want to see him, that's all. Just hold him. Just once." Erin wiped her eyes then shot to her feet. "Don't you get it? Manheim and Kilburn were right to do what they did. Girls like me should never have babies."

Raina rose and took her arms. "Erin, please—"

The sound of footsteps turned their heads. A man in a white coat escorted by Scanlon and flanked by the social workers was walking toward them up the hall. Carrying a bundle.

CHAPTER 131

Slumped in his deck chair, Scanlon stared out across the back lawn. The air held a chill that seeped to his bones, yet he sat unflinching, taking in the scent of damp earth and fallen leaves overlaid with a hint of wood smoke.

Even were he blind, he'd still know when autumn came to New England. Even without seeing the mandatory pumpkins and potted chrysanthemums on every doorstep, the leaves flitting down like so many frenzied monarch butterflies. It was the air that told him. The rawness it carried. The melancholy. The scent of decay.

He needed to get out here one day soon and take care of these leaves. Autumn clean-up had never been one of his favorite chores but it seemed he had even less energy for it these days. Not much energy for anything actually.

Behind him the glass door slid aside and Peg came out, bearing two glasses of red wine. She handed him one, pulled a chair over, and sat beside him.

"So the baby was hers?" she said without preliminaries.

Scanlon nodded. "DNA test was conclusive. It's hers." The reunion he'd witnessed that day at the hospital was the one bright note in the aftermath of this sordid case, taking his mind, however briefly, off Farrington's involvement and the lies he'd been hiding all these years.

Peg sipped her wine. "What will happen to them?"

"We haven't found a home prepared to take both of them. At this stage it looks like they'll go to the shelter."

"As long as there's no chance they'll end up with *her.*"

The venom in her tone drew his gaze to her face, a visage twisted by years of grief. Or was it more than that? Condemnation? Vengeance? A victim clinging steadfastly to old wounds. Was this what he had looked like all these years?

"Honestly, John, I still can't fathom what you were thinking? If Social Services made the decision and *forced* it on you, I could understand. But that you'd actually go to them and *request* they allow the girl and baby to stay with her..." She shook her head. "How could you leave them with that woman for a single day, let alone two weeks?"

A host of responses sprang to his lips. Because Erin needed someone and had bonded with Raina. Because Raina had saved the girl's life, and been instrumental in helping uncover Manheim's racket and finding Liam DeMarco's killer. That because of Raina, the police now had a real hope of reuniting other stolen babies with their mothers.

None of which Peg would want to hear.

Clutching her glass, she glared at him. "Being denied a child of her own was the one way that woman had been forced to pay for what she'd done. The *one* way I could feel justice had been served. And you had to take that from me as well."

Scanlon stared out over the lawn. So many truths she would not want to hear. So many truths he'd been forced to withhold.

But there was one she would need to face eventually. Assuming he could find the courage to tell her. God knew he'd been struggling with it himself. Still, perhaps the moment had come.

"Peg, there's something I need to—"

"No wait, please." She set her glass down, swung in her chair, and took his hand. "I'm sorry. Please forgive me. None of that was what I came out here to say."

He waited, startled by her change of mood. A look on her face he'd not seen in years. A look that might almost be hope.

"There's something I need to say to you." She dropped her gaze. "I...I know things haven't been good between us for quite some time. I know I've been a burden to you—"

"Oh, Peg, don't—"

"No, it's true. I know it is. But at the same time I know I couldn't have done any better. I tried, John, truly I did. You have to know that."

"Of course I know it. Peg, what on earth—"

"Wait, let me finish, please. You see..." She swallowed. "I've been doing a lot of thinking lately. Ever since this whole thing began; with the girl I mean. John, I believe I've finally found a way for us to move forward." She clutched his hand. "What if we took them?"

He frowned. "Took what?"

"Not what – *who*. The girl and her baby. What if they came and lived with us?"

He was speechless a moment. "You aren't serious."

"Why not? John, think about it – we've got Rick's old room, the guest room for the baby. Why couldn't we take them? We may be old, but we're not that old."

For a moment all he could do was stare.

She reached up and cupped his cheek. "My dear sweet

man, don't you see? We could be a family again."

A family.

Inexplicably a chill washed over him. "I had no idea…"

"John, I need this. Please. Give me back what she took from me. Someone to care for. Something to live for."

A hard shell closed around his heart. "We could've adopted or fostered a child at any time in the last ten years. You know I would've been more than happy to."

"Yes, I know. All I can say is I wasn't ready. I think you'll agree with me on that."

"But you're saying…now…"

"Yes, that's exactly what I'm saying. I've thought it through and I can honestly say, yes, I'm ready."

He gazed at her face. He'd not seen this measure of joy in her eyes for over a decade. The truth would douse that light forever, destroy her completely. Plunge her back into a well of despair from which she would possibly never emerge.

The truth. One which he alone knew. Safely buried for all these years.

With Farrington gone, was there any reason it had to be told?

CHAPTER 132

Raina heard the car pull into the driveway and hurried to the door before Erin could answer it. The social workers weren't due until ten – they wouldn't be welcome if they'd showed up early. Bad enough this was happening only days after Erin had been reunited with Cody. Raina wouldn't let them take the pair a moment sooner than the time they'd arranged. Assuming that's what they were coming for. But what else could it be?

She hung her head. Whatever their purpose in coming today, she had absolutely no say in the matter. If they'd decided to renege on their two-week agreement and take Erin and Cody sooner, there wasn't a thing she or any of them could do about it.

She opened the door and let out her breath at the sight of Alec climbing the steps. He'd been there every day of the week they'd had together – sharing meals, going for walks, even holding the baby at times. But facing the moment it would all have to end was a trial he might have chosen to spare himself. She was glad he hadn't.

With a strained smile he stepped through the door and

kissed her cheek, then set down the box he was carrying and took off his jacket.

His gaze swung at once toward the living room where Erin sat holding the baby. "How's she doing?"

Raina closed the door gently behind him. "Toughing it out, pretending she's come to terms with it all but the cracks are showing."

He looked back down at her. "What about you?"

Biting her lip, she shook her head.

"They haven't told you what it's about?" he said.

"No. They just called and said someone was coming to discuss our situation." She forced a smile. "Hey, it could be good news I suppose – they may have found a foster home prepared to take both of them." Her smile faltered, both at the thought how unlikely the possibility was and that it wasn't what any of them wanted to begin with.

"But at this point she's still thinking of giving Cody up for adoption?" he said.

"Rather than bring him to the shelter, yes."

He turned to face her. "Raina, you know if there was any way I could…"

"Yes, I know."

"It just wouldn't be—"

She silenced him with a finger to his lips. "None of this is your fault."

"Or yours." He smiled sadly. "So why do we both feel like shit?"

Helplessness gnawed at her heart. As a welcome distraction she nodded at the box he'd brought. "Is that for me?"

"Actually it's for Erin. I thought it might cheer her up."

She brushed a stray lock of hair from his brow. "You're a

keeper, you know that, DeMarco."

"I was hoping you'd feel that way." He clasped the hand she'd placed to his cheek. "Raina, I know we haven't had much time to discuss it, but I hope you know that, whatever's coming, I'd like to stay a part of your lives. Both yours and Erin's. If you want me, that is."

She moved into his arms, held him so long a measure of her despair dissolved away. The minute she stepped back it was there again.

She motioned him toward the living room.

Erin looked up at their approach and pushed to her feet. Raina took Cody from her arms, giving her a chance to greet their visitor.

Alec handed her the box. Surprised, she set it down on the coffee table and opened the lid. With a look of confusion she lifted out some of the books it contained.

"I'm not sure I ever mentioned it," he said, "but I'm a high school English teacher." He gestured to the books and shrugged. "If you still want to get your high school diploma, I'd be happy to tutor you. And, if you're still thinking of becoming a writer I'll be happy to coach you in that as well."

She stood a moment staring back at him, then threw her arms around his neck.

The door bell rang. Raina returned the baby to Erin and went to answer it. She opened the door and recoiled a step. Recovering, she looked past the man on the porch. He was alone.

Her jaw tightened as she looked in his eyes. "Yes?"

"Raina." Scanlon nodded a greeting. He arched his brows. "May I come in?"

So polite. Did she have a choice? She stepped aside and let him enter.

She watched his face as he spotted Erin and Cody seated on a chair in the living room. Incredibly, she thought she saw him smile. A part of her wanted to believe it was pleasure at seeing mother and child reunited. But another part wondered if it was pleasure of a different sort – knowing he'd soon be depriving her of their company. It seemed he would have his justice after all.

Alec had taken up position beside them, clearly not happy to see the man. The tension in the air was palpable.

Raina mustered the will to speak. "So what can we do for you, Chief?"

"Actually it's you I need to speak with. But perhaps..." He turned to her. "It might be better if we spoke in private."

She shook head. "Anything you have to say to me you can say in front of them."

He nodded as though he'd expected no less. "Fine. Can we sit down at least?"

She led him into the living room where they all took seats on the couch and chairs. From across the coffee table, Erin shot Scanlon a fearful glare. Refusing to return his greeting, she went back to tending the baby.

By the twitch of his brow, the rebuff seemed to affect the man. He recovered quickly, handing Raina an envelope. She opened it and scanned the document it contained. So that's what this was all about.

"It's another agreement with Social Services."

"*Temporary* agreement," she corrected him. Whatever their reason for granting it, she'd not allow him to pretend this was anything but a brief reprieve.

Erin looked up. "You mean I can stay?"

Raina glared at the man before her. Damn him for giving the girl yet another false glimmer of hope. "How long this time, Chief?" she said. "One week? Two? How much longer are you going to torture us?"

To her surprise he looked away, the haunted expression back on his face. He opened his mouth, then closed it again. She'd never seen him at a loss for words. Could things be even worse than she'd thought? "What? Tell me."

"There's something you haven't..." He took a deep breath. "Before Deputy... Before Craig went to meet you at the lake that night, I spoke with him at length in my office. He told me something he believed would keep me from interfering, stop me from blowing the whistle on what he, Manheim, and Kilburn were doing. I'm ashamed to say, it very nearly did. Thankfully I came to my senses in time."

Raina returned Alec's frown, unable to fathom where this was going.

"What Craig told me..." Scanlon looked down, then up again. "Ten years ago, the night of the accident in which Rick was killed..." He forced himself to meet her gaze. "You weren't driving the car. Rick was."

She heard the words, felt them like dull raps against her head, but their meaning refused to register. "I...I don't understand."

"Craig was the responding officer, the first on the scene. Even the witness who saw your car go down the embankment and called 911 never actually went down to the crash site. Craig was the only one. When he got down there he found Rick had been thrown from the car but you were still inside. Firmly strapped in the passenger seat."

"The *passenger* seat?" The words were starting to have an impact. Her heart beat faster. "Then how—"

"Both you and Rick looked in bad shape but to Craig's untrained eye you looked worse. He knew that if you died,

Rick would be charged with vehicular manslaughter. His life would be ruined."

Her leap of insight struck like a blow. "He swapped us around?"

"He pulled you from the car and simply told everyone you'd been the one behind the wheel." The man winced. "He even took glass and cut your face to make it look as though you'd gone through the windshield."

Raina fell back against her seat. "My god. Why would he do such a thing?"

"For me. When he joined the force I pretty much took him under my wing. We were close even then. He knew how much I loved Rick, how proud I was of him – his scholarship, his dreams for the future. He knew all that would be destroyed with a felony conviction."

"So he pinned it on Raina instead," Alec said. "And just how would he get away with that?"

"When the paramedics arrived on the scene they were so busy trying to save you both they didn't notice any clues to the switch. Craig filled out the accident report to take care of the rest. Given it was your mother's car, and with the reputation you had at the time, he figured no-one would question that you had been driving. It pains me to say he was absolutely right."

"All these years..." She stared into space. "I just... I can't..."

"There's more," Scanlon said. "I'm sorry I couldn't have told you this sooner but I wanted to be sure it was going ahead before I said anything."

God, what now? "To be sure what was going ahead?" she said.

"In light of Farrington's disclosure I've put things in

motion to reopen your case."

Raina stared back, her capacity for shock surpassed for the day.

"It'll take time, but ultimately your conviction for Rick's death will be overturned."

"My conviction? Overturned?" Her brain wouldn't process.

"What it means, Raina, among other things, is you'll be free to foster Erin and Cody." He looked from one stunned face to the next.

"Are you serious?" Alec blurted.

"The extension from Social Services covers the interim until the matter's officially resolved."

"My god. I can't believe it." Raina shook her head, then looked over at Erin. "You can stay."

"For real?" The girl pushed to her feet. "Until I'm eighteen?"

"Longer than that." Raina was on her feet the next instant. "As long as you want."

As the two came together, Alec joined in their embrace.

Scanlon gave them a moment, then rose. "Raina, I...I just want to say..." But seeing as no-one was listening any more, he simply nodded. "I'll keep you informed of further developments."

Raina barely heard his words. By the time she'd broken away from the others and turned around he was at the front door, pulling it open. She ran to catch him.

Before he could step out, she took his arm and turned him back. "I can see why Craig might have thought his secret would..."

A sudden surge of anger engulfed her. Ten years she'd been living with this. Ten years of enduring a guilt so intense, a future so bleak, at times she'd thought to end it all.

Yet none of that had been Scanlon's fault. In a way he'd been as much a victim as she had – they'd both been lied to. Having learned the truth, he *could* have gone on protecting Rick's name. Instead…

 As the magnitude of his actions sank in her anger abated. Once again she felt overwhelmed. "All you had to do was forget what Craig told you. Say nothing. No-one would ever have known the truth."

"I don't think Rick would've wanted that. Do you?"

Her throat clamped tight. She looked away into the living room – at her new future, at all he had given her – then back up at him. "Thank you," she said.

Scanlon nodded and put on his hat. "Take care of them, Raina."

ACKNOWLEDGMENTS

As always my first round of thanks goes to my critquing partners, Alison Manthorpe, Mary Gudzenovs, and Kathy Blacker, without whose support and encouragement I might never have seen this project through.

A huge thanks also to my beta readers Louise Mrdjen, Patrice Glass, Tania Kolega , Gayle Santic, Anna Harders, Lyn Craig, Liz Jones and Pam Barton for their valuable feedback. And to my editor, Ruth Kennedy, for helping to refine and polish my efforts.

Above all, my love and appreciation to Michael for his unwavering support.

ABOUT THE AUTHOR

Born in New York, Diane Hester is a former violinist with the Rochester Philharmonic and the Adelaide Symphony. Her debut thriller, RUN TO ME, was short-listed in the 2014 Daphne du Maurier Awards. She now lives in Port Lincoln, South Australia with her husband Michael. Visit her at www.dianehester.com